# CHAPTER 1

IF THE PHRASE "Murder Capital of the World" ever comes up in conversation, you can be sure Evansfield, Vermont—population 1,333—will never be mentioned. But just as root canals, taxes, and power-obsessed politicians are a lamentable fact of life everywhere these days—it's true that no place on earth is immune to unnatural deaths.

So, it probably shouldn't have surprised the good citizens of Evansfield, Vermont—although it actually did—when not long ago a violent murder occurred in their midst. That was when Verity Cade, dairy farmer, found herself involved in her very first murder investigation. Thereby discovering the darker side of "quaint" rural towns. Places often too small to appear on a AAA road map. Communities where everyone knows everyone else's most intimate secrets.

*Or at least they think they do.*

To her surprise, Verity discovered that interviewing suspects and shadowing possible killers was, well, rather exciting. Six of her friends agreed. After all, who can walk past an incomplete jigsaw puzzle without adding a piece?

Long story short. After discovering the who, why, and how

of the murder that shocked the entire county, Verity and her sister amateur sleuths established Evansfield Private Investigations with high expectations of continuing their crime-fighting efforts.

Unfortunately for them, but much to the relief of Sheriff Fred Bailey, crime proved disappointingly thin for many months. Thus, it fell to the novice investigators to accept cases less urgent than those involving murder. Such as locating missing car keys, intervening in a dispute between neighbors over an aboveground swimming pool, or tracking down the thief of a stolen engagement ring. (Eventually found beneath a couch cushion.) Even recovering a kidnapped pooch was less interesting than they'd hoped. The dog turned out to be less kidnap victim than escape artist.

And so, after many months lacking any real criminal activity, Verity's thoughts were far away from murderous mayhem as she drove her little blue Ridgeway truck down Main Street on her bi-weekly dairy deliveries. Milk, cream, her popular hand-churned butter and fresh eggs were packed into the back of her truck. Her final stop of the day was Sunny Whitaker's café.

Before she reached her turn—the alley between the Cat's Cradle Café and Chaundra Adebe's Antiques Emporium—she frowned at an unexpected sight and hit the brakes. An immense chrome-and-carnation-red bus blocked the narrow alley. The bus was so wide its sides nearly touched the buildings' walls.

"Seriously?" Shaking her head, amused and frustrated in equal parts, she steered into the nearest parking spot. She scooted off the driver's seat and dropped down to the pavement to assess her options for reaching the café's delivery door.

Locals optimistically called this part of Main Street the "shopping district." But it was just one block long, a single row of eight tiny shops and small businesses. Clapboard storefronts designed to attract tourists had been stained patriotic hues of

# KATHRYN JOHNSON

# THE DEATH of a BAD EGG

THE HAUNTED FARMHOUSE MYSTERIES    BOOK TWO

Cover design by Kim Killion

Published by Oliver-Heber Books

0 9 8 7 6 5 4 3 2 1

colonial blue, barn door red, and antique white—intentionally faded to look appropriate for an 18<sup>th</sup>-century New England village.

Until now, Verity had been so focused on the behemoth bus, she hadn't noticed the line of people standing outside the café door. Very odd indeed, she thought. The crowd stretched along the cobbled sidewalk in front of the recently reopened *Historic Wayfarer's Inn* with its lovely wrap-around porch and window boxes overflowing with jewel-bright red geraniums. The line didn't seem to be moving. Several people peered lackadaisically into the display window of Fumiko Oto's *Knit One Purl* yarn shop. Others stared impatiently at movie posters in front of *The View*, a single-screen movie theater. The theater presented only vintage flicks because the owner couldn't afford first-run features.

Verity stood beside her truck, perplexed by the crowd. *Good grief!* Even on Sunny's popular Five-Buck Fridays, there was never this large a crowd. Tourists, she guessed, passengers from the excursion bus that was currently hogging her alley.

Sighing, she walked over to the bus and peered up into the tinted glass in the door. But there seemed to be no sign of the driver. He was probably inside the café eating his lunch. She supposed she could storm in there and make a scene, demand he move his bus so she could get through, but it didn't seem worth the effort. She knew another way around behind the café.

With a shrug, she climbed back into her truck, drove to the end of the block then turned into the gravel path that led down to the wide alley behind the row of shops. A ramp up to the café's rear door led directly into the kitchen, making it unnecessary to push her metal trolley through the busy dining area.

Verity rolled the trolley down from the truck's bed, grabbed a crate of milk bottles and swung it onto the footplate of the trolley. She stacked a second crate on top of that. Then two canvas bags stenciled with the green Cade Family Farm logo. The café's order of twelve dozen eggs, tubs of creamy yellow butter and old-timey glass jugs of whole milk and rich cream was her largest order of the day. She'd already made home deliveries to eight local families who preferred purchasing their dairy products, fresh from her farm, rather than by way of area supermarkets. Just a quart or two of milk, sometimes also a dozen eggs or a pint of cream.

She side-eyed the nose of the bus sticking out from beside the café and shook her head. *Oh, Ervin, I hope you didn't bite off more than you can chew.*

Ervin Tewksbury was a true New England character. After retiring to Vermont and moving in with his sister's family, he had supplemented his Social Security income as an odd-jobs man. Unfortunately, he lacked any real experience in plumbing, electrical work, or carpentry. When no one would hire him, he decided to become an inventor. After months of work on an astonishing number of inventions, he filed for their patents. Sadly, every one of his "original" designs had already been invented *and* patented by other people. He next announced he would start his own business, although it was never clear what sort of business that might be. How he imagined he might scrape together start-up money, Verity had no clue.

Then came the monumental day when Ervin won the state lottery. Before anyone could ask how he might use his prize money, he had up and bought himself a shiny Silver Blaze Deluxe touring bus. Today must be the beginning of his inaugural tour.

Verity rolled the loaded trolley up the ramp to the rear door of the café. Her long strides up the squeaky planks woke up a big Maine Coon cat sunning itself on the upper landing; its Lucifer-green eyes glared annoyingly at her before it dashed away down the ramp. Verity let herself in through the screen door.

The kitchen was hot, steamy and noisy. She dodged around two of Sunny's waitstaff and the busy cook, placed her sparkling-clean glass bottles of cream and milk into the larger of the two commercial refrigerators along with eggs she'd collected early that morning and homemade butter.

Folding the empty canvas bags, she tossed them into her cart and turned to leave.

"Wait! Verity don't go!" a breathless voice called.

"The check can wait, Sunny. I can see you're busy." She waved over her shoulder and grabbed the trolley by its handles.

"No!" Sunny grabbed her arm. "You don't understand. This is an emergency!"

Verity had never heard her friend sound so desperate. Worried, she stopped short and turned to face her.

# CHAPTER 2

"WHAT'S UP?" Verity studied her friend's face. It took a lot to unnerve Sunny.

"I'll tell you what's up." The café owner snagged a hand towel off the side of the sink and mopped her forehead. "You'd think a swarm of locusts had just landed. Fifteen minutes ago, Ervin's tour bus comes rumbling up to my door—no warning at all, I might add—and dozens of tourists rush in, fighting for tables and scaring my waitstaff half to death."

"Scaring them?" Verity laughed, relieved that the emergency was no more serious than an overabundance of customers.

"She's not kidding!" A teenage server in blonde braids and blue jeans waved toward the dining room. "It's like Voldemort and his minions out there."

"These tourists!" Sunny huffed. "The way they act, you'd think they owned the place."

"It can't be that bad." Verity pulled out a stool from the stainless-steel prep counter. "Here, sit down and catch your breath."

"I can't! I had to tell half of the mob they needed to wait outside for a free table. You must have seen how many people are still standing out there. We haven't even taken all the orders for those who found seats." She groaned and threw her hands into the air. "Listen, sweetie, I know you've got a lot to deal with at the farm. But I'll pay you any amount of money if you'll stay for just an hour and help out."

Verity slung an arm around her friend's shoulders. "You don't have to pay me, silly." She thought for a moment. If it had been January, she would have been hard pressed to get all her chores done before dark. But with the extra hours of sunlight in July, and since she'd already finished the rest of her deliveries, she could surely spare Sunny one hour.

"Tell me what you need me to do."

Sunny pulled an order pad and pen out of the pocket of her blue gingham apron. "Any table that still has menus, take their order. I've been training two new girls, so I've numbered the tables until they learn them. Just write the table number on each order. Oh, and tell the customers, no separate checks today. They can work out who owes what for themselves."

"Got it."

Verity took the customers' orders at the first three tables she came to, picked up their menus and delivered the order slips to Sunny, who was now helping her cook in the kitchen.

*Easy-peasy! Anyone can do this waitressing gig.* She grinned. *Hey, maybe I'll even get tipped!* She moved on to a new table where two couples sat, menus stacked in the center of the table. When she asked what she could get them, they looked up at her with blank expressions.

"Oh!" one of the women said, giving her a panicky look. "Sorry. I guess we just got so busy chatting we haven't—"

"It's okay," Verity assured them. "I'll come back after you've had a little more time to..." She waved a hand at the menus and started to turn away.

"Hold on a just a sec," one of the men shouted. "We're ready. I'll take a burger with everything and fries."

The other man quickly added, "Ditto." He elbowed the woman who had apologized for their not being prepared with their orders.

"Oh, why not?" she said. "A burger, but no fries. A side salad?"

"Of course." Verity said. "Three burgers, one with side salad." Smiling, she turned to the remaining woman at the table. "And you, ma'am?"

"Oh dear, I just don't know." She reached for a menu. Her three companions glared at her.

"It's okay, take your time." Verity counted silently to ten. Slowly. The woman made desperate noises in the back of her throat and ran a crimson nail down the list of sandwiches, then the salads...then the entrees.

Verity tapped her toe.

"Ummm. What about the tuna-melt special—it's really yummy," Verity suggested. The woman shook her head and made a face. Verity tried again. "Local folks just love the liver and onions."

"Oh, I just can't decide." The woman pouted. "Maybe the meatloaf? No, you can never depend on meatloaf in a little road-house like this."

*Roadhouse?*

Verity rattled off a list of options she knew by heart. She cast apologetic looks at customers at nearby tables who were now glaring murderously at the woman. Hands beckoned frantically toward Verity.

"Listen," Verity said after the woman vetoed three more of her suggestions, "while you're making up your mind, I'll just step over to another table and take their ord—"

"No!" shouted Miss Indecisive's three companions, making Verity jump.

"Mattie, make up your damn mind right now," one of the men said, "or you'll go without lunch."

Mattie ordered fried chicken. Then wrinkled her face in dissatisfaction. Verity turned away before she could change her mind yet again. She thrust the order slip at Sunny as they dashed past each other.

"Thanks!" Sunny gasped, rushing back into the kitchen. The mouth-watering smell of grilling meat wafted through the dining area. Verity salivated, suddenly hungry.

She was on her way back across the room to another table when a hand came out of nowhere and seized her by the shirt-tails. "Hey, honey, we've been waiting long as anyone. How about doing us next?"

She spun around, appalled. The owner of the hand, still gripping her shirt, leered up at her from his seat. From his expression, she had no doubt that he was fully aware of his request's double-entendre. She could ignore the words, but not the hand.

Stepping away, she roughly brushed off his big paw. It took every bit of self-control to not call him out, loudly and angrily, in front of everyone in the café. She didn't want to make things worse for Sunny.

"I'm on my way to help table five," she said firmly. "You'll be next, sir."

"Now hold on there, missy."

*Missy?* Verity clenched her teeth and scowled at him.

He stood up from the table, planted snakeskin cowboy boots shoulder-width apart and gazed down on her with a smug expression. Until this moment, she hadn't taken notice of his overall appearance. As warm as it was that day, he wore a leather jacket, open in front to display a broad chest. A New

York Yankees t-shirt was tucked into fitted jeans. His hair was long, held back in a man-tail by a plain rubber band. His clenched jaw looked capable of biting off a table leg.

She held her ground, refusing to give him the satisfaction that his intimidation tactics were working. "Sit down. Sir." Somehow, she hid the tremor in her throat.

He leaned toward her and lowered his voice. "You probably aren't used to the way things work in the big city." She felt fingers slip inside the front pocket of her jeans. Shocked, she jumped back.

Which was when she saw Jason Grimalski, one of her young farmhands, moving like a house afire across the room toward them. It wasn't hard to guess what was about to happen.

"Jason, no!" Verity shouted, holding up her order pad like a stop sign. With her other hand she tugged a ten-dollar bill out of her pocket and tossed it onto the man's table. "It's alright, Jason. No harm done. The *gentleman*—" and she didn't try to hide her sarcasm "—is going to sit down and wait his turn like everyone else." She gave the tourist the same steely glare that had made an angry bull think twice about messing with her. "Aren't you, *sir*?" But *jerk* is what she thought.

Jason either didn't hear or he ignored her, which was unlike him. He was a serious, well-mannered, hard-working guy, just like his twin brother, Jerry. Now in their twenties, they had worked part-time for her husband before Mark died, almost two years earlier, in a terrible accident. Twins they might be, but their personalities were light years apart.

Jerry was a good-natured, sweet introvert who loved reading, enjoyed his solitude, and was constantly picking up stray or injured animals. Jason, a classic extrovert, thought nothing of starting up conversations with strangers and loved being the center of attention. Girls flocked to him. He dated prolifically and was a fan of mafia flicks. And, like the crime bosses in the movies he loved, Jason had a temper. Once he let loose, there was little chance of stopping him.

But she had no choice now. Verity stepped between the two men. "Stop, Jase! I'm sure Mr., ummm, Mr.—"

"O'Halloran. Rudy O'Halloran," the man bellowed, fists on hips. "And I don't need a woman to protect me from a country bumpkin like *him*." He jabbed a finger toward Jason.

Outraged, Verity opened her mouth to respond, but O'Halloran continued his rant.

"What's with this hick town anyhow?" he boomed. "First, that so-called historic inn we're staying in has no liquor, not even beer or wine. Then—" The woman seated at his table shot O'Halloran a pleading look. She reached out as if to tug him back down into his chair, but he ignored her. "Then we can't get anyone in this rinky-dink joint to take our orders, even with generous encouragement! Something wrong with my money, lady?"

Verity blinked in disbelief while stiff-arming Jason, her hand pressed to his chest to keep the two men apart.

Thankfully, Sunny materialized at her side. "Now, sir, Mrs. Cade has asked you politely to sit down and wait your turn. I'll need to ask you to leave if you can't do that."

O'Halloran rolled his eyes. "Do you believe these people?" He waved toward Verity, Jason, and Sunny for the benefit of the rest of the room.

A few of the other tourists made vague sounds of acknowledgement but no one gave their traveling companion much reason to feel they were on his side.

Sunny—ever the peacemaker—turned and whispered to the woman who had encouraged the man to sit down. "If you can persuade your...uh, friend to sit down, I'll be more than happy to provide a bottle of wine for your table and take your order."

Verity was unconvinced that placating the idiot would make things any better.

O'Halloran's face was still flushed a deep red in anger, but he apparently felt he'd made his point. He grudgingly stepped back toward his table.

She felt Jason lunge against her palm.

"Don't let him get to you, Jase," Verity hissed. "Leave it."

"Isn't right," her farmhand muttered. "Behaving like that." Then much louder, "You deserve a good whipping, mister. Teach you some manners!"

O'Halloran laughed, and it was as cold and mean a laugh as she'd ever heard. "It'd take more of a man than you, boy."

Mrs. O'Halloran, if that's who she was, leaned out of her seat and tugged her husband down into his chair with surprising force. "Don't screw around!" she rasped in his ear, loud enough for anyone nearby to hear. He shot her a nasty look but stayed seated.

Verity's arm, still locked to hold back Jason, felt as if it might fall off. She looked the young man in the eyes. "Go back to work, Jason. I'll see you at the farm. Sandwich makings in my fridge if you're hungry." She didn't want him staying another minute in the café, even if just to order takeout.

He drew a deep breath, staring down at his work boots as if willing them to move on their own volition. Finally, he took a step back from her and spun around. Verity watched him cross the little dining room in four furious strides. He slammed the café door behind him. Through the wide bay window overlooking the sidewalk, she watched him shove angrily through the crowd still waiting outside.

The room had fallen deadly still during the tense confrontation between the two men. Now, as if the sound on a TV had been suddenly switched from mute to full volume, everyone started talking at once. A tickly bead of sweat rolled down Verity's back. Usually, the swirling of the ceiling fans above the diners was enough to make even the hottest summer days tolerable. But the row between the two men seemed to have driven up the temperature in the room at least another ten degrees. Verity knew the diners' impatience at the delay of their food would only increase with their discomfort.

She set to work rapidly taking orders, one after another. When everyone's choices had been sent to the kitchen, she coordinated delivery of plates to tables with the other waitstaff, while Sunny returned to assist her overwhelmed cook.

Verity ended up staying nearly two sweaty, exhausting hours before Sunny finally pulled her behind the pastry display case.

"You should go now, Verity dear. I'm so sorry for that nonsense earlier. You didn't buy into a brawl when you agreed to help me." She puckered her lips as though she'd bitten into a lemon. "Please apologize to Jason for me, too."

"It's no big deal." Verity forced a laugh. "Jerks will forever be jerks. It's in their DNA."

"New Yorkers," Sunny groaned. Referring, Verity realized, to the origination of the tour.

"Hey, I know plenty of great people from New York City." She smiled. "Some may be brusque or a bit demanding. But that guy's outrageous behavior has nothing to do with his being from the Big Apple."

"Well, wherever he got that attitude, it sucks." Sunny sighed and absently swiped a damp rag across the glass showcase displaying donuts, pies, and cakes. Tossing down the cloth, she reached inside for a cherry tart and slice of her Vermont-style cheesecake, drizzled with maple-syrup glaze. She dropped them into a little white cardboard box and thrust it at Verity with a smile. "Anyway, thanks so much. I owe you much more than these."

*No, you don't,* Verity thought as they walked together, back through the kitchen. Hadn't Sunny been there for her all those times when she so desperately needed a shoulder to cry on? Without her gentle words of solace in that first year after Mark died, she wasn't sure she would have been able to carry on. With the farm. With...anything.

"Call if you need me again." Verity tucked the dessert box into her egg crate.

"Right. Like you can tell your cows to milk themselves."

"Almost. Thank goodness Mark had those computerized Robo-Milkers installed. They've been a life saver." Verity wheeled her trolley toward the rear door but couldn't help noticing a troubled look returning to the café owner.

"You're not still upset about that guy, are you?" she asked. O'Halloran and the woman with him had eaten quickly and left soon after, thank goodness. They took their unopened bottle of wine with them. A prize they definitely didn't deserve.

"Not really upset," Sunny said. "It's just that I heard complaints from others in the tour group as I circled the tables. Not directed at *me*," she added quickly when Verity's eyes widened. "Comments about the inn's lack of a liquor license. Henry should never have opened the inn without securing his licenses enabling him to serve alcohol. You can't advertise a *world-class wine cellar*—" she sketched air quotes "—and then tell people they can't have a beer or glass of wine with their meal in the inn's dining room."

"Oh my!" Verity sighed.

"To be honest, it's not entirely Henry's fault. He told me he'd applied well in advance for both A and C licenses—for spirits, and for wine and beer. But the State of Vermont won't grant him either until the town council signs off on the application."

Verity didn't need to ask why the delay. Much heated discussion had monopolized recent town meetings.

Half the residents applauded Henry Brockhurst's purchase of the long-neglected Wayfarer's Inn. It had been a terrible eyesore for over seventy years. The restoration must have cost a fortune, but the results were amazing. When it became obvious to everyone that its opening would bump up the flow of tourists, local business and shop owners were thrilled. They could foresee a healthier local economy. But the other half of Evansfield's residents—farmers, older folks, and families with young children—objected vociferously. Streets that had remained narrow since colonial days, they argued, would become clogged with the inevitable increase in traffic. Possibly to the danger of young children and livestock.

The one thing both camps agreed on was that they wanted to keep the small-town feel of Evansfield. Which was the reason many current residents had moved here from large cities or remained living in this town where they'd grown up.

"I'm sure it will all get sorted out in time." Verity hoped she sounded confident. The town council was known for dragging its feet whenever emotions ran high, afraid of offending one camp to satisfy the other. *You can't please everyone!* A lesson well-learned today.

Verity rolled her trolley and empty crates down the ramp to her truck. She was anxious to return to the farm for reasons beyond her usual chores.

In a weak or possibly insane moment, she had agreed to let Ervin, the Vermont Elite Tours Director, bring his customers with children to visit her farm. "As an educational bonus," he announced grandly. "All the best tours feature cultural enrichment." Which might be true. But she suspected the idea of using the Cade Family Farm appealed to him because he knew she wouldn't ask him to pay for the use of her property.

In preparation for the visit, she intended to make sure Jason and Jerry were on hand to help her supervise. Meanwhile, she would store potentially dangerous tools, set up barriers in strategic areas and post signs to indicate restricted access. Best to avoid accidents, if possible, rather than deal with the aftermath. Having witnessed Mr. Rudy O'Halloran in action, she could foresee a lawsuit if someone tripped on a rake or got a foot stepped on by a cow.

She caught up with the Grimalski twins in the sunny pasture behind her chicken yard. Jason, still in a black mood after the incident at the café, nevertheless assured her that he and Jerry would be on hand the following day. She spent nearly two hours child-proofing her property the best she could, then posted cautionary signage for the adults.

Finally satisfied with her efforts, she allowed herself an icy glass of lemonade, sweet and fruity, and the slice of maple cheesecake Sunny had gifted her. With a little smart planning, she mused while sitting in her porch swing and licking the last creamy smear from her fork, what could possibly go wrong?

# CHAPTER 3

AFTER SEEING off her two farmhands at 5:00 pm Verity was about to go inside for her supper when she remembered a problem she'd put off dealing with for weeks. The source of her concern was in the milking barn but had nothing to do with her cows or any of the equipment there.

It was rats. Or mice. She couldn't be sure which. Maybe both.

Mark had always taken charge of vermin control. Foxes, the occasional coyote and more commonly raccoons, mice and rats, moles and voles were an issue. He protected their cows and chickens from the larger critters by diligent fence mending and, when necessary, his shotgun. To rid the farm of smaller nuisances, he laid traps. They had agreed no poisons would be used that might contaminate their vegetable garden or harm birds, neighborhood pets and children.

She had suggested they simply procure a cat or two from their neighbors, whose barn cats happily produced litter after litter of sturdy kittens. But Mark worried she would make a pet of a cat and bring it inside the house. Thereby rendering it (according to him) pampered, lazy, and useless. If she was honest, she probably would have done just that. Who can resist an adorable, fluffy little kitten?

Although the Grimalski boys now offered to manage the traps for her, there was always a chance she'd be the one to find a maimed, half-dead, squirming little body. Disgusting! Growing up in a single-family, 100% mouse-free suburban home, she had never even seen a wild rodent—squirrels didn't count—until moving to the Vermont farm with Mark. And so, erring on the side of tenderheartedness, she had turned down her farmhands' offers of rodent-squishing devices, hoping for a better solution.

But now the resident beasties were flagrantly breeding in her barns and sheds! She saw two or three each day, skulking around. Fat gray little things with beady eyes that observed her fearlessly. One would think the critters might wise up to the fact that the larger their numbers, the less food they'd each have. It was only a matter of time before their ballooning population necessitated human intervention and ended their days of feasting and cushy barn-life.

Her most serious concern—would the purity of her herd's milk be compromised? So far, neither her own tests of the milk, nor the safety checks performed by the co-op dairy's driver at each pick-up, had revealed harmful bacteria levels. But if she lost the income from the co-op, her big moneymaker, there was a real danger she might lose the farm. And keeping the Cade Family Farm in healthy operating condition was the single most important thing in her life. She owed it to Mark. The farm was, in a way, what had brought them together. They shared a deep, almost sacred love for the land and animals. Now that she was solely responsible for all of it, she had to protect it however she could.

Verity checked the automated Robo-Milkers to make sure all three machines were functioning properly. She drew a sample and tested the raw milk from the largest stainless-steel collection tank. Thankfully, it passed muster and she felt a moment's relief. But as she was leaving the tank room, firmly closing the door behind her, a gray-brown flash raced across the wide wooden floorboards.

"Yee-ikes!" she screeched, performing an inelegant Texas two-step to avoid tromping on the mouse. Even though crunching it underfoot—*eeeuuugh!*—would have served the purpose of eliminating at least one of the invaders.

As the critter skittered away to safety, another thought occurred to her. Did mice and rats bite? She expected they probably did. Would they bite her poor cows? She didn't have a clue.

There were so many gaps in her training as a farmer. She had only started learning about the vast and surprisingly technical world of modern agriculture after they married. Because Mark had reserved so many of the farm's chores for himself, she had little or no experience with such things as mending fences, ordering the right kind of chicken feed, or programming the milking machines. Luckily, her two farmhands took over these tasks immediately after the accident. They were so intent on helping her, she actually had to order them to show her how to do some of the jobs.

But the rodents—it was her procrastination that had allowed them to have the run of her property. And whether or not she liked her options, she had to do *something* about them. Fast!

"Argggh!" she growled in frustration and stomped her foot, sending up a cloud of dust and straw chaff.

"Oh, darlin' girl, what's wrong?"

Verity jumped and nearly fell against the metal cooling pipes leading into the tank room. "Anna Louise!" she gasped at the silky drawl that seemed to come from everywhere and nowhere at once. "Don't do that."

"Do what?" A silvery mist in the dim interior of the barn took the form of a young woman with a waterfall of luxurious blond curls. Anna Louise Putnam snapped open a beribboned pink silk fan and peered over it, her lavender eyes the picture of innocence.

Verity sighed. "You know I hate it when you and Percy sneak up on me."

Anna Louise shrugged her delicate shoulders. Clearly any attempt to scold her into behaving was a waste of effort.

The hazy figure standing before Verity was the wife of the farm's other resident ghost, Percy Putnam, a Civil War officer whose family had owned the farm before the Cades. Sharing a house with the unliving took some getting used to. The couple tended to appear suddenly and often at inconvenient times. They had assured her that they would reveal their existence only to her. Verity told herself she was adjusting reasonably well to the situation, for someone who'd never believed in ghosts.

Today, Anna Louise's floor-length ruffled dress resembled a ballgown more than anything a 19th-century farmer's wife might wear. The Virginia-born ghost possessed a refined fashion sense. Not that the love of beautiful garments was unusual for a woman. It was *how* she acquired her wardrobe that mystified Verity. Apparently, all Anna Louise needed to do was think of a new outfit and—*voila!*—she appeared in it. Today's choice of dress was an apricot muslin with velvet flocking, ivory roses and delicate embroidered green vines over the bodice. Lacework of a particularly intricate pattern encircled her slender throat and wrists. Layers of petticoats held the skirts far out around her ankles.

"I didn't sneak up on you," Anna Louise objected. "I merely came to your rescue when you screamed."

"Did I really scream? It was just a mouse. I didn't need rescuing."

Anna Louise's aura shivered. "Nasty things those." She wrinkled her nose.

Deceased circa 1878, the Putnams first appeared to Verity on the one-year anniversary of Mark's death. They explained that they were afraid she would sell the land to the town's physician for his new medical center. At the time, Verity's finances had been in such bad shape she feared she would have no choice but to sell.

Fortunately, she discovered the value of her mother-in-law's collection of rare porcelain figurines—*thank you, Karen, dear!*—and the auction money paid off most of the loan Mark had secured for the computerized milking system.

"What will you do about the mice?" Anna Louise asked, casting her eyes warily across the barn floor. "You probably have rats, too."

"I really don't want to set out traps or poison, but they're taking over my barn."

"Why don't you just get a kitty-cat?" Anna Louise produced a surprisingly realistic purring sound in her throat.

"I guess I should, although Mark thought it was a bad idea." Verity smiled, imagining him gazing down from heaven and shaking his head in dismay. "Maybe a pair of sweet kittens?"

"No," Anna Louise said firmly. "Not kittens. The rats would eat them for breakfast."

"Really?" Verity was horrified.

"Figuratively speaking, darlin'. No, you definitely do not want kittens if you need instant results. You must procure for yourself a cat old and wise enough to have been trained by its mother to hunt. A large, aggressive, experienced, bloodthirsty—"

"I get the picture," said Verity. "A veteran ratter." She had never owned a cat. Didn't know anything about taking care of one. She had heard that barn cats were feral, or close to it. She supposed they must fend for themselves, living off their catch? Maybe that was good. She wouldn't need to buy cat food.

She thoughtfully chewed the corner of her thumbnail. "I guess I could start by asking around town, or at church. Maybe post a notice on the café bulletin board?"

Anna Louise tossed her head, sending her long, shimmering curls quivering. "That will take far too long. You just leave it to me!" The ghost twinkled out of sight before Verity could stop her.

"Oh, bother!"

Anna Louise—well, both of the Putnams, actually—had an unfortunate history of mischief and innocent mistakes. Based on past experiences, Anna Louise was likely to return with the entirely wrong kind of rat-hunting creature. Like a pit bull. Or mongoose. Or sharp-beaked raptor!

# CHAPTER 4

BY THE NEXT morning Verity had heard not a peep from either of her housemates. *No news is good news?* She could only hope. She had little time to consider her rat/cat problem. Today was the dreaded farm tour.

She had only agreed to hosting Ervin's tour because this was all about education. She believed children should know where their food came from. Adults, too, for that matter. Ervin was right in this respect; she was in a position to provide a valuable learning experience. A wholesome, family adventure the little ones would cherish for the rest of their lives.

She planned, first, to introduce the families to her farm animals and the various food items she produced on her farm—milk, cream, butter, eggs. Then she would give an informative talk; her visitors would learn why healthy, fresh food was not only good for them but tasted better than overly processed grocery-store fare. She had even baked the previous night, planning after her talk to set out a plate of homemade oatmeal cookies along with paper cups of cold milk.

When the immense red tour bus with its gleaming chrome embellishments lumbered up her gravel driveway later that morning, it looked even bigger than on the previous day. The monstrosity nearly filled the entire space between her buttermilk-yellow farmhouse and the milking barn. She stood ready to greet her guests as the bus noisily heaved to a stop. But she was surprised to see so many adult faces peering out at her through the tinted windows. What had happened to this being an event for children?

As Ervin was descending the bus's steps, she could hear him loudly addressing his people, aided by a lapel microphone.

"Now folks, I guarantee you'll have an amazing time at the famous Cade Family Farm. The amazing Verity Cade will be your hostess. Just let me check in with her and we'll get on with this amazing tour in just five minutes."

Verity giggled. *Amazing*—clearly the word of the day! Poor Ervin sounded rattled.

As he crossed the yard toward her, she studied his oddly gaunt face. "Is something wrong, Ervin?"

"No. Well...yes." He coughed to clear his throat and clicked off his microphone. "You see, last night there was some trouble at the inn. Not a good start for my debut tour."

"Oh?" she said.

"Hope you don't mind," he continued in a low voice. "I encouraged more of the adults to join us for the farm tour. You know, get the bad taste out of their mouths."

*Bad taste? Trouble?* "What kind of tr—?"

He waved off further conversation. "Let's just get them off the bus and you can, ummm, do whatever you planned to do with them. I'm sure the grownups will be as enthusiastic as the kiddos."

"How many do you have, total?" She stared uneasily at the bus, trying to count heads through the windows.

"Uh, well. Fifty, give or take."

"Oh." She frowned. That many people wouldn't fit on her

porch for milk and cookies. Did she even have fifty cookies? Fifty paper cups? Milk, at least, wasn't a problem. Maybe she could seat them on the lawn and stand on her front steps to deliver her talk?

"Ervin." She reached out and grabbed his arm when he started to turn back toward the bus. "What exactly happened at the inn?"

"Nothing you need worry about." He looked as if he was trying to smile but his mouth more resembled a death rictus. "I've got it under control. Sheriff Bailey has been informed and—"

"The sheriff?" she gasped. This did not sound good.

But before he could explain, three youngsters tramped down the steps from the bus and ran across the yard toward the tractor barn.

Verity counted to ten. When no adults followed to take control of the escapees, she gritted her teeth. She might even have sworn under her breath. "Ervin, you keep the rest of your group together while I chase down those three before they get into monkey business."

He chuckled. "Good luck!"

She could have strangled him.

By the time she reached the doors on the tractor shed, a chunky little boy in cut-off jeans and t-shirt had managed to roll open one of the doors and squeeze through. The two little girls in his entourage followed him inside. Excited squeals ensued but soon turned frightened.

"It's too dark! I'm scared."

"Whoooo!" teased what she assumed was the boy's voice. "I'm a ghost."

"Nooooo!" a high-pitched voice shrieked. "Stop it!"

Verity shoved both doors open, letting in the brilliant July sunlight. "It's alright, guys. No ghosts." She hoped. "But I'm afraid this barn is off limits. We're going to visit a different one though, and some awesome animals. Would you like to see my cows and chickens?"

"Do you have any llamas?" one of the girls asked. "I love llamas."

"No llamas. Sorry," Verity said.

"Bunny rabbits?"

"No bu—"

"Tractor!" the boy shouted with glee.

Verity spun around in time to see two bare legs clambering up into the seat of the rusty green John Deere. "Oh, for heaven sakes!"

Where were their parents? Was she supposed to babysit as well as entertain the whole group? "You there, little boy, what's your name?" She tried to project as much authority as she could. "Get down from that equipment immediately. You could hurt yourself."

"That's Morgan," one of the girls announced helpfully. "He's always in trouble."

"Vroooom, vroom!" Morgan mimicked engine noise and reached for the steering wheel. A blue sneaker stretched down toward the throttle.

"No! Stop that!" Verity shouted. The chances of him getting the tractor started were close to impossible. But she couldn't risk him falling. Or somehow getting the thing rolling and endangering the two girls, who seemed torn between joining him in his fantasy or fleeing from the angry lady farmer.

Verity reached up to lift Morgan off the tractor and back down to safer ground. "Here, I'll help you."

"No! Get away!" He kicked viciously at her.

She backed off, shocked. The toe of his sneaker only grazed her, but that wasn't the point. "Hey! I said get down. *Now!* I'm an adult—you have to listen to me!"

He howled with laughter and started fiddling with the controls. Desperate now, she came up with only two options. Physically knock the kid off the tractor seat and onto his little keister. Or dash outside in search of reinforcements. The first felt like a much more satisfying solution but might be illegal.

As it happened, neither was necessary.

A mystified expression suddenly crossed the boy's face. He stiffened as his entire body lifted up off the tractor seat and into the air. His arms swinging wildly, feet dangling, he franticly kicked air.

"Morgan's flying!" the taller of the two girls shrieked. "Look, look!"

His eyes wide, mouth forming a silent 'Oh!' the boy revolved in the air like a human corkscrew. He twisted round to look behind, beneath, and all around himself, meanwhile levitating five feet off the barn floor as he rose in a smooth arc away from the tractor and toward Verity.

It didn't take her long to figure out what was happening. She hid a smile as Morgan lowered, ever so slowly, until the tips of his sneakers gently touched ground.

"Hey, how'd you do that?" he demanded.

"Wasn't me." She made a face at him. "Ghosts."

He wrinkled his nose at her and snarled something that might have been a cuss word. Then he bolted out through the barn doors. His two companions chased after him, screaming.

Releasing a long breath of relief, Verity closed her eyes. She rubbed a knuckle into the throbbing spot above the bridge of her nose.

"Percy," she whispered, "I know that was you. Thank you." No answer. "Although I'm sure I could have handled him." *With a little help from the National Guard. What a little demon!*

Still no response from her savior. Not that it mattered. Far better if the two wandering souls remained invisible and unheard of for the next hour or two.

Verity reclosed the barn doors and marched across the yard toward Ervin. His group had clustered around him in the blistering sun beside the bus. Heat waves rose up from the chrome. Several in his party were fanning themselves with what appeared to be a brochure. Before she let them move an inch, she would have a stern word with them about proper behavior and safety precautions for guests at a working farm. And she'd give them a chance to apologize for allowing the children to run amok.

But as she moved closer to her visitors, she saw that, far from looking mortified and apologetic for their lapse in parenting, every single one of them was glaring at her.

"There she is!" the young tractor cowboy shouted. "Sh-she grabbed me! Hard!"

A woman with long sandy-brown hair, wearing a polka-dot halter top and shorts, stepped toward Verity. "Who gave you the right to lay a hand on my child?" she blustered. "I heard you yelling at him all the way from here!"

*Then why didn't you come and take control of him?*

"He was playing with dangerous equipment. He, or the children with him, might have been hurt." She kept her voice as calm and free of emotion as possible. "When I asked him to stop and get down from my tractor he refused."

Mom took a moment to assess this new information, which was apparently quite different from what her son had shared with her. Abruptly, she turned and flat-handed her son upside the head. "I told you to behave yourself, Morgan. One more stunt like that and I'll take away your phone."

*A kid that age has his own phone?* He looked to be no more than five years old. Verity restrained herself from a satisfying eyeroll.

"We all need to pay attention to safety rules on a farm," Verity said firmly. "Just like at school or in your own home where you have rules that—"

"I'm sure there will be no more incidents," Ervin inserted quickly, with a pleading look toward Verity. "Now, let's move along, everyone. And please stay together. There's so much amazing stuff to see here."

Before she could finish her rules speech, Ervin was hurrying his customers along toward the milking barn. Verity whipped out her cellphone to call the twins and warn them that the mob was on its way toward them. She could only hope that the rest of the tour would go more smoothly.

In retrospect, she really should have known better.

In the cow barn, two teenage boys vaulted over impromptu barriers Jason and Jerry had erected earlier that morning. They rushed at the cows, windmilling their arms and shouting, "Moo! Moo! Mo-o-o!" Unaccustomed to such behavior from humans, the animals crowded away from their attackers, jostling each other, their soft brown eyes wide with terror. Again, no adult stepped forward to stop them and Verity was forced to act. Jason herded the boys back behind the barriers and lectured them about paying attention to the posted "No Admittance" signs.

"Morons. Probably can't read," Jerry muttered under his breath.

The chickens left the visitors unimpressed. "Filthy, ugly things, they are," one of the women snorted.

"But they sure taste good," a man laughed.

A toddler somehow crawled into one of the coops—*memo to self, find the hole before a fox does*—sending the hens clucking in hysterical panic. The curly-haired cherub giggled and screeched, "Chickie...chickie, chickie!" Verity thrust herself through the crowd of unconcerned onlookers who seemed charmed by the rugrat's close encounter with farm life. Before

Verity could reach her, the child was clutching an egg in each hand, which she gleefully smashed against the wooden hutch.

After order was restored—but not Verity's nerves—Jason hitched the flat-bed haying wagon to a tractor. Everyone piled on and they rode across the bumpy field to the brook that bordered the Cade property. Which turned out to be a brilliant idea. For nearly an hour the younger members of the crowd (as well as some adults) entertained themselves by paddling in the stream, trying to catch tadpoles, water striders, and the trout fingerlings with which the water had been stocked.

Finally, Verity unloaded the group onto her front lawn. She announced that a snack would be served after a short talk about the importance of family farms. Only a few people seemed interested in what she was saying. Most of the adults took this as an opportunity to check messages on their phones. A few chatted loudly among themselves, forcing her to shout to be heard.

Exhausted by the effort of playing hostess and educator to a less than appreciative crowd, she cut short her lecture and invited everyone to come forward to the porch for milk "straight from cow to you!" And homemade cookies. "One each, please!" she chirped with strained cheerfulness. "We need to make sure there's enough for everyone." Her cookie rationing was met with a chorus of disappointed groans.

Verity looked around for Ervin and found him ringed by half a dozen tourists. She tried to get his attention, waving toward the bus, hoping he'd get the idea and herd everyone on board. She didn't think she could take another minute of this. Her head ached, fit to splitting open. Ervin continued to ignore her awkward semaphores.

As Verity pushed her way between people to reach him, she caught the tail end of a conversation between two of her visitors.

"The least the woman could do," the man was saying, "is offer a choice of adult beverages."

*This is a farm, not a bar!*

She stopped short but was unwilling to trust her ability to carry on polite conversation. The moment she got Ervin alone she'd tell him to forget about asking her to host another farm tour. Ever!

As though he read her thoughts, Ervin glanced toward her anxiously, then announced the bus would leave as soon as everyone was on board.

Verity breathed. Really breathed for the first time in over an hour.

She walked around her yard, picking up paper cups and napkins from her lawn. Two men lagged behind, lost in conversation. She overheard the word "robbery." She automatically tuned in, thinking they might be discussing the mysterious trouble Ervin had mentioned earlier.

"Did you hear whose rooms were broken into?" the taller of the two men said. He looked to be sixtyish, his trim gray hair almost silver. The word 'dignified' came to her mind.

"Don't know for sure," grumbled a red-haired man she'd seen standing next to Morgan's mother earlier. Morgan's father, she guessed, given father and son's shared coloring and features. "Ours for one. And a young couple's room down the hall from us."

They continued walking toward the bus.

Verity surreptitiously followed them.

"My wife left her purse in the room when we went downstairs to dinner," Mr. Morgan continued. "Stupid." He rolled his eyes.

*Man-to-man, always blame the woman.*

Morgan's dad continued. "No big deal, I guess. MasterCard is expressing a new card. She also had some cash in her purse.

But that young man sure was steamed. He was the one who blew up in the café yesterday. Swears this tour is some kind of scheme to fleece him."

"The two of you should sue the inn," his friend said conversationally as they clumped up the bus's steps. "No security at all, far as I can tell. Apparently, the town doesn't even have a real police force."

Minutes later, Verity was still thinking about the break-ins when the mega-bus roared to life. It rolled down her driveway, trailing a river of diesel fumes and spitting gravel from beneath its huge tires. She lifted a hand in an apathetic wave.

Exhausted, she turned toward the comfort of her farmhouse. She yearned for a cup of hot tea and an even hotter bath but she couldn't get the conversation she'd overheard out of her mind.

She wondered if there was any chance the sheriff might fill her in about the robberies. Maybe he'd ask for the EPI's help? They were, after all, experienced investigators now.

# CHAPTER 5

LATER THAT SAME DAY, while harvesting early sweet corn from her kitchen garden, Verity wondered if she should talk to the inn's owner. Just to see if there was anything she could do to help. Although how that might be possible—short of nabbing the thief—she had no idea. She felt so bad for Henry. Imagine being sued just months after opening!

The restoration of the Victorian-era inn, which had fallen into ruin and finally been abandoned by an earlier owner in 1955, had only recently been completed by Henry. He had poured his enthusiasm and a truckload of money into giving it a new life. Verity (along with most of the town) attended the open house celebrating its re-opening. She wasn't the only one impressed with the results.

She worked her way down another row of cornstalks, remembering that festive day.

Henry had lovingly retained the 19th-century floorplans and design. Gingerbread scrolling embellished twin cupolas. The faded clapboard exterior now gleamed in a pale yellow, offset by dark-green shutters and pristine white veranda railings. All of his color choices, he announced proudly, were based on hand-tinted daguerreotypes of the original inn.

Inside, antique fixtures and fireplaces were refurbished. His contractor found the original gaslight sconces and crystal chandeliers gathering dust in the basement. Cleaned, polished, and wired for modern electricity, they were reinstalled in the parlor, dining room, library and sitting room. He shrewdly kept the clawfoot bathtub in the shared bathroom in an upstairs hallway, to preserve the ambiance of the era. However, Henry added ensuite bathrooms in the largest four rooms. Updating all the plumbing and wiring throughout the inn had kept local contractors busy for months.

Verity could only imagine the cost.

She and Mark had made do with the original plumbing and fixtures in their farmhouse. Pipes banged. Timbers creaked at changes of temperature or humidity. Hot water was undependable. But she dearly loved the old place. And every little sound or structural temper tantrum reminded her of him. Her Mark. And made her smile.

She picked two dozen ears of corn, the husks still green, silks just starting to turn brown. They were so ripe with natural sugars, the field smelled like a bakery shop. Slinging her basket over the crook of her arm, she turned toward the house. She would husk and parboil all but one of the ears (saving it for her dinner), then bag and freeze them after they cooled. Nothing was better than hot corn on the cob on a cold winter's day.

She sat on her back steps shucking the leathery husks away from the golden kernels, one cob after another, lost in the mechanical chore while her mind churned.

Thinking...thinking...thinking.

If she warned Henry about what his guests were saying with regard to his lack of security, maybe he could do something to improve it. Even if he did, though, members of the town council who were already against granting Henry his liquor license might use the thefts as another excuse for refusing his application. They could claim that reopening the inn attracted crime to the town.

Verity shook her head. *Stop worrying about everyone else's business,* she told herself. It was all she could do to keep up with her own responsibilities. She also wished she could see a way to increase her farmhands' wages. The brothers never complained about taking on extra work after Mark passed, even though she couldn't afford to increase their salaries.

An hour later, after storing her golden bounty of corn in the big chest freezer in her pantry, she tugged on her Wellingtons and walked out to the milking parlor to check on the Robo-Milkers for the second time that day. All three machines were occupied with bovine customers, while other cows lingered nearby, presumably waiting their turn. Or maybe just socializing. Who knew with cows? Seeing her ladies so peacefully unconcerned with life always made her smile. They seemed to have recovered from the teenagers' antics earlier that day. Thank goodness.

When Mark first told her he was considering installing the computerized milking system, she hadn't believed robots could possibly do the same job as milking by hand or with traditional electric suction milkers. These had been dairy farmers' standard methods for decades. But with Robo-Milkers, Mark explained, cows voluntarily walked into a stall, allowed the machine to clean their udders, attach suction nipples, and siphon off their milk.

No way, she thought.

But Mark visited a working farm in New Hampshire that had just such a system and swore it was amazingly efficient. And no, the cows were not traumatized or hurt, as she'd imagined.

"Their farm's herd is much larger than ours, Veri," he reported. "But that just means we need fewer units. And going hi-tech will save us so much time. Time we can use for other jobs on the farm. Or free both of us for much more enjoyable activities." The wicked sparkle and promise of pleasure in his eyes always made her blush.

They planned to try getting pregnant as soon as the big loan was paid off. But her dreams of having a family had evaporated into the air. The freak accident that ended her lovely Mark's life meant there would be no babies. No family. Ever.

She sat down heavily on an overturned tin bucket. The sudden wave of grief was sometimes still too hard to bear.

"Miss Verity, are you unwell?"

She slowly looked out from sad thoughts. A streak of brilliant sunlight slanted through the doorway that led out to the cows' paddock. Blinking away tears she searched for Anna Louise, the source of the voice. What she saw was a very large, levitating amber cat.

Verity squinted at the frantically squirming creature. Even more disturbing was the way it floated in the air. It reminded her of little Morgan, plucked off the tractor by Percy.

"Anna Louise, what are you doing to that poor animal?"

"Oh, sorry, did I startle you again? I forgot to make myself visible after I found your ratter." The air stirred, shimmering in silver waves. Particles coalesced into the shape of Verity's deceased tenant.

This time, Anna Louise Putnam wore a tan-and-blue calico dress, over which was tied a starched white pinafore. Beside her appeared her handsome young husband in full uniform of the Army of the North. Dark-blue wool coat and light-blue trousers with a thin red stripe up the outside of each pant leg. Scabbard and sword strapped to his hip.

Percy doffed his forage cap to Verity in greeting. He had

told her, avoiding the most horrendous details, that he had survived many bloody battles during the American Civil War. He met his beloved Anna Louise on his way back home to Vermont, while tramping through the Virginia woods.

How the couple had died only a few years after they married, they couldn't (or wouldn't) tell her. The mystery of the cause of their deaths appeared somehow connected to their inability to move into the afterlife, as the dead are supposed to do. Since their physical demise, they had remained in Evansfield on the farm that had once been theirs in life.

The cat began to struggle with more energy, limbs flailing, claws raking the air. Anna Louise hurriedly dropped it to the barn floor with an annoyed wrinkle of her nose. "Its name is Lady Macbeth," she stated.

"You're kidding." Verity observed the animal doubtfully. It definitely wasn't a kitten. Neither was it the sleek stalker of vermin she'd pictured in her mind. She wondered if the fat thing could move fast enough to catch any but the most decrepit rodent.

No sooner had that thought occurred to her than the cat sprang across the floor with impressive speed and agility. It dove headlong into a pile of hay, presumably after prey that Verity hadn't even seen.

"Oh, well then." Verity smiled. "Looks like she'll do."

Seconds later Lady MacBeth backed her rump out of the straw, sending a puff of dust and golden motes into the air. A limp, furry prize clenched in its toothy jaws, the cat trotted away with an air of having proven herself.

"And how did you know she'd be so good at her job?" Verity asked.

"Its owners told me," Anna Louise began. But seeing the horrified look on Verity's face, she added, "What I meant to say was, I *overheard* the woman talking with a neighbor. She was having a strange sort of party on her front lawn. I think she must have shifted every stick of furniture out of her house and put price tags on it all."

"They called it a yard sale," Percy added for Verity's benefit.

"I see," she said, holding back a smile.

"The cat was in a cage with a sign on it—*'I need a new home.'*"

"And why were they giving away their cat?" Verity didn't want a defective cat.

"The family is moving and can't take the animal with them," Percy supplied. "I also overheard the owner talking to a neighbor."

Verity eyed the two ghosts with suspicion. "You're sure you didn't make yourselves even a little bit visible to get this information?"

"We know the rules, darlin'," Anna Louise tittered. "Only in an absolute emergency."

"We don't want to attract undue attention any more than you do," Percy assured her with a military officer's solemnity.

"I waited until the cat's owner was bargaining with a neighbor over a bookcase," Anna Louise said. "Then I snatched up the cat before anyone else could." She looked terribly pleased with herself.

"You just *took* their cat?"

"Percy left a note promising it was going to a good home."

"At the Cade Family Farm," he added. "I signed your name."

"*You what?*" Verity gasped.

"Well, we couldn't very well sign our names, seeing as we're dead." Anna Louise arched a brow as if she thought Verity rather slow in the head. "Don't you think that would raise suspicion?"

"Forgery was a necessary precaution," stated Percy firmly. "An anonymous adopter wouldn't make sense to the woman."

Verity supposed that was so. With a sigh she looked around the barn. Lady M was nowhere in sight. She hoped cats weren't like dogs she had read about, who sometimes traveled miles to reunite with their human family. She really did need the feline's services.

When she turned back to face the ghosts, they seemed less... less what? She couldn't quite put her finger on it. Less *substantial?* Yes, that was it. And sort of wobbly. It was almost as if she was watching images on a TV with only rabbit-ear antennae. *Odd.*

Then again, a lot of what happened with ghosts seemed strange.

"We'll have to see how she does," Verity said. "If she spooks my cows or attacks the hens, I won't keep her."

"I'll tell her to mind her manners," Anna Louise promised. *As if,* Verity thought, *you are an expert on proper behavior.*

Percy just grinned at his wife, in full rapture of her, as always.

## CHAPTER 6

THE NEXT DAY, Verity headed off on her deliveries, planning to save her two commercial stops—the Wayfarer's Inn and Cat's Cradle Café—for the end of her route. She was anxious to hear from the horse's mouth about the rumored thefts. This particular horse being Sheriff Fred Bailey. Maybe he'd tell her whether the thief she'd overheard the two men talking about had been arrested. She was certain she would find Bailey at the café—his usual breakfast stop.

Verity was relieved to find the tour bus nowhere in sight, leaving the alley alongside the café open to her use. She drove through, unloaded, pushed the trolley into Sunny's kitchen, and unpacked her order while the café staff called out friendly greetings to her.

Verity peeked out through the kitchen door into the dining room, but the sheriff wasn't there.

"Fresh croissants on the prep island," Sunny called to her from behind the cash register. "Two have your name on them."

"Thanks!" Verity bagged a pair of the flaky pastries, gathered her crates and canvas bags, then wheeled back out the door and down the ramp. She leaned against the truck's cab and munched happily on one of her croissants. *Buttery yumminess!* The second one would be even better with coffee, at home.

The inn was virtually next door and had similar access for deliveries. She didn't really need to move her truck. But she noticed that two large, galvanized garbage cans behind the inn had rolled onto their sides. Trash littered the bare ground around them, standing in the way of her trolley when she wheeled up to the inn's rear entrance.

Strange, she mused. There had been no high winds recently to topple them. And she hadn't heard about dogs or raccoons recently ransacking neighborhood bins. Anyway, Henry and his staff would have known to make sure the lids were tight, to prevent just such a mess.

"Oh bother," she muttered.

Verity pulled work gloves out of her truck's console. With effort, she heaved up the first heavy can and stood it on the cement slab where it belonged. Thankfully, the remaining contents stayed inside. She was preparing to scoop up as much of the spillage as she could when she saw a shoe sticking out from the mess. A Reebok, to be precise, white with red striping. It looked almost new. Too new to throw out.

She moved closer.

Just above the athletic shoe she saw a khaki pant cuff. She peered around the second toppled trash can and behind it lay the rest of a person. The man in a black t-shirt and chinos lay motionless on the litter-strewn ground.

"Oh jeezus!" She drew a sharp breath stumbling backward, her heart racing.

Her first thought was one of the tourists had drunk too much the night before and passed out behind the inn. But why would any of Henry's guests be outside in the service alley? She forced herself to move closer again, her eyes fixed on the man's torso, hoping to see his ribcage inflate with rhythmic breaths.

Nothing.

"Sir? Do you need help?" she whispered.

Silence.

Verity studied the side of the man's face that wasn't planted in dirt and pebbles. Of course she recognized him. Rudy O'Halloran. The man who had made such a fuss in the café, insisting upon being served before others. Trash talking her town. Baiting Jason until they nearly came to blows.

Feeling suddenly dizzy and short of breath, she thrust a trembling hand into her jeans pocket, fumbled out her cellphone and punched 911 with her thumb. While it was ringing, she leaned down over the man. She told herself she probably should feel for a pulse, but she cringed at the thought of touching him.

The emergency operator responded and Verity focused on keeping her voice from cracking while she answered the woman's questions. Her exact location? Did she know the unconscious person's name? Had she already called the police? Did she attempt CPR?

*Oh God! CPR. Of course!* Some first responder she'd make. She hadn't even considered taking steps to revive him. She closed her eyes to concentrate on the rapid flow questions but that made her feel nauseous and even more dizzy.

"As best you can tell, ma'am, is the person breathing?"

Her own breaths sounded so loud and raspy she found it hard to hear anything else. Adrenaline surged through her in powerful electric jolts. She had an idea and rushed back to her truck, her fingers gripping her cellphone hard for fear of dropping it and losing the connection. Reaching into her truck she found the small mirror she kept in her glove compartment then ran back to the man. Holding the mirror to his nose and mouth, she waited for a wisp of fog to bloom on the glass.

The mirror remained clear.

"I'm pretty sure he's dead," she said. "Oh, God! Please hurry."

*Idiot*, she scolded herself. *Please hurry?* What did it matter how long it took for help to arrive? It was already too late for Rudy O'Halloran.

The ambulance arrived less than a minute ahead of Sheriff Fred Bailey and two of his deputies. The sheriff slid a puzzled look at Verity, who sat on the rear bumper of her truck, out of the way of the EMTs.

The sheriff approached the body just as one of the medical techs stood up from examining the man.

"Well, Jack?" Bailey said.

"Gone," the tech responded.

"How long?"

A shrug.

Apparently, the two men knew each other and had established a tidy verbal shorthand.

The EMT angled his head left then right, as if giving the question more thought. "At a guess—maybe six, seven hours. Doc will know better."

"So-o-o, late last night," Bailey said, although it sounded as if the observation was just for his own benefit. He looked along the alley, then up at the inn's rear-facing windows, and finally at the six-foot-high fence that separated the rear entries of the commercial businesses from a neighborhood of single-family homes.

"This the way you found everything, Mrs. Cade?" Bailey said without turning to look at her.

"Yes, Sheriff. Well, pretty much anyway." Thankfully, her voice sounded a little steadier now. "I righted one of the trash cans and started to pick up trash before I saw the...um...dead person."

Bailey squatted low over the body, peering at the man's face. "You sure 'bout that?"

She nodded her head before realizing he couldn't see her. "I'm sure," she said.

While waiting for help to arrive she had, however, done something else she wasn't sure the sheriff would approve of. She used her phone to take pictures of the body, the toppled metal can and scattered trash, the rear door and windows of the inn, a huge rusty-green iron dumpster, and several sections of the ground. The alley had never been paved; its surface was packed dirt and gravel. Some spots seemed to her rougher than others, sort of chewed up. Maybe by truck or car tires? Or Ervin's bus. Then again, the disturbance could have been the result of a scuffle. Maybe.

"You'll send me the pics you took." He turned and gave her a 'gotcha' look. "Right?"

She scowled at him. The man knew her too damn well. "Of course, Sheriff." She sent off the photos while his guys decorated the area with streamers of yellow crime scene tape and blocked off entry into the alley.

She hadn't been much use in saving Rudy—for which she truly felt bad, even though he had been a creep. But he probably didn't deserve to die, as young as he was. Probably not much over thirty years old. And with a wife. That part made her sad. But she could at least make life a little easier for the sheriff and his deputies. Whether the tourist had suffered a heart attack, accidentally injured himself, or something more sinister had occurred, Bailey was responsible for the investigation.

He stood up and strode across the open space toward her. "Does Ervin, Henry or anyone else know about this?"

"I assume not," she said. "I haven't seen a soul since I got here."

"My dispatcher told me you ID'd the fella."

Verity had been so shaken she couldn't remember half of what she'd said to the 911 operator. "I guess I must have. His name is Rudy O'Halloran. I saw him in the café yesterday. He was less than subtle when introducing himself."

"I heard something 'bout that from Sunny Whitaker. A troublemaker, she said. I'll be wantin' to talk to both you gals later."

Just then, the inn's rear door flew open and Henry Brockhurst stepped out onto the landing, his white hair mussed and standing up on end, his thin face cherry red. If he had been a cartoon character, he would have just received a high-voltage electrical shock.

"What's this all about, Bailey?" He waved at the scene below, letting everyone know he was unhappy they were on his property. "I have paying guests who have a right not to be disturbed by all your ruckus so early in the morning."

Then his line of sight angled down toward the ring of people standing around a figure who definitely wasn't standing. Henry visibly flinched. His ruddy cheeks paled.

"Lordy. That man there, he's not moving."

"We've noticed, Henry," Bailey said dryly.

Verity would have laughed had the situation not been so serious. Long-time poker buddies, the two men enjoyed nothing more than ribbing each other. Apparently, not even death changed that.

"Don't come down, Henry," Bailey called up to the inn's owner. "I'll be up to talk with you in a little while. Just one question. Any of your tourists gone missing?"

Verity flashed Bailey a confused look. Hadn't she just told him whose body was lying there? But a second later it came to her—he wasn't asking for the name of the victim. He wanted to know if someone else had suddenly disappeared. Someone who might have been involved in the man's death or witnessed what had happened last night.

Henry backed toward the open doorway, shaking his head, eyes fixed on the body. "Best I go...ah, check on my guests." He wobbled and grasped the wooden door frame for support.

"Right," Bailey shouted back. "You can get a closer look at him later, if I need you to verify his identity." Not that Henry looked like he *wanted* a closer look. The sheriff turned back to Verity. "What's the doc's ETA?"

"The 911 operator said he's on his way." She looked over at the body and again felt unaccountably sorry for the man. "Can't the EMTs take him away now?"

"No. We need official time of death." He checked his phone. "Thanks. Just got your pics." When he turned back to her, he frowned. "What is it, Mrs. Cade?"

She sighed. "Sheriff, I told you I didn't touch him, but—" he narrowed his eyes at her "and I didn't. Honest. So don't stare at me that way! But anyone can see there's a lot of blood under his head."

"Noticed that, did you? Right, so we're probably lookin' at a fractured skull. Cause unknown."

She hesitated. Having no training or experience in law enforcement, she felt out of her element discussing what might or might not constitute a crime scene. Who was she, owner of a tiny dairy farm, to offer her opinion on anything like this? She nipped at her bottom lip nervously.

"Just say it," Bailey growled. "What's on your mind? I can see you're ready to pop."

And she was. She really wanted to tell him what she had observed in the minutes before he and his team arrived. But one thing she'd learned about Fred Bailey—he absolutely hated it when anyone provided a possible explanation for a suspicious situation before he thought of it.

"I was just thinking—why *here*? Why was O'Halloran outside behind the inn when there's nothing to see but a trash dumpster and recycling bins and the backside of a dusty old fence? What was the attraction?"

"Stepped out for a smoke?" he suggested, then looked almost contrite at the lightness of his chosen words. "OK, I get it. You get a kick out of puzzles. Mysteries. Things that don't make sense to you. That's why you ladies formed your little club." He smirked at her.

She glowered back.

"Hey," he continued, "the man probably had a few drinks too many. Ran into somethin' hard like that dumpster over there after stumbling into the alley by accident. He hits his head, falls unconscious to the ground. If he was out for long and the injury serious enough, he could have bled out in no time."

"But if he hit his head on the dumpster," she said, "which, as you can see, is a good twenty feet away from where he's lying, why isn't blood over there, too?" He scowled, already looking annoyed at her. Not good. In for a penny... "And exactly how did he get to the middle of the alley without leaving a trail of blood?"

"Because he didn't go down right away," he snapped. "The man's dazed, staggers around for a few seconds before he drops. Who knows about the goddamn blood? Don't you worry, missy...Mrs. Cade," he quickly corrected himself when he saw her eyebrows shoot skyward. "My guys will take samples from everythin' 'round here. We'll find out what he collided with." His eyes narrowed and slid toward her when she didn't agree with him. "What now?"

Verity drew a deep breath and scanned the scene again,

checking her theory, before returning her gaze to the body on the ground. "He's facing the wrong way."

Bailey let out a long, weary breath. "What do you mean the *wrong* way? Is there a right way to fall down?"

She sketched a line in the air with her finger from the ugly green iron dumpster—the largest and most obvious surface with sharp corners and rusty edges—to the body. "Say, he stumbles, hits the back of his head over there. Then staggers forward and away from the point of collision."

"He mighta turned and stumbled backward." He demonstrated by rocking back on his heels and pretending to trip.

"True. But whether he's moving forward or backward, that is the direction in which he would naturally fall. Head leading his body. It's a matter of momentum and gravity. We fall in the direction we're moving."

Bailey said nothing, but she could sense the man's simmering annoyance.

Dare she risk trying again? "Look at how he's lying. His head," she said slowly, "is pointing toward the dumpster, not away from it."

A beat passed. Then another.

The change in the sheriff's posture was almost imperceptible. He shifted from one foot to the other. His left shoulder lowered a fraction of an inch. She smiled; he got it.

"I see what you're saying," he mumbled. "Far from conclusive though."

"Of course," she agreed, meekly.

He leaned against her truck, his thumbs hitched in his pants pockets and closed his eyes—concentrating. "Someone mighta snuck up on him from behind and brained him. That's what you're thinking?"

"It's at least a possibility."

His eyes snapped open. "Sure hope you're wrong. Un-be-lievable paperwork if it's murder."

"Fred!" A shout came from down the alley. Dr. John Evans had arrived.

Mark had told her that the town had been named in honor of one of the physician's ancestors, back in the 18th century. Ever since then, a member of the Evans family had lived in Evansfield and provided the community with medical care.

The father of two teenagers, John Evans had lost his wife the previous year, making him the most eligible bachelor in the area. His boyish good looks, even in his forties, and athletic appearance had lured many a female patient away from physicians in Springfield, the nearest city. Verity expected the single women of Evansfield wouldn't rest until they saw the good doctor remarried. Each of them hoping to fill the position herself.

Any attraction she personally might ever have developed toward Evans had been squelched months ago when she experienced a rare display of the man's temper. He had since then apologized to her, and they were now, if not exactly friends, at least cordial neighbors.

Verity observed the doctor as he approached them. Deep wrinkles marked his broad forehead; his lips were tightly pursed. She wondered if these signs meant he already knew the man whose body he had come to examine.

"Thanks for gettin' here so fast, Doc," Bailey said. In fact, they had been waiting for over half an hour even though Evans's office was five minutes away. The sheriff ducked under the crime scene tape, brushing past the waiting EMTs. Verity followed because no one had told her she couldn't.

The doctor held out his hand to shake with the sheriff. "I would have been here sooner if—oh, good morning, Mrs. Cade, didn't notice you over there—if I hadn't needed to inventory my prescription samples. Someone broke into my surgery last night. I wanted to record the missing items so I could give you a list straight away."

"That's awful," Verity jumped in. "Did they do much damage?"

Bailey shot her a back-off glare.

"No. It appears they knew what they were looking for. Just went after the drugs they could sell easiest."

"You got the list on you?" Bailey took out a battered black notebook from his hip pocket.

"You probably don't even need to see it to guess most of the stolen items," Evans said, handing Bailey a slip of paper. "They cleaned out my supply of Oxycodone, Fentanyl, Xanax and Seconal. Samples of some antibiotics, too, but they may have thought those were something else."

"I didn't get a report of a theft," Bailey said. "Why's that?"

"I only walked into my office after I got the call to come here. Just stopped to pick up my bag, then saw the cabinets open." Evans shook his head. "It was quite a shock, I can tell you."

Bailey returned the notebook and list to his pocket. "Can't say as I remember you ever havin' a break-in before."

"Never did. The locks I installed years ago have always been enough to deter mischief makers. This wasn't the work of local kids. Like I said, whoever it was, they knew what to take for best profit on the street. They would have been in and out in five minutes. You'll come by and take a look, won't you, sheriff?"

"Sure thing. My boys'll dust for prints. But if you're right about the thief knowin' what they were doin', they likely were smart enough to wear gloves." Barely taking a breath, he gestured toward the body and switched topics. "Take a gander at this fella and tell me what you can."

Evans dropped a what's-she-doing-here look on Verity.

"I should go," she murmured. "And let the two of you get on with things here."

Bailey put out his hand, surprising her with a touch on her arm. "No, stay please, if you can. I may have a job for you." She had no idea what he had in mind. In the past, the man had done everything he could to keep her and her friends out of official investigations.

The doctor walked over to the body and set his bag on a less garbage-y area of ground. He pulled on gloves, squatted. Elbows braced on knees, he studied his patient. "Know his name?"

The sheriff gave a grunt of acknowledgement. "Mrs. Cade identified him as a Rudy O'Halloran, one of the group of tourists that came up from New York on Ervin's bus. They're stayin' at the inn. His wife is inside, not yet apprised of the situation."

Verity hung back, less than keen on looking again at the dead man. If they rolled him over, what would she see? Blood, she could tolerate. When you worked with animals, you got used to bodily fluids of all sorts. Human brains and splintered bone, not so much. Her stomach burbled at the thought.

The doctor ran gloved fingers around O'Halloran's skull, jaw line, throat. He examined the underside of the man's head wound, then carefully eased him onto his side so that he could lift his shirt to peer in at his chest.

"Well," he said, "no question the man's dead. I'll fill out the death certificate and send it over to your office by noon. It appears he took a vicious blow to the back of his head. I guess you saw that." The sheriff nodded. "A blunt object is my guess. Something heavy. Probably one whack would have done it but— I can't tell—there may have been additional blows. You're sending him to Springfield for the real-deal forensics and autopsy, I hope."

"Yup."

*Thank God*, Verity thought. During an earlier murder investigation, Bailey had been satisfied with the local coroner's assessment of cause of death, even though the elected official had no medical training.

"You have a possible murder weapon?" Evans asked.

"Nope. Not yet sure what we're dealin' with. Accident, assault, or somethin' else. If anyone was out here with Mr. O'Halloran last night, would be nice to know who." He shoveled the fingers of his right hand through the remaining strands of his graying hair and looked up from the body. "I'll be over to your place later, John, to look at your break-in."

Verity waited for the doctor to leave then, "You said you need me for something, Sheriff?"

"Maybe. Not so sure now," Bailey murmured distractedly. "You go on with your day. I have to give Mrs. O'Halloran the bad news."

SOMETHING WAS TROUBLING VERITY. And it had nothing to do with the gruesome scene behind the Historic Wayfarer's Inn. It involved the incident in the Cat's Cradle Café the day before.

Bailey hadn't been in the café when Rudy O'Halloran was slinging insults at the town and everyone in it. He hadn't witnessed Jason going ballistic or how the place felt as if it might erupt into something like a Western-movie saloon brawl. The sheriff hadn't heard the threat in Jason's voice or O'Halloran's sadistic challenges, egging on the younger man as if he welcomed a fight.

But everyone in the crowded café had heard them. And word of their confrontation already would have gotten around town faster than the cartoon roadrunner escaping from Wile E. Coyote. Sooner or later, the sheriff must realize how serious the shouting match had been. Verity felt sick at the thought. Because she knew how guilty that made Jason look, now that his tormentor was dead.

Of course, she also knew her farmhand was more talk than

action. Never once had Jason shown disrespect or anger toward her, no matter how dirty the job she asked him and his brother to do. Although, she had to admit, the Grimalskis' respect for her was most likely due to their continuing loyalty to Mark. They had started working for him part-time, as teenagers. The two boys worshipped him. After her husband's death, the brothers became super-protective of her; they seemed to feel it was their job to make sure nothing bad ever happened to her again. Sweet of them, yes, but unnecessary, not to mention impossible.

Maybe this was the reason she had backed off from immediately sharing with the sheriff her observation of the alley's broken surface. Because it just might point to murder rather than an unfortunate accident. In her heart, she didn't want to believe that anyone in her town was capable of murdering another human being. Perhaps she wanted to protect Jason, as he and his brother protected her. Even if she broke the law by doing it.


Later that afternoon, Verity called for an emergency meeting of the Evansfield Private Investigators. They would gather in her kitchen, the largest room in the old farmhouse. A massive oak trestle table dominated the center of the room, easily seating all seven members and providing ample room for munchies.

The table's worn top had served generations of Cade women as their preferred command center for egg sorting, butter churning, preparation of family meals and for feeding seasonal farmhands. On its scarred surface families threaded popcorn garlands to loop around Christmas trees and dyed eggs to hide at Easter. It had stalwartly hosted both joyous celebrations and solemn wakes.

The beautiful Sheridan mahogany table in the dining room seemed to Verity too formal for everyday use, practically demanding her mother-in-law's blue Wedgwood china and delicately etched lead crystal. After Mark's parents passed away, he and Verity always ate their meals in the kitchen. And now that she was the only one living in the farmhouse—the only *living* soul, that is—setting a single place in the dining room seemed ridiculous. Even when she invited friends over for coffee or a meal, everyone gravitated toward her cheerful yellow kitchen with its country-blue French floor tiles.

In preparing for the EPI's meeting, Verity took the precaution of reminding Lieutenant and Mrs. Percy Putnam, deceased, to remain out of sight. She was well aware of the couple's desire to join her investigators and wanted to nip that notion in the bud. She shuddered to think of the consequences, if her friends (not to mention the rest of the world) discovered she was sharing her home with two ghosts!

The EPI had arisen from a small group of her delivery route customers. What had started as a joint effort to solve the baffling murder of one of their own evolved into an unofficial support group for the understaffed local sheriff's department.

Initially, Sheriff Bailey had flat-out refused their help. ("Interfering" and "meddling" were how he described their efforts. At least those were the repeatable words.) But he eventually recognized the advantage of having reliable volunteers capable of relieving his staff of a few of the more mundane and time-consuming community duties.

As soon as everyone had their coffee or tea and selected a pastry from the tray of day-old cinnamon bear claws, cherry danishes, and double-fudge brownies from the café, they settled into their seats. All eyes turned expectantly to Sunny Whitaker, their usual spokesperson, who remained standing.

"We have only one item on today's agenda," she began solemnly. "I assume, by now, everyone has heard that one of our visiting tourists passed away last night." She waited for murmurs around the table to quiet before continuing. "His name was Rudy O'Halloran. This morning, Verity discovered his body in—"

"Oh, Verity, it was *you* who found the man? How awful!" Kate commiserated. "I hope it wasn't too—" she wrinkled her nose "—you know, gory."

Verity tried to give their youngest member, mother of two little girls, a reassuring smile. She feared her effort wasn't very effective. "It wasn't pleasant. But I wouldn't say the scene was particularly bloody." *Thank goodness.*

"My source told me his whole skull had been smashed in!" Mary Beth Loop said with far too much enthusiasm. "If you watch CSI shows religiously like I do, you'll know that Verity has probably understated the violence of the death scene. Blood and brains must have sprayed all over the—"

"You don't know *that*, MB," Sunny cautioned. "Let's not get carried away by gossip."

"It's not gossip," Mary Beth protested, "the mayor got a full report from Sheriff Bailey." Mary Beth was married to Mayor Rupert J. Loop.

"Verity was there," Denise pointed out, "and Rupert wasn't. I want to hear what she has to say."

Denise Delaney, the town's chocolatier, owned Denise's Chocolate Designs. How she stayed so fit with all that yummy chocolate around, Verity had never understood. Although... Denise did run at least three miles every day before opening her shop, so that might have had something to do with her trim shape.

"Are they doing an autopsy?" Chaundra Adebe asked.

"The sheriff requested I come to his office and make a formal statement," Verity explained. "While I was there, he said they've already sent the body to Springfield, requesting an autopsy to determine exact cause of death. And, of course, he's reviewing other evidence from the scene."

"If our own coroner were performing the autopsy—" Mary Beth paused to take a mammoth bite of cherry pastry then mumbled through a full mouth "—I thertainly would volunteer to athitht him."

Denise hooted. "That's just absurd, MB! The mayor may be our elected coroner—though God knows how that happened—but he isn't a trained forensic specialist and neither are you."

Mary Beth looked sheepish. She swallowed before speaking this time. "I'm sure I could at least examine a head wound and determine something, well, useful. Like, maybe the murder weapon?"

Fumiko Ota threw her hands into the air. "Denise right, MB! You only expert in TV murders!" Although the Japanese-born owner of Evansfield's knitting-and-yarn shop sometimes struggled with her English, today she seemed to be expressing herself clearly enough.

Mary Beth's plump cheeks flushed.

Chaundra patted Mary Beth on the arm. "Let's hear what Verity has to say about the incident," she repeated. "Since she is the one who discovered the body."

"Right," Sunny seconded firmly. "For all we know this was just an unfortunate accident. Veri dear, fill us in, please."

Verity took another sip of her coffee, which had already begun to cool. Scalding hot and lightened with her own cows' rich cream—no sugar, thank you—was how she liked it. She set down her mug and looked around the table at her friends.

"First of all," she began, "I didn't call for this meeting to organize our involvement in this situation because the sheriff hasn't asked for our help. At least not yet. I think we should honor his wishes by staying out of his way. In our last big case—"

"Our *only* real case," Denise said. "Lost pooches and car keys don't count."

"In our *former* case," Verity corrected, "we got a bit pushy by investigating behind Sheriff Bailey's back."

"Because we had no choice," Chaundra insisted. "He claimed the only possible cause of death was suicide. We knew better. But he wouldn't listen to us."

"True," Sunny agreed. "But the Sheriff's Department is Evansfield's only official law enforcement. Bailey has a right to tell civilians to butt out of his investigations."

Mary Beth pouted. "But we're smarter than him."

"Some of us may be," Denise whispered.

Kate giggled and elbowed her.

"The point is," Verity continued, "he has agreed to let us look into local issues like quarrels between neighbors that get out of hand, lost pets, stuff he doesn't have the time or patience to deal with. They aren't criminal offenses. We're merely acting as community support."

"Agreed," Sunny said briskly. "But in case he should ask for our help, we should be prepared. So, bring us up to date on what you know."

Verity cast a wistful gaze at the fat bear claw sitting untouched on her napkin. Studded with plump raisins, riddled with cinnamon, and coated in a vanilla glaze, its deliciousness called to her. She breathed in and swore she could taste its sweet, gooey-ness without taking a bite. Reluctantly, she tried to focus on the information her investigative associates needed to know.

As Verity described the grim scene in the alley, she sketched in pencil on a pad of paper she had brought with her to the table. Clearly, the emerging picture would never hang in an art gallery. A stick-figure represented O'Halloran's body in relation to the rear door of the inn. She drew more shapes—a square, a rectangle, a circle and long spikey line—while describing the toppled-over trash cans, big green dumpster and fence line running parallel to the alley.

"Sorry." She blew out an exasperated breath on examining her pitiful efforts. "I fear my artistic talents haven't advanced since kindergarten. Kate's girls could do better."

"It doesn't matter," Chaundra reassured her. "All we need is the basic idea of the scene. Did you think to take photos?"

"Oh, right!" Verity put down her pencil, moving it and the paper pad to the middle of the table. "I did."

She picked up her phone, clicked on her Gallery, then passed it to Sunny. "What doesn't show up well, and I can't draw for you, is the way the ground around the body looked scuffed or dug up. It seemed to me there had been a struggle. That would also explain why the trash cans had been knocked over."

Mary Beth scrunched up her face, looking disappointed. "Where's the blood? Pictures of any crime scene include markers to show all the locations where blood—"

"Give it a rest, MB," Denise groaned.

"No, she's right," Verity said, giving Mary Beth a smile because she looked so crushed. "I took the photos before the sheriff and his crew got there. The only blood I saw had seeped from beneath O'Halloran's head and it hadn't spread far. The sheriff said his guys would test the whole area for traces. Until he has more information—and who knows if he'll share it with us—this is all we have."

Sunny said, "Did the sheriff mention anything about whether he suspects this might or might not have been an accident?"

"He was inclined to think the man's death was due to his own making."

"Ah," intoned Mary Beth. "Technically, a classic misadventure."

Everyone ignored her.

"What about you, Verity?" Denise asked. "What were your thoughts at the scene." She held up Verity's phone showing one of the views of the alley.

"To be honest, I initially thought it looked as though the man had been attacked. Struck suddenly from behind with something hard enough to break more than just skin. But then, why the scuffed-up dirt if he'd been surprised?"

"Surprised maybe, but still conscious and on his feet?" Chaundra suggested. "He could have turned and fought back."

"That's possible, I guess." Verity retrieved her phone from Denise and clicked through the photos to the closeup of the scattered gravel and dirt. She studied it for a moment, but nothing definitive came to mind.

"Did Bailey even listen to your idea about the man being assaulted?" Kate asked.

"He did," Verity admitted. "And I think he took it seriously. But he definitely wants to wait for the autopsy before deciding how to proceed. The one detail we didn't discuss was the odd condition of the alley's surface. He might not have noticed it. And you know how touchy he can be if anyone points out that he's missed something important." She shook her head.

"Woe betide bearer of truth," Fumiko intoned darkly, sounding like a Greek oracle.

They all stared at her.

Kate shivered. "Ew-w-w-w. That gave me chills."

Verity took advantage of the lull in discussion to seize her bear claw and take a big bite. *M-m-m-m!* The pungent cinnamon and overkill of sugar hit the back of her throat as she chewed and swallowed. She rolled her eyes in rapture.

"It might not have been a fight. A vehicle that takes off fast will chew up the ground," Denise pointed out. "The thing is, we don't know if whatever disturbed the ground happened last night when O'Halloran died or weeks ago."

"But we had heavy rains the day before yesterday. If those marks were already there before it rained, they should have washed away. And they looked fresh to me."

Fumiko was frowning while nibbling daintily at pieces she'd pinched off her brownie. "You say wound on back of man's head. Like he surprise by killer?"

Verity nodded. "That's one possibility. Or he turned his back on the person because he trusted them or didn't view them as a threat. The man was a loudmouth and a bully. I actually can't see him being afraid of anyone."

Chaundra shook her head, sending her short black curls jiggling. "I can't see anyone intentionally turning their back on a stranger in the middle of the night, especially if you were arguing with them."

"She's right," Denise said with conviction. Verity knew she had taken martial arts instruction for years. "You never take your eyes off an opponent. And he was in an unfamiliar place. He'd have been extra cautious."

Another thought struck Verity that left her feeling strangely troubled, although she couldn't say why. "How can we be sure only two people were in the alley?"

Kate's eyes widened. "You mean like a gang came after him? Oh gosh, too bad there were no witnesses."

A moment of silence ensued as they all considered this new scenario.

"Oh God!" Sunny cried, making everyone jump. "Jason. Jason Grimalski." She turned to look at Verity, who wished her friend had kept her mouth shut. "At the café, you had to stand between Jason and that horrible man to stop them from fighting."

"Young Jason?" Kate looked shocked. "*Your* Jason?"

Verity tried to keep her voice free of emotion. "For those who haven't already heard, Rudy O'Halloran made a ridiculous scene in the café. Jason wasn't happy with the man's rudeness." She avoided making eye contact with anyone. "I'm sure their faceoff wouldn't have amounted to anything." *Liar*, she thought.

A rumble of thunder drew her attention to the kitchen window. Outside, ominous clouds smudged the sky. The wind had risen, flicking dust and grass clippings at the glass, foreshadowing a summer storm.

When Verity looked back at the group, Sunny was studying Verity's flushed face. "We all know dear Jason couldn't have had anything to do with that man's death. That wasn't my point," Sunny said. "But Jason threatened the man in front of dozens of witnesses. People will remember. If the sheriff starts asking around, someone's bound to tell him about the incident."

"That man has a one-track mind," Chaundra said shaking her head. "He gave me a terrible time about an outdated zoning law. Nearly shut down my shop on a technicality. Once he gets it into his head that your farmhand held a grudge against the victim—"

"I don't think we should jump to any conclusions," Verity said quickly. "Jason would never act on words spoken in anger. He was defending the town as much as standing up for me and Sunny. Once Jason left the café, I'm sure that was the end of it."

"But you can't *know* that!" Kate insisted, her voice shooting up an octave. "It really doesn't sound good for poor Jase. And who can say if it was just him or he had a friend with him. Jason has loads of buddies."

"And the Grimalski brothers are, like..." Denise held up two fingers as if welded together. "They practically cast each other's shadow."

True, Verity thought. The twins were inseparable. But would laid-back Jerry agree to attack the man who had argued with his brother? She didn't think so. However, just the possibility sickened her.

Chaundra stood up and started collecting used paper plates and napkins from the table. "Jason might have a short fuse, but he's not a killer. I've paid him to move shelves for me and reorganize displays in the emporium. He couldn't have been nicer. And didn't he once do something for you in the bookstore, Kate?"

Kate bobbed her head and smiled. "Yeah, he read a story to some of my kids. He was so sweet with the little ones in the Kiddie's Korner." Kate pinched her lips together. "I just...I just can't imagine either of those boys intentionally hurting anyone."

"Unless someone threatened or hurt his brother," Denise said grimly.

Verity held up a hand. "Please, there's no use speculating when we know so little about what happened or why."

"So, we do *nothing*?" Mary Beth sighed, clearly disappointed.

"We've already agreed that we're not officially involved in the investigation," Sunny reminded her. "But I think the sheriff might be ok with us quietly talking to folks in town. If anyone saw or heard anything suspicious, we can pass that information along to him."

"Someone should keep track of everything we find out," Chaundra suggested. "I'd volunteer, but the summer is my busiest time of year. I'm about run off my feet."

"I have some free time," Kate offered. "My girls are signed up for summer day camp."

"I thought your husband didn't like you investigating with us," Mary Beth said.

"After our success in an actual murder investigation, and all the press we got, Tony came around." Kate blushed furiously. "With a little encouragement in the bedroom."

"O-o-o-o-o!" the others responded.

Verity laughed so hard tears trickled down her cheeks. "The job of information coordinator is all yours, hot stuff."

## CHAPTER 8

AS SOON AS her friends left, Verity headed out to the milking barn. The sky had darkened to a venomous ashy crimson. Thunderheads were mounting in the west, looking like they meant business.

The Grimalski brothers had already left for the day, without knowing they had been a topic of her friends' conversation. She tried not to think about all their troubling speculations but she'd seen the rage in Jason's eyes. And she knew what angry young men were capable of.

She found a note from Jerry in the barn, letting her know the Daisy Dairy tanker truck had come by to pick up the day's milk. She checked the receipt the driver had left for her, showing his test readings of the milk's purity. All looked good, so far. She breathed a sigh of relief but searched for telltale signs of rodents anyway. After ten minutes she'd found none. Thank goodness! Maybe Lady Macbeth was actually doing her job.

After flushing the main collection tank, she drained the contents of the smaller auxiliary tank into it. The Robo-Milkers would now continue to add more of her cows' sweet milk. A dozen of her lovely fawn-and-white Guernseys were milling around in the open milking parlor, several awaiting their turn in the three automated stalls. She looked for Molly, her problem child, but the cow didn't seem to be around. She was the only one of the herd that hadn't adjusted to the new machinery. Verity milked her by hand, twice a day, or asked one of the boys to do it for her.

Verity didn't mind the extra ten minutes of work to milk the cow the old-fashioned way. The rhythmic motions of her hands gently pulsing the cow's teats was relaxing—for both of them, she imagined—but seemed particularly therapeutic for the human. Mentally undemanding, the chore freed her mind to drift pleasantly. These moments of calm, little gems to be mined from the substrate of her busy mind, gave her a chance to recharge.

But first, she needed to find her cow.

Verity stepped outside the milking parlor and through the door to her yard. A low rumble then sharp crackle of thunder hurried her along. She circled around the outside of the big yellow barn to the right. Down the grassy slope she went, beside the original stone foundation that had been built with rocks dug out of the surrounding fields, and into the lower level of the barn. Decades earlier, this had been the original milking parlor.

Mark told her that this partially underground area was also where the herd had once sheltered during fierce Vermont winter storms. Although unheated, when the space was packed with the warm bodies of the big animals, the air stayed surprisingly warm. These days, she heated the new milking parlor, which also guaranteed the modern collection lines and tanks didn't freeze up. She liked to think that the cows' sonorous moos on chilly winter days were their way of thanking her for their cozy lifestyle.

As soon as her eyes adjusted to the cool, dim interior of the lower barn, she saw Molly standing patiently, as if knowing her lady-farmer would come for her. "Hello, girl. Been waiting long?"

Molly did not deign to respond.

"Sorry. Serious things are afoot. Seems we have another murder in town. Most unpleasant."

"Most mysterious and exciting!" That wasn't Molly.

"Percy, is that you?"

"At your service, ma'am." Lieutenant Percy Putnam glimmered into sight in his smart dress uniform of Lincoln's Army. No wonder, she thought, Anna Louise fell in love with him—even though he had fought on the wrong side. At least, according to her Southern father.

Molly didn't seem to mind the ghost's presence, so Verity set to milking her.

Anna Louise had told her all about their romance. How it broke her heart when her father refused to bless her marriage to a Yankee. She had run away with her lover and never returned to her birthplace. Verity got a lump in her throat whenever she thought about how sad it must have made the young woman—having been forced to choose between her family and the man she loved. But it was even more tragic that the couple had died while still in their twenties. And she had thought that Mark's death at thirty-four was unbearably young!

In a strange way, she felt comforted by the ghosts' presence—even if only in their spirit forms. They were, after all, Mark's ancestors. His family. Indeed, the Putnams were sometimes annoying, meddlesome, and added complications to her life that she might well have done without. But they also could be fun to be around and seemed so much nicer than some living people she knew.

"Where is Anna Louise?" she asked Percy, hoping for a report on her new barn cat's progress in depleting the rodent population. Although she had seen neither mice nor rats that day, she could feel them lurking deviously in the shadows, waiting for her to leave the barn. Just the thought made her skin itch.

"Percy," she repeated, "your wife. Where is she?"

"I'm, uh, actually not certain. Perhaps she is taking a nap, up at the house?"

"Percy?" She observed him dubiously. "You know I can always tell when you're lying. What's she up to now?"

"Nothing of import, Miss Verity." He looked away, his attention suddenly absorbed by an old rake standing in a corner.

"She's in town snooping, isn't she? Admit it. I don't want her getting in the sheriff's way." She continued Molly's milking, the musical ping and stream of warm milk filling the pail. Then the truth struck her. "You two were listening in at our meeting this afternoon, weren't you? I thought I told you to—"

"You said we must not be visible to your friends," he stated, as if she needed a reminder. "You didn't see us, did you?"

"No, but...but you were eavesdropping on us."

He stared at the toes of his shiny black boots. His image flickered for a few seconds, as if he were a light bulb about to fail.

"Percy, dear, I've already told you that you two absolutely cannot be part of our investigation team. I notice that your shade seems a bit uncontrolled. Flickery. If you are accidentally seen, Ervin's next business venture will be ghost tours! Is that what you want?"

"Lord, no!" he said. "Although my bride, as you have experienced on numerous occasions, is never bashful of the limelight."

And that was an understatement.

Although it must be hard for them to not know why their spirits were lingering in the world of the living. Or how they had died. Perhaps Anna Louise acted as she did to distract herself from her fear over their futures.

Verity often wondered why the two ghosts had never appeared to Mark. If they had done, wouldn't he have told her? And why choose her? They had claimed they felt dutybound to look after her, now that Mark was gone. Which sounded very considerate. But she wasn't entirely convinced. The pair could be secretive and had a habit of causing mayhem.

Although, to be fair, they had also once saved her life.

Verity set aside her questions about the couple. She needed to make sure they didn't interfere with anything the sheriff might be doing.

"Listen, Percy, I'm sure there will be a time when I need your help. But not now. You have to concentrate on finding out why you and your bride are the only ghosts in town—in the State of Vermont or the entire country, for all I know."

"I realize something has gone awry," he admitted, standing to attention and bracing his left palm on his sword's hilt at his side. She had to admit he cut quite the manly figure. "There must be a reason why we haven't moved along to the other side." He scowled up at the barn's cobwebby rafters. "I fear it's not a good one."

"Let's not assume the worst," she said quickly. "I've already told you that you're welcome to stay here on the farm until you go off to...wherever it is you're going." She was struggling to be tactful. Hopefully, wherever they were destined to move on to would be the good place, not the other one.

A new thought came to her. What if it were possible for another ghost to haunt her house? Was there any way Mark could come to her, in spirit? Even if he couldn't eat, sleep, or make babies with her, at least she wouldn't be so lonely.

Her Evansfield neighbors were—for the most part—lovely, generous, friendly people. And she adored her animals and the work she did on the farm. Being outside in the fresh air with nature, providing wholesome food for people—that was the best.

But she and Mark had been so very happy together. She had believed the years stretched out before them, promising joy and years in which to build a family.

She coughed to clear the sudden tightness in her throat. Blinked away the tickly bit of moisture in her eyes that wasn't yet tears. Going all maudlin would do no one any good. Verity moved her stool back from Molly and patted the cow on the rump to let her know they were done.

Percy studied her face with concern. "I'll go find Anna Louise," he offered quickly.

"Good idea," she murmured, unable to hide what he must have already seen.

Percy had barely dimmed from sight when she sensed movement behind her. She spun around to see Lady Macbeth, her tail twitching, body poised in a crouch as if preparing for an Olympian pounce. But as hard as she looked, Verity saw neither mouse nor rat.

Before she drew her next breath, a mouse skittered into the middle of the old milking parlor's floor, let out a surprised squeak when it saw the furry hunter, raced around in a diversionary circle, and hightailed it across the barn floor. The big yellow cat flung herself forward with impressive strength and a swipe of claws.

And missed.

Instead of giving chase, Lady M simply curled up on the floor, as if disgusted with her own shoddy performance.

"Hey, lazy bones, what's up with you? Not in the mood for a chase?" Verity walked over and sat on the floor beside the cat. Lady M roused herself to stand and twice circle her new mistress—butting her head against Verity's knee, backside, elbow and then hand—before crawling into her lap. A low, contented rumble issued from the animal's throat.

Verity stroked the thick mustard-gold fur and smiled. "Aw!

You like being with people, don't you? I know your family said it was too much trouble to take you with them. Just between you and me, I think that's a terrible excuse for leaving a family member behind. Tell you what, Lady M. You can be part of my family. One human, two ghosts, and a yellow cat. Sounds good to me!"

## CHAPTER 9

THE BARK of the storm proved worse than its bite. Ground-shaking thunder, howling winds, a sky so dark it might have been doomsday. But after a five-minute shower, the weather passed, leaving in its wake a fiery sunset that deepened into purple dusk.

It wasn't yet fully dark when Verity heard a vehicle pull off the road and down her gravel driveway. Standing in her kitchen, she peered through the dining room window to see the sheriff's SUV roll past. Dinner had been a salad of butterhead lettuce, fresh-picked tomatoes, sliced cukes, and red peppers—all from her kitchen garden. Happily, she'd finished eating before he arrived. She set off to find out what had brought him to her farm, unannounced.

He was already on her back porch by the time she opened the mudroom door.

"Sheriff Bailey. Come on in. Coffee?"

"No. Thanks anyway. Can't stay long. This investigation is..." He removed his hat and flapped it as though to shoo away an annoying swarm of insects, or thoughts. He followed her up into her kitchen, talking as they went. "I need to ask a favor of you, Mrs. Cade."

"Ask away!" Even before he'd stepped into her house, she decided she wouldn't mention the troubling discussion she'd had with her friends about Jason and O'Halloran at the café. No sense putting thoughts into his head.

"It's the wife of the deceased," he began. "I'd be grateful if you'd talk with her. Questions need answerin'." He paced halfway around her kitchen table, then back again. "About her husband. Who might want to hurt him. What he was doin' in the alley, middle of the night. Did she see or hear anything at all that might give us a clue what happened out there?"

"She won't talk to you?"

"No. Well, in a way, yes." He stopped and planted his feet, as if it took an effort to discontinue circling her table. "She's just so upset I can't get much out of her. As soon as she tries to speak, she bursts into tears again. I feel like I'm torturin' the poor woman."

"Can Dr. Evans prescribe something to calm her?"

"She refuses to see him. Seems to look on any kind of medicine as a drug and says she won't take it."

"What about Social Services?" she suggested. "They're wonderful at supporting survivors. They helped me so much—"

"After Mark's accident. Yes, yes, of course. But the woman has shut down, locked herself in her room at the inn. Won't open the door to anyone including me." He flapped his uniform hat again. "Feel like an idiot, shouting through a closed door at her. I could haul her into my office and hold her there until she gives me the minimum information I need, but that seems cruel."

"It might even be illegal," Verity said.

"You think so?" He scratched his head. "But then I was

thinking she might open up to another woman." She could hear hope in his gruff voice.

"It would be better if someone she knew spoke with her. She must have made friends on the bus tour," Verity suggested.

"She says not. Ervin tells me she texted him, insisting he curtail the tour and take everyone back to New York City. Apparently, some of the others on the bus agree with her. They want their money back." He slapped his hat back on his head. "But just as many want to stay and get what they paid for—five more days in scenic New England and an old-fashioned Fourth of July celebration. Hoo-boy! Mr. Ervin is not a happy camper, let me tell you."

"I'll bet Henry isn't doing cartwheels either," she said. "A murder in his dream inn during its very first year after the reopening."

"Technically not *inside* the inn, but close enough, and don't you start droppin' the 'M' word. Not yet. I'm not convinced that's what we're lookin' at." He flashed her a stern look.

"Sorry," she murmured. "Anyway, I'm sure both Henry and Ervin are scared to death their businesses will be destroyed."

He stared down at his hands. "It doesn't help these tour folk have already started postin' complaints on Facebook, Tik Tok, and Insta-what'sit. 'Never gonna book another trip with this crappy tour company!'"

Verity sat down to think and tried to ignore the sheriff as he resumed looping her table. He was making her dizzy.

There was, she decided, little she could do to help either of Evansfield's entrepreneurs. But maybe by talking with the dead man's wife she could uncover information that would point the blame away from them. Away from Jason, too. Either because it really was just an accident or because someone they didn't yet know about had a reason for wanting Rudy O'Halloran dead.

"You honestly think she might talk to me?" Verity asked.

"Worth takin' a chance." He rubbed the flat of his big hand over his sweaty face. "I don't want to make the poor woman any more miserable than she already is. But you know as well as I do, I won't get far investigatin' this man's death if the person closest to him won't tell me what I need to know."

"Alright," Verity said, "I'll talk to her. Can it wait until tomorrow morning?"

"I'm afraid if we wait, she'll up and leave town. Even if Ervin refuses to take his tourists back to the city early, she might get her own ride. Then where will I be?"

"Up a creek without a proverbial paddle?"

"You betcha."


"Mrs. O'Halloran?" Verity called through the door to Room 201 of the Wayfarer's Inn.

After three tries, she had still received no response. Bailey stood silently at her side, convinced the woman was in the room. He signaled Verity to try again with a chin nudge toward the closed door.

"My name is Verity Cade. I hate to disturb you, Mrs. O'Halloran, but it's very important that I talk with you. I'm sure you will feel better if you know exactly what happened last night." *But will she really?* Verity thought. Talking wouldn't change the fact that her husband was dead.

As before, no response came from behind the door.

Verity looked at the sheriff and shrugged.

"Tell her that I've left so the two of you can speak in private," he whispered. "You know, woman-to-woman like."

*Woman-to-woman?* Verity mouthed, narrowing her eyes at him.

His face colored and he dragged a hand over his jaw. "Aw hell, word it however you want. You know what I mean."

"Right," she said quietly.

"I'll be downstairs with Henry. Maybe there's somethin' more he can remember 'bout last night." But he sounded less than confident.

Verity gave him a weak smile. She hated the idea of disturbing the poor woman, who clearly only wanted to be left alone to mourn in her own way. It didn't seem all that long ago that she had felt the same way. Losing Mark was the worst thing that had ever happened to her. No one and nothing could permeate the black fugue into which she had sunk. Weeks went by before she was able to have anything close to a normal conversation with anyone. She got by with one-word responses:

"You just let us know what we can do for you, Verity. Hear?"

"Sure."

"Would you like someone to stay with you?'

"No."

"Seriously, honey. You shouldn't be alone."

"Unnecessary."

"Shall I put some of this food in your freezer for later?" The neighbors had brought a month's worth of casseroles to her door. "You'll never be able to eat all of this before it spoils."

"I know." She had been so proud of herself. Two words in a row!

As difficult as it had been to deal with the constant flow of pity, she at least had been surrounded by friends and in the comfort of her own home. This woman was alone in her misery, trapped in an unfamiliar town. Verity leaned her head against the door, her eyes closed. She swore she could feel waves of pain and sorrow passing from inside the room through the wood panel and into her own body.

"Mrs. O'Halloran, I met you at the café when I was waiting on tables." She paused. Would the woman remember her? "I just...well, I just wanted to tell you how very sorry I am, how sorry everyone in Evansfield is for your loss." She drew a shaky breath. "And to let you know I understand what you're going through. My husband died not long ago in a freak farming accident."

She might as well have gripped a live, high-voltage wire. With those words, memories rushed back with a painful jolt. The image of the old tractor lying on its side in the dark field. The horrid realization that Mark was trapped under it, crushed beneath its immense, iron weight.

Verity caught her breath but forged on. "It was very sudden, his death. No warning at all. No chance to say good-bye. The pain was unbearable. So, I know, *I really do know how you must feel.* I wish I could offer you..." Her throat closed up. Her eyes burned like hot coals. She swallowed and somehow forced out a few more words. "I don't know what I can give you other than a few minutes' comfort. If we could just sit and—"

The latch clicked. The door to the guest room opened a crack.

Verity was resting so hard against the door she nearly fell into the room. Steadying herself with a hand to the door jamb, she swallowed and dabbed at her eyes with the back of her free hand, then gingerly pushed the door open the rest of the way. The young woman inside stepped back, thin arms clamped at her sides, her face, pink and wet with weeping, contorted in agony.

Suddenly, Verity wanted to be anywhere but here. Reliving her own pain through another woman's loss. But she had promised the sheriff she'd do what she could to find out something helpful for his investigation into Rudy O'Halloran's death.

"I apologize for, ah, for my behavior," the woman said thickly. Her voice curled in on itself, flower-petal soft, subtly southern but not so much as to call it an accent. Her eyes were so red and swollen, Verity couldn't tell what color they were. Her brown hair hung in strings around her face. She was wearing a loose t-shirt with a New York Yankees logo on the front and oversized pajama bottoms. Verity wondered if either or both had been her husband's, and her heart wrenched.

"Please," Verity said, "you don't need to apologize."

"The sheriff is only trying to do his job, I guess," the woman said. "I just want to go home. This trip has been a...a nightmare." She broke into sobs, shaking head to toe as she stumbled away from the door.

Verity hesitated at the threshold, not knowing whether she should step inside or leave the woman to her grief. The poor thing looked barely able to keep to her feet.

Verity stepped into the room, easing the hallway door closed behind her. She lightly touched Mrs. O'Halloran on the arm, guiding her toward the upholstered settee in the middle of the room. They sat down and Verity took the woman's nearest hand in her own, at a loss for what to say now. Until she stopped weeping it seemed brutal to force her to answer questions.

"You're right," Verity said at last. "It is Sheriff Bailey's job. But if you don't feel up to talking with him, it can wait."

"Really?"

"Of course. It's just that the sooner he has some questions answered, the more likely he is to find out what led to your husband's...death." She had barely stopped herself from saying *murder*. Which, she was becoming more convinced, was the real cause of the man's demise. Her mind kept replaying the scene she'd come upon in the alley. The position of the body. The deep wound in the back of his head. And then there was the offensive personality of the dead man. How many enemies had he made during his lifetime with his obnoxious attitude and bullying?

"Jennifer," the woman said. "Call me Jennifer, please. I'm not missus anyone now," she added miserably.

"Oh." Verity swallowed. "Well, alright, Jennifer. And you can call me Verity. Or Veri, like some of my friends do."

"The sheriff told me that Rudy was in an accident," Jennifer said, barely above a whisper. "I don't really understand. How did it happen? Was he in a car with someone? Or..." She raised both hands in a confused, pleading gesture.

"I don't think anyone knows yet," Verity said. "As soon as the sheriff has a clearer picture of events, I know he will tell you."

The woman grabbed a fistful of white tissues from a box sitting on the cushion between them. The carpet was littered with balled-up, used ones, tossed haphazardly like a flurry of windblown flower blossoms.

So distracted had Verity been by the woman's grief when she entered the room, she initially hadn't taken in any of its details. But now she could see how spacious it was, a suite really, with more than enough room for a king-size bed, a freestanding wardrobe to make up for having no closet, a writing desk and dressing table, as well as space for a settee, a pair of occasional chairs, and coffee table. The walls were papered in damask roses, edged in cream wood trim. A rumpled comforter had been tossed off of the bed. Open suitcases revealed a disarray of clothing.

Verity tensed, realizing the distraught woman had been watching her survey the room. "Oh, I'm sorry, I just—"

"It's a mess, I know," Jennifer mumbled, rubbing her eyes with her knuckles. "I can't seem to, you know, stop crying long enough to tidy up."

"Of course, no one expects you to function normally under the circumstances. I was just curious about the room. I haven't been inside the inn since the renovations," she fibbed. "It's very pretty."

"Oh, yes. I guess it is." Jennifer grabbed another tissue, dabbed at her eyes, blew her nose. "You said, your name is Verity. That's an unusual name. Does it mean anything? I suppose it's a family name?"

"No. I think my parents just liked it. It means 'Truth.'"

Jennifer's eyes widened. "How...interesting."

Verity had an idea. "Speaking of which, I'm sure you're just as anxious as the sheriff is to find out what happened to your husband last night."

"Of course I am!" Jennifer gasped, leaping to her feet. Her worried expression segued to an offended glare. "Are you saying because I couldn't talk to the sheriff, he thinks I don't care what happened to Rudy? I *loved* my husband!"

"I'm so sorry, Jennifer. That's not what he thinks, not what anyone thinks," Verity rushed to assure her. "I just wonder, since you obviously *do* care—" she considered her words carefully, avoiding any mention of possible causes of the man's death "—you might want to help us work out the details of the final hours of his life."

"*Us?* You work for the sheriff's office?" She frowned.

"Not really. Sheriff Bailey just thought you might feel more at ease speaking with me. Because of our similar losses." A point that she and Bailey had not discussed, but it sounded convincing enough as soon as she said it.

Jennifer sat down again and folded her hands over the knees of the baggy gray PJ pants. The clothing looked slept in. Verity remembered being unable to dress for days after Mark's accident. She worked, slept, and ate in the same worn flannels until she could smell herself and, disgusted, threw them in the trash.

"He, your sheriff that is, came off sort of...bullish," Jennifer said sheepishly.

Verity pressed her lips together to keep from smiling. "He's a big guy; sometimes size alone intimidates." And sometimes Bailey intentionally used his size to his advantage. "Would you be willing to chat with me, over a cup of tea, coffee, or something stronger? We can go downstairs to the dining room, if you like." It would be good to get her out of the room, away from the too-intimate possessions of her dead husband.

Jennifer sent her a teary smile. "I sure could use that last option. But you won't find any booze here. Or haven't you heard?"

"Sorry, I forgot." How could she? Wasn't that what O'Halloran had been hollering about in the café besides his stupid food? The inn had no liquor license.

"It's okay." Jennifer shrugged and sniffled. "One of those in-room coffee makers is over there on the dresser." She waved a hand in that direction. "Tea bags, too. I prefer tea, and you might be wise to have the same. Dishwater would taste better than what comes out of those coffee pods." Jennifer almost smiled again but the emotion failed to reach her eyes.

Still, Verity felt as though she was making headway. Just by getting her talking. Seeing even a little less misery in the woman's eyes seemed a good sign. "I'll make the tea," she offered. "Do you want sugar and...hmmm...no refrigerator in the room, I see. So, I guess there's no milk. Maybe one of those powdered creamer packets?"

"Neither for me."

Before long they were back on opposite ends of the settee, each with a leg angled up on the cushions to enable them to face one another. Verity allowed her attention to leave the grieving woman and drift around the room again.

It definitely was a disheveled mess, then again, she'd always found it hard to keep things in order when living out of suitcases. However, through the bathroom door, she could see a cosmetic kit upended on the countertop beside the sink—lipsticks and tubes of foundation and assorted clamshells of either eyeshadow or blush. Nearly half of the containers lay helter-skelter on the floor. Verity tried to imagine how that might have happened. Jennifer O'Halloran, in a blind rage at the unfairness of life, wailing at the injustice of her loss. Snatching up one item after another and hurling them, until she ran out of strength to do anything but cry.

"Sorry, neither of us have ever been very tidy," Jennifer mumbled.

"Oh, please, it's the least of—" she'd almost said 'your worries' but stopped herself just in time. "Listen, I'll never win a prize for my housekeeping. It's one of my weaknesses. Another is chocolate truffles. You should try Denise's at the candy shop next door." *They're to die for. No, don't even think of saying that.* And why, for gosh sakes, was she talking about chocolate at a time like this? But she just wanted to make a connection with the woman, find a way to get her to relax and keep her talking.

Jennifer tossed down another used tissue, blew her nose in a fresh one, dabbed at her red-rimmed eyes. "Maybe I will. Tomorrow, if I'm still here." She picked up her cup of tea, cradled it in both hands and sipped, looking heartbreakingly fragile. "Alright, Verity. I'll try to do better now. Ask your questions."

"Maybe you should start by just telling me what you remember about last night."

"Well, the evening started out nice." One corner of Jennifer's mouth twitched upward. "We ate here at the inn. Nothing to write home about, by the way. I had Vermont Roast Chicken. Rudy ordered Marvelous Meatloaf. He said it wasn't bad but not marvelous. Then again, he's a—I mean, he *was* a meatloaf freak. Slap ground meat on a plate and he's a happy camper." She paused as if remembering a special moment.

"Anyway, I felt restless after dinner and went for a walk through town. Rudy was never one for walking, for walking's sake. He always had to have a goal, a destination."

"I'm like that, too," Verity said. "I walk to my kitchen garden to pull weeds or plant stuff. I go out to the chicken coops for eggs. I like strolling to church if the weather is nice."

Jennifer looked at her as if amused. "Hmmm. Anyway, when I got back to the room, Rudy was already asleep, which surprised me because he's the original night owl. A real party boy. But to be honest, this town doesn't have much nightlife."

Verity smiled. "No, indeed it doesn't. You need to drive into Springfield to find a bar, and I have no idea where the nearest nightclub is. Go on."

"Well, I found a postcard with a pretty photo of the village green, in the drawer beside the bed, and wrote a note to my mom. I took it downstairs to the front desk where they have a box for mail to be dropped off. By the time I got back to the room, it was dark outside and I decided to read in bed."

"Having the light on didn't bother Rudy? You said he was sleeping."

"Oh, yes, he was. Believe me, that man can sleep anywhere, anytime. Broad daylight or pitch dark. Doesn't matter to him." This time, she didn't catch her own slip, making Verity twinge in sympathy.

"So, you read for a while?"

Jennifer snorted. "All of ten minutes. Then I was out like a light."

"And Rudy was still here, in the room with you?" Jennifer nodded in the affirmative and sipped her tea. "But he must have left the room sometime before morning," Verity said. "Did you see him leave? Or go with him somewhere later in the night?"

Jennifer's eyes filled again. Her lower lip trembled. "Oh, damn. Sorry, Verity. This is really h-h-hard."

"I know, I know." Verity reached forward to rest a hand on her knee. "You're doing great. I just want to be able to come up with a timeline for the sheriff. He needs to determine where Rudy was at critical moments during the night."

"I understand." Jennifer sighed and brushed tangled strands of hair out of her eyes. "No, I didn't see him leave. I don't think I even turned over in bed when he left the room. The last I saw of him, he was sound asleep, b-b-beside me!"

Verity was about to give up. She had found out nothing at all helpful to pass along to the sheriff. But maybe if she could get the woman talking about something less painful... "Tell me about Rudy? Where did the two of you meet?"

Jennifer focused on the mug of tea, cupped between her hands. She blinked away tears and gave her a weak smile. "Oh, Rudy, he was quite the charmer. We met at a bar in New York City and I knew right then he was the one. Those green Irish eyes of his, so flirty, full of mischief. I was a goner." She set the empty mug on the floor in front of the couch. "He was a really smart businessman; you'd probably never guess that. Owned his own business before we met, sold it and started a new business. Sold that one, too. He did real well for himself, for a guy who never got past tenth grade."

"Sounds like. What was he currently doing for a living?" Verity wondered.

"Nothing. He retired young, not yet forty. And because he had made so much money, I didn't need to work. Mostly we take trips...took trips." She bit her bottom lip. "Visited friends. He has loads of friends, just about everywhere." She seemed incapable of not talking about her husband as though he was still alive. Verity remembered doing that, too. More than a year had passed after the rollover accident, and she was still talking about Mark as if he had just stepped out of the room for a minute. Whenever that happened, the realization of what she'd said hit her like a slap in the face and brought on a flood of bitter-sweet memories.

But Rudy O'Halloran was a very different man than Mark Cade. Verity hadn't forgotten the brash, repellent Rudy who had confronted her in the café. Honestly, how many friends could a man like that have? And if he did have buddies, what sort of people were they? Who would willingly accept a jerk like that into their life? One person, at least, did. Jennifer clearly loved the man. She must have been blind to his faults.

"Ummm, did your husband have any enemies? Anyone who might want to harm him?"

Jennifer's eyes saucered. "Enemies? I don't think so. I mean, he could be a little bossy sometimes, sure. You saw him in the café; he gets tetchy when he's hungry. What man doesn't, right? But enemies?" Her brow puckered. She stared at Verity. "Why are you asking a question like that, if it was an accident? This wasn't a mob hit or anything like that, right?"

Verity nearly laughed. "Not likely, here in Vermont dairy country. I just thought you might know someone, possibly connected to his former businesses, who didn't get along with Rudy. Or maybe they held a grudge or he owed money to them?"

Jennifer considered this, lifting serious eyes to the ceiling. "I hadn't thought about any of that. I still know next to nothing about his businesses. I was never that curious about how he made his money or who he might have worked with, or hired, or anything like that."

"You never thought to ask him?"

"I did, once or twice, but he kept stuff like that to himself. Said I wouldn't understand. And anyway, he was ready to sell out and retire by the time we hooked up. The business stuff never mattered to me." A look of horror flashed across her face. "Oh God! Verity, do you really believe someone could have had a reason for attacking him? I assumed, because of what the sheriff said, an accident is what he called it. I thought that meant—I don't know—he'd fallen and hit his head. Or got run over by a car."

"Well...I don't know." Verity was sure the sheriff wouldn't want her to give out information about the investigation until he was ready to do so. She leaned in with a gentle smile. "Jennifer, thank you so much for talking to me. This has been very helpful. I'll pass all of this along to the sheriff. Maybe, if he needs anything else, you'll feel more comfortable talking to him. He's really a good guy."

Jennifer reached out and clasped Verity's hand. "Please tell him I'm sorry for being so difficult. Thank you for the chat, Verity. I do feel a little better."

But Verity was unable to say the same for herself. She felt emotionally drained. And after nearly an hour of conversation with Jennifer, it seemed to Verity there was a lot about Rudy O'Halloran even his wife didn't know.

# CHAPTER 10

THE NEXT DAY, after Verity told Sheriff Bailey what she'd learned from Jennifer O'Halloran, she couldn't help sensing that something was wrong. What that something was, she was unable to say but it felt vaguely unpleasant and was impossible to grasp—like oil slick over water.

Rudy's fatal accident—or murder, if that's what it turned out to be—was of course wrong in itself. But she was sure that her unease came from more than the man's unexplained death. Maybe talking to someone about these odd feelings would help. But Jason and Jerry were working in the upper field, far from the house. And she hadn't seen her phantom roommates since yesterday, which was worrisome in itself. One never knew what they might be up to.

*Oh!* Another idea struck her. What if the Putnams had finally made their way to the other side?

After a two-second spurt of celebratory relief—*no more vexing ghosts, yay!*—a sad sort of emptiness came over her. Of course, she knew they needed to move on to the Afterlife. Eventually. But she had grown accustomed to their presence. What if she never saw them again? It would be like losing a mischievous younger sibling you complained about to all your friends. Until they were no longer there. Then you desperately missed them.

No, she decided, there must be something more bothering her than the passing of the most horrible man she'd ever met or a pair of AWOL ghosts. She tried to put her unease out of her mind and focus on her work.

Later that day, she shut the hens into their coops for the night, all cozy and safe from marauding foxes, and herded her cows into the barn. It hit her as she walked back to the farmhouse that she hadn't seen Lady Macbeth since the previous day.

She returned to the barn, calling the cat. Usually, it immediately appeared and trotted over to her. Not that Lady M was a particularly obedient cat. And she didn't believe the animal had developed a special affection for her. The creature's punctuality likely had more to do with the outrageously expensive little cans of Moist & Yummy Tuna cat food she'd bought to supplement the—*yuck!*—mouse snacks. Even a cat should have a delicious, balanced diet, right?

Verity felt rather bereft by the time she returned to the house and sat on the mudroom steps, prying off her mucky boots. She and Lady M hadn't been partners in mouse extermination for long, but she admittedly had grown fond of the little lioness with her thick golden fur and iridescent green eyes. The animal had wandered through the various outbuildings across her property, diligent in pursuit of her quarry. She seemed to feel quite at home. But what if Lady M had decided she didn't like her new home? Could she have returned to her former family?

Just then, an immense 18-wheeler roared past her house on the narrow country highway, trailing an effusion of brown dust and noxious fumes. Verity shuddered. Her arms goose bumped with an ominous chill, in spite of the warm summer air.

What if Lady M, in a blind dash after her prey, ran into the street at the wrong moment? Although cars and trucks usually slowed down to the posted thirty-miles-an-hour speed limit through town, they sometimes gained another twenty by the time they reached her farm. Her mouse-catcher wouldn't be the first critter to lose its life to a speeding vehicle.

She closed her eyes feeling sick at the thought.

The next morning, the cat still hadn't shown up, although the food Verity had left for it was gone. No doubt the mice had enjoyed a feast, along with their new freedom.

As soon as she fed the chickens and gathered their eggs, she loaded her truck with special orders for the Wayfarer's Inn and the Cat's Cradle Café. This was her second commercial delivery within two days, due to an uptick in orders from both businesses.

If this kept up, she might be able to afford a down payment on some new equipment for the farm. Or maybe she would arrange an overhaul for her two remaining tractors. Jason and Jerry had long ago talked her into selling the third machine, the one that had rolled over on Mark. She hadn't needed much convincing. She couldn't bear to look at the green monster. Besides, she would never risk injury to either of her young helpers.

Verity drove straight to the Wayfarer's Inn. When Henry had called the previous night, he sounded almost desperate. "I don't know if I've got enough eggs for my breakfast crowd," he wailed. "These folks are raving about how fresh my eggs are. I don't want to disappoint them."

"I'll have your eggs there by eight o'clock tomorrow morning," she promised. "Earlier if necessary."

"Most of them aren't even up at that hour." He sounded relieved. "Eight will be fine."

Verity parked in front of the inn since the alley was still blocked off with traffic cones and yellow crime scene tape. She couldn't imagine what the sheriff expected to discover that he and his deputies hadn't already found. Maybe he was beginning to doubt his initial belief that the man's death had been due—as Mary Beth put it—to misadventure.

As she was climbing down from the cab of her truck, the tour bus rumbled up behind her and stopped, its airbrakes wheezing like an aging smoker. Ervin, in vivid red vest and cap to match his bus's fiery trim, trotted down the inn's steps toward the bus. A woman in dungarees and black t-shirt stepped off the bus and greeted him.

*The driver?* Verity thought, surprised for some reason. *Don't be sexist, Verity.* And this woman looked particularly capable of driving anything, no matter how huge.

She was easily six feet tall and as broad-beamed and muscular as any man. Over her short ponytail she had tugged down a black baseball cap. Her bare arms sported an impressive display of colorful tats—red and green dragons breathing fire up one arm, serpents coiling down the other.

Passengers in sunglasses, beachy hats and daypacks rushed down from the inn's veranda and started climbing on board. *Early risers. Good for them!* Off on a fun day trip, no doubt.

Verity glanced back at the bus driver and her boss, amused. She tried to imagine Ervin, so much smaller and more conservative in appearance, interviewing this Valkyrie of a woman for the position of his driver. Maybe he'd been afraid *not* to hire her. She giggled.

Verity unloaded a crate of eggs from her truck bed and carried it past the dapper little tour owner and his employee, who were deep in conversation. From the little she overheard, they seemed to be discussing the day's itinerary.

Ervin looked up and saw her before she reached the inn's steps. "Verity, come meet my driver, Sue Brown." He waved her over. "Sue, this is Verity Cade, producer of the best farm-fresh milk and eggs in the county."

"That may be a bit of an overstatement, but I'll take the compliment." Verity shifted her grip on the crate to hold out a hand for Sue to shake. "We have many wonderful dairy farms in the area."

"A lady farmer. Good for you!" Sue beamed at her, the smile transforming her from a little terrifying to a gentler soul. "My grandaddy had a farm out in Nebraska. Steer mostly, I think. Had to give it up when none of the kids wanted to take it over."

"That's a shame," Verity said.

The Cade Family Farm also would have been given up if she hadn't fought to keep it alive—as much to honor Mark's wishes as for her own love of the beautiful property. She supposed she loved it all the more because she didn't have children.

"Do you drive for a living?" Verity said. "Great for seeing the country."

"It can be," Sue agreed, "depending on the routes and the bossman. Ervin here's pretty easy to work for. But highways these days are like navigating f-ing bumper-car rides. People don't know how to drive." She shook her head in dismay.

Verity nodded her understanding. "I can't say I'd enjoy that. Anyway, I'm a homebody at heart."

"I hear you!" Sue smacked her on the back, and the force of her arm swing nearly knocked Verity and her eggs off the curb.

Ervin grabbed her arm just in time. "You alright, Verity? Sue, she don't know her own strength. Isn't that so, Sue?" He chuckled. "Mighty handy for keeping these tourists under control," he whispered.

The driver looked away, as if she thought the comment inappropriate.

"Well, I'm glad to meet you, Sue," Verity said. "If Ervin gives you some time off while you're still in town, come on down the road to my farm and I'll show you around. I'd love to chat about your adventures."

The woman blinked at her as if surprised and suddenly looked bashful. "I might do. Have to see what the schedule allows."

"Of course." Verity started to turn away toward the inn's steps but was forced to wait while three more people rushed down them to board the bus. While she waited, she figured she might as well gather a little information for the sheriff. "Ervin and Sue, I wonder if you might have time before you leave for your day trip to answer a few questions."

"Sure thing," Ervin said cheerfully, sticking his thumbs in the pockets of his vest and puffing out his chest.

Sue nodded her assent, although with less enthusiasm.

"The night Rudy O'Halloran died, did either of you see him?"

Sue looked at Ervin. He answered for both of them. "We were dog tired after finishing the day's activities with this crowd. I turned in early as I could. You, too, Sue—I imagine."

"Yeah," she mumbled. "Slept like a log. Woke up early to all sorts of ruckus and emergency vehicles parked out back of the inn."

"So, your room overlooks the alley behind the inn?" Verity said.

"No," Ervin jumped in. "I couldn't ask Henry to give her a prime room. She was okay with having a cot in the basement. That right, Sue?"

The driver nodded and shifted her feet before looking in through the bus's open door. "Hey now," she called up to her passengers, "no fighting over who's gonna sit next to who! Behave yourselves in there."

This generated hoots of laughter from within and a proud smile from Ervin. "Told you she's really good with them," he said. "Keeps them in order, she does. Don't know what I'd do without her."

"Nice." Verity wanted to get back to her interrupted questions. She turned to Ervin. "Your house is on the other side of the fence separating the alley and Winfield Estates, right?"

"That's right," Ervin chirped.

"You didn't hear any unusual noises or voices coming from this way during the night, did you?"

"Nope."

"By the way," Sue said, this time with a little steel and considerable impatience in her voice, "your sheriff already asked me all sorts of questions. And I told him the same thing. Didn't see or hear nothing."

"OK," Verity said, unsure why the woman's friendly mood had changed. The crate was dragging heavily on her arms, but she didn't want to put it down on the ground. "It's just that Sheriff Bailey asked a few of us who occasionally act as support for his department to gather additional information. His department is a little short-handed these days."

Ervin looked back and forth between Verity and Sue, as though he, too, sensed rising tension between them. He gave his driver an anxious smile. "Mrs. Cade here is quite the local celebrity since—"

"A celebrity farmer?" Sue grinned, and it wasn't the pleasant kind.

Ervin stared at his driver, as if trying to figure out whether she was joking or serious. "Naw. You see, she's one of our local amateur detectives. She's already solved one murder in Evansfield. Verity Cade is one clever lady. Maybe she'll solve this new one."

"Now, Ervin," Verity cautioned him, "no one knows what caused the man's death. Not yet."

"A sleuth, is she?" The driver smirked and looked her up and down. Verity couldn't tell if she was angry, annoyed, or just bored with the conversation.

Sue propped her tree trunk of a leg on the first step of the bus and looked over her shoulder at Ervin. "Why don't you rustle up the stragglers, Mr. Ervin, and we'll get on over to Ye Olde Maple Sugar Shack in time for the tour and the lunch you booked."

"Oh yes! Good idea," he agreed. "I'm on it!" He turned to Verity as they made their way together up the inn's steps. "Sue don't like to be made to wait. Likes things done the way she wants when she wants." He shrugged. "No difference to me. I'm the boss, sure. But she's right. Gotta keep things moving. This is a premium tour, after all."

Verity smiled at him. Well, at least he seemed to be enjoying himself.

He held the door open for her. She glanced back toward the bus. Driver Sue stood on its top step, glaring at her. And all Verity could think was, *What did I say that blew up that conversation?*

# CHAPTER 11

VERITY FOUND Henry in the kitchen. To her delight, Sunny and Denise were with him.

"Hey there!" she crowed as she came through the door. "Just the people I was hoping to run into before the morning was over." She had called Kate but only got her voice mail. She hoped Sunny might have heard from her with information she'd gathered from the EPI members.

Henry immediately seized the egg crate from her and started packing eggs into his fridge.

"Oh, Henry, let me do that for you," she said. "I'm sure there are other things you could be doing with all these guests to care for."

"You can say that again," he muttered, turning back to face her. Now that she got a good look at him, she noticed the dark shadows beneath his eyes and deep worry creases across his forehead. His graying hair shot out over his ears at odd angles and appeared uncombed. "I definitely need to hire more staff. I just finished changing bed sheets and cleaning two bathrooms. The public rooms still need vacuuming."

"Why are you doing housekeeping chores?" Denise said. "I

thought Alma Frank and your granddaughter were working as chambermaids."

"Alma had to take her kids to camp before she could come in today. And Crystal—" he shook his head, his expression grim "—she's too young. I don't want her in the rooms. Had to let her go."

"But she was so excited to have a summer job," Sunny objected. "And she's very conscientious. When I hired her to help me at the café for a few weekends, she worked hard and got along with every—"

"Not gonna happen," Henry snapped. He looked around the room as if he'd lost something then bolted out of the kitchen.

"I wonder what's got his undies in a knot," Denise said, watching him disappear. She squinted at Verity.

"I haven't a clue. Sunny, anything to report from Katie?"

"Not really. Everyone has a theory about how O'Halloran died, but no one actually saw anything."

"Oh, too bad." Verity looked from Sunny to Denise, then nipped at her bottom lip.

"What?" Denise grinned in anticipation. "I've seen that look before. You know something. Spill!"

"I'm not really sure," Verity admitted nervously. She didn't want to be like so many in the town, a gossip. "I was out in front of the inn when the tour bus arrived to pick up Ervin's people for an excursion. Ervin was acting a little strange."

"Ervin *is* strange." Denise laughed.

"Yeah, well, stranger than usual. And his driver is a bit of an odd duck." Verity thought for a moment. "Sue, that's the driver's name, looks like she could be a bouncer for a bar. A big woman, lots of tattoos. Sort of intimidating."

"You're scared of her just because she has tattoos?" Denise laughed. "I have tats."

"And you aren't intimidating?" Sunny teased.

Denise rolled her eyes.

"I have nothing against tattoos." Verity thought for a moment. "I might have said something that offended her. She was all cheery and smiles when Ervin introduced us. Suddenly she changed." She shuddered, remembering how dark and angry the woman's eyes had turned. "I've never seen such a rapid mood swing. It actually was a little scary."

"Oh my, are you alright, sweetie?" Sunny studied her face. "You turned pale just now. I guess she really did frighten you. Did she say anything threatening?"

"Not at all, and I'm really fine." Verity shrugged with a show of nonchalance but heard a tremble in her own words. She cleared her throat and concentrated on steadying her voice. "It was just so weird. The thing is, she was in town the night O'Halloran was killed. Henry has given her a bed here, in the basement. Sheriff Bailey told me yesterday he'll be interviewing all of Ervin's travelers, but he didn't mention the driver. I'm going to ask him if he's interviewed her or knows anything about her."

"Good idea," Sunny said. "We shouldn't try to talk to her until he has a chance to." The café owner let out a long sigh and absently rubbed the pad of her thumb over a discolored spot on the marble countertop. "Poor Crystal. She's going to be so unhappy having lost her summer job. Maybe I should ask her if she'd like to come to the café and help me for the rest of the season."

"She's only fifteen," Denise reminded her, "she can't serve wine or beer at the tables."

"I realize that and would never ask her to. But she knows how to work my old cash register and tend the pastry counter." Sunny had found an antique cash register at Chaundra's emporium. They both thought it would add old-timey flavor to the café that complemented the pressed-tin ceiling and cute bistro tables and chairs. Customers seemed fascinated, watching their tabs being rung up on a machine that wasn't a computer. "Anyhow," Sunny continued, "the girl can take food orders and I'll handle requests for adult beverages."

"Oh," Verity said, just then seeing Henry's granddaughter appear in the kitchen doorway with a timid smile. "Hey there, Crystal."

"Sorry, wasn't eavesdropping. I just came in to see how Grandpop was doing and heard my name and—" She lifted one shoulder and looked shyly at Sunny. "I heard you mention the café, Ms. Whitaker."

"So-o-o, what do you think? Would you like to work for me the rest of the summer? With your grandpa's permission, of course."

"Sure." The girl walked over to the kitchen island and lifted the cover of the white cardboard box Sunny had brought for Henry's guests. "Yummy. Can I have one of the chocolate eclairs? Please, please?"

"Go for it, sweetie!" Sunny beamed at her. "There's more where those came from. In fact, Henry rushed off before I could ask him if these will be enough for today."

"Gotta be tough, getting fired by your own grandfather," Denise commiserated.

"Denise!" Sunny and Verity said at the same time.

"Well, she's right," Crystal said, biting into the end of a ginormous eclair and distributing a circle of dark chocolate ganache around her mouth. She chewed and swallowed, then wiped the frosting off her lips with a napkin. "He didn't need to do that. I handled things okay. I shouldn't have told him what happened."

Frowning, Verity turned toward her friends to see them looking at her with equally concerned expressions. "What happened, Crystal?"

"Oh, it was that guy just being weird." The teenager focused on her pastry as if it were the only thing that mattered in the world.

"What guy?" There was grit in Denise's tone. The town's chocolatier held her fists locked at her sides.

Of all Verity's friends, Denise reacted the fastest and most forcefully to a perceived insult or threat. Often using more than words to show her disapproval of whoever had raised her hackles. Denise wasn't as big as the woman bus driver. But she was tall and fit and capable of putting up a good fight, if it came to that. In fact, Verity suspected Denise sometimes hoped for a brawl.

"Who are you talking about, Crystal dear?" Sunny asked in a calm voice that belied the tension in the muscles along her jaw.

"The one that got himself killed," Crystal murmured, licking up globs of custard filling as they escaped from the pastry shell. "Serves him right. I guess Grandpop thinks so, too. He just hasn't said it, at least not to me."

Verity stepped closer to the girl and spoke as gently as she could even as she steamed inside. "Can you tell us what he did, Crystal? Please?"

The girl narrowed hazel eyes at her then looked away. "Why?"

"Because it might be something the sheriff needs to know. Unless you've already told him."

Crystal propped one hip on a barstool tucked up to the kitchen's island, the picture of indifference. "No. I didn't tell Sheriff Bailey. It was nothing. Seriously." She licked her gooey fingers. "Mmmmm. These are the best ever, Ms. Whitaker. I'm going to have one every time I work for you—even if I have to pay for it."

Verity knew teenage avoidance tricks when she saw them.

She had used such tactics herself, much to her mother's consternation. "Why don't you let us decide if it was nothing. Your grandfather looked pretty upset a few minutes ago. I'll bet he's worried about you."

"He worries too much. I'm not a kid anymore."

"You're fifteen!" Denise exploded, making them all jump. "That's still a kid!"

Sunny held up her hand to signal Denise to cool it. Although she probably suspected Denise wasn't capable.

But Verity couldn't let this go, even if Crystal's life wasn't, strictly, her business. She knew what it was like to be fifteen and a girl. School, your friends, clothes, parties, who were the couples and who were the nerds or the popular kids. Kid stuff was sometimes tough but, mostly, you could handle it.

Unfortunately, at fifteen you weren't always ready for the situations some adults threw in your path. When you were a kid and feeling confused about how to respond to a situation, it sometimes seemed best to let an incident slide. Don't make a fuss. Everyone will forget about it. It will just go away. Or so you think.

"I know you feel like an adult, working here and at the café," Verity said. "I'm sure your grandfather is very proud of you. But if Mr. O'Halloran stepped out of line, said or did anything that made you uncomfortable, the sheriff should know about it. One of us can go with you if you like."

"Why does it matter? He's friggin' dead!" Crystal groaned, scrunching up her face. "Oh, alright, but plea-ea-ease don't make a big deal about it."

She polished off her pastry in two more bites then needed a minute more to swallow and use a paper towel to clean her face and hands of custard and chocolate.

"Since you won't stop bugging me," Crystal said with a resigned sigh, "this is all that happened. I was cleaning rooms, changing sheets, spritzing air freshener and restocking the little shampoos and coffee pods. And cleaning bathrooms, of course, they're the worst." She rolled her eyes and shuddered. "But Grandpop needed help and he was paying me a whole lot more than Sunny." She winced. "Sorry!"

Sunny smiled at her. "Family connections never hurt."

"Yeah, I guess. Anyway, I had to do Alma's rooms in addition to mine, until she got back from carting her kids around town."

"That was nice of you," Sunny said softly. She looked toward Denise as though she feared the chocolatier might re-erupt at any moment. Denise's lips were so firmly pressed together they were turning purple.

"Yeah." Crystal nodded in agreement. But then she dropped her gaze to the floor and wrinkled her nose, as if she smelled something disgusting. "Anyway, I always knock first. You just never know what state of—" She flushed petal pink. "It can be kind of embarrassing if someone's lounging around in their altogether, you know?"

"Of course," Verity said. "So, you knocked."

"And no one answered, so I knocked again. Still no answer. So-o-o, I wheel my cleaning cart into the room. That guy, Rudy, steps out of the bathroom." Crystal's cheeks deepened to a raspberry hue. "He's wearing one of the inn's fancy terrycloth robes."

"Oh no!" Sunny whispered nervously, like you do when watching a movie and sense a scary part coming up.

Crystal barked out a laugh that wasn't the funny-ha-ha kind of laugh. "Yeah. So, he's trying to be all friendly like, complimenting me and telling me how pretty I am. And I know when someone is lying—I'm not dumb. But for crying out loud, he's like *ancient!* So, gross! Argh!" She made a gagging sound.

Denise laughed and earned another dirty look from Sunny.

"Did he touch you?" Verity asked softly. "Hurt you?"

"Like I'd even let him near me!" Crystal's pretty eyes widened, as if she suddenly realized what the three women with her in the kitchen had been thinking. "No way! No, he grabbed for me but I was too fast for him. I threw the stack of sheets and towels at him and told him he could make his own freakin' bed."

Verity stepped up and hugged her. "You did great." She was prepared to back away if she sensed any awkwardness on the girl's part. But Crystal nestled into her embrace.

"Well, that does it," Denise growled. "If he weren't already dead, I'd have killed the creep."

"Of course, you would, dear," Sunny said sweetly. "If I didn't get to him first."

"I shouldn't have told Grandpop," the teenager repeated, her voice muffled in Verity's t-shirt.

Sunny and Denise turned questioning looks to Verity, but she was sure all three of them were thinking the same thing. *Was there a better motive for attacking a man than to punish him for abusing a child?*

# CHAPTER 12

LATER THAT SAME DAY, Verity's cellphone rang while she was collecting eggs from her chicken coops in the field behind her kitchen garden. She brushed the worst of the dust and chicken poo off her hands then checked her caller ID before answering.

"Yes, Sheriff?"

"I think it's time we compare notes, providing you have anything useful for me."

"I do. Sort of. I think." Crystal's experience had been weighing heavily on her mind. "Although it may or may not mean anything for your investigation."

"You didn't notice anything in particular about the alley when you first came upon the crime scene the other morning— did you?" he asked. "Of course, you did," he added when she hesitated a beat too long. "Why do I bother asking?"

Verity scooted one of her hens off its nest and palmed two warm eggs in her free hand, giving herself time to think of an answer that wouldn't set off his famous temper.

"I knew you'd notice the way the ground was scuffed up," she said quickly. "I didn't want you snapping at me for mentioning something so obvious." She had decided to wait until she saw Bailey in person to tell him about O'Halloran's attempt to seduce little Crystal.

"I don't snap," he snapped.

"You do, but so do I," she admitted, "when I'm stressed."

"I'm not stressed, missy; just doing my job."

She bit her tongue. Man, she hated when he called her that. "Of course you are. Anyway, I was thinking that I should meet with my field agents once more before—"

He laughed. "Your *field agents?*"

She was more than a little offended now. "What would you call the members of Evansfield Private Investigations? Would you prefer investigators? Sleuths? PIs? Or maybe gumshoes?"

"I wouldn't dare say." He rushed on before she could respond. "You ought to know that you can't really be considered private investigators. That requires a license in the State of Vermont, and you ladies, to my knowledge, aren't qualified to get one." He sounded short of breath, his lungs puffing in and out noisily as if he was walking fast. She wondered where he was. "Never mind. It's probably a good idea for you ladies to first discuss whatever you learned in town, then just give me a summary."

"You'd be welcome to join us when we meet." She grinned, knowing how uncomfortable he'd been in the past when he was alone with her whole group. Poor man.

He coughed, which, she suspected, was his futile attempt to camouflage another laugh. "I'm not sure I'd survive even fifteen minutes as the lone male with that bunch. Best you bring me your report after you meet with your friends."

"Coward." She foraged another three eggs and stood up. Her Rhode Island Reds had done her proud today.

"I know when to take a risk for my community," he grumbled through the phone, "and when to shelter and live another day."

She chuckled. "Fine. I'll see who is free this afternoon for a quick debriefing. I should be able to catch you up by tonight."

She started back toward the house, pausing at her kitchen garden to pluck two ripe tomatoes and drop them into the string bag hanging from her jeans belt. With the lettuce and cucumbers and sweet red peppers she had picked earlier, she'd have a fine side salad to accompany her supper omelet. That was one good thing about living on a farm, you ate well if the weather cooperated.

She looked around her yard on her way to the back door, hoping for a glimpse of Lady Macbeth. She still hadn't seen the cat, and neither had the twins. Jerry had offered her a gentle warning that she shouldn't get her hopes up; the animal might not return at all. Verity sighed, wishing Lady M well, wherever she was. She was sure it was her fault the cat had disappeared. Obviously, she was a bad cat mother. She must have done something wrong. The animal had wandered off in disgust at her stupidity.

Verity's thoughts returned to the sheriff and the investigation. If O'Halloran's death wasn't due to a freak accident, they should be looking into who might have wanted him dead. Starting with whoever had the strongest motive. Henry? His name had leaped into her mind the moment she realized he knew what O'Halloran tried to do to his granddaughter. But what about Crystal herself? She had been embarrassed by what he tried with her and might have felt (although without cause) ashamed. However, she doubted the girl would have been capable of taking down a grown man.

She was strangely comforted, though, by her suspicions that Rudy had spent a lifetime offending people. Thereby widening the field of suspects, if indeed murder was involved. He was a truly vile person. Even his wife must have found him a hard man to live with, although Jennifer seemed desperately sad that he'd died.

*Missy,* Verity thought, her squirrely mind jumping back to her conversation with the sheriff. The word was vaguely pejorative, a snide reference to her gender. Good grief! You'd think they lived in a nineteenth century prairie town.

She had tried to stop the sheriff from using it—on her or anyone. One memorable time, Denise took a swing at him and only just missed punching him in the face. Now Verity could laugh at the fiasco, which had nearly landed the candymaker in jail for assaulting an officer of the law. She was just thankful the man was starting to take their group of volunteers a little more seriously.

Before summoning the other six members, she washed and checked her freshly gathered eggs for signs that one had lingered too long in a coop and begun to form a chick or had rotted. Sometimes a broody hen was particularly clever at hiding her treasures. Over time, Verity had developed a talent for scoping them out. She rarely missed a bad egg these days.

With egg inspection done, she phoned Sunny and explained the sheriff's request for a summary of their findings. "I'll start the telephone chain," Sunny agreed. "We can meet here in the café, right after lunchtime rush. Say, two o'clock?"

They gathered in the little flower garden behind the café, fenced in from the alley. As it turned out, there were nine in attendance instead of the expected seven. Seven living souls; two deceased. Verity squinted at the faint silhouettes twinkling within the shadows of Sunny's rosebushes. So much for discouraging the two ghosts from attending their meetings.

As the legitimate members of the group arrived, each

woman dropped $4.00 in a basket and picked up a treat to accompany their coffee or tea. Verity set her latte and lemon-curd danish on one of the wrought-iron tables and casually walked over to the rose bushes. She leaned in close and sniffed.

"You won't smell anything," Mary Beth sang out, "hybrids aren't like the aromatic old-fashioned roses I carry at my nursery." The mayor's wife was a wiz when it came to any kind of plant. It was the rest of life she struggled with. When not working at her beloved nursery, Mary Beth preferred to live in the world of her CSI shows.

"They're so beautiful, I can't help trying," Verity answered, but then lowered her voice. "Apparently, neither can you two. Didn't I tell you to stop spying on us?"

"Why, whatever do you mean, Miss Verity?" cooed Anna Louise, flipping open her favorite beribboned fan. The delicate, pierced ivory screened her pert nose and pretty lips.

"We don't mean to intrude," Percy assured Verity in a whisper, even as he beamed affectionately at his wife. "Do we, my dear?"

"Not in the least. We were, as it happens, simply passing by when—"

"Rubbish!" hissed Verity, far louder than she'd intended.

"What's wrong?" Sunny turned to stare at her. "You don't like my roses? The yellow ones are called Princess's Pride. Mary Beth ordered them special for me, this spring."

"No, no," Verity said quickly, nuzzling the delicate petals. "They're absolutely gorgeous. I, ummm, thought I saw a Japanese beetle on one, but it was just a trick of the light." She dropped her voice again. "You are *not* to show yourselves. Understand? Now dim that glimmer or you'll—"

The ghostly sparkles flitted out.

Verity huffed. *Ghosts!*

"Let's get started, everyone," Chaundra called out. "I can't stay long. Hattie is guarding the emporium for me, and she tends to nod off in the middle of the afternoon."

"And I'll need to relieve one of my helpers who has kids to pick up from swim class," Sunny added.

Verity watched Kate select a blueberry muffin from the tray of goodies. She fished money from her jeans pocket and added it to the kitty. When they had first started meeting to talk about crime, Sunny had been way too generous, supplying pastries for free. Even though she claimed the yummies she donated were day-olds, Verity knew that wasn't always the case. And anyway, her stuff was way too scrumptious to throw it out less than twenty-four hours later. The local food bank always scrambled for any leftovers she could give them, regardless of age.

"Alright then, I'll go first, shall I?" Verity sat down, took a sip of her creamy latte and glanced longingly at her pastry, regretting she hadn't already taken a few bites. Why did she never learn!

First, she shared with her friends her experience with Ervin and his driver. Then she reminded them of what she'd seen in the alley that the sheriff now seemed to be taking more seriously. "There's more. But Sunny should share what happened in the inn's kitchen this morning when Denise and I were with there with her."

The café's owner gave a solemn nod then brushed her blonde curls back from her face, all business now. Denise leaned forward in her chair, as if she might jump in at the first opportunity, but Verity shook her head at her in gentle warning. The confectioner frowned and lifted a shoulder in a reluctant shrug of compliance.

"The three of us were in the kitchen with Henry," Sunny began. "He was acting miffed about something and seemed super distracted. We had no idea why. But his mood appeared to have something to do with his granddaughter, Crystal. I think most of you already know her?" Nods all around. "Anyway, she had been working as a chambermaid for him, but he told us he'd recently fired her."

Fumiko shouted something that sounded like: *Hai-cho!* Perhaps an obscenity in Japanese? "What he do that for? She good kid!"

"You'll see in a minute," Verity promised. "Go on, Sunny."

"Right. So, then Henry needed to go off to finish the cleaning chores, since he was shorthanded, and Crystal joined us. She admitted that the reason Henry wouldn't let her continue working as a chambermaid was because of a problem with one of their male guests."

"Mr. Creepo Rudy!" Denise burst out, unable to hold back any longer. "Do you believe *that*? And Crystal only fifteen! I could have strangled the—"

"We know!" they chorused.

"At first," Sunny continued, glaring a warning at Denise, "the poor girl pretended that his attempts to cozy up to her hadn't bothered her. Crystal assured us that she was tough and had managed things on her own."

"She must have been terrified," Kate whispered. "I would have been." Her voice rose suddenly, gaining starch. "But if anyone, I mean *anyone*, tried that stuff with my girls—"

"Of course," Sunny said quickly, patting Kate's arm comfortingly.

"Did Crystal report the incident?" Chaundra's ebony skin looked stretched taut across the sharp angles of her face.

"No, and neither did her grandfather, apparently." Sunny looked at Verity. "Maybe you should explain the rest. I need to get out front to my customers." She sniffed once and her eyes looked a little red as she left to go back inside the café. Verity could tell that repeating the story had upset her more than either of them had expected.

"I can't believe Henry didn't do anything about that man's behavior," Denise said.

"I think Verity's point is—maybe he did." Kate stared at the crumb-covered napkin in her lap, as though she couldn't figure out where her muffin had gone.

Chaundra turned to Verity. "Do you really think that's possible?"

"What's possible? What are you talking about?" Mary Beth sputtered, crumbs spraying from her mouth.

Kate sighed. "MB dear, we're still talking about Henry." She paused, giving their friend a moment to catch up. "Henry's granddaughter was, um, she was made uncomfortable by that awful Mr. O'Halloran."

"Un-com-fort-able?" Mary Beth chewed on the word and gazed skyward. "Oh! You mean he tried to...like kiss her or something?"

"Maybe a lot more, the fucker!" Denise shouted.

"Shush," Chaundra cautioned. "We're supposed to keep things on the QT."

"Ask me if I care!" Denise looked around the circle of concerned faces. "He's *dead*. I'm glad he's *dead*. And you should be, too. We all should be hysterically, joyfully thankful that the world is rid of at least one man who takes advantage of women and kids!" Denise was on her feet by now, marching back and forth across the garden's flagstones between rows of orange lilies and long stalks of purple foxglove, her arms swinging like machetes. Innocent blossoms flew like frightened birds.

Sunny reappeared in the doorway, hands on hips. "What on earth is going on out here?" She stared at the group, then narrowed her eyes on the figure in yoga duds, her cropped red hair sticking straight up as she zipped back and forth like a crazed fairground shooting alley duck. "Oh," she said.

"Denise is a tad upset," Kate explained.

*Understatement of the year*, Verity thought.

"I can see that. Well, everyone inside my café can hear you, Denise. Now sit down and shut up." Sunny's voice turned gentler at the apologetic look she got from her favorite truffle-maker. "Listen, we're all pretty upset, but you're not doing any good by raving like this." She took a step forward and lowered her voice even further. "We are supposed to keep what we discover to ourselves. Remember? For the sheriff's ears only."

"Oooh," Mary Beth cooed, "so-o-o James Bond."

"That's *For Your Eyes Only*. Not ears." Verity normally would have smiled at Mary Beth, except she didn't feel like smiling, given what they'd been discussing.

"We can't afford to leak information to the public," Sunny reminded them again. "Sheriff Bailey might disband the EPI if he thinks we're sabotaging his investigation. And we don't want that, do we?" Heads shook. "Denise?"

"No. Sorry, 'course not. I just get so steamed." Denise sat down in a sulk.

"Verity, see if you can hammer some common sense as well as professionalism into this group."

"Yes, ma'am," Verity said. She would have added a snappy, military-style salute had it not been for the dour expression on the café owner's face.

Verity waited until Sunny again left and the rear door of the café firmly shut. She took a deep, cleansing breath and was sure she heard others doing the same. Sunny was, of course, right. They needed to settle down and get to work. Emotion wouldn't crack this case.

"So, here's the thing," she said at last. "In case you haven't already figured it out," she glanced pointedly at Mary Beth, "we're worried that Henry might have felt he needed to protect his granddaughter."

"Grandpapa's job to do that!" Fumiko stated, her black eyes

shining. She pounded the knuckles of one hand into her other palm for emphasis. "Family honor demands."

"Yes, well, the law is funny about things like how much protection is appropriate, as well as when and in what form. Murder is considered overkill." Verity winced at her own pun and feared she wasn't quite getting her point across.

"I'm still not sure I totally understand," Mary Beth said meekly.

"What Verity means," Chaundra volunteered, with a cautious glance in Denise's direction, "is, just because you're angry at what a person does, you can't go beating them up or killing them."

Denise sat stiffly on her iron garden chair and looked away.

"The thing is—" Verity said "—Henry could have reported the incident to the sheriff. And Bailey would have acted on the complaint. But if Henry took it upon himself to go after Rudy with the intent to injure or kill him, and if he actually *did* kill him—"

Denise opened her mouth, and Verity gave her the squinty-eyed death-stare in Sunny's absence.

"I'm not going to shout," Denise whispered hoarsely. "I am calm. *Very, very* calm. Can I please say something?"

"You may," Mary Beth said, with a regal wave of her plump hand before anyone else had a chance to respond.

"Good. I am going address the logic of this situation." Denise straightened up, tugging down the legs of her yoga shorts. "I want all of you to imagine our sixty-something-year-old Henry. Weighing 130 pounds soaking wet, if that. How do you think he would have fared in a fight with that six-foot orang-utan Rudy?"

They looked at one another. "Not too great, I guess?" Kate murmured.

"Exactly!" Denise folded her arms over her chest in satisfaction.

"But he might have done it with help," Chaundra suggested solemnly. "Henry has lots of friends in Evansfield who care about him and Crystal."

*Enough to murder for them?* Verity thought. And yet, she couldn't dismiss this possibility. Who could say what might have happened in the alley that night if emotions (not to mention testosterone) ran high enough.

# CHAPTER 13

IT WAS NEARLY 4:00 pm on the 3$^{rd}$ of July before the Daisy Dairy co-op truck arrived to pick up the day's milk. Verity stood beside the driver in her tank room, watching nervously over his shoulder as he drew a small sample and tested her ladies' creamy product.

"Are we good?" she asked, as he entered the results on his iPad.

"Passed with flying colors." Brian —she had noticed his name on the embroidered patch on his denim jacket—smiled at her and loped off to bring his hose in from his truck and attach it to the big stainless-steel tank. He was a new guy on her route. A little less friendly than the regular driver but he seemed nice enough and obviously knew what he was doing. He wore dark-framed eyeglasses that made him look vaguely pedagogical. Sort of the Clark Kent version of Superman, but with less obvious muscle.

She let out a long breath of relief; the purity of her milk was still more than just acceptable. But without her resident mouser she worried it would only be a matter of time before the rodent population again mushroomed. She didn't know for certain that the rodents would harm the milk, but their presence couldn't possibly be good for it.

"I hear you've had some excitement recently," Brian commented later as she walked him back to his truck. He looked at her curiously. "An unexplained death, as I hear it?"

"Sadly, yes. Sorry, I can't talk about it yet. The sheriff has asked us to—"

"I understand," he said. "I have to say, little Evansfield is fast becoming famous, or maybe it's infamous." He chuckled but looked contrite when she didn't smile. "Apologies. Bad taste, I guess?"

"Everyone is just curious, wanting to know what happened to the man who died," she said. "I get that."

"Of course. I guess I'll just have to wait until you crack the case." He winked at her. Maybe he was friendlier than she'd thought? Whatever. It seemed the story of her involvement in the previous year's murder had spread beyond Evansfield's town lines.

"You'll be the first to know. Well, among the first," she amended with a smile.

"Good enough. You take care, ummm, Mrs. Cade." He hesitated a beat before hauling himself up into the truck's elevated cab. She wondered. Had he been waiting to see if she'd invite him to use her first name? *Oh, please, just call me Verity.* Or ask him to come inside for a cup of tea? No. That couldn't be right.

Shaking her head, she watched him back the big tanker around and turn north onto the road, away from town.

She checked in with Jason and Jerry. They were mowing the yard surrounding the farmhouse. She had never asked them to do this, but they took it upon themselves to keep her lawn from reaching knee high. She insisted, however, that they leave the flower borders around the house and her kitchen garden for her to maintain. The boys were well-meaning but knew less about flowers than about corn, hay, and alfalfa.

The previous spring, wanting to surprise her, they had "trimmed and weeded" the perennial bed under her parlor windows. She returned home from her egg route to find the tender tips of her sprouting irises and peonies chopped off and lying on the compost pile.

Today, before her helpers left for the day, she confided her concerns about the vermin situation now that Lady M had deserted her. They did their best to reassure her.

"You've got as modern a closed milking system as possible, from cow to dairy," Jerry said. "Once the Robo-Milker sterilizes the cows' teats, draws the milk into the sealed pipelines and storage tank, there's no way mice or rats can harm it."

"You're sure?" she asked. "What about their droppings getting into the cows' feed?"

"Now that might become a problem," Jason admitted. "If you can't keep cats on the job, we definitely should set traps or—"

"No poisons," Verity insisted. "We've been over this before. The chance of harming other animals or kids who wander into the barns is just too great."

"Alright then. What will it be? Cats or traps?" Jerry folded his arms over his chest and gave her as no-nonsense a scowl as the sweet-natured young man could muster.

"Maybe Lady Macbeth will come back?" she said hopefully.

"Who?" the twins chorused.

"Lady Macbeth, that's her name. The yellow cat who was—"

"You named her after a Shakespearean murderess?" Jason hooted.

"Why not?" she said haughtily. Not only was it an appropriate moniker, she thought it was quite classy. And anyway, she couldn't admit that a ghost, not she, had named the cat.

Her farmhands just looked at each other.

Jerry sighed. "That cat's not coming back. You can forget about her. We'll ask around town, see who has a litter that's old enough to start earning its keep."

"But if we can't find cats for you," Jason insisted, "or they don't do the job, it's gonna be traps."

"Oh squish," she muttered.

Feeling a little depressed at the thought of her AWOL kitty and surfeit of mice, Verity drove back into town to meet with Sheriff Bailey at his office across the village green from the Cat's Cradle Café. She couldn't stop thinking that whatever she had done to make Lady M leave might also send replacement felines scampering for a better home.

Sheriff Bailey looked up from his desk with a hangdog expression when she stepped into his office. "Thought you might've forgot about our meeting." He shoved aside a veritable avalanche of paper that looked like reports of some kind. Yellow forms, green spreadsheets, graph paper.

"Forget you, Sheriff? Never. I'm not interrupting anything important, am I?"

"Just damn paperwork. Gets worse every year."

"Your deputies can't handle some of it? Or—"

"I don't trust those idiots to do anything right. And Harriet, she always reminds me that arrest reports and traffic citations aren't in her job description; she's the receptionist, and that's that! Bev needs to concentrate on taking calls and doubling up as dispatcher."

Verity smiled. "Bless their hearts." The two women had

been a fixture at the Evansfield Sheriff's Department long before Verity came to live in the town.

"If you say so." He made a lopsided pile from the paper and shoved it to one side. "You first. What do you and your lady-friends have for me?"

"My *investigators*," she said with emphasis, "and I have a few other items of my own to pass along to you." She started with the least important things they had discussed at the café earlier that day. Including a few unsubstantiated rumors about the thefts from Doc Evans' office and one totally implausible rumor that Ervin was using his bus tours to smuggle cocaine into Evansfield. Then she paused for a moment to gather her thoughts for the sensitive conversation to come.

"Good. Thank you for this, Mrs. Cade." Bailey put down the pen he'd been using to take notes. "Now, here's what I've—"

"I'm not done," she said quickly, but immediately had second thoughts. She hated to even suggest that Henry or his grand-daughter might have had anything to do with O'Halloran's death.

"Go on then." Bailey waved a big hand at her.

"I was delivering Henry's order of eggs and milk to the inn this morning." She tried to keep her tone neutral but already heard a revealing quaver in her voice. She knew he heard it too, because he lifted his big head along with an impressive collec-tion of jowls to fix her with a steady gaze.

"Henry was running around like a headless chicken," she continued. "His cook was off somewhere and he was short a chambermaid. No," she revised, "short two chambermaids because he'd fired one and the other was carting her kids around town. So, he was trying to do all the work himself."

"I feel bad for the man," the sheriff said, "but what does this have to do with the O'Halloran investigation?"

She bit down on her lower lip. "Maybe nothing?" she said

sheepishly. He gave her an even more impatient get-to-your-point flap of his hand. "Anyway, Sunny and Denise were in his kitchen when I arrived, delivering pastries and chocolates."

His eyes widened. "And here I was interviewing the lamest collection of applicants for positions in my department when I could have been at gourmet central."

"The deliveries were for the tourists staying at the inn, Sheriff." She knew if he had joined them in the kitchen, there would have been a lot fewer sweets for the inn by the time he left. Snatching a few freebies now and then never counted as theft in his mind. "As I was saying, the three of us noticed that Henry was in an unusually horrid mood. Maybe due to more than being worked off his feet. He told us that he had fired his grand-daughter Cry—"

Bailey choked on a laugh. "He did what?"

"He told Crystal she couldn't work at the inn anymore." She held up a warning finger to caution him against another interruption. "Because Rudy O'Halloran tried to grab the girl in his room."

The muscles in the sheriff's jaw tightened. His eyes hardened, the pupils swelling. "He what? No, that's impossible. I would have heard about it if anyone reported an incident like that."

"Well, they didn't—report it that is. We had to coax the story out of Crystal. She finally told the three of us what happened."

"You sure she wasn't makin' it up? Lookin' for attention?"

Verity turned a face of stone on him. "She was really upset, Fred Bailey! Of course, she pretended it didn't matter. She acted like she was in control of the situation, but you *know* she couldn't have been. You can't ignore a kid who tells you something like—"

"I'm not ignorin' a thing!" he objected, rocketing out of his chair. On his feet now, he planted palms on his desk blotter and leaned over it toward her, his big, anger-bloated face turning an alarming shade of purple. "I just wonder if you realize what that might mean for this investigation."

"*Of course,* I know what it means!" she shouted, jumping up from the visitor's chair. "Why do you think I'm telling you? I hate bringing this to you, I really do. It makes Henry a suspect."

"Maybe Crystal, too," Bailey growled.

"Oh, no. No, no, no!" Verity jab, jab, jabbed a finger at him like a knife blade, punctuating her words. "You can't possibly think that little girl had—"

"I'm not accusing either of them, yet. But Mrs. Cade, what if he tried again? What if that man caught her outside in the alley, alone?" Bailey came around the desk toward her in three long strides. "What if she was forced to fight him off?"

He was sweating now, steaming in his own juices on this hot July day. He was a generously apportioned man, always a bit florid, with a nose full of broken blood vessels that spoke of someone who liked his beer a little too much. But she had never once seen him drunk on the job. Now he was intoxicated, but not on alcohol. Drunk on his own fury. She feared she had miscalculated how he might react when he learned that something this dangerous had happened on his turf, nearly under his nose.

*Please, don't kill the messenger!*

He spun away from her, cursing, pacing back and forth within the tight space between her and his desk.

"I'm sorry, Sheriff, I know how serious you are about the town's welfare, about keeping us safe. I should have—"

"Don't apologize," he growled. "I needed to know this." He stopped pacing and closed his eyes in thought. "Okay. Here's what I'm thinkin'. Crystal might have grabbed whatever was handy, slugged him with it. Self-defense. Just tryin' to get away from him in the alley."

Verity collapsed backward into her chair and slid down, scowling into her lap. His temper tantrum had exhausted her. And now he was building in his own mind the worst possible scenario.

"You don't think that's a possibility?" he said. "I sure do."

This was not the direction she had believed he'd take. She sighed. "Let's just say that I...I think it's a less likely possibility than—"

"Than what?" His eyes narrowed on her. "You don't like my theory? Alright. I have another one for you." He leaned down into her space. "O'Halloran catches Crystal out in the alley. Maybe she's takin' out the garbage for Gramps. Given this second opportunity, Rudy attacks her. Henry hears her screams or maybe just a strange noise he can't identify. He looks out through a rear window and sees O'Halloran all over the girl. In a rage, Henry races down to the alley, picks up a brick or shovel or hammer and beats the man's brains out."

"I don't like that one either," she whispered miserably.

"Course not! Neither do I. But it's as good a motive for endin' that man's miserable life as any I can think of."

"You're not going to arrest Henry, are you?" she asked weakly. "If I hadn't said anything to you about...about what O'Halloran tried to do."

"But you couldn't *not* tell me." He was speaking in a more normal voice now, almost kindly. His eyes had lost that crazed look. "You might have held onto their secret for a little while, but you're not one to turn your back on the truth."

"I know. That's what makes this so hard."

"Anyhow," he chuckled, "that big-mouth Denise would have come to me, if you hadn't."

Verity smiled, just a little. "Deni definitely couldn't have kept this to herself. And Sunny is as much a stickler for honesty as any of us."

"That's the only reason I'm lettin' you and your friends have anythin' to do with the work of this department," he said. "You know the value of the truth. And justice. And you want to help this community stay safe."

"We do," she echoed softly, and felt a little better, knowing that he understood her. "What are you going to do now, Sheriff?"

"For the moment, I'll continue as before with the investigation. I got no proof that either Henry or his granddaughter had anythin' to do with that man's death. If I find out that either of 'em was involved, or someone else tried to teach the man a lesson on their behalf, there will be arrests." He paused. "Are we good now, Mrs. Cade?"

"Yes, I guess so," she said. "We'll just keep doing our thing—eyes and ears open, relaying anything of interest to you."

"Good on you." He returned to his desk and sat down heavily. The chair complained. To her mind, it should have been replaced with something sturdier a long time ago. If it ever gave way under the big man, it wouldn't be a pretty sight for either of them.

She stood up to leave but then remembered. "You haven't given me *your* report."

"No, I haven't. Somethin' came to mind while we were talkin'. I need to do some research before I know if what I meant to tell you has anything to do with this mess. I'll let you know if it's important."

# CHAPTER 14

THAT EVENING, before night had well and truly settled in, Verity turned her attention to her kitchen garden. The Seychelles pole beans she had planted in May had produced a cracker crop, plenty to keep her fed through the end of summer and well into the winter. Two-thirds of her mid-summer harvest she had already parboiled and frozen. She picked the remaining pods from the gracefully twining beanstalks then cut off the vines at ground level before pressing more bean seeds, with the pad of her thumb, into the soft fertile ground. If the weather stayed mild into September, she had a good chance of getting a second crop before the first frost, and that might tide her over for green beans into next spring.

She enjoyed observing the stages of a plant's life from seed to embryo to maturity and, finally, to a fruiting plant. Seedlings grew so rapidly in the mild Vermont summers, she was amazed by the changes she saw from one day to the next.

Her squash and pumpkins would need another month before they were ready to harvest. The tan, pear-shaped Waldorf winter squash and much larger gray-green Hubbards kept for many months in her cool, frost-free root cellar. She also stored potatoes, beets, turnips, carrots, and parsnips there. Whereas storing her corn, tomatoes, cauliflower, broccoli, beans, and peas required freezing or canning. The latter being the more time-consuming and a chore she didn't look forward to. But she never failed to feel grateful when January, February, and March—the lean months—rolled around. Having a fully stocked pantry and freezer meant fewer trips to the grocery store, and money saved. And she always had fresh eggs year-round.

Life was good.

Tired and not wanting to fuss over cooking anything but a simple meal, she made herself a spinach-and-onion omelet, toasted two slices of Sunny's amazing whole-grain bread, and sat down to enjoy her supper as night closed in around her.

Before she took a bite, she sensed she was no longer alone in her kitchen. "I'm eating," she said, a little annoyed at the interruption.

"We're dead, darlin' girl, not blind."

She sighed. "Anna Louise, whatever you have to say to me, can it please wait until I've finished my perfectly lovely omelet?" She forked a bite of rich yellow egg into her mouth and savored the creamy, slightly salty flavor of her hens' fresh eggs.

"Miss Verity." Percy flashed into view alongside his wife. "I believe you will want to hear what we have to say without delay."

"Says the man who has forgotten what it is like to be tired and hungry," Verity muttered and chomped down on her buttered toast.

"Now that is such an unkind thing to say to the departed!" Anna Louise stomped a dainty satin slipper.

*Sometimes, she can be so cute.* Verity couldn't resist teasing the ghost, just to enjoy her drama-queen reactions.

"You asked us to spy for you," Percy reminded her, "and we have followed your orders."

Verity raised a brow. "As if snooping isn't what you two would be doing anyway?"

Anna Louise huffed her offense and propped white-gloved hands on her hips. "Well, I never!"

Today, the pretty ghost had eschewed plain muslin and homespun gingham for an ankle-length gown. The bodice was pinched in so tight at the waist Verity was amazed its wearer could breathe. Then again, she supposed that was irrelevant, as Anna Louise had stopped breathing over a century ago. But she had to admit the gown was lovely. Its skirts fell in a waterfall of pale rose taffeta ruffles from waist to hem. When Anna Louise moved, Verity was sure she counted at least a half-dozen petticoats beneath the billowing hem.

"You know," Verity began, hiding a smile, "as sweet as that dress is, blue really is your color, Anna Louise. It brings out the lavender in your eyes. So lovely."

"Oh?" Anna Louise blinked at her then stared down in a dissatisfied way at her definitely-not-blue skirt. "You truly think so?"

Percy laughed. "She's joshin' you, my sweet bride."

"No, she isn't!" Tossing her blonde curls Anna Louise flicked her fan at him in annoyance. "You told me I looked perfect. Men! You've no fashion sense at all."

"I *am* playing with you." Verity laughed. "You look absolutely lovely today. But it's also true that your eyes have a special sparkle when you wear blue."

"Then I shall save blue for special occasions." Anna Louise giggled, looking better pleased with herself.

Having distracted the two of them long enough for her to finish eating her meal, Verity pushed her plate away. "OK. Tell me what's so darn important."

They stepped closer to her. She felt a familiar rise in the air temperature between the two glittering specters and her own body.

She had always thought that the presence of ghosts—if one believed in such things—would generate a marked chill in the air. At least, that's how the presence of spirits was portrayed in movies and TV shows. But she had discovered quite the opposite to be true. She often felt a subtle rise in the ambient temperature when they were around. Only rarely did the air temperature drop when they appeared.

These fluctuations seemed linked to their emotions. A rare coolness meant the couple was upset, frightened, worried, or angry—which almost always meant trouble of one sort or another. Warmth signaled they were excited, happy, or just glad to be with her. Although now that she really thought about it, both moods had presaged unfortunate incidents. You just never knew with ghosts. So temperamental! They made teenagers seem like monks by comparison.

"Out with it," Verity encouraged them. "I really do want to hear what you've discovered."

The pair beamed at her.

"We were relaxing on the veranda of the inn," Anna Louise began, twirling around twice in her fluffy skirts, "just enjoying the lovely sunshine, wishing for two icy mint juleps while we listened to conversations around us."

"A woman started talking to your friend Kate, the bookstore lady," Percy interrupted impatiently. "About the dead man who was found—"

"*I* am telling the story!" Anna Louise gave her husband a pointed look.

"My sincerest apologies, my love." He bowed, one hand pressed to his uniform jacket over his heart.

"I shall continue," Anna Louise stated, tipping her nose toward the ceiling. Rather elegantly, in Verity's opinion. "As other people joined the conversation, we noticed that few hesitated to speak ill of the dead. The man was not well liked at all. I remember saying to myself..." Little frown lines appeared at the bridge of her nose. "Oh dear, what was it I said to myself? I do wander so in my narratives, don't I?" She peered imploringly over her fan at her husband.

Percy took up the story. "We were trying to observe who might have a particular grudge against the dead fellow when the big coach returned with the rest of their group." Percy's eyes lit up. "Such an invention that coach is! Absolutely magical, the way it moves without a single horse or mule to pull it!"

*He gets sidetracked as often as she does!* "Please, Percy, get to your point," Verity prodded, gently.

"Ah yes. The returning passengers disembarked, then went inside the inn with the rest of their group for dinner. But Mr. Ervin stayed behind to talk with his lady driver."

"Sue is her name," Verity said.

Anna Louise side-stepped in front of her husband. "I remember now! When Mr. Ervin commented that he thought their excursion went well, the driver responded, 'At least no one tried sneaking a flask on board like before.'"

"Mr. O'Halloran's name was mentioned," Percy supplied, over his wife's shoulder. "Anna Louise left that part out."

"I *would* have said it if you had given me a chance!" she sputtered.

"Never mind," Verity said. "I get the idea. So, O'Halloran was already making trouble even before the tour arrived in town."

"Yes!" Anna Louise cried. "Sue told Mr. Ervin she'd warned the man he wasn't allowed to bring whiskey on her bus, but he just laughed at her. And when she insisted that he hand over his flask, he only pretended to put it away but continued drinking on the sly."

"Obviously there was animosity between the driver and O'Halloran," Verity mused.

It surprised her that Ervin wasn't on the bus for the trip from New York, but perhaps he'd been busy making last-minute arrangements for his day trips. Of even more concern to her was the possibility that Sue's verbal confrontation with O'Halloran on the bus might have later resulted in physical violence.

"Is there anything more you need to tell me?" She was tired and, despite the ghosts' information, she longed for her bed.

"Oh, my yes!" Percy continued. "It seems an older woman on the bus scolded Mr. O'Halloran and threatened to get him booted off the tour."

Having witnessed O'Halloran's temper in the café, Verity could easily imagine his reaction.

Percy's eyes darkened. "According to the driver, Mister O'Halloran tried to snatch the woman's phone out of her hands when she took a picture of him. Miss Sue ordered him to sit down and leave the woman alone, and if he didn't, she threatened to drive him straight to the nearest police station."

Verity shook her head. It seemed everywhere Rudy O'Halloran went, trouble followed. "I guess Ervin and Sue will report the incident to the sheriff when he questions them."

"No," Percy said, "Miss Sue asked her boss to say nothing about what happened on the bus."

"Actually," Anna Louise added with a little shudder, "she didn't *ask* him, she *ordered* him to keep his mouth shut. I think little ol' Mr. Ervin is afraid of her."

"That woman is two heads taller and twice his weight," Percy said. "Miss Sue could have picked up your friend Ervin and thrown him like a leaf."

*Maybe that's exactly what she did do,* Verity thought. *Just not to Ervin.* She recalled the terrible wound on the back of O'Halloran's head.

# CHAPTER 15

VERITY KNEW she should tell the sheriff what she'd learned from the Putnams. The confrontations between O'Halloran and both the bus driver and the older woman on the bus might be important to the investigation. Problem was, Bailey would demand to know how she'd gotten her information. She couldn't admit that her source was two dead people. *Argh!* So, she needed to keep these disconcerting incidents to herself until she could figure out if, or how, they were involved in his death. By then she might come up with a good way to tell him that didn't involve ghosts.

Meanwhile, she had much more pleasant things on which to focus.

The July Fourth Cake Auction was a longstanding Evansfield tradition that Verity loved. She had agreed to bake two cakes. According to the rules, these must be made from scratch. No store-bought cakes, and the use of boxed mixes was strictly forbidden.

By the time she arrived at the village green with her contributions, the lush expanse of grass was already crowded with what appeared to be every resident of the town. She drove around the green twice, searching for a parking place. The festivities were well underway.

Charcoal grills billowed smoke redolent of hickory and charred meats. She imagined the usual hot dogs, hamburgers, rings of kielbasa and barbecued chicken. Her mouth watered. Even from the cab of her truck, she could see big bowls of what were probably homemade coleslaw and potato salads, as well as bags of potato chips, paper plates and cups, coolers of soda, and beer. All piled on top of long, folding tables that had been trucked in to supplement permanent picnic tables.

The high school band occupied the old bandstand, which had been draped in red-white-and-blue banners and surrounded by huge cement pots of vivid red geraniums. The young musicians were playing a collection of patriotic songs and marches that had been jazzed up from their original versions, probably to hold the teenagers' interest. Game booths ranged around the perimeter of the park. Children of all ages played at ring toss, horseshoes, and whack-a-mole; older kids clustered around a shooting gallery, Space-Bounce trampolines, and a trailer that had been made into a Haunted House.

Verity finally lucked out and spotted a car leaving a parking space at one end of the green. Thank goodness, she thought, hastily pulling the Ridgeline into the opening before anyone else grabbed her spot.

Although today was a non-working holiday for most residents, farmers rarely got a break, and she was no different. Instead of having the entire morning to complete her usual chores, she'd needed to reserve two hours for her baking. And, of course, she'd given Jason and Jerry the day off to be with their family—which added their jobs to her own. She had been out of bed and working since 4:00 am.

Out of breath by the time she reached the auction table, she handed over her cakes to Mary Beth, who served as chair of the committee.

"Oh my, don't those look amazing!" Mary Beth's eyes dilated as though she'd taken a hit of something more potent than sugar fumes.

"Thanks, MB. I wasn't sure I'd make it in time. When does the auction start?"

"In an hour. You had plenty of time."

Verity looked around at the expanse of picnickers. Some of Ervin's tourists had commandeered a pair of temporary tables directly across the road from the inn. A few kids were roasting marshmallows on sticks at one of the park's stone fireplaces.

"I should label these for you," Mary Beth was saying. She whipped out a pack of small white cards and a black marker from the kangaroo pocket in her fire-red apron.

"Oh, I'm so sorry!" Verity gasped. "I totally forgot. I was supposed to label my cakes."

"Not to worry. I'm re-writing the tags on everyone's cakes. Makes them look uniform. And it's easier for me to read my own writing when I announce each cake and its baker during the auction."

Mary Beth tended toward ditziness most of the time, but when it came to organizing an event like this, she somehow got her act together.

"Now, tell me what they are. Start with this one." She pointed to Verity's sheet cake.

"Applesauce with raisins and chopped walnuts and cream cheese icing."

"Oh, I may need to bid on that one myself!" She carefully printed Verity's name and description of the cake. "And the other one?"

"A burnt-sugar layer cake with caramel frosting."

Mary Beth chuckled. "I'll need to describe that one in more

detail for our tourists," she said. "I know the locals will appreciate the classic Vermont recipe. I think it was popular back in the early twentieth century, wasn't it? I've never made it myself. Too complicated, I seem to recall."

"Mark's mother taught me all the tricks. The recipe does require a lot of steps. Like, caramelizing the sugar to bring out the rich flavor. It's the process of almost 'burning' the sugar that gives it the strange name. The first bite I took of my mother-in-law's version, I couldn't believe how delicious it was."

"Well, I know *that* one will bring on some hot bidding. All for a good cause!" Mary Beth carefully completed the second label in dark block letters. "We're giving the auction's proceeds to the new children's wing of the hospital in Springfield—Elvira's favorite charity."

"Lovely," said Verity. Just the mention of their friend, the good doctor's wife, who had died so tragically months earlier, made her a little teary-eyed. Elvira Evans hadn't been the nicest person in the world, but she had done a lot for her community.

Verity looked away at the festivities to give herself a moment.

Mary Beth moved closer. "You don't seem in a holiday mood, Verity. Why don't you grab a hot dog or burger off the grill over there. Find a place to sit down and enjoy yourself."

"I'm okay. I need to share something with the sheriff. Just...well, he's not in a listening mood these days." On the other hand, Verity thought, a nice juicy hamburger sounded wonderful. She couldn't remember eating anything since breakfast, and somehow it was now the middle of the afternoon.

"I thought you briefed him yesterday." Mary Beth slid cakes around on the display table to match an invisible design in her mind.

"I did. This is something else. I'll explain later. I see some of

Ervin's people over there. I think I'll have a chat with them then see if I can find Sheriff Bailey."

"If it's Mrs. O'Halloran you're looking for," Mary Beth called after her, "I haven't seen her all day. Poor dear, she must be miserable—everyone else celebrating the holiday."

*She's probably on the phone trying to make funeral arrangements back home,* Verity couldn't help thinking. *How sad.*

If she had been in Jennifer O'Halloran's shoes, she wouldn't want to remain in the town that had been the scene of her husband's death for one minute longer. Then it struck her that fleeing Evansfield was the opposite of what she, herself, had done when she lost Mark.

Verity was so startled by this epiphany that she missed a step and nearly tripped on the uneven ground. Her own experience with the death of a loved one wasn't the same as Jennifer's. Jennifer had no roots in Evansfield.

So, why was the woman still here? It didn't make sense. Verity didn't think the sheriff would have forced her to stay in town. Was she so overwhelmed with grief, she couldn't make herself take the necessary steps to immediately return home without taking the tour bus back to New York City with the group? Maybe she had a reason for waiting. Maybe she had asked the sheriff if she could take her husband's body home with her. But until the investigation was complete and the forensic report filed, Rudy's body wouldn't be released to next of kin.

Lost in thought, Verity watched the park's cobbled path pass beneath her red sneakers as she walked. She wasn't sure why, but she suddenly felt a need to talk to the feisty photographer who had confronted Rudy on the bus. Preferably without Ervin listening in.

On her way toward the tables claimed by the Elite Vermont Tours folks, she wove between gaggles of children, screaming their way from booth to booth with the carefree abandon that came with being let loose by their adults. Delirious with their freedom, they were experiencing a golden time in their little lives. Just across the street in the inn, a woman had barricaded herself with her grief.

*Such a contrast in emotions!* Verity mused.

Verity's mind spun with a mishmash of information and theories—none of which seemed connected or yet made sense.

She stopped to watch the youngsters throwing water balloons at their school principal, his head poking through the center of a bullseye—a very popular game and money earner for charity by the looks of it. She moved on to stand behind lines of gawky teenagers waiting to try their hand at archery and the giant carnival mallet that clanged a bell if they smashed it down hard enough.

She felt a little nervous about questioning the woman from the bus, if she could even find her. Watching the youngsters was her way of delaying the interview. *Killing time.* Another phrase —*killing it*—meant doing a great job at something challenging. How had such diverse definitions come about for the same word as murdering a person?

Living things, when killed, felt pain and bled. Time didn't feel pain, did it? *Killing it* was a good thing. Killing people wasn't. The English language was perverse.

*Stop it!* she told herself. *This isn't helping.* What was it about this investigation that had her so rattled? *Stay focused.*

The two ghosts had only described the person who snapped photos of O'Halloran as an older lady. But now Verity saw at least six women over fifty years of age seated at the aluminum tables occupied by the tourists. She looked around for Ervin, and then for Sue.

No Sue. But Ervin was crossing the road toward the inn's steps, where Henry stood observing his approach with a grave expression. The two men immediately became absorbed in animated conversation. Good, they would be occupied for at least a few minutes.

On her way past a sizzling grill, she stopped to pick up a paper plate. She used a long-handled spatula to choose a burger and lay it on top of half a potato bun. She added a squirt of ketchup, a slice of ripe tomato, lettuce leaf, and a fat dill pickle spear, then casually approached the table occupied by the most gray hair. A bowl of potato salad nestled in a second bowl filled with ice to keep it cool. It looked like the kind Sunny served at the Cat's Cradle Café, rich with creamy mayo, chopped hard-boiled egg, onion and celery. Yum!

"Help yourself," one of the women invited, glancing up at Verity. "And have a seat." She had long hair pulled back in a ponytail and wore overalls emblazoned with American flags. Verity thought she remembered her from the farm tour. One of the moms.

"Well, thank you." Verity smiled. "I thought this table was reserved for the tour group."

"Not at all. My name is Amy, by the way. And I know you're Verity Cade." The woman patted the bench beside her. "I was just telling Marta here that she missed a great tour of your farm."

"I have too much trouble walking over rough ground these days," Marta said, pointing to the walker folded up at her end of the table. She looked to be in her eighties—although her alabaster skin was only finely wrinkled and her eyes sparked with intelligence.

"Oh, I'm sorry you missed visiting me," Verity said. "I don't know how long you'll be in town, but if you stop by sometime before you leave, I'll be glad to give you a personal tour. Just the areas that are easiest to navigate. I promise."

"That would be very nice," the older woman said. "But I wouldn't want to keep you from your work. I hear you're trying to run your farm on your own; that must be frightfully difficult. Such hard work."

"It can be. But I love it. I doubt I could ever give it up. Every day is different, and I adore being outdoors so much of the time."

"Well, that's the important thing, isn't it?" Marta said with a firm shake of her crown of white curls. "Finding something to do with your life that you can enjoy."

"Here, here!" Amy chimed in.

Marta grinned mischievously. "Amy here was just telling me that your farm is haunted."

Verity caught her breath. A shot of fear-driven adrenalin rushed through her. "I...no, I mean—wherever did you hear that, Amy?"

The woman was laughing uproariously and waving a hand in the air as if signaling she needed to catch her breath before answering. "Oh, that's what a couple of kids on the farm tour were saying. Weren't they, Cindy?" She nudged the woman seated on her other side.

Her friend chewed the bite of hot dog she'd just taken and shook her head. "Some nonsense about a floating tractor or flying boy. Whatever," she mumbled.

"No, I'm sure there was a ghost somewhere in their story," Amy insisted. "Along with a crazy lady farmer. That must be you, Verity." She winked at her. "Kids. What they dream up!"

"Yes, very funny." Verity felt her pulse gradually return to normal. What would she ever do if people actually discovered the truth about Percy and Anna Louise? "Ummm, which reminds me of something else funny. A story I heard about your group's trip up here from New York City."

"Oh?" Amy's green eyes flashed with sudden interest. "What kind of story?"

"Something involving that man who died the other night,"

Verity said. "How he snuck alcohol on the bus against the rules? And another passenger objected to his behavior, called him out. Was that you, Marta?"

Marta's expression altered abruptly. Her sweet, sunny smile morphed into a scowl. "I told that jerk to knock off his drinking. It wasn't that kind of tour. We had families on board, for goodness sakes."

Amy patted the older woman's hand. "Now, now—speaking ill of the dead doesn't sound like you, Marta." Verity watched the exchange of quick looks between the two women.

"Speaking the truth isn't the same as speaking ill of a person," Marta countered. "He was a vile, vile man!"

Amy sighed. "I can't argue with you there."

"I'm wondering," Verity said, finding the opening she was looking for, "about something else I heard—that one of your group took photos, catching him in the act, so to speak."

"That, again, would be me!" Marta yipped, proudly. She fished through a big black leather handbag hooked to her walker and pulled out a flip-type cellphone. "Look at this!"

After a few clicks on an app, she displayed a video for Verity. The audio was so muffled she couldn't, at first, make out the words, but she was able to clearly see Rudy glugging from a leather-covered hip flask. Then a voice seemed to come from the person holding the camera. Rudy O'Halloran whipped around in his bus seat, his face crimson, lip curling in a malicious snarl.

He shouted (and this was easy to hear), "Mind yer bees wax, old lady!" Launching himself from his seat, he lunged toward the camera lens as if to grab the phone or swat it out of the photographer's hand.

The screen jerked then went dark.

Verity's hand flew to her mouth in shock. "Oh, my! Were you alright, Marta? He didn't hurt you, did he?"

"Oh, no-no! That nice driver made sure of that. He stopped the bus right then and there and—"

"She," Amy corrected.

"Are you sure, dear? Goodness such a big strong lad!"

"Lass." Verity corrected. "Her name is Sue. Ervin introduced me to her."

Marta shrugged. "Not that a man couldn't have a name like —do you remember that old song? Johnny Cash, I think."

"A Boy Called Sue," Cindy laughed. "My dad was a huge Johnny Cash fan. He near died laughing whenever he heard the song. Go on, Marta. Sorry to interrupt."

Marta's attention appeared to have drifted across the park toward the inn where Ervin and Henry were still deep in conversation. "I suppose Mr. Cash has nothing to do with that awful fellow's death."

"Probably not," Verity said, desperate to bring the woman back to the topic at hand. "You were saying that the driver came to your rescue?"

"Oh, yes!" Marta's clouded eyes brightened. "That he did!" Verity and Amy exchanged amused looks but neither corrected her a second time. "Our driver immediately pulled the bus to the side of the road and stopped. He came straight back down the aisle between the seats, stood in front of that awful man and told him in no uncertain terms that he was of a mind to throw him off the bus."

"And that made O'Halloran stop drinking and leave you alone?"

"For all of five minutes," Amy grumbled. "Right, Cindy?"

"Yeah, then Rudy was back to taking furtive sips of whatever he had in that flask and grinning like a fool. Like he believed he'd pulled one over on everyone. Ha!"

"Rich people think they can do anything they please, no matter it hurts others." Marta patted Amy's hand. "Not you, my dear Amy. You are a lovely woman with the nicest manners." She aimed a critical look at Cindy who, by now, was wolfing down her third hotdog.

"Why thank you." Amy beamed at her fellow traveler. "And I'm proud to know you, Marta. Such a grand lady. You remind me of that actress on the British show where they live on a grand estate and have tons of servants. Don't I wish! Honest, you're just like her—so elegant and just a little spicy."

All through the conversation, Verity wondered whether any of these women could possibly have had anything to do with O'Halloran's death. Obviously, they found the man detestable. But she decided she couldn't imagine any one of them capable of attacking and killing him. Not even if they ganged up on him. (And wouldn't that have been a picture!)

"Marta, I probably should have said something sooner," Verity began at the next pause in conversation, "but I'm helping our sheriff and his deputies gather information about Mr. O'Halloran and the night he died."

"Someone done him in!" Marta sounded just like a character out of an Agatha Christie novel.

"Oh, no, I'm sure not. Murder? You really think so?" Amy asked, wide-eyed.

"Well, it may be one possibility," Verity said. "No one really knows yet. The sheriff is still searching for any information that might help him determine whether Mr. O'Halloran might have been alone that night and simply had an unfortunate accident, or if—"

"Someone bumped him off!" Marta finished for her, with zeal and a twinkle in her eyes that Verity found a bit disturbing.

Amy frowned. "I'm not sure I'd want to help the sheriff, even if I did know something. Why should any of us care that the man's dead?"

*It's what we do,* Verity thought but didn't say. *We reach out for the truth in spite of what we think of the victim.* "I guess it's just human nature," she said in a quiet voice, "you know, to try and make sense of our world."

"Sorry, you're right of course." Amy looked down at her hands, folded on the tabletop. "I honestly have no clue what happened that night. I take sleeping pills whenever I'm traveling. I don't sleep well in a strange bed. Never have. I didn't wake up until nearly ten o'clock the next morning."

Verity asked, "Where is your room in the inn?"

"One floor up, overlooking Main Street." She pointed toward the front of the inn; Ervin and Henry were still talking. "Up above the lounge and foyer. I heard nothing that night once I closed my eyes."

"Marta, what about you?" Verity asked. "Where is your room?"

"Oh, I'm only one flight of stairs up, too. The owner, Henry, dear sweet man, apologized for not being able to offer me a ground-floor room. I guess when he renovated, he didn't think about that. I told him he really ought to have accessible rooms for those of us seniors who may need them."

"Yes, he should," Verity agreed. Although when she first saw the beautiful renovations, she hadn't thought of that. "And do you also overlook the village green?"

"Oh, no, I asked for a quiet room, away from the road."

Something teased the back of Verity's mind. "Then your windows look out on the alley?"

Marta gave her a mysteriously cagey look. "Ye-e-es."

"You didn't happen to take any photographs or videos through your window, did you?"

Marta's smile shone brighter than the July sun. "I most certainly did!"

Amy was staring, her eyes bopping back and forth between Verity and her elderly friend, growing wider with each question and response. She looked like she was following a pickleball match.

Verity could hardly contain her excitement. Any nervousness she had felt earlier was forgotten. Her heart pounded. Her mouth turned dry. "And did you wake up because you were alarmed by something you heard or saw below in the alley?"

"Why yes—it was most alarming, Mrs. Cade. I put on my bathrobe to make myself decent, threw open my drapes and right away started filming the scene below."

"Oh, Marta!" Amy cried. "Why didn't you tell the sheriff this? He'll want to see what you recorded!"

"You think so?" Marta looked up into the treetops above the picnic table, as if she'd find an answer there. "I didn't think he'd really care about seeing an old lady's silly videos. My hands aren't very steady. Everything looks as if I'm filming during an earthquake." She blinked as though another thought had just struck her. "Isn't it amazing? I didn't even know I could take moving pictures with my telephone until we were on our way to Vermont. One of the little boys sitting near me on the bus showed me."

"But about the video you took out the window in your room —" Verity said, grasping the woman's fragile hands in her own and giving them a gentle squeeze to encourage her to concentrate "—you need to let the sheriff see it."

"Oh, alright, if you really think I should," Marta said.

"You should!" Amy and Cindy shouted.

Marta looked amused. "Then I shall bend to your will, ladies. Actually, it was all quite fascinating in a scary sort of way. But I could tell the sheriff had everything well in hand. After all, he was right there supervising his deputies and the emergency folk." Her gaze shifted to Verity. "You were there, too, farmer lady!"

Verity swallowed back a shriek of dismay. "Me? You saw me

and the sheriff that night?" Perhaps the lady wasn't as sharp a tack as Verity had assumed. She didn't wait for the woman's response. "Ummm, Marta, what time was it when you were filming your video of the alley?"

"I'm not entirely sure but it was certainly light out and I'd say it was definitely before I had my breakfast. Yes, it must have been before breakfast because I was still in my bathrobe. Didn't I just say that? I was awakened by the sounds of sirens and then loud voices outside. And when I looked out my window, there was a body on the ground and people rushing around, unreeling yellow tape and—"

Verity sighed with disappointment. "*That's* when you were filming with your phone. The morning *after* his death? Not during the night when it actually happened."

"Well, yes, I suppose that's right. Didn't I say it was morning? Anyway, I don't think a little telephone camera could work in the dark, could it?"

"Some do," Amy said weakly. She looked at Verity and mouthed 'sorry.'

Verity let out a long sigh.

# CHAPTER 16

VERITY FELT the need of a good, strong cup of coffee to clear her head. Talking to Marta, as lovely and well-meaning as the woman seemed, had left her feeling more than a little disoriented. One moment, Verity thought she'd come across a reliable witness. The next she became convinced the woman was two eggs short of an omelet.

Verity had desperately wanted Marta's video of the alley to reveal an argument, a physical struggle, anything supporting the clues she and the sheriff had observed at the scene of O'Halloran's death. She knew she shouldn't have jumped to conclusions. That was bad investigative technique.

She left the ongoing picnic and games on the village green and walked across the street to the Cat's Cradle—the only reliable source of brewed java in town. Starbucks had yet to plant itself on Main Street—and she, for one, was glad of it. The arrival of a mammoth coffee chain would drastically cut into Sunny's business. And what would Verity ever do without the little Cat's Cradle—source of juicy gossip, perpetual comfort, and buttery pastries to accompany a mug full of Sunny's delicious dark-roast coffee dredged in Cade Family Farm cream?

Verity stepped through the door, setting the silver bell above tinkling. Today, there were plenty of free tables. Apparently, the outdoor festivities were keeping most folks busy and fed.

"Hey there!" Sunny called to her from behind the glass case displaying today's choice of croissants, bear claws, assorted pastries and muffins the size of small grapefruits.

"You're stuck inside for the day?" Verity made a sad face. "It's beautiful out there."

"I know, but I'm happy to hold down the fort while I give my staff time to spend with their families. They deserve it."

"You're such a good boss."

"I am, aren't I?" Sunny beamed. "Anyway, I'll shut down for two hours later today while the parade passes by. I can get my fill of holiday hoopla then. But I'll reopen for a few hours to accommodate the dinner crowd. All hands on-deck then! So, Verity dear, what can I get you?"

"A large coffee, cream, no sugar as usual and—mmmm, let me think—one of those enormous bear claws." The scent of cinnamon, nutmeg, and sugar was making Verity's mouth water.

"Bear claw it is!" Sunny laughed. She set one of the pastries on a plate and handed it to Verity with a napkin. "I think we all need a little extra energy on a day like this. Is everything OK?"

Verity lowered her voice and stepped closer to the spotless glass case between them, taking care not to rest her burger-greasy fingertips on it. "Let's just say it's as good as possible, given the sheriff still has no idea what happened to Rudy O'Halloran." Only four customers sat at the little bistro tables, and they were halfway across the room. Still, she didn't want their conversation broadcast publicly

"Well, I'm sure you're doing all you can to help. And I'm staying on alert here. If anyone in town knows anything, they won't be able to resist telling their friends."

"Right." She looked around the dining room. "I worry that time is running out for the sheriff," Verity whispered. "The tour group will be leaving in two more days, according to Ervin's original plans. I don't think the sheriff can force all those people to stay in town. They've already given their statements."

"But surely," Sunny pointed out, "he can get in touch with them later, if he needs to."

"I suppose. But the distance is bound to make his job more difficult."

Sunny glanced around at the tables, making sure her customers were content with their meals. She turned to her young helper who was arranging donuts in the far end of the display case.

"I'll be in back if you need me, Sarah," Sunny said.

"No probs," the girl said with a smile.

Sunny crooked a finger at Verity. "Come on back with me. I want to hear more about what's been going on since we last met."

Verity followed the café owner toward the beaded curtain that separated the dining room from the Employee's Only area. The strings of brightly colored wooden beads clattered as they passed through. Verity felt a frisson of annoyance at the normally pleasant sound and blamed her own edgy mood.

"Have any of our investigators discovered new information?" Sunny asked.

"No. I'm sure Kate will call if she learns anything."

The kitchen was uncharacteristically quiet, no sign of the chef or other staff. At the far end of the long open area was a cozy nook with a round white plastic table and two chairs. The waitstaff used it for short breaks, but today it was covered with receipts and bank statements. Sunny brushed them into an accordion file, and they sat down.

Verity placed her precious bear claw on the table and resumed their conversation. "I thought I had come across something groundbreaking, but it turned out to be nothing."

"Tell me about it."

She related Marta's story. How she had taunted Rudy on the bus by taking a video of him drinking from his illegal flask.

"Wow! She's a gutsy one, isn't she? That man had me terrified the other day." Sunny thought for a moment. "I'm pretty sure I've seen the woman you're talking about in here—tiny and sort of frail, isn't she?" She didn't wait for confirmation. "If he'd hit her, she would have snapped like a twig."

"Would even Rudy have been that stupid? With all those witnesses?" Verity blew out a breath of exasperation. "The driver put him in his place, at least temporarily. But you're right. I wouldn't have wanted to cross that man. He could easily have held a grudge and waited for a chance to pay back Marta for calling him out."

"He definitely seemed the type. Vengeful." Sunny shook her head. "Thank goodness he didn't get a chance."

"There's more," Verity said. "I learned from Marta that her room is at the back of the inn, overlooking the alley. She used her phone to take a video out her window."

"Oh, my!"

"At first, it sounded as though we actually had a witness to whatever happened in the alley." Verity poked at her pastry, considering her strategy—bite around the delicious crunchy edges first, or tear the bear claw in half to get straight to the soft middle with maximum cinnamon exposure. "Then I realized she was filming the morning-after events. I checked what she recorded on her phone, just to be sure. She filmed the sheriff's department, EMT's, me, and Doc Evans."

"Oh brother!" Sunny laughed. "That's worthless." But her face almost immediately brightened.

"What?" Verity asked.

"I was just thinking—what if Marta wasn't the only person taking pictures?"

Verity nibbled the crusty-sweet edge of the claw. "Don't you think they would have mentioned it to Bailey or his deputies by now?"

"Maybe. Maybe not. Marta didn't."

*True*, Verity thought.

"Think about it!" Sunny sounded increasingly excited. "If someone recorded whatever happened to O'Halloran that night, they might later realize there were reasons why they shouldn't tell the sheriff. Like, filming the scene made them look bad. Or—I don't know—it somehow implicated them in a crime. I really think we should follow up on this, Veri. We need to find out who else had a room overlooking the alley or might have wandered outside around the time O'Halloran died."

Verity broke off a piece of bear claw, popped it into her mouth and chewed while thinking. Sunny's suggestion felt like a long shot. What were the chances?

"I don't want to do this on my own," she said after savoring the delectable mouthful. "Two people should work together, interviewing the inn's patrons. To provide a witness to the conversation. Could you spare an hour to—"

"Don't you even go there, Verity Cade. If I survive the rest of this day, I'll collapse on my bed as soon as I close up at seven o'clock."

Verity smiled sympathetically. "I get you, but it will be a short rest. Remember, fireworks tonight!"

Sunny closed her eyes and sighed deeply. "Of course. How could I forget? No chance of a peaceful, early night. Listen, why don't you try Kate or Mary Beth?"

"MB is hosting the silent cake auction and announcing the winners before the fireworks display kicks off. Kate has little kids." Verity took another bite of her claw. Was anything more comforting and delicious? "I think Chaundra mentioned she would be out of town tonight. I'll ask Fumiko. She's usually up for an adventure."

**CHAPTER 17**

FUMIKO OTA HAD no children and wasn't married, which honestly surprised Verity. The Japanese woman had such lovely, delicate features and luminous black eyes. Verity secretly coveted her sleek, ebony hair. She was a smart businesswoman, too. Fumiko had brought her yarn business with her from Tokyo, and it had become an instant success with knitting and crocheting fans, attracting customers from across the state.

Her shop, Knit One Purl, was three doors down Main Street from the café, in the opposite direction from Denise's chocolate shop. Fumiko was locking her front door when Verity walked down the street from the café.

"Closed for the day?" she asked, making Fumiko jump. "Sorry, didn't mean to startle you."

Fumiko gave an exaggerated shudder of her whole body. "It no matter. I jumpy all day."

"Any reason why?"

Fumiko shook her head. "Hate firecrackers. Hate boom-boom-boom!" She pantomimed explosions with finger-waving jazz hands.

"I know, it can be unsettling," Verity said. "Why not watch from a distance where it's less noisy but just as pretty?"

"Better, much better. I watch from New Hampshire." She smiled to let Verity know she wasn't serious. Maybe.

"I saw the amazing cake you made." Verity rolled her eyes. "My gosh, it looked like a scale model of a real pagoda. It's going to set off a bidding war, for sure! Are you staying for the announcement of the auction winners?"

Fumiko shrugged. "Ah, no. Whatever money it make, that ok. Good for hospital, yes?"

"Absolutely. So, you're on your way home now?" Verity asked.

"My new little doggie, she hate firecracking worse than me. She so-o-o frightened. Hide under bed. She cries and cries." Fumiko imitated the little dog's whimpering. "I go comfort her."

"I was hoping to get your help questioning a few people who are staying at the inn. But I understand if you need to take care of your pup—"

"Oh!" Fumiko's dark eyes sparked with their own version of fireworks. "More investigating?" She looked at her watch. "One hour, maybe more. I got time! No firecracking until dark."

"True," Verity said. "If you're sure you can spare the time. What's your doggie's name?"

"She is Shikoku Ken. I call her Shiko."

"Awwww. That's so pretty. I think I saw her the other day with you. She looks a little like a spitz but smaller."

"She thinks she princess. So-o-o spoiled!"

Verity chose not to point out that Fumiko was the only one who could be blamed for spoiling the dog since she lived alone. Instead, she briefly explained what Marta had done. "I'm hoping she isn't the only one who was curious about the goings-on behind the inn and might have taken pictures. Only during the early morning hours when Mr. O'Halloran met his end."

"Sunny, she tell me what he like." Fumiko's entire face scrunched into an expression of pure revulsion. "Disgusting, rude man."

"Admittedly, he wasn't very nice," Verity agreed. "But killing someone because of their lack of social skills, that's a bit much."

Fumiko frowned. "Much what? You do not make sense, dear Verity. You must finish your sentences."

Verity smiled and shook her head. "I was trying to say that murdering a person isn't an appropriate response to bad manners."

"Ah, why you not say first time?"

"Sorry," Verity smiled and gave her friend a one-arm hug. Verity was sure that if *she* ever moved to a country where another language was spoken, she would be hopeless. "Next time, I'll choose my words more carefully."

"I should hope so!"

Henry looked up from the reception desk in the vestibule when they walked in. Verity saw him grimace before he checked himself and plastered on an exaggerated smile. "How can I help you ladies?"

"Some information, Henry, if you don't mind."

He looked pained. "I don't have time for these constant interruptions," he said crankily.

Fumiko squinted at him. "You don't want killer found? You not good citizen!"

Verity touched her on the arm. "Fumiko, I'm sure that Henry wants to h—"

"Sheriff Bailey said I didn't have to talk to you," Henry snapped.

"Did he really?" Verity tilted her head, studying him through narrowed eyes.

"He told me I wasn't legally required to talk to you women about the accident the other night." The inn's owner made shooing motions with his hands, as if he expected her to run away like a chastened schoolgirl. She didn't budge. "If Bailey has questions," he added impatiently, "he can bring them to me directly."

"Ri-i-i-ght." Verity drew a calming breath that didn't quite do the job. "You see, there's a problem with that, Henry. The sheriff is so busy overseeing the setup for tonight's fireworks and filling out all those forms involved in an unexplained death *on your property*, he can't possibly come over here and talk to people. And he has more questions for a few of your residents. That's why he sent us, unofficially of course, to chat with folks."

Henry crossed his arms over his chest and locked his jaw in a display of defiance.

"But here's what we can do," she said sweetly. "I'll call Sheriff Bailey and let him know that since you and your residents are unable to speak with us, you will arrange for everyone to meet him at his office and—"

"No!" He looked horrified. "I can't possibly do that! It's far too disruptive."

She just looked at him and waited for him to come around.

"Ohhhh!" Henry finally growled. "Just...just go on, ask me your questions and let me get on with my work."

"If you're sure you don't mind." She blinked at him innocently. "All I need to know from you is—which of your guests had rooms facing the alley on the night of Rudy's death."

"But that's private information," he complained. "I can't give out customers' room numbers to the public."

Now he was really trying her patience. "And I understand

completely, Henry. Just give me names, no room numbers. That's alright, isn't it?"

"I-I don't know. I suppose so." He scratched the back of his head. "Well, alright then. Four rooms are on the alley side of the inn, two on the second floor and two on the third floor. All my other rooms face Main Street."

"Excellent!" Verity said. She took out her pocket notebook. "And the customers' names?"

"Mrs. Marta Schultz—that's a single," he said, now apparently resolved to cooperate. "And Mrs. Jennifer O'Halloran— the deceased's widow." As if she needed a reminder.

"Yes? And the other two?" she prompted when he hesitated.

His pale eyes darted nervously around the vestibule, as though the hotel ethics police might jump out from behind the coatrack and arrest him for revealing classified information. She wondered if there was a reason for his being so close-lipped, other than to protect his customers' privacy. Could it be he was hiding something? Or was he worried that one of his guests might say something that would come back to bite him?

"Henry?" she nudged.

"Alright. Yes. Then there are the Dentons, Mr. and Mrs. with their two children. Their room is one of my largest—an ensuite bathroom, queen bed with two cots at no extra charge." His expression brightened with pride. "And lastly, Mr. and Mrs. Anderson have a rear-facing room."

"Perfect!" she said, snapping shut her notebook. "Thank you, Henry."

"That not so hard!" Fumiko gave the innkeeper an approving nod. She reached out as if to pat him on the back, but he spun away, scowling and sputtering on his way toward the kitchen.

Verity could hear the festivities continuing outside on the village green. The shrieks of children interspersed with the

Evansfield high school band's rendition of *She's a Grand Old Flag.* Someone was singing—rapping, actually—to the beat of the percussion section. She could feel the thud-thud-thud of a base drum in her stomach.

Fumiko turned to Verity, her face lighting up. Verity felt a moment of apprehension but told herself that a little enthusiasm could only be a good thing.

"What the plan, Verity? We split up list? You take two rooms, I take two. We grill witnesses." Fumiko punched the air. One. Two. Three. "Make them spill their guts!"

Ironically, that *had* been Verity's plan—although without the ruthlessness she had just observed from her partner. Verity quickly switched to Plan B.

"I think it's best if we stick together," she said, tactfully. "Less chance that way of forgetting something important." *And, hopefully, no one will get pummeled.*

"Oh!" Fumiko smiled. "Good idea. Who we start with?"

"We don't need to question Marta again," Verity said. "I've already spoken with her. And Mrs. O'Halloran, I'm sure, would have already given the sheriff any video or photographs if she had them." She thought for a moment. "The family with the two kids, the Dentons, they're probably outside now. Let's knock on doors and see if we can find the Andersons at home."

They climbed the curving staircase, covered in plush dark red carpeting, to the second-floor landing. Verity turned to her right and stopped in front of the first door.

"Oh, for heavens' sakes," she muttered. The unhelpful Henry had failed to mention one thing. The residing guests' names were written in ornate script on cute little plaques, decorated in red, white, and blue and attached to their door. All she'd needed to do was check the doors to know who was inside.

As they soon discovered, the Andersons' room wasn't on the

second floor. Verity and her co-sleuth climbed yet another flight of stairs.

Eyes shining, Fumiko nearly skipped up to the appropriately labeled door and knocked—three short, sharp raps. *She is enjoying herself way too much,* Verity thought.

"Yes?" came a sleepy sounding woman's voice from inside.

Verity hoped they weren't interrupting the couple's nap...or possibly a more entertaining activity. "Sorry to bother you, Mrs. Anderson," Verity called through the door. "If you and your husband could just spare us a moment, I'd really appreciate it. We're working with the local sheriff's office and need to ask you a few questions."

"Now!" Fumiko shouted when the door didn't immediately spring open. Verity threw her partner a *stop-that* look.

"Good cop, bad cop." Fumiko shrugged.

Verity's gaze drifted toward the hallway ceiling, in hope of divine intervention. She should have asked Denise to come with her. Even Denise was capable of being diplomatic, on occasion.

The door opened six inches. Half of a face appeared in the crack. "What is it?" a woman whispered. "My husband is sleeping."

"Likely story," Fumiko said in a bass movie-cop voice.

Verity shifted to her left, placing herself between Fumiko and Mrs. Anderson. "I'm very sorry but the sheriff would like to know if there's any chance—"

"We already talked to him. We neither heard nor saw a blessed thing that night. We were asleep then...just like we were a minute ago."

Verity tried again. "Yes, but we were thinking—" She felt Fumiko's needle-sharp elbow in her ribs. Verity planted her feet and tried to ignore the painful jabs. "If you or your husband heard anything at all, you might have gone to the window to check it out before returning to bed."

"I might have, but I didn't."

"We know what you do!" Fumiko accused, hopping up and down. Verity could feel the vibrations in the floorboards. "We know you take pictures of brutal murder. Admit it!"

Verity swung around to glare in disbelief at her erstwhile mild-mannered partner. She slashed fingers across her throat. But Fumiko seemed oblivious to the cease-and-desist signals.

"Good lord! Are you people crazy?" the woman cried. "I told you; we were asleep."

"What the hell is going on out there?" a groggy voice called from inside the room.

"Now see what you've done!" the woman snarled. "Why do you think people ask for a room in the back? They want peace and quiet! Lot of good it did with those children screaming up and down the stairs. This was supposed to be a restful trip to the country." She was in full-rave mode by now. "But no! First, we're trapped on a bus with Mr. Obnoxious for three hours. Then he gets himself killed. And now it's ridiculous questions from amateur Sherlocks!"

Verity grabbed Fumiko by the arm and pulled her away from the door. "We're so sorry to have disturbed you, ma'am."

The woman slammed the door shut.

Breathing hard and flushed with embarrassment, Verity spun to face Fumiko. "I hope," she managed between gritted teeth, "you have a very, *very* good reason for your behavior."

"Yes." Fumiko nodded her head slowly up and down, her eyes still fixed on the Anderson's door. "Those people most suspicious."

Verity opened her mouth to say something. Nothing came out. She closed her eyes and wished away the throbbing in the center of her forehead.

# CHAPTER 18

ALTHOUGH FUMIKO PROTESTED that she wanted to stay and continue helping Verity interview others of the inn's guests, Verity finally convinced her that a pet owner's first duty was to her pet. Traumatized little Shiko needed her.

Relieved that she would be free to talk to the Dentons without her partner's Gestapo tactics, Verity knocked on the Denton family's door. Getting no response, she walked downstairs, out through the front door of the inn and into the glorious late-afternoon sunshine in search of the family.

The activities on the town green appeared to be winding down. Booths were closing. The cake auction tables lay bare. Verity idly wondered who had offered the winning bids on her two cakes.

Young children had by now overreached the limits of their energy. A little boy sobbed into his fists while frantically trying to escape his stroller. Two little girls in pigtails protested to their mother that they didn't need a nap. The fire department's blazing red truck rumbled past on Main Street without its siren shrieking. She supposed EFD volunteers were on their way to the field on the outskirts of town where the fireworks were being set up. It would be at least three hours before dark when the display could begin, but she expected the elaborate preparations took a long time to complete.

She scanned the park, looking for a couple with two children. To her regret, she saw the boy who had caused so much trouble on the farm tour. He was accompanied by two adults and a little girl who could only have been his younger sister. *Please don't let that be the Dentons.* But after another quick scan of the dwindling crowd, and seeing only local families, she sighed and approached the foursome.

They sat at a picnic table shaded by lofty old elms, enjoying ice cream cones. Verity strode over, fingers crossed that this wouldn't be a wasted effort. "Mr. and Mrs. Denton?" she asked.

The woman looked up over her scoop of neon-pink ice cream. Her relaxed posture immediately went rigid, her sun-flushed cheeks paled. "I haven't let Morgan out of my sight all day, I swear. If you've had any more trouble at your farm—"

"No, no." Verity laughed, feeling a little sorry for the woman. "No problems at the farm." Other than an AWOL mouser, a perpetually stubborn milk cow, and two ghosts who were incapable of staying out of trouble.

Which reminded her that she must leave for home soon and finish a few more chores before the fireworks started. She hadn't collected eggs that day and she needed to call the twins to make sure they were still coming to work for her tomorrow.

Verity turned her attention back to the Denton family in time to see the boy slip nimble fingers into his mother's purse, where it sat on the picnic table bench between them. With a sly glance at his mom, who was conveniently focused on Verity, he deftly pulled out a ten-dollar bill and tucked it into his pants pocket.

*The little devil!*

Verity wondered how many opportunities he found to steal.

Maybe from people who weren't even his parents. She squinty-eyed him. He noticed her disapproving look and made a face at her.

"Mrs. Cade? Is there something you wanted to say?" Mr. Denton said.

Verity snapped her eyes up from Mr. Sticky Fingers. "Yes. Actually, there is." Keeping her tone light, she explained that she was helping the sheriff with his inquiries into the unfortunate death of Rudy O'Halloran. "The sheriff is just trying to follow up on all possible leads. It turns out one of your fellow travelers took videos of the alley behind the inn."

"I bet it was that Marta women," Mrs. Denton said casually between licks of her melting ice cream.

"She's quite the busy body," Mr. Denton added, but not in an unkind way. "I suppose the old thing has little else to do with her life. She took photos of everyone on the bus."

"A man got kild'ed," the boy screeched gleefully. "I see'd out the window when the cops came. I wanted to go downstairs and look at the blood—Dad said there might be lots—but they covered him up." He looked deeply disappointed.

Verity stared at the child, not knowing what to make of this.

Mrs. Denton shook her head. "Boys. Why they delight in gore is beyond me."

"Anyway," Verity said, hoping to steer the conversation back on track, "the sheriff was wondering if any strange sounds from the alley might have awakened you that night. Since your room faces the alley and you might have had a window open, you could have—"

"I did think I heard *something*," Mrs. Denton mused. "It sounded like an argument between people who'd had a little too much to drink. I could have dreamt it, though. By the time I roused myself enough to really listen, the sounds had stopped. I fell back asleep within minutes."

"I sleep like the dead," Mr. Denton stated. "Always do. No help from me, I'm afraid." He chuckled and finished off his ice cream cone with two loud crunches.

"And the children, they didn't see or hear anything? Didn't mention being awakened by anything during the night?"

"No," the two adults chorused.

"I see'd the man get murdered," the boy repeated.

"Oh, Morgan, don't be ridiculous!" his mother laughed. "You couldn't have. You were sound asleep at that hour."

"Was not. I looked out the window. I did!"

Mr. Denton glowered at his son. "Stop it, Morgan." He turned back to Verity. "He's recently started making up these wild fantasies. We don't believe a thing he says. I can't wait until he outgrows this phase."

Morgan was bouncing up and down on the picnic bench as if he were on a spring. "I *did* see the man get dead. I did, Dad!"

His father looked distressed. "Come on, finish that ice cream and let's all go back to the inn. You need a time out, young man."

"But Da-a-a-d!" Morgan whined, staring at the sugar cone in his hand that held only an inner pool of melted chocolate mush. He threw it on the ground. "Two guys in the alley!" he shouted defiantly at his father. "One guy hitted the other guy. Really, really hard!"

His father's face turned as red as the geraniums on the bandstand. Whether in anger or embarrassment, Verity couldn't tell. He leaned across the table and shook a warning finger in his son's face. "That's it, Morgan. Not another word."

Mrs. Denton's hand shot out and smacked the boy on the back of his head. "He's just fishing for attention."

"Mo-o-o-m!"

Verity winced. She didn't want to get the kid in worse trouble. But with so little evidence to rely on, she hated to pass up even the unlikeliest clue.

"Mr. Denton," she interrupted as calmly as her racing heart allowed. Was it really possible she'd found a witness? "Please, may I ask your son just a few questions? If it turns out this is all a fantasy, allowing him to finish describing the scene will do no harm."

"No," he said, "we're not going to continue this ridiculous conversation. I don't want to encourage my son to make up any more of these outrageous—"

"But if there's anything at all that could help Sheriff Bailey with his investigation—" she lifted her palms in a pleading gesture "—surely, we should let him determine whether or not it's useful?"

Mom and Dad looked at each other doubtfully. "Fine," said the boy's mother. She turned to her husband. "She's right, Ted. It can't hurt. I'm sure a man in his line of work has heard his share of fabrications. He won't be taken in by a five-year-old."

Verity caught a glimmer of dismay in the boy's eyes. What was more hurtful than not being believed by your own parents? Even if you only ever told the truth on rare occasions.

She stepped toward her possibly unreliable witness and knelt beside his bench. Hoping to reduce the palpable tension in the air, she lowered her voice to just above a whisper. "Morgan, it's terribly important that you tell me exactly what you saw. Not what you *think* you saw. Not what you would *like* to have seen because it might sound more exciting. Do you understand?"

"I see'd it," he repeated solemnly, but without answering her question. "Them, I mean."

"Alright. Good. So, you saw two guys?"

"Yup!" He blinked lashes so long and lush they could only look natural on a child. His gaze was pure innocence, and he suddenly seemed pleased. Because he was glad someone was listening to him at last? Or because he was up to his usual mischief? His father looked ready to cuff him again.

"Did you see their faces?" she asked.

"Naaaaw!" He giggled. "It was dark, you silly."

His mother squeezed her eyes shut and shook her head.

"Of course," Verity said. "That really was very silly of me. But maybe you saw their clothes, even just a little bit of color?"

He shook his head. "They was wearing black."

It was true that O'Halloran had been wearing a black t-shirt, and his chinos were a very dark brown. They might have appeared black in the darkness. Was the assailant, if there was one, also in black? Or was this, too, just an invention of a desperately imaginative child?

"Did you see one person strike the other?" She held up a finger before Morgan could answer. "Think carefully. Remember, only exactly what you saw, in the dark."

"Yes! I see'd!" He hopped off the bench to his feet, nearly coming down on top of the mess he'd made in the grass by dumping his ice cream cone. He couldn't seem to stop bouncing.

"Is it possible that you might have just *thought* the two men were fighting—" she held up another wait-for-it finger "—because the next day you heard a man had died in the alley?"

"No-o-o!" Morgan ceased jitterbugging. "I really, really see'd him do it! He sneaked up behind the guy—" he demonstrated in a low crouch "—like this. And he smacked him hard on the head. I heared it!"

"Was the window you looked out open or closed?" Verity asked. A chill of anticipation spider-walked up her spine. She was aware of the father's body language, every muscle tensed. A coiled human spring, prepared to release at any second.

"Open," Morgan said firmly. "It sounded cool. Just like on TV. *Clunk!*"

She already knew the victim had been struck on the back of the head. So far, the boy's story rang true. She hoped his father would let him finish.

"And he felled on the ground. And...and the killer guy bended down and smashed him again and again, and he—"

"Now that's enough, son. The lady doesn't want to hear any more of these gruesome fairy tales of yours."

"But it's true!" Tears filled the boy's eyes. "Dad, I did see—"

"Enough!" barked his mother. "Come on, we're done here. It's off to the room for some quiet time." She seized Morgan's arm while his younger sister stood silently by, eyes wide, her ice cream cone dripping down her arm. "Bethany, finish that ice cream and come along with your father."

"Please, just one more question," Verity begged even as the boy was being dragged away. She ran to catch up with mother and son.

"You have until we reach the door to our room then that's the end of it," Mrs. Denton called over her shoulder. Which wouldn't be long at the rate the woman was sprinting across Main Street, leaving her husband to bring up the rear with their daughter.

"Morgan," Verity shouted, "you said you didn't see either person's face. Is that right? Are you sure?"

The child was sniffling now. No longer interested in talking after being scolded, perhaps suspecting punishment as soon as Mom had him alone. He dragged his feet, scuffing the ground with the toes of his shoes and making little mewling sounds in his throat as his mother hauled him along.

"Please. It's important, Morgan. I believe you." Verity wasn't sure she did. But if a little reassurance bought her anything they could use, why not give it a shot? "Did you see hair color? Any skin that wasn't covered by clothing? There was a security light behind the inn, the kind that comes on when someone moves. Maybe it wasn't totally dark down there."

Mrs. Denton flew up the steps to the inn's veranda, her hand still wrapped around her son's forearm. She reached for the front door.

"Wait!" Morgan shouted so loudly his mother stopped in shock and looked around nervously as if afraid people would think she was abusing her son. But they were the only ones on the veranda, everyone else having gone off to their rooms or in search of dinner. He wriggled his arm out from her grasp and spun to face Verity. "Guy that got hit, he had yellow hair. Other guy weared a hoodie."

"Thank you, Morgan," Verity breathed out. "And thank you, Mrs. Denton. If the sheriff needs to talk to any of your family, he'll be in touch. And Morgan—" she smiled down at him "—I'm sure you'll remember to tell Sheriff Bailey exactly what you told me. The truth. No stories, yes?"

He gave her a wobbly smile but it appeared sincere. "Yeah. I promise."

Verity watched the couple herd their offspring into the inn. She collapsed on one of the pretty green rocking chairs on the porch and thought about the boy's claim to have witnessed the murder of Rudy O'Halloran. Was any part of it true?

At first, she had dismissed his story of what he had seen below the family's room in the alley, just as his parents had done. But the urgency in his voice, and the hurt and shame at not being believed—those felt authentic.

# CHAPTER 19

VERITY WAS STILL SITTING on the inn's shady porch when she took out her phone and called the sheriff's office.

His dispatcher, Beverly, answered. "I haven't seen the boss for hours. I expect he's out at the fairgrounds with Vincenti & Sons, the fireworks company. He and the deputies are keeping the kids away, making sure our young'uns don't try to get too close to the explosives or bother the pyrotechnic guys."

"Thanks, Bev, I'll catch up with him there."

She found Bailey, talking with one of the pyros on the Vincenti crew. When he saw her step from behind an ambulance and start across the open field toward him, he nodded to the other man and strode over to meet her.

"Any developments?" she asked him.

"Should be even better than last year's show." He grinned, all little-boy excitement, and she could so easily imagine this bear of a man as he must have been forty years ago. "These guys really know their business. Much more professional than the company we hired last year."

She tipped her head to one side. "I meant, anything new about the investigation."

"Oh. Right. Nothin' that can't wait." He stared distractedly at the busy explosives experts rushing around the field.

"Well, I have something," she said, "maybe. At least I hope it's something."

She first described interviewing the unhelpful Andersons at the inn. Fumiko had insisted they were acting suspiciously, but Verity thought they were probably just annoyed at having their private time interrupted. Fumiko's bad cop act hadn't helped. Then she told him about the Dentons.

Initially, Bailey showed no more interest in this interview than in the first. His eyes beneath the stiff brim of his cap wandered the field, at last coming to rest on two of the Vincenti crew nearby who were weaving fuses together and connecting them to what looked like little cannons half buried in the ground. She itched to seize him by the arms and give him a good hard shake to make him pay attention to her, but she feared startling him. An involuntary swing from either of the man's formidable arms would knock her flat.

When she got to the part in the boy's story about the killer repeatedly hitting the downed man, presumably O'Halloran, the sheriff finally turned to her with a long, hard stare.

"Come again?" he said.

"Morgan Denton told me—risking the fury of his already upset parents, I might add—that he saw two men in the alley the night of O'Halloran's death. Guys, he said, so I assume he believes both were men. Both wore black or very dark clothing. One, he thinks, had yellow hair, which sounds like O'Halloran. The other with a hood pulled up over his head. It seems unlikely that two men other than O'Halloran and his assailant would be in the same place and at the same time as O'Halloran was killed. Wouldn't you say, Sheriff?"

He gave an almost imperceptible nod. "Go on."

"The one with the hood hit the other guy on the back of his

head, likely with something other than his hand. Morgan said it made a loud, hollow sound. *Clunk.* O'Halloran fell to the ground, then the other man leaned over him and struck two more blows." She thought for a moment. "Wait. No, that's not right. Morgan didn't say how many, but it sounded as though he witnessed at least two additional whacks."

Bailey's expression morphed from childish exuberance to funereal gravity. He said nothing but stared off across the field for so long she wondered if he'd forgotten about her.

"What? What are you thinking, Sheriff?" She stepped closer to better hear over the pounding of a nearby power shovel.

"Autopsy came in 'round noon," he said. "Shocked me since it's a holiday but I guess someone's still workin' today. Thank God."

"And?" She had stopped breathing.

"The victim died from multiple blows to the head. Pathologist says, the first one probably stunned O'Halloran, not fatal. He's almost positive the victim would have gone down though. Maybe only for a moment. Or maybe he was unconscious and unable to defend himself—no way to know. At least two more blows followed, he says. Crushed in his skull, killing him." The pupils of Bailey's eyes contracted to tiny black points. His full attention was on her now. "What else did the kid say? And how old is this Morgan?"

"He's five years old. But," she added quickly, "even at that age kids can be very observant. His mother told me she may have been awakened by arguing voices. She shrugged it off and went back to sleep but I think her son woke up to the same sounds outside their window. Morgan told me he couldn't see faces. Which makes sense, dark as it must have been."

"Alright then." Bailey hiked up his belt and pants, in a

getting-down-to-business gesture. "Did you pick up on a sense that the kid was making up the whole thing?"

"No. Morgan had already invoked his father's wrath for creating stories on earlier occasions. I could tell Morgan knew he'd be punished if he told another tall tale. But when I asked him questions about that night, I think he figured he'd take the risk and tell me what he'd seen. I also thought he was just happy to have someone listening to him and taking him seriously."

Bailey chewed his bottom lip. "He definitely said it was two men? Not three or more?"

"Yes, two. I can't remember him actually using the word men though. He said, 'guys.' You don't think a woman could have done this, do you?" As soon as she said it, she pictured Sue, the bus driver, and realized how wrong she was to assume only a man would have resorted to such violence.

"You don't think gals can kill?" Bailey cracked a laugh. He started moving back toward the road when one of the pyro crew commenced working on a ground display near where they'd been standing.

Verity followed him. "No, of course, you're right," she said. "I suppose I was thinking of the strength necessary to actually knock a hole in a person's skull." Just saying those words made her feel sick.

"Hey, listen," he said, "even a lady farmer like yourself could smash in a bloke's head with the right weapon and a jolt of rage-born adrenaline. You're plenty strong, and lots of women work out in gyms and play sports." *Or drive buses*, Verity thought.

"True," she said, reluctantly. "Anyway, I hope this helps, Sheriff."

"Of course it helps. If this kid is tellin' the truth, we now know this was no accident. I'll be lookin' for a murderer." He came to a stop now that they were well clear of the preparations of the field. "Clever little bugger. The boy may be our only witness. My bad for not questioning kids."

As if an enormous electrical cord had been pulled, all the noises from drills and digging and foreman's shouts stopped. In the sudden silence, Verity heard footsteps moving quickly away from them. When she turned to see who they belonged to she saw Sue walking away in long strides.

How close had the woman stood by them...listening? And for how long? Did she hear their conversation about a witness? Verity looked at the sheriff. He was talking on his phone now and seemed not to have noticed Sue's presence.

The bus driver's sudden appearance might mean nothing. Still, if Sue had been in any way involved in Rudy O'Halloran's death, and she believed a witness might be able to identify her, what might she do to silence that person?

# CHAPTER 20

VERITY LEFT the field and the sheriff, torn as to whether she should share her concern over the bus driver with Bailey. Her mind-your-own-business gene was warning her to say nothing. She had no proof that the driver had attacked Rudy in the alley or anywhere else.

*Let it go, Verity.*

The sun was already hanging low over the treetops, turning the sky above them a ruddy mauve. In less than an hour, the fireworks would begin. Before then, she needed to tuck in her critters for the night.

The chickens were never bothered by the brilliant flashes in the sky or the loud bangs and crackling sounds of fireworks. Their little brains seemed triggered by more primal situations. A fox or raccoon prowling outside their fence always set off a raucous panic with feathers flying everywhere. Usually, she arrived in time to run off the intruder before it dug its way inside the coop.

She hadn't needed to defend her hens from larger predators, so far. But other farmers told of birds lost to marauding coyotes.

A farmer five miles north of town swore he'd chased off a mountain lion. She found that one hard to believe.

Chickens were funny little things. Her Rhode Island Reds had proven themselves, for the most part, even-natured and occasionally even affectionate, allowing her to pick them up for a quick cuddle. Their one pet peeve, if chickens could be said to have peeves, was the bi-monthly shifting of their wheeled coops to fresh grass, even though the change in real estate gave them a whole new world of juicy bugs, worms and sweet green shoots to eat.

Occasionally, one or two of her hens went broody and aggressively refused to give up her eggs. Then, any attempt by a human to steal them earned the person a painful pecking. Verity understood. She'd be pretty upset if someone tried to steal her babies. In spite of the hens' occasional moodiness, she found them entertaining and made a point of visiting her flock every day, so she would seem familiar and unthreatening to them.

As darkness began to fall, her hens naturally sought out their roosts. She shooed stragglers into their henhouses and latched the doors. Foxes started hunting at twilight.

Her cows were another matter entirely when it came to fireworks. The gentle creatures, as big as they were, easily spooked in response to almost anything. An unfamiliar animal or person entering their paddock. A backfiring truck. A birthday party balloon bobbing in the wind across their field. They just didn't like anything new or unexpected.

Every once in a while, a passerby would get out of their car, climb over the fence and try to approach a cow as if it were a big dog. If one animal in the herd took fright and broke into a run, a Guernsey stampede might ensue. A 1,200-pound cow running in blind fear is capable of knocking down fences, people, or injuring other animals in their desperation to get away from a perceived threat. One time, a tourist had lifted his toddler over the fence and coaxed the child to "go pet the pretty cow." Luckily, Verity was working near enough to run interference. She returned the child, unharmed, to the oblivious parent before her cows became aware of the little intruder.

*People can be such idiots!*

Dogs like Fumiko's pooch weren't the only animals to hate thunderstorms and pyrotechnics. Feeling the vibrations of the deep booms through the ground, cows sometimes went a little crazy if left out in the field. At least hers did. They weren't exactly happy in the barn, where the slightly muffled noise still reached them. But enclosed by familiar walls, they seemed less bothered by the erratic explosions, and the colorful flashes in the sky weren't visible.

It took her longer than usual to bring the herd in from the field without the help of Jason and Jerry, but the task eventually was accomplished. She was looking forward to driving back to the fairgrounds to watch the fireworks with her neighbors. But first, she needed to get out of her work clothes.

After a tepid shower to cool down from the heat of the day and rinse off the usual detritus of farming, she pulled on blue denim shorts, a red short-sleeve blouse, and navy-blue sneakers. Her friends often competed with each other by wearing eye-catching, fun jewelry during the holidays. Sparkly snowflake earrings during the winter. Miniature blinking jack-o-lanterns and black cats on a necklace for Halloween. A brooch or decorative hair ornament of hearts and doves for Valentine's Day.

She had nothing that sparkled or blinked for July 4th, but she remembered the necklace and matching earrings Kate and her girls had made for her one summer. Red-white-and-blue beads alternated along a clear fishing line; easy to loop over her head. When she pulled the matching earrings from her jewelry box, she remembered the girls had added tiny pieces of red and silver foil tinsel that caught the light. If anyone made fun of her dime-store choice of jewelry, she didn't care. She thought it was adorable that the girls had wanted to make anything for her.

"To thank you, Aunty Veri—" Sarah, the older of the two sisters, sang out when presenting the baubles to her "—for all the yummy eggs you bring us!"

*So cute!* Of course, she had to wear their gifts. She'd probably run into Kate and her husband with the girls tonight.

Verity parked her truck on the field south of town, among dozens of other vehicles. Ervin's bus, decorated with patriotic flags and streamers, had already arrived and dropped off its passengers. Refreshment booths and souvenir vendors ringed the car park. She carried a blanket with her to spread on the ground and a bottle of water for rehydrating after the warm day.

Verity stepped around blankets that had been spread across the grass, folding chairs, and coolers stocked with sodas and beers. She searched the crowd for friends. After her eyes finally adjusted to the deepening dusk, she spotted Mary Beth and her husband the mayor; they had brought lawn chairs, which looked like the kind that could be reclined to better view the sky. She gave them a wave but marched on until she finally saw a cluster of other familiar faces. Denise, Chaundra, and Sunny sprawled on a huge canvas tarp. They had even managed to coax Fumiko into coming. (Sans pooch.) Kate sat with her family on a nearby blanket.

"You're the last one!" Denise chimed.

"We thought you might not make it in time," Chaundra said.

"Wouldn't miss this for the world," Verity assured them.

The Fourth of July had been one of Mark's favorite holidays. They attended the fireworks every year, bringing icy-cold beer, chips, and her favorite non-chocolate candy, Jelly Bears.

Sitting on their blanket, she'd scoot back between his legs and lean against his chest, her head nestling into the curve between his biceps and shoulder. Heaven!

They stared up at the fiery bursts of color, pointing out their favorite designs, oohing and ahhing at the intricate displays. Lost in each other as much as in the brilliant show overhead. At some point, they forgot about the crowd around them. Verity could always count on Mark sneaking as many kisses as he could until their friends started teasing them with chants of "get a room!" Embarrassed, he'd stop and whisper in her ear, "Later." The devilish twinkle in his brown eyes, revealed in a flash of light above them, promised more fun. Her heart thrummed with lust. And love.Making love at home after the fireworks became a tradition for them.

Verity sighed and blinked away tears before they could fall. What a lovely man. She supposed she would always miss him. *Always and forever, my darling.*

Leaning back on her elbows, she drew a deep breath to steady herself then looked around to see who else she knew in the crowd. It seemed that the entire town was here. And off to one side were Ervin's bus-people. They were nesting as a group on a mosaic of matching white towels, obviously borrowed from the inn.

*Oh boy!* She wondered if Henry knew his luxe Egyptian cotton bath towels were lying in a dirt field.

Observing the group more closely, Verity frowned. Were some of them missing? She hoped they hadn't decided to pass on the show because they felt uncomfortable mixing with the locals.

A moment later, Verity realized who she had unconsciously been searching for. Jennifer O'Halloran. She chided herself for even thinking the young woman who had closeted herself in her room since her husband's death would join their festivities. *I certainly wouldn't have been in the mood!*

Then Verity noticed the Dentons with their two young ones, Morgan and Bethany. Mom was trying to get them to sit down with her but the two kids kept bouncing to their feet and pointing up the field to a vendor who was selling candy apples, spun sugar, and ice cream bars. Finally, Dad gave a sharp order and both kids plopped down on their bottoms in a sulk.

Verity looked away for a moment, then a movement caught her eye. She turned back and she saw the little boy snake an arm toward his mother's purse. In a flash he was in and out, with something balled in his fist.

"Why that little imp!" He was still up to his mischief.

"Something wrong?" Sunny asked.

"Morgan Denton, that little boy in the red t-shirt. Twice today, I've seen him raid his mom's purse."

"A criminal in the making." Something changed in Sunny's eyes, as if a thought had occurred. "You don't suppose..."

"What?"

"The rooms that were broken into. The thefts. You've heard about them. Maybe he takes advantage of opportunities outside of his family to enhance his allowance."

Verity nipped at her lip pensively and sat up straighter. She twisted around again to watch Morgan. He was cozying up to his mom, gazing up at her with a loving, heart-melting smile. The perfect angel.

"I guess it's possible," Verity admitted. "But wouldn't his parents wonder where he was while he was making off with loot from people's rooms? Anyway, he couldn't have broken into the doc's office and stolen drugs. He's only five years old!"

"Kids get into all sorts of trouble. Just five, you think? He seems pretty big for his age."

Their discussion was interrupted by the first big *boom*. In spite of Verity's delight in being here with her friends, she felt the backs of her eyelids tickle. She hadn't expected to be quite so emotional this year. In many ways, she felt as though Mark was right here beside her. Sitting on their special blanket, enjoying the show with her.

And yet he really wasn't, was he?

And he never would be again. She blinked hard—two, three times—wiping away tears with the back of her hand as the tempo of the explosions increased. *Dammit, Verity! Now isn't the time to go all maudlin.*

She felt Sunny watching her. Verity reached out and squeezed her friend's hand. *I'm fine*, she mouthed. Sunny nodded her understanding.

It was then, while her eyes were still a little glassy and not quite focusing properly, that she saw *them*.

Two figures stood among the seated and reclining crowd, holding hands and staring in rapture up at the sky. She told herself this wasn't possible. *Shouldn't* be possible. Because whenever each new burst of neon color lit the pair as silhouettes against the brilliant sky—they seemed far too solid for their normal spectral selves. And much too obvious not to be seen by everyone in the crowd around her.

"Oh, no!" She clapped her hand over her mouth. *N-no, no, no!*

"What's wrong?" Sunny asked.

"Nothing," she breathed. *Everything. Oh crap!*

Sunny turned to stare across the field in the direction Verity had been looking. Luckily, the glow from the most recent shower of blue-and-green sparks had faded, returning the night sky to a dense velvety black shroud.

"I don't see a thing." Sunny gripped Verity's wrist and frowned up into her face. "You're tight as a piano wire. Do the fireworks scare you? Is that it? You want to leave?"

For a moment, Verity thought everything was okay. If Sunny couldn't see the two ghosts, neither could anyone else. When she got home, though, she definitely would have a word with the Putnams about being more discreet.

*Boom! Boom! Boom!* Three rockets shot into the air, igniting the sky in red, yellow, and orange fire. The audience cheered their approval.

"Oh, look at that cute couple in old-timey costumes," Kate cooed between detonations to her two girls. To Verity's horror, she was pointing right at Anna Louise and Percy. "See the pretty lady in the long dress and the man in uniform?"

Verity sucked in a sharp breath, aware that Sunny and others nearby must have heard Kate. Sunny was intently scanning the crowd. "Oh, I see them!" she yipped. "How cool is that. They've come in period costumes. They must be reenactors. I love it!" She elbowed Verity.

Verity did not love it.

*Wait until I get hold of those two,* she fumed.

She wanted to rush across the field and order them back into invisibility but that would only draw more attention. She gnashed her teeth. They had promised not to play games, to only let *her* see them. Except for emergencies. Like that one time when a murderer had come close to killing a second victim —her.

She was debating whether, if her timing was perfect, she might be able to reach them in a moment of total darkness between the brilliant strobe-like effects of the fireworks. She could order them to turn invisible and go home. But before she was able to move, the two ghosts began to flicker, dim, then brighten again—almost like holograms—before disappearing entirely.

*Huh?*

Holding her breath, Verity turned to look at Sunny and

Kate. But they seemed to have lost interest in the couple and were transfixed by an even more dazzling display overhead. A fluttering American flag surrounded by gold starbursts. The crowd went crazy, bursting into applause.

Verity frantically scanned the field as the light slowly faded again. She saw no sign of her ghosts but they most definitely had stood there, as bold as could be, a minute earlier.

"I'm going to kill them," she whispered under her breath.

# CHAPTER 21

THE FIREWORKS DISPLAY ended with a glorious finale and the crowd quickly dispersed. Verity lingered. She had volunteered to help clear away the clutter of food wrappers, soda cans, and other litter from the field. Fortunately, most people cleaned up after themselves but some either couldn't see their leavings in the dark or simply assumed someone would tidy up after them. The clean-up team came with their own flashlights, gloves and trash bags.

Denise was one of the supervisors. "You look frazzled, Verity. We have more than enough volunteers to finish the job. Go home and get some sleep, girl."

"You're sure you have enough help?"

"Heck, I sent away half of my volunteers already," Denise insisted. "They were tripping over each other."

Verity thanked her and turned toward the parking area. She watched a few of her neighbors exchanging cheerful greetings and chatting about the show. Everyone seemed to agree this was the best fireworks event ever in Evansfield, the same things they were saying after last year's display. She smiled. It felt reassuring to see people in a good mood and feel the kindness in the air.

The fire department volunteers remained to assist the professionals who had designed, set up, and controlled the elaborate presentation. They would comb the area for spent shells and for duds that hadn't exploded and might be a danger if a child found them or a tractor ran over them. A pungent, sulfurous smell still clung to the air, mixed with the tang of gunpowder. The aftermath of all the explosions. Verity sat in her truck for a few minutes, letting the last of the crowd drive away while she tried to figure out how to impress upon the Putnams that they simply couldn't take foolish risks as they'd done that night, just because they liked mixing with the living.

Finally, she started the engine and drove across the tire-rutted grass, then onto the two-lane highway toward town. She wished she could have felt totally immersed in the night's happy buzz, but the murder continued to prey on her mind. Driving north along Main Street, she turned her mind to working on what she was going to say to Anna Louise and Percy. The more she thought about them, the more furious she became. If they had any sense, they'd make themselves scarce until she had time to cool off.

*Stupid ghosts.*

Every shop window and home through the center of town was dark. The silence enrobed her in a sense of peace. Her annoyance with the pair eased as she drove. Her eyelids slid lower and lower, exhaustion hampering her will to stay alert.

A shout from somewhere outside of the truck shattered her reverie. She popped open her eyes, shocked to find she'd nearly fallen asleep at the wheel.

She hit the brakes, her heart pounding as she frantically scanned her surroundings for the source of the cry. Had she hit someone?

Her headlights picked out a shape in the road. But it was still twenty feet ahead, to her relief. Startled eyes glowed back at her. A deer? A bear? She eased her foot back onto the accelerator, letting the truck coast a little closer while she tried to figure out what it was.

Whatever it was, it stood in the road on two legs. Not a deer after all. Not big enough to be a bear rearing on its hind legs. The cold-white beams of her headlights spotlighted pale blue shorts and a frilly white top, bare legs, bare feet. A woman. And she was staggering down the middle of Main Street toward the truck as if drunk.

Verity brought the Ridgeline to a stop well before reaching the woman, so as not to startle or chance hitting her.

A pale heart-shaped face gazed up at Verity through her windshield, eyes squinting into the headlights' glare. The woman waved frantically. "Help!" she croaked. "Please. Please help me!"

Verity was already out of the truck and rushing toward her by the time she realized who it was. "Mrs. O'Halloran? Jennifer? What's wrong? Has something—"

"H-he. He!" The woman pointed behind her but Verity saw no one. "Oh, God! He tried to *kill* me!"

Verity didn't ask further questions. A dark, deserted country road was no place for a conversation. She tucked an arm around Jennifer O'Halloran's back, led her to the truck and helped her up into the passenger seat.

Running around the front of the truck, Verity jiggled her cellphone out of her jeans pocket and speed-dialed Sheriff Bailey. No answer. She left a curt message, "Call me. Now!" and rang off. If he was awake, he would. If not, she'd find out what was going on, then call 911. Someone would have to respond, holiday or not.

The woman in the seat beside her was shivering violently, even though it was still near eighty degrees outside.

"Jennifer, tell me what happened." Verity shifted into drive and powered on. "Who is 'he' and what's going on?"

"I don't *know!*" she wailed. "Oh, God, why is this happening to me? Rudy is dead and now someone is coming after me! I'm so afraid. I just want to go home."

"Did you recognize this person, this man?"

Jennifer shook her head violently. "It was too d-dark. He... he came up behind me." She was doubled over in the truck's seat, sobbing so hard Verity could hardly understand her words.

"Alright. You're safe now. I'm taking you to my house and—"

"What if he's *following* us?" Jennifer wailed, staring wildly through the truck's windows. "He might attack you, too!"

Verity glanced up at her rearview mirror. The black night closed in behind them as soon as the truck's taillights passed along the road. No headlights followed them. The road ahead appeared empty. She supposed it was possible that someone who didn't want to be seen might turn off their vehicle's lights and tail them. She saw no one walking in or along the road. Nothing moved in the darkness. At least, nothing she could see.

She tried to swallow, but her throat had gone stone dry. Her fingers, locked around the steering wheel, ached. She attempted to loosen them but it was no use.

She needed to find out exactly what had happened. Who attacked her? Why? Wasn't it important to get details while they were still fresh in a victim's mind? Isn't that what Mary Beth always said when she was jabbering on about her CSI shows? But she suspected Fred Bailey might want her to wait until he arrived before asking Jennifer anything more about the assault.

*What to do? What to do?*

She steered into her driveway and stopped barely a foot away from her back porch steps.

In case someone really was following them, she wouldn't give them time to catch up while she parked in the garage and then walked across the dark yard with an unsteady woman in tow.

Verity ran up the steps and unlocked the door then reached down a hand to help Jennifer up onto the porch and into the house. She slammed the door behind them and locked it.

"Oh, I'm s-so cold!" Jennifer cried. "Why do I feel like I'm freezing? It's freakin' July."

"You're in shock. Come on." Verity gently led her through the mudroom and up the plank steps into her kitchen. "Sit," she said. When the woman didn't move, she repeated her order with less drill-sergeant brusqueness. "Jennifer, please, before you fall over, sit down while I make us some tea. You're safe now." And just then her phone rang.

"You know how much I hate being woken out of a sound sleep, don't you, Mrs. Cade?" a gruff voice greeted her.

"I do, Sheriff, but—"

"So, what you're about to tell me, woman, had better be worth my lost sleep."

"It is." Tucking the phone under her chin, she held the electric kettle under the tap to fill it. "Jennifer O'Halloran is here with me, at my place. She's been attacked. I can put her on the phone if you want." Although, she doubted Jennifer was capable of carrying on a coherent conversation. Her voice had already gone raw from crying.

"No. I'll be right there. I can hear her bawlin'. If she's injured call for an ambulance, if not... Never mind. I'm comin' soon's I pull on my pants."

Not an image she wanted to dwell on.

Verity ended the call. She felt the still-sobbing Jennifer

watching her while she grabbed three mugs out of her cupboard, set out milk, sugar, sweetener packets. *Earl Grey*, she thought, then changed her mind to Chamomile. Much more calming.

The heart-breaking sobs had by now weakened to soggy gasps.

"Tea first," Verity said, "then talk. By the time you finish your first cup, the sheriff will be here. I promise."

"Are you sure no one followed us?" Jennifer fixed anxious eyes on the inky-black kitchen windows.

Verity sucked in a sharp breath, shocked by what she hadn't noticed outside in the darkness but now couldn't miss under her bright kitchen lights. A vicious red line circled the woman's throat.

"This looks like an old house," Jennifer rasped. "Probably dozens of ways to creep inside."

"You're safe," Verity repeated. She was trying to remember if, before leaving the house that night, she had locked every door, every window. It probably didn't matter. How hard would it be for someone to break a windowpane or unscrew a latch? Now she was frightening herself! "Ummm, would you like me to call for medical help? Or drive you to the hospital in Springfield?"

"No!" Her tear-filled eyes shot wide. "I-I don't want to go outside again. Not tonight. I told you, I just want to go home." Not, Verity understood, to the inn. To her real home, wherever that was.

The electric kettle switched off. Verity poured steaming water into two mugs and dropped in tea bags. The inflamed flesh across the front of the young woman's throat unnerved Verity. She set a mug of tea in front of Jennifer and sat down at the oak table, choosing a chair cattycorner from her guest to be close to her and also face her. She slid a box of tissues toward her and tried not to stare at what had to be a fresh injury on her throat.

Jennifer plucked out a handful of tissues and blew her nose. "It was awful," she mumbled into the soggy wad. "I thought I was a goner."

"Do you want to talk about it?" Verity asked after a moment.

Jennifer shook her head. But then, "Have you ever believed you were going to die, Verity?"

"I guess I have, but I try not to. We all do. Die, I mean. Right?"

"But not like Rudy, like I almost did." She shuddered and sipped the hot tea, gripping the mug with both hands. Her breathing seemed less desperate and watery. She stared into her mug.

"What happened, Jennifer? Were you in your room when he...you know." With everyone else at the fireworks display, the inn would have been virtually empty. No one around to hear a call for help.

"I didn't think I'd go to the July Fourth stuff," Jennifer whispered. "I just wanted to be alone."

"Of course." Verity patted her hand.

"But then I heard the sounds of fireworks and saw the colored flashes in the sky from my window. So, I went downstairs, sat on the porch and watched for a while." A faint smile teased her lips. "They really were beautiful. Like huge tropical flowers blooming in the sky."

"Yes. It was a great display this year." Was that where she had been attacked—on the veranda?

"I could hear people cheering. Happy sounds—you know?" Jennifer sniffed and shrugged one shoulder, her palms still cupped around the mug, as if she needed its warmth. "Suddenly, I just wanted some company. I started walking down the street, looking up into the sky to try and figure out where the field was. I'd heard people talking in the hallway outside my room, how the fireworks would be somewhere south of town." Her face tightened and red-rimmed eyes swerved toward the dining room windows that looked out over the driveway.

Verity had heard it, too. The crunch of tires grinding toward the house. "It's okay, Jennifer. That'll be Sheriff Bailey."

"How do you *know*? Oh, my God, what if it's *him*?"

Boots pounded up her back steps; something punched her back door. *BAM! BAM! BAM!* Verity instinctively tensed.

Jennifer rocketed to her feet, her fingers releasing her grip on the mug before she set it down. Tea sloshed across the table. Verity lunged for the toppling mug before it hit the floor.

"Mrs. Cade, it's me—Sheriff Bailey. You ladies alright?"

"Sit down," Verity said, "I'll be right back. I'd know that bullhorn of a voice anywhere."

Jennifer grimaced at the mess on the table. "Sorry."

Verity ran down into the mudroom and let Bailey in.

"How's she doing?" he whispered. "You call for an ambulance?"

"She said she doesn't want one, only wants to go home. I think she's just plain terrified and wishes she were back on familiar territory."

Bailey's tight nod sent his chins wobbling. "Where's she from anyway?"

"I don't know. I would have said New York City, that's where the bus tour started. But I guess Ervin's customers may have come from anywhere."

Jennifer was wiping up the spilled tea with a fistful of paper towels when they stepped into the kitchen. "I'm so sorry, Verity. I really am trying to calm down. Could I please have more tea? I think it's helping." She tossed the soggy towels in the trash can, grabbed a fresh tissue and blotted her eyes and nose.

The sheriff observed her solemnly. "Please, sit down, Mrs.

O'Halloran. Can you tell me what's going on? I understand you told Mrs. Cade here that someone assaulted you?"

Jennifer nodded and pressed her hands to the tabletop as she lowered herself shakily into her chair. She took three deep breaths then opened her mouth but closed it again without speaking. She pressed her lips together.

Seeing her reluctance to speak, Verity used the moment to pour hot water into a clean mug and plop in a fresh chamomile teabag. "Tea, Sheriff?"

"No." He hadn't taken his eyes off the silent woman.

Verity set the mug down in front of her guest, then stood off to one side and rested a hand on the woman's thin shoulder. "Mrs. O'Halloran was just telling me that she changed her mind at the last minute about going to the fireworks."

Bailey's heavy iron-gray eyebrows drew down, making him look all the more like a jowly bulldog. "Were you planning to walk to the field?"

Jennifer nodded.

"Alone or with someone?"

"No one was left at the inn to walk with." She looked up at Bailey. "Listen, I'm not an idiot. There are cities in this country where I wouldn't even think of walking at night on my own. But here, it seemed so peaceful. Frogs croaking, crickets or grasshoppers or whatever the hell they are making those chirpy summer sounds. Safe, I thought. Right?" She seemed lost in the memory of a quiet moment before it happened—whatever *it* was.

"So, you started walking..." he prompted.

"Yeah. I'd probably gone a quarter mile. I could see the fireworks but by then they sounded like the show was about over. You know—crazy-loud, the big finale, the whole sky lighting up red, white, and blue with overlapping explosions. That's probably why I didn't hear his footsteps coming up behind me. But I sensed something and—" She looked down at her folded hands on the table. Her lips pressed together so hard they appeared glued together.

"And?" said the sheriff. Verity could tell he was afraid Jennifer might shut down, permanently.

"And he was just there." Jennifer's voice sounded distant, barely audible. "Maybe thirty feet behind me. I couldn't see his face when I turned to look. I mean, it was so-o-o dark. And whoever it was, he didn't say anything. I just kept on w-walking." Her voice cracked. "If it had been somebody from the tour, they'd have said something, don't you think? Like, 'wait up, we can walk together.'" She stared up at Bailey, wistfully. Then down into her tea. But she didn't try to pick it up, as though she was afraid she might spill it again.

"I know it's hard to talk about something like this," Verity said softly. "But it's important the sheriff gets as much information from you as possible." She flicked a finger toward the woman's throat, a none-too-subtle attempt to direct the sheriff's attention toward the injury.

Bailey regarded her with puzzlement. She finally gave up, realizing it probably looked as though she was trying to dislodge a particularly sticky insect from her fingertip.

"I am trying. I really am." Jennifer grabbed her tea, took a quick swallow, then firmly replaced the mug on the table. "The faster I walked the faster he walked. Before I knew it, he was right behind me, breathing on the back of my neck just before he grabbed me and pulled me to a stop. He tugged my necklace tight around my throat. I-I couldn't—*oh, God!*—couldn't catch my breath, let alone shout." She pressed quivering hands over her face. "I tried to fight him, I did. But the more I struggled the tighter he yanked on the chain."

And now, the sheriff's gaze fell to the woman's throat—and Verity saw understanding dawn in his widening eyes.

"You must have fought back hard," Verity said. "You got away from him."

Jennifer seemed not to have heard her. She was gulping down air, lost in reliving the attack. A trembling hand lowered from her tear-stained face and curled around her throat in a protective gesture.

"It's ok," Verity crooned softly. "It's over."

Jennifer tossed her head wildly. "I don't know what would have happened if my necklace hadn't snapped. He must have been thrown off balance when it came away in his hand. I heard him hit the ground, hard, and curse. I was already running. I just knew I had to get as far away from him as I could."

"Did he chase after you?" Bailey had been standing all this time. Now he pulled up a chair and sat facing the victim. Verity stayed beside her, keeping one hand on her shoulder, hoping this might give her some comfort.

"Maybe? I think he started to but got spooked by people returning from the fireworks."

Bailey brightened. "Was a helluva crowd. Best year yet!" He immediately lost his smile at a piercing look from Verity. "Can you tell me anything at all about what he looked like, Mrs. O'Halloran? His height, weight? What he wore? It was a man, you're sure?"

"Definitely a man." She coughed to clear her throat. "He grabbed me like he...like he meant to—" she winced and blinked up at Verity. "I don't think he meant to kill me. Not then at least."

*An attempted rape?* Verity thought, feeling sicker by the moment.

"Did you see a car, any sort of vehicle he might have been trying to pull you toward?" the sheriff continued.

"No. No car. But I was pretty out of it by then."

Verity added, "She was staggering, sort of weaving around

in the middle of the road when I saw her. I thought she might be having trouble breathing. I made her get into my truck."

"And you saw no one in the area, Mrs. Cade?"

"No. Not a soul. Not since I left the fairgrounds."

Bailey rubbed a hand over his chin. "Mrs. O'Halloran, do you think you might be able to identify the man if—"

"Do you not get that it was freakin' dark?" Jennifer stared at him in disbelief. "Your stupid country roads. Not a single streetlight! I couldn't see my own feet." She sighed. "I don't know. Maybe he was, like, medium tall. Taller than me. He might have been wearing a hoodie, but I'm no longer sure."

"I'm sorry," said the sheriff. "I just need to make sure I'm not missing anything that could be helpful."

"Well, you're *missing* my husband's killer. And if it weren't for this nice woman here, there's no telling what might have happened to me!" Her eyes had lost their desperation and now flashed with furious exasperation. "I need to go home and make arrangements for Rudy's funeral. I'll take the next train or bus, call a cab, whatever it takes—you can tell that idiot tour director I'm leaving. He can keep his outrageous fee. I just want to get as far away from this nightmare town as possible."

"Wait, Jennifer!" Verity glanced questioningly at the sheriff but he didn't stop her from continuing. "I need to ask one more time. Is there anyone we should know about, anyone who might have a reason for wanting to hurt you or your husband?"

Jennifer launched herself out of her chair. "No! I already told you."

"But someone clearly has a grudge against one or both of you," Verity insisted.

Jennifer looked from Verity to the sheriff then back again, her expression a mask of confusion and helplessness. "Listen, I have no idea who would want to do this to us. But my staying here isn't going to help you find Rudy's killer." She spun around and marched out through the kitchen doorway. They could hear the hollow sound of her steps crossing the mudroom's board floor. The outside door slammed.

*What the hell!* Verity thought.

Minutes earlier, the woman had been scared to death of being outside. And with good reason. Verity exchanged a worried glance with the sheriff. "I don't want her walking back into town alone."

"Me neither," he said. "I'll catch her up and drive her back to the inn."

BY THE NEXT MORNING, Verity was halfway through her first cup of coffee and still had seen neither of her two resident spirits. She found their absence particularly irritating because she had been all revved up to give them a well-deserved piece of her mind. But it was hard to keep her anger at full boil when the target of her fury had literally vanished, and she had no way to find them. Anyway, their lack of common sense had become less a priority after the attack on Jennifer.

While sorting eggs for her home delivery customers she thought about the O'Hallorans and how terribly wrong their lives had gone, almost from the moment they arrived in Evansfield. Rudy O'Halloran murdered. His widowed wife assaulted but—thank goodness!—not seriously injured. It was so bizarre! Stuff like this just didn't happen in little Evansfield.

But it had happened. And thanks to the autopsy, they now knew for sure that Rudy had been murdered.

Bailey had shared with Verity key points of the pathologist's final report after depositing Jennifer back at the inn. Unable to sleep, he called her. The report stated that although O'Halloran's blood was rich with alcohol the night he'd died, the head injuries he'd sustained couldn't have been caused by a fall. A drunk person might take a tumble and hit their head, resulting in minor or serious injury. But the nature of the multiple blows to O'Halloran's skull indicated a much different scenario. One that actually matched the scene little Morgan described.

Score 1 for the little guy.

Now, after far too little sleep, Verity snapped shut an egg carton with the Cade Family Farm logo on its lid and her thoughts spun in yet another direction. The assault on the murder victim's wife couldn't be a coincidence. Two people from the same family attacked within days of each other? No. The events couldn't have been random. They were planned. But to what end? And by whom?

There were significant similarities. Both attacks were violent and carried out from up close. Which seemed to indicate they were personal in nature. Rudy was struck with a club, brick, or maybe a rock. Jennifer had nearly been strangled, using her own necklace. Hands-on assaults. Only the weapon changed. The only really important difference being—the second attack hadn't been successful. Did this mean Jennifer was still in danger? Would the thwarted killer return to finish the job?

*Oh God!* Just the thought gave her chills.

But again, why? If the killer was after something of value the couple had in their possession, what good would murdering them do? Jennifer said the man who jumped her didn't speak a word to her; he demanded nothing of her. Was this then some weird kind of revenge plot? What could the couple have *done* to mark them both for death?

Verity mulled over all of this and more while filling another stack of egg cartons.

She was nearly done when, out of the blue, another possibility fluttered annoyingly into an already confusing flock of theories.

Maybe it wasn't about having something of value. Was it possible the O'Hallorans *knew* something that someone urgently wanted to keep secret? Was Rudy killed to silence him? Maybe this was why Jennifer had been so desperate to leave Evansfield. Jennifer feared she would meet the same fate, because she knew what Rudy had known. What secret could possibly be so damning to make a person risk committing two murders?

Verity's head hurt. Nothing made sense. The one result of all her brainstorming was a very strong suspicion that Jennifer O'Halloran knew things she hadn't told her or the sheriff.

Having finished preparing her delivery, Verity tossed the remaining cold dregs of her coffee into the sink and poured herself a fresh, steaming cup. Just the aroma was fortifying. Her morning java, doused with a healthy pour of her cows' rich cream, was so sweet and smooth her cuppa deserved to be called dessert. She savored every swallow as she dressed in her favorite straight-leg jeans, navy blue t-shirt, and comfy cotton socks. Downstairs again, in her mudroom, she bent to step into her wellies and stomped her heels down inside the boots.

When she straightened up, a faint glimmer caught her eye. Two figures slowly emerged within the dim room, garbed in work clothes as practical as her own. Percy in a flannel shirt and canvas pants. Anna Louise in a patchwork blouse and denim overalls, looking far more subdued than her usual flamboyant self.

Although relieved to see them, Verity propped fists on her hips and narrowed her eyes at the couple. "Well, it's about time! You two are in one heap of trouble. What got into you last night? Why did you come out of your shades in the middle of a crowd like—"

"Oh, Verity," Anna Louise whimpered. "We never—"

"It's no use apologizing now for your little tricks," she scolded. "Luckily, everyone was so into the fireworks they paid little attention to you. Never do that again or you—" She couldn't think of a suitable punishment for ghosts. After all, they were already dead. "Or you'll be sleeping in the barn with the cows!"

Anna Louise tried again. "But we—"

"I don't want to hear excuses." Verity shook a finger at them, feeling a little silly for the schoolmarm-y gesture. "Promise me. Never, ever again!"

"Sadly, we cannot give you our word," Percy said in a voice much calmer than her own. "More's the pity, Miss Verity."

"What does that mean?" A rush of heat filled her face.

"He means," Anna Louise cried, "we seem to have lost control of, ummm, of ourselves."

"Huh?" When, Verity thought, have these two ever been in control of anything? They were two souls helplessly stuck between the living world and their final destination. Wherever that might be. Then it struck her. "You're claiming you didn't intentionally make yourselves visible to the whole town?"

"We surely did not, Miss Verity." Anna Louise dropped her gaze mournfully to the floor. Her long, golden curls quivered over wan cheeks. The ghost's lavender eyes brimmed with tears, giving them an almost lifelike shine. "We wanted to join the celebration but hadn't meant to become visible. And you see, w-w-we need to *think* ourselves out of our shades before living folks can see us. What happened last night wasn't our doing. It wasn't normal."

*Is anything normal in my life?* Verity shook her head.

Percy reached out and gently took his wife's hand in his.

"We were standing there, invisible even to you, as far as we knew. Watching the fireworks and having a grand time. Then we short-circuited."

Verity narrowed her eyes at Percy, then at Anna Louise. "Short-circuited? How did you even come up with that word? You didn't have electricity back in your time."

"True," Percy agreed, "at least not as you use it. There was the telegraph, but that's neither here nor there. My point is, we went to the library to try and find out what went wrong."

"Last night wasn't the first time this happened, you see," Anna Louise added helpfully.

Percy continued, "We searched for reasons why our shades might come or go without our intending them to. The only explanation that made any sense was what I read about electrical current."

"Personally," Anna Louise commented, "I don't believe in electricity. I think it's—what do you call it—fake news?"

Verity rolled her eyes. "But electricity has nothing to do with your being dead or in limbo, does it?"

"I should think not," he admitted glumly. "However, when one understands so little about one's present circumstances, one grasps at straws."

"I suppose one does." Oh Lord, now she was beginning to talk like them. Verity glanced at her watch. She was going to be late for her deliveries. "I wish I could help you, but I have no idea what's causing your visibility issues."

She turned to leave with her crates of egg boxes but sensed a presence still behind her by the time she'd reached the back door.

"We will help you," Percy offered, "so you can help us."

"You can't follow me outside," she reminded him. "What if Jason or Jerry sees you?"

"We're still visible?" Anna Louise sighed. "Oh dear. I had thought we—"

"You mean, you don't even *know* whether or not you're visible?" Verity turned to look back through the doorway and saw their figures flickering like malfunctioning neon bulbs. She set down her eggs on the porch and stepped back inside, closing the door behind her.

"You see?" Percy said dolefully. "One minute we're invisible—the next minute someone asks us where we bought our adorable costumes." He cringed, looking deeply offended.

"The worst was right after the fireworks last night," Anna Louise murmured. "A little girl saw us and started crying. When she tried to point us out to her mother, we beat a hasty retreat, I can assure you."

"Well, thank heavens for that."

"But what should we do?" Percy asked solemnly. "How do we stop this from happening?"

Verity shook her head. "I don't have a clue. But until we figure out what's going on, the two of you need to stay inside this house. Agreed?"

"Yes, ma'am, I believe that is a wise strategy," Percy said. "Although we did agree to help you gather evidence about the murder."

"I know. And I really could use your help. But if people realized I was living with... Never mind. We've already discussed this. You know we can't risk that happening."

Percy bowed his head with a resigned sigh. Verity looked at Anna Louise who just turned away. Not a good sign.

"Anna Louise? What are you not telling me?"

The lieutenant's wife pursed her lips and her eyes misted over. "I'm terribly frightened, Miss Verity." She grasped her husband's hand and pressed it to her breast. "What if we fade away and never come back? What if we are suddenly just... gone?"

Verity was puzzled. "Isn't that what you both want? To be released from the world of the living and go off to heaven...or wherever you're destined to go?"

"This is true." Percy sighed, looking truly miserable. He wrapped his free arm protectively around his wife. "But we can't be certain we'll still be together in the afterlife. If by staying here on the farm with you we can be sure to have each other—"

"I understand," Verity said quickly as her heart gave a sympathetic leap. "I would absolutely feel the same, if I were in your situation."

"You see, Miss Verity—" Anna Louise smiled at her "—although we surely miss our earthly lives, we find it quite agreeable being here with you, in our spirit forms."

"Why thank you." She was, apparently, an excellent ghost landlady, if not an excellent cat mother. "Now please, you two, stay here. Out of sight. Maybe I can do a little more research and come up with an answer to why you're losing control of yourselves."

Verity carried her eggs the rest of the way to her little blue truck. Before setting out on her delivery route, she stopped in at the milking barn to check the Robo-Milkers. Although deeply troubled by the couple's revelations, she couldn't ignore her most critical work

Everything looked good here. According to the digitally stored data on the machines, half of her herd had already passed through one of the three automated milking stations that day. She checked the gauges on the stainless-steel collection tank. Plenty of room remained before the co-op dairy's afternoon pickup.

She drained off and bottled milk for her customers who preferred raw milk over store-bought pasteurized. She sold the whole milk, each bottle with its own cap of cream before she sealed it. Her customers loved the heavy cream for their coffee and baking. On other days she would remove cream from a quantity of her milk, rendering the remaining milk "skimmed" and use the cream to make her popular Cade Family Farm hand-churned butter. Sunny's standing order for butter contributed to the luscious texture of her pastries at the café. With the inn now open, she had gained a second large order. Her business was, thankfully, 'in the black' now. An immense relief to her after the financial struggles of previous years.

By nine o'clock she had finished loading deliveries and started into town.

First stop, Dr. John Evans' house. His receptionist buzzed her in through the medical office's door at the back of the big house. She could hear voices as she passed by the medical office's inner door and climbed the steps to the kitchen. John's teenage son and daughter were nowhere in sight. Perhaps sleeping in, as she remembered so often doing at that age. She found John's payment for the family's milk and eggs in an envelope on the kitchen island and slipped it into the fanny pack strapped around her waist.

Her next stops, the café and then the inn.

Back in her truck, she tossed the empty canvas sacks on the passenger seat and drove down Main Street. The sun was blazing this July day, its glare challenging her dark sunglasses. She flipped down the truck's windshield visor. Her dazzled vision calmed down. She hadn't gone far before she saw the glint of something bright on the road.

Curious, she checked her rearview mirror then the road ahead to make sure no vehicles were coming from either direction. She climbed out, leaving the truck in Park, the engine idling. If the source of the glitter was glass, she'd kick it into the gutter so one of the neighborhood kids wouldn't puncture a bicycle tire. But it wasn't glass. It was a thin gold chain.

Her heart skipped a beat.

Squatting like a baseball catcher, she carefully used the penknife she always kept in her jeans pocket and lifted the necklace from the road's burning-hot surface. A single small medallion hung from its center. She held up the chain to examine it. The necklace was no longer a closed loop, the clasp had broken, and maybe some of the links were missing, too.

One thing she *was* quite certain of—this must be the necklace Jennifer O'Halloran had been wearing the previous night when she was attacked. Verity remembered all too vividly the thin red line that had cut into her flesh. How fortunate the woman had been to get away from her assailant.

An icy finger crept up Verity's spine. And to think the sheriff believed Jennifer O'Halloran would be safe at the inn! Verity could kick herself for not insisting the young woman remain with her at the farmhouse. There, at least, she and her two farmhands could watch over her.

A car horn blasted.

Startled, she looked up to see an SUV sitting in the middle of the road behind her truck. She waved an apology at the driver and jumped into the cab. Carefully, she laid the chain on top of her empty canvas bags before continuing to drive.

As soon as she had parked in front of the Cat's Cradle Café, she fished a clean plastic sandwich bag out of her console, picked up the chain again with the pocket-knife blade and slipped the necklace inside.


Verity phoned the sheriff's office. She left a message with his receptionist, saying she wanted to stop by. Harriet told her she expected Bailey to return momentarily.

"He's stepped out for a smoke," she explained. "We have a new no-smoking regulation." Verity was sure this must be Harriet's doing, certainly not a new rule instituted by the ardent cigar-puffing Bailey. Harriet's bailiwick was any- and everything that happened in that office; she ruled her domain with an iron will.

The receptionist wasn't at her desk when Verity reached the department's offices after quickly finishing her deliveries. Verity walked straight through the reception area and into Bailey's office without knocking, just because she knew how much he hated her doing that. It was so darn easy and gratifying to get him riled.

Grinning at the gnarly face he gave her, she tossed the bagged necklace on his desk.

"What's this?" he grunted.

"If you hurry before Jennifer leaves town, you can ask her if this is the necklace she was wearing last night."

"Where'd you find it, Nancy Drew?" His payback for the missing knock.

"In the street, not far from where I found her staggering around in a daze last night."

He nodded, looking a little less like killing her. "Something came up you should probably know about," he said.

"Oh? I hope it's a clue to what the hell is going on, because I sure can't make any sense of it."

"I was thinkin'," he said while his thick fingers poked speculatively at the plastic baggie, "technically, anyone could have offed that idiot Rudy. I haven't heard one word of admiration about the man."

"Not that he deserved to be offed," she reminded him.

"True. Any-who, I ran a check on the least helpful individuals in Ervin's travel group. Talked to several, some you've already mentioned. The Andersons for one. But I figure their lack of cooperation was because they were so irritated at bein' woked up. I can sympathize, seein' as I'm like a bear comin' outta hibernation, anyone wakes me."

"As I have discovered," she commented dryly. "So, what did you find out?"

He made her wait for a beat, as if for dramatic effect. "Ervin's bus driver, Susan Brown, has a criminal record."

"Does she now." She could easily believe it. The woman clearly enjoyed intimidating people and sounded like she might be dangerous.

"She did three years in prison for a series of B&Es in Pennsylvania. Made off with a heap of stuff from people's homes over a period of years. Apparently, she was pretty good at it. The local cops took a long time to catch up with her."

"Was anyone hurt during the break-ins?" Verity asked.

"No. She only broke in during the day while most folks were at work. Took cash, valuables she could fence. Probably in and out in minutes."

"Is she still on probation?" Verity sat down in one of the two visitors' chairs, sensing this conversation was going to take longer than she had expected. "If that's what it's called."

"Yup. Which may be why she wouldn't want to get involved in a murder investigation. If her probation officer heard she was mixed up in a serious crime, that could land her right back in jail."

"Are you going to have another conversation with her?" Verity asked.

"Absolutely." He squinted at her. "I know you want to help, Mrs. C. But your sittin' in on this interview isn't a good idea."

She shrugged, pretending not to care. Sue had made it obvious that she didn't like her. But Verity thought how satisfying it would feel to see the driver squirm as Bailey interrogated her. Still, she supposed she should be more sympathetic.

She'd read how hard it often was for newly released prisoners to find employment. Maybe Ervin didn't even know about her incarceration. If he found out, would she lose her job driving for his tours?

"I have too much to do today anyway." She shrugged. "The twins will be justified in accusing me of not doing my share if I don't get back to the farm pronto."

## CHAPTER 23

VERITY HAD BARELY STOPPED her truck beside the Grimalski brothers' army-green Ford pick-up when Jerry came running out of the farmhouse's back door. It wasn't unusual for her two farm hands to let themselves inside her house. She'd always told them they were free to raid her fridge, grab a cup of coffee, or use the upstairs bathroom, the only one in the farmhouse. But the urgency of Jerry's speed toward her put her immediately on alert.

"What's up?" she said, thinking the worst. "Did one of you get hurt?"

"No, nothing like that." Gasping for breath, Jerry looked back at the farmhouse. "We think someone broke in."

"Seriously?"

"Yeah. We were signing off on the milk pickup with the co-op driver when I looked up and saw someone pass behind the parlor window."

"Oh." She was getting a bad feeling about this, and it had nothing to do with there being an intruder in her house. At least, not in the way the boys were thinking. "Did Jason see this, ah... person, too?"

"No, not at first," he said. Verity was already moving toward the house, Jerry sidestepping to watch her face while they talked and walked. "Jase said you probably just got home earlier than expected. But that was stupid; your truck wasn't here."

"I see." She scowled up at the windows facing the long gravel drive that ran between her sunny yellow house and barns. Nothing moved.

Verity was about to look away when an oval shape, details indistinguishable in the sun's glare, appeared in her bedroom window. What she could see of the clothing was dark colored, maybe black. It looked as though a high collar or hood framed the face and hid the hair. Her first reaction was relief. Neither of the Putnams would be caught dead—she cringed at the pun—wearing anything so twenty-first century. Then her brief respite from worry evaporated. *A hoodie.* That's what the little boy had said the killer wore.

Verity broke into a run. "Is Jason still inside?" she shouted.

"Yeah, why?"

"I just saw someone. Upstairs. My bedroom. I hope your brother's alright."

They flew up the porch steps, through the back door. Without stopping, she grabbed the wooden handle of a heavy iron shovel propped in the corner beside the mudroom's stairs. Jerry took the lead. She was inches behind him when the door flew open and a hooded figure barreled down the steps from the kitchen, colliding with them.

"Hey, man, watch out!" Verity knew that voice.

"Jason? What's going on?" she shouted, scrambling to catch her balance before she hit the hard floor. Jerry landed on his backside with an '*ooomph.*' Then it struck her. "Were you just now looking out my bedroom window?"

"Yeah, I heard a car pull into the drive and wanted to see who it was."

Breathing hard, she stared at him and set the shovel aside. She was relieved that no one had broken in. And, probably, it was only a brief glimpse of one of the ghosts through the window that had alarmed her two farmhands. The important thing was—neither of them had come face-to-face with Anna Louise or Percy.

Almost immediately, though, that feeling of restored calm faded and suspicion danced its sticky fingers up the back of her neck.

"What are you wearing, Jason?"

"This? My old high school track sweatshirt." He laughed. "It's too hot for a day like this, but the hood keeps the hay from falling down inside my shirt. Itches like crazy."

She studied his face. A dark scratch on his left cheek she hadn't noticed earlier created a red track through his beard stubble. She tried not to connect the dots that were starting to spin in her head like numbers in a TV lottery tumbler. Rudy O'Halloran had been attacked and killed by a man in a dark hoodie—if Morgan, their only witness, could be believed. Jennifer was nearly killed by a man, maybe also in a hoodie. In her frenzy to escape, could she have gouged her attacker with a fingernail?

*Oh please, God, no!*

"Did you find anyone upstairs?" Jerry was asking his brother. Both of her farmhands seemed unaware of her rising panic.

Jason shook his head and pulled the black hood off his tousled sandy-brown hair. "Nope. Not a soul up there."

Jerry frowned, looking past his brother's shoulder toward the kitchen door. "I was sure I saw someone in there."

"I thought so, too," Jason said casually. He turned to Verity. "Guess we were both sun-dazed. The light gets to you after a while. I searched every room though, no worries."

Verity had stopped fretting over ghosts and intruders. Her

mind had gone to an even darker place. She hated what she needed to do next. But did she have a choice? "Jason, can you tell me where you were last night?"

"At the fireworks of course, right Jerry?"

"Uh, sure, we both were there. Along with the rest of the town." Jerry chuckled but looked at her questioningly. As if he was uncomfortable with the direction the conversation had taken.

"Were you two together the entire time?" she asked. "Every minute?"

The two young men looked at each other.

"Not *every* minute," Jason said impatiently. "I brought Cindy Duncan to the fireworks. We sat off by ourselves. At least, as far away from the crowd as we could and still get a good view of the lightshow."

"And after the show?"

"Cindy and I went to her house. I was with her all night, if you need to know." His voice had turned sharp, suspicious.

She turned to Jerry. "So, during the fireworks, you couldn't really see Jason."

"That's right. So what? What's this all about?" Jerry huffed. "You sound like a TV cop grilling a crim."

"I'm not grilling anyone." Even as she said it, she could hear the defensiveness in her tone. "I just need to know that you aren't involved in—"

"In what?" Jason snapped, glaring at her.

She sighed. This was not going well. "You've probably already heard that the wife of the man who recently died was assaulted last night."

"Yeah, and what's that got to do with us?" Jason snapped.

"Her assailant wore a black hoodie." She let that sink in.

Jason laughed but his reaction felt delayed, if only by

seconds. Was he calculating a response and that was the best he could do? Laugh? Jerry just looked annoyed.

"You can't be serious." Jason stepped into her space and glared down at her. A tiny muscle twitched at the corner of one eye. "You do realize that every single person in this town under the age of thirty has at least one hoodie in their closet?"

"Of course. But this is important, guys. The sheriff has reason to believe that the person who killed Rudy O'Halloran was wearing dark clothes and a hoodie. And his wife has given a similar description of her assailant."

Jerry threw up his hands in a show of disgust. "This is insane. Mrs. Cade, you *know* us. Why would either of us try to hurt that poor woman?" She noticed he didn't ask the same question about Rudy.

"I don't know," she said slowly. "Why would anyone? It doesn't make sense to me either. If someone had a bone to pick with her husband, why go after her? And if she has enemies, why kill her husband?"

She looked from one to the other of her young men. They refused to meet her eyes.

"Listen, guys, I know you're both good people. But the sheriff won't overlook that fight you had with Rudy in the café, Jason. You threatened the man. In front of witnesses! And that happened less than twenty-four hours before he died." Both young men started to speak at once, but she put up a hand to silence them until she finished. "*And now* the sheriff is treating O'Halloran's death as a homicide. You must see how this looks."

"I don't give a damn how it looks!" Jason shouted. "I didn't kill the jerk. And I don't go around attacking women. Ever!"

Verity sucked in a deep breath, wishing she'd never started this conversation. She felt terrible for accusing Jason. She would volunteer in a heartbeat as a character witness for either of them. Ten years younger than her, they had become almost like brothers. The pair had been unconditionally loyal to Mark since they were teenagers and started helping him around the farm. And once Mark was no longer around, they'd been equally loyal to her.

"We have stuff to do," Jerry muttered, turning toward the outside door. "Let's go, bro. That barn door hinge won't mend itself."

"No, wait!" Verity cried. "I'm sorry if I've upset you. I really am. I think you should both call it a day. The sheriff will discover who's behind these crimes. But he has to remain unbiased."

Jerry stared at the worn planks under his feet.

Jason shifted from one foot to the other but still avoided her eyes. "You think he's going to question me?"

"He might. He's talking to everyone. He can't eliminate anyone from the investigation just because he likes them. Or I like them." She gazed fondly at the two young men. "You both are really very special to me; I hope you know that. I'm sorry for hurting your feelings."

"Yeah, well," Jerry said, "I guess this stuff has gotten a lot of people nerved up."

Jason spun around and clomped out through the mudroom door without another word.

"Oh, no," Verity sighed.

"Don't worry," Jerry said after a moment. "He'll get over it. He always does. I better go. Family dinner tonight at Mom's house." He gave her a sullen wave and slouched away.

She stood in the doorway, watching the Brothers Grimm (as half the town referred to the two Grimalskis) disappear around the corner of the house in the direction of their truck. Not for the world would she ever harm those two. But Jason's flash temper deeply troubled her. Was it possible in a fit of rage he might have...

*No!* She couldn't let herself think like that. She just couldn't.

# CHAPTER 24

SITTING ALONE in her kitchen after her two farmhands had left, Verity took a deep breath through her nose, then let it out between her lips to a count of ten. She repeated the breathing exercise, trying to generate soothing thoughts. No matter how hard she tried, she couldn't drive from her mind the image of the fresh scar on Jason's cheek. She was almost certain it hadn't been there when she last saw him, which was the day before the fireworks.

If a woman was fighting for her life, she instinctively went for one of two places on her attacker's body. Claw at his face and try to gouge out his eyes. Or aim a swift immobilizing kick to his crotch.

However, pitching hay down from the loft into the cows' troughs while wearing a hoody as armor made sense. The ends of dry straw were as sharp as knife tips, capable of piercing skin. The result was more painful than a paper cut. The boys were right, too, about the ubiquity of sweatshirts with hoods. They were everywhere.

Which meant the person Morgan saw in the alley and Jennifer encountered could have been anyone. But Verity was immobilized by the possibility that Jason's terrible temper might, for once, have gotten him into serious trouble.

She sat feeling helpless, for how long she couldn't have said, before she sensed their presence.

"Hey, you two," she whispered disconsolately, looking up at the two ghosts.

"How did you know we were here, sugar?" Anna Louise said. "We were ever so quiet."

Anna Louise wore a sweet yellow frock and a straw bonnet tied with a wide satin ribbon over her blonde curls. Percy sported civilian clothes—buff-colored trousers, shirt, and a trim vest. Shirt sleeves rolled to his elbows revealed the muscular forearms of a farmer who had worked hard on his land. She had to admit he cut a truly handsome figure.

"It doesn't matter. Sometimes, I just know. Did you realize that my farmhands saw one of you through an upstairs window?"

Percy looked at his wife. "I told you so."

"You said we must stay in the house, and we were." Anna Louise pouted. "I just wanted to see what those clever boys of yours were up to. We try to keep track of them whenever you're not here, you know. They just happened to look up at the window before I could duck out of the way."

"It's not your job to supervise my hired help," Verity said with a heavy sigh.

"Apologies." Percy's response sounded far too casual.

She slanted him a dubious look.

"When we were alive," Percy explained, "we hired extra help during the haying season, sometimes for spring planting as well. We needed to make sure they were doing their jobs properly. Sometimes you aren't here to supervise your workers."

Verity shook her head. "So, you've been standing in for me as lord of the manor?"

Percy puffed up his chest. "No need to thank me."

It just didn't pay to exert yourself with a ghost. You never won.

"Just please be more careful in the future." She caught the two of them glancing guiltily at each other. Verity narrowed her eyes. Was there something else they weren't telling her? More importantly, did she really want to know?

"Miss Verity," Percy said tentatively, "we have some news for you."

"Oh?" She stood up and all but threw herself across the kitchen toward her basket of calming herbal teas. Instinct and experience told her she'd soon need to settle her nerves.

Picking a teabag—Lavender-Chamomile, perfect!—she dropped it into her favorite blue ceramic mug and flicked on the electric kettle.

Anna Louise retrieved an ivory-and-gold fan from within the folds of her skirts. "As you may recall, darlin' girl, you requested news relevant to your...what do you call it? Your case?" She held the fan in front of her face and side-glanced at her husband.

Percy cleared his throat. "First, might I say that we admit to already knowing about the Widow O'Halloran having been hurt."

Verity observed the two ghosts suspiciously. "Of course you know. Because you were eavesdropping on us when I brought her home with me last night."

"Yes, well," Anna Louise admitted with only the faintest of blushes, "we innocently overhear quite a lot. Such as your farmhands' conversations. Did you know both of your young men are courting? Oh, and one of their ladies—"

Now this was just getting annoying. "Will you get to the point, please!" The kettle burbled then shut itself off; Verity poured steaming water over the teabag. The scent of lavender wafted across the room.

Anna Louise made two impatient flicks of her fan. "Oh, alright. Your young men were quite upset about the O'Halloran woman having been hurt. They are such sweet and sincere fellows."

"I know they are," Verity said over a lump in her throat. All the more reason to doubt either of them could ever intentionally harm another human being. She took her tea with her into the living room and sat heavily in the worn leather chair. "Is *that* your news? The Grimalskis were discussing their concern for Jennifer O'Halloran?"

"No," Percy said, having followed her by way of a shortcut through the interior wall between kitchen and living room. She'd nearly forgotten they could do that. "I confess, ma'am, that I left the house for an hour today."

"Of course, you did," Verity said. Why did she bother trying to enforce rules?

"I am perfectly cognizant that this was against your stated wishes." He rushed on, "But I believed my spectral aura was under control. And as my darling wife has already reminded you, we did promise to investigate for you."

"So, what did you find out?" She took a sip of her tea a little too soon and scalded her throat. Her eyes watered with pain.

"The bus driver was talking to the O'Halloran woman," Percy said. "The driver told her that she overheard the sheriff talking with you." As if to gauge the effect of his words, Percy stared into Verity's eyes. Which, she could attest to, is very disconcerting—when the one doing the staring is a dead person.

"Go on." She blew on her tea. "By the way, the driver's name is Sue."

"Yes. Sue. She told the widow that she thought the sheriff

would soon make an arrest because he had found a witness to her husband's murder."

"Oh no!" Verity knew the sheriff would hate this. He hadn't intended to release that information to the public. But as long as the driver didn't know the actual identity of the witness, maybe this wasn't too bad.

"A little boy," Anna Louise said helpfully. "He's one of the children on the bus tour."

"No, no, no!" Verity groaned. The sheriff had warned her, as well as the boy's parents and the child himself, that no one was to mention his having seen the crime.

Anna Louise frowned. "We thought you would be pleased. Isn't this good news? Surely, an arrest is imminent if there is a witness."

"Not as imminent as I'm sure the sheriff would like. No one is really sure how much the child actually saw."

"It was quite strange, I must say." Even Percy looked a bit shaken now.

"What was?" She couldn't imagine what would rattle a soldier who had seen some of the bloodiest battles in the American Civil War. Well, other than seeing television, which still freaked out the two of them.

"I think the driver expected the other woman to be happy to hear the news."

"Sue was probably trying to cheer Jennifer up," Verity said. "It's been a tough week for her—all things considered." And *that* was an understatement.

"Well, the widow lady surely was not happy." Percy's pale blue eyes suddenly sparked with mischief. "She looked like she'd seen a ghost."

Anna Louise smacked him playfully on the shoulder with her closed fan. "O-o-o-o, you are so naughty."

"Only joshing." Percy's grin disappeared at an unappreciative look from Verity. "She acted startled, maybe even frightened."

No doubt because Jennifer was concerned for Morgan's safety, Verity thought.

She set her tea mug on the lamp table beside her and looked around for her phone. Then remembered she'd left it in the kitchen. "I need to warn the sheriff that his investigation has been compromised. If the killer were to find out Morgan might be able to identify him, the child could be in danger."

"Perhaps the little imp needs a bodyguard. Percy would make a brave and dashing protector." Ann Louise fluttered her long eyelashes at her husband. He visibly melted and turned a fetching shade of pink.

"Calling that child an imp is a kindness," Verity muttered. "I don't suppose either of you ever saw the movie, *Home Alone*?"

They gave her a blank look.

"But we do know about moving pictures," Anna Louise giggled. "We sometimes sneak into the theater on Main Street. Will you take us to see that picture?"

Verity recalled the many painful pranks the child star had played on the two burglars who invaded his family's home. "Absolutely not. I don't want to give you two any ideas. And unfortunately, I think either of you acting as a bodyguard is a recipe for disaster. What if you lost control of your visibility again?"

She pushed up out of the comfy leather cushions and paced the living room. "I'll figure out some way to tell Bailey what you overheard, without revealing my source. He can decide what to do about Sue leaking information."

"I do hope nothing happens to the child," Anna Louise exclaimed.

Percy said nothing, just scowled solemnly at the floor.

"At the very least," Verity said, "Morgan's parents need to be informed that others know he saw something the night O'Halloran was killed. Maybe the sheriff will assign one of his deputies to watch over him."

But that wasn't the end of it. Because minutes later, Jennifer O'Halloran phoned Verity, giving her yet another reason for connecting with the sheriff.

**CHAPTER 25**

IT WAS Italian Night at the Cat's Cradle Café and Verity guessed that was where Sheriff Bailey would be. The man had a prodigious capacity for food; it might be hours before he put down his fork and returned to the business of law enforcement.

She drove to the strip of shops lining the west side of Main Street and parked. As she had expected, the Cat's Cradle was hopping. She pushed open the door. Before the overhead bell ceased its happy tinkling, a wave of oregano, garlic, olive oil, and roasted tomatoes wafted over her.

*Oh, my!* Her mouth watered.

Two long tables had been installed to accommodate Ervin's tourists. Locals seemed to be doing their best to squeeze into the little eatery's remaining space, four people sitting at round bistro tables that normally accommodated two customers. All of Sunny's tables sported perky red-and-white checkered table-cloths and an empty chianti bottle holding a red candle. Drops of wax ran decoratively down the sides of the dark green glass. Little wicker breadbaskets holding crusty baguettes added to the room's rustic European mood.

Verity scanned the room for the sheriff but didn't see him.

Sunny waved at her from behind the glass bakery case. She looked a lot calmer than she had on the night she begged Verity to help her.

Verity smiled and wove between tables toward her friend.

"Don't worry," Sunny said with a wink. "I finally got smart and commandeered a few temporaries. Each of my regular staff brought a friend, eager to put a few extra dollars in their pockets this summer. Everything seems to be running smoothly, so far."

"Good. Looks like you've pulled off another great theme night. I bet you'll get plenty of requests for a repeat." Verity looked around the busy dining area again. "Have you seen our illustrious sheriff tonight?"

"Table 7." Sunny pointed. "I sat him and Penny behind the potted palms for a little privacy. They arrived over an hour ago. The man hasn't stopped shoveling pasta and meatballs since then."

Verity laughed. "He'll make you a rich woman!"

Sunny made a face. "It's an all-you-can-eat buffet, Veri." She gestured toward the rear wall of the café and the row of steaming chafing dishes.

"Oh my!" Verity winced. "I stand corrected. He'll put you in the poor house."

"Not to worry. His wife eats so sparingly, I figure they'll consume an average of two normal meals."

"Do you think it's safe to approach him now that he's been so well fed? I need to talk to him about something important."

"Better you than me, sweetie. But hey, at least there are plenty of witnesses. He probably won't draw his sidearm on you."

"Very reassuring."

On her way across the dining room, she checked out the selection of food on the hot and cold serving tables. She lifted the first stainless-steel lid and found Sunny's famous meatballs swimming in pungent marinara sauce. A choice of spaghetti or rotini nestled beneath the next lid. Another heated tray displayed lasagna, delectably gooey with mozzarella and ricotta cheeses and Italian sausage.

Verity decided she really needed a hot meal. Like, now! She fixed herself a generous plate of lasagna, adding tossed green salad, a few pepperoncini and garlic bread. Picking up plastic utensils wrapped in a red paper napkin she walked her dinner across the crowded room.

"Good evening, Sheriff and first lady of law!" Verity said, stepping around a tall palm. She hoped her cheerfulness would be contagious.

Sheriff Bailey grunted, swiped his mouth with a napkin and lifted one big paw as if to wave her away.

"Oh, Verity, how nice to see you!" Penelope Bailey decisively gripped her husband's shirt cuff and tugged his hand down. "Pull up a chair and join us. It seems like such a long time since we've had a chance to visit."

Penny was everything her husband was not. Slender to his bulk. Petite to his six-foot-and-then-some stature. Exuberantly jovial and cordial in contrast to his unpredictable moodiness. The one characteristic they shared was a willingness to come to the aid of anyone who asked for their help.

"I see you every Thursday when I deliver your eggs and cream," Verity reminded her.

"Well, yes, but you always burst through my kitchen door like a wayward tornado then disappear in a flash. Such a busy young woman you are!" Her eyes sparkled with sincere fondness.

"That's farming for you." Verity sat down and arranged her plate and plastic flatware in front of her. Penny poured her a glass of water from the pitcher on the table. "Thanks. You know how it is. Always something to do. On the bright side, I'm never bored." Wasn't that the truth!

"Well, I've finished eating, but Fred is only on his third plate." Penny rolled her eyes. "Or is it your fourth, dear? No matter, it's good to see him thinking about something other than that awful murder." She shook her head and clucked her tongue. "So very disturbing for our little community."

"It certainly is," Verity agreed. She felt the sheriff's suspicious gaze even as he forked another meatball into his mouth. She took a deep breath for strength. "Sheriff, I'm afraid we need to talk about—"

He slapped his fork down on the table. "Good grief, Mrs. Cade. Can't it wait until I've finished my meal?" He turned to his wife. "I swear, this woman intentionally times her news bulletins to coincide with my sleep and mealtimes."

Penny tipped her head to one side, observing her husband patiently. "Now Fred, let Verity have her say before you read her the riot act. I'm sure she wouldn't come looking for you unless it was important."

"Actually," Verity said quickly, "I was hoping you'd step outside with me, Sheriff, for just a moment. So we can talk in private."

His eyes widened. "Great God a-mighty! Penny has already heard everything there is to know about this case. Unlike the rest of this town's gossips, she is the soul of discretion." This earned him a gentle smile from his wife.

"I didn't mean in private from Mrs. Bailey. I meant out of hearing range of everyone else in this room." Even a few overheard words had the power to balloon into the most ridiculous rumors.

"We might use the Cone of Silence," Penny suggested, deadpan.

The mouthful of pasta Verity had been about to swallow

came dangerously close to spraying across the table. She shielded her mouth with one hand until she recovered. "*Get Smart*, right?" she laughed.

"Just tell me what the hell's on your mind." Bailey reached into the breadbasket and broke off a hunk of baguette. He dredged it in olive oil before tearing into it like a grizzly awakening from hibernation.

Verity stared at him. Clearly, she would have no success getting him away from the table any time soon. She took a deep breath and plunged on, taking care to lower her voice.

"You recall our questioning young Morgan Denton about what he saw the night of O'Halloran's death?"

Bailey made a circling motion with one hand while he chewed.

"Well, it seems someone we didn't know about was listening in."

Bailey swallowed and really focused on her for the first time. "Interesting. I assume you have a name?"

"The bus driver, Susan Brown."

"And you know this how?"

Which was the question she'd been afraid he'd ask.

Verity tried not to stumble over her next words. "I, ah, overheard a conversation between the driver and Jennifer O'Halloran." This itty-bitty lie was the best she could think of to avoid mentioning a ghost as her source.

The sheriff looked at his wife, at his empty plate, then at his wife again. Penny shook her head, firmly. With a show of reluctance, he pushed his plate away. "Got to save room for dessert."

His wife laughed but said nothing. Wise woman, Verity thought. Never stand between a man and his dessert.

"What did those two gals say?" he said. "Word for word, if you can."

All Verity could do was repeat what Percy had related to

her. "Sue told Jennifer she could expect an arrest of her husband's killer very soon. Because you, Sheriff, had found a witness to Rudy's murder."

He balled up his napkin and tossed it in disgust onto the table. "For cryin' out loud! Why can't people mind their own business?" Heads turned at nearby tables. Bailey's next words dropped several decibels. "Was that all?"

Verity was almost afraid to continue. "She told Jennifer that the witness was a boy. And...she may have mentioned Morgan's name. I'm not sure."

Bailey glared at the backs of his hands.

Penny looked at Verity. "Not good?"

Verity shook her head.

The sheriff looked up after another minute. "Might not be a problem. Isn't the tour leaving tomorrow? That'll put the kid and his family out of harm's way, if the perpetrator is still in our area. Jennifer will leave on the bus, too. Can't say I'll miss that bunch."

Verity was already shaking her head.

"What?" Bailey snapped. "You're enjoying their company?"

"Not really. What I was about to say is, Jennifer won't be on the bus tomorrow because she intends to leave tonight. She called me and said she hopes to get a ride to the train station. There's a train that will get her back to New York City by 11:00 pm." She paused, unsure how to word the next bit, without lighting the sheriff's fuse, again. "When Jennifer leaves isn't important. At least I don't think so. What matters is Morgan's safety. If Sue or Jennifer mention to others in town that the boy witnessed O'Halloran's murder—"

"Oh, Fred," Penny whispered, "that little boy could be in terrible danger."

"My dear, you have a talent for statin' the obvious," he said.

"Soon as I finish my dessert, I'm gonna warn Master Morgan's parents to keep an eagle eye on the lad."

"No," his wife countered, "you are going to them *now*. No dessert for you until after you deal with this emergency."

Bailey looked crestfallen. "But, but I—the cheesecake!"

His wife gave him a look that Verity, personally, would never ignore. He, apparently, felt the same. "Oh, alright, I'll go. Mrs. Cade, you want to come with—" he glanced at her full plate, as yet untouched "—no, s'pose not. You eat. I'll be back after I talk with the Dentons."

# CHAPTER 26

PENNY KEPT Verity company while she ate. The sheriff's wife chattered on, choosing topics unconnected with the recent crimes. A new recipe she wanted to try—sausage-stuffed green peppers. Lessons in watercolor painting she had recently begun at the town hall. And then, "I hear that Fumiko Ota has a new yarn in stock that will be perfect for this winter. Imported from Japan in a half dozen luscious colors. I can't wait to get my hands on it."

"What sort of project do you have in mind?" Verity asked between savory mouthfuls of lasagna.

"A shawl, I think. I'll need to feel the wool to decide on a pattern and choose a color." Penny smiled dreamily then chuckled. "It's not as if I need another shawl. But I love knitting, it's so calming." She looked at Verity. "I don't suppose you have time in your busy life for hobbies."

"Free moments are rare," she agreed. "But I do make time for a bit of knitting at the end of some days, when I have the energy."

"Are Jason and Jerry enough help? I'm sure you could use more hands on that farm."

"As long as they continue working their current hours, the farm is fine." She shrugged. "Sometimes I can hardly catch my breath. In December and January, I get a break."

Penny sipped her after-dinner coffee and gave her a sideways look. "I worry that Fred is taking advantage of you, Verity."

"Why?" She sensed that the woman had been working up to this topic.

"You have so much to do as it is. The farm is your world, not to mention your source of livelihood. All this investigating that you and your friends do for him—you especially—must rob you of time you badly need for necessary chores."

Verity smiled. *Smart lady.* "I guess it might get out of hand if I let it. But I tell Fred when I can't spare the time. Anyway, I feel good knowing I'm helping our community."

"You certainly helped Dr. Evans' family after Elvira passed."

Verity looked away, feeling uncomfortable with her praise. "It was important to everyone to find out what happened to her. If I hadn't stepped up, I'm sure others would have. This town is so special. We truly care about each other. It's why I'll never leave. Why I hope I'll never *need* to leave."

Penny patted her hand. "I couldn't have said it better myself. Just remember that you can say 'no.' Sometimes the sheriff needs others to draw limits for him." She winked at her.

Verity couldn't help thinking how lucky the two of them were. Penny and Fred understood one another; being together made each of them a better person. She wondered if there would ever come a time when she could accept another person into her life in an intimate way. She would never stop loving Mark, that went without saying. She would always feel so very grateful for having been loved by such a wonderful man. Could a person hope to find that near-perfect match of personalities and loving companionship more than once in a lifetime? Somehow, she doubted it.

She finished her meal and thanked Penny for her companionship, then left the sheriff's wife circulating the dining room, greeting friends. Verity paid Sunny for her meal and wished the café owner luck with the rest of the evening. When she turned toward the front windows of the café, she saw Bailey standing outside with Jennifer O'Halloran in the shade of an old elm tree. Two big gray suitcases stood beside her.

Verity joined them on the sidewalk. "Looks like you're heading home." She didn't know what else to say, except... "I hate that you've had such a miserable week with us. But if you ever feel like—"

"Don't. Please." Jennifer contorted her face into an angry scowl. "No way will I ever set foot in this town again."

Verity let out a long, weary sigh. "Oh, Jennifer, I'm so very sorry."

The young woman looked up and down the street, shifting with obvious restlessness back and forth between her sandaled feet. She wrapped trembling fingers around the extended handle of one of her wheeled suitcases, as if she needed support just to stay upright.

"Mrs. O'Halloran has called for an Uber," the sheriff explained. "The driver hasn't shown up yet."

"As if that's not obvious," Jennifer grumbled. "If he doesn't come soon, I'll miss my train." Her doe-eyes brimmed with tears.

Verity stepped a little closer, feeling the need to offer comfort but sensing a hug wouldn't be welcome. "There isn't much call for paid drivers out here in the—"

"I can see that," the woman snapped. "Fuck these boonies! What am I going to do?"

Verity looked at the sheriff but he didn't seem to get her silent message. "I can drive you to the station," she offered at last. "Really, it's not a big deal. Thirty minutes or less. Will that get you there in time?"

"Just," Jennifer said with a whisper of a smile. "It'll be close. I'd sure appreciate the ride."

The sheriff cleared his throat. "I would have offered one of my men to drive you but we're already down a man 'cause of—" He broke off, as if unsure he should finish the sentence. "He's on protection duty."

Jennifer gave him a look that Verity couldn't read. Probably irritation with the man for not offering *her* protection.

"Oh, one more thing, Mrs. O'Halloran," Bailey said. "I'll need your home address and a phone number where I can contact you."

"Why?" She peered distractedly down the length of the street.

"In case new information turns up about the person who attacked you. Or about your husband's killer. Might well be the same person. Either way, you need to know who this person is and what they look like, for your own safety."

Jennifer's eyes shot wide open. Now he had her attention. "You think I might still be in danger even after I get back to New York?"

"I'm not sayin' you should be afraid," he said quickly. "Just, on the off chance this person tries to contact you, as a precaution, you understand."

"Oh." She dug into her purse with trembling fingers and pulled out a pen and small notebook then jotted down the requested information. She tore off the page and handed it to him. "That's my mother's address and phone number at the top. She's asked me to come and stay with her for a few weeks, so I won't be alone. My apartment in New York City is the second address. My cellphone number is still the best one no matter where I am."

"Good idea, stayin' with your mum for a while," the sheriff said gently. "Bein' with family is what you need now."

Jennifer closed the little notebook and returned it to her purse, then stared at the ground. For a moment, Verity was sure she was about to burst into tears. From inside the café, lively conversation and laughter seemed to intrude on her grief.

Jennifer drew a deep breath and blinked away threatening tears. "Yes, sir, I do believe you're right about that."

Verity gave her a moment to compose herself then pointed toward her blue truck, across the street. "Well, looks like your Uber isn't coming. That's me. Here, let me take one of those suitcases." Together they wheeled the bags to the Ridgeline. Verity hefted them into the open bed. She had intended to purchase a cover for it soon after she bought the vehicle. But immediately after Mark's accident it had been all she could do to keep the farm going. And later, she'd just never gotten around to finding one she liked. If it rained on a delivery day, she simply threw a tarp over everything.

"You're leaving from the Bellows Falls station, right?" Verity asked, just to be sure. "That's the closest with connections to New York."

"Yes, please." Jennifer climbed into the passenger seat while Verity got behind the wheel. "I sure am grateful, Verity. Not just for the ride today. You were so sweet to me after my husband... Anyway, I guess you know how it feels."

Verity felt a tightness at the back of her throat. "Yes, I do understand." She started the engine and backed into the street.

After they had driven a mile or so, Jennifer continued their previous conversation. "When you told me about losing your husband, I didn't think much about it. My own grief being so overwhelming. Guess we don't need to talk about shared sad times, but I want you to know that you probably saved my life, coming to my rescue as you did after that horrible person attacked me."

"I'm sure if you had knocked on any door in town and asked for help, they'd have gladly brought you into their home and called the sheriff."

"You seem so sure of that." Jennifer sniffed and swiped at her nose. "I wish I could feel that positive about the goodness of people."

"I believe most people are willing to help others."

"If you say so," Jennifer murmured, turning her head away to look out the window as dusk fell around them, purpling the western sky beyond the soaring line of emerald-green pine trees.

Neither said another word for the next fifteen minutes. Then—

"Oh my!" her passenger proclaimed on a whoosh of breath.

"What?" Verity glanced away from the road at her passenger's anxious face.

"I just thought of something I probably should have told the sheriff before I left town."

"You can call him." Eyes back on the dark road, Verity tilted her head toward her own phone, sitting on the console between them. "Go ahead. He's on speed dial."

"I don't want to bother him in case it's nothing important."

"Well, tell me, and I'll pass it along to him, unless it's absolutely urgent that we call right now."

"The thing is—" Jennifer paused as if searching for the right words "—I don't want to get anyone in trouble. I just—well, I saw something the other day while I was holed up in the inn." She bit her bottom lip nervously. "Some kids, a girl and a boy, were playing in the hallway—you know, squealing and tearing around and generally raising a hullabaloo like kids do. And then it suddenly got real quiet."

"Oh?"

"They reminded me of my kid brother. When you didn't hear him or know where he was, you could be sure he was up to no good. Anyway, I didn't see any adults around who might be in charge of the youngsters. So, I went to investigate. I found them playing in the hallway linen closet. Where the maid keeps fresh sheets and towels."

"I'm sure they couldn't hurt anything in there. Although," Verity added, "if the staff stores cleaning supplies there, they shouldn't be messing with them."

"Sure. But that's not what the sheriff needs to know. When I peeked into the closet, the boy was showing the girl a man's watch. He also pulled out something from a box pushed behind rolls of toilet paper. At first, I thought it was play-money."

"Hmmmm," Verity said.

"I didn't think much about it at the time. Two kids playing, right? No big deal. But now I'm wondering if it might have been real money. And a watch was one of the things reported stolen along with cash from the guests' rooms, including Rudy's and mine."

"Did you say anything to the kids?" Morgan and his sister, it had to have been them. She was pretty sure that the Dentons' son and daughter were the only young children staying in the inn.

"No. Once I decided they weren't doing anything danger-ous, I left them to it. Too many other things on my mind."

"Of course," Verity said. "But you're right, the sheriff should know about this."

In another five minutes, they arrived at the little railway station. Verity parked under the yellow glow of a streetlight, facing a door marked 'Passenger Lounge.' Only two other cars were in the lot. She could already feel the rumbly vibrations of an approaching train through the pavement. *Good, just in time.* She opened the driver's-side door.

"Oh, please, don't bother getting out," Jennifer said. "I saw how you opened the latch at the truck's back. I can manage the suitcases." She climbed down from the cab and peered through the surrounding darkness toward the station's entrance with what looked like relief. Verity couldn't blame her in the least.

"Take care, Jennifer," Verity called after her.

"Oh, I will. You can be sure of that."

And that, thought Verity, is that. She'd probably never see Jennifer O'Halloran again, which was a shame. She had liked her; they might have become friends.

# CHAPTER 27

AFTER DROPPING off Jennifer at the railway station, Verity returned to the farm and stumbled through her end-of-day routine, caring for her animals and herself. She didn't fully realize until then how deeply the murder and second act of violence had exhausted her. And yet, when she lay down in bed that night, she found she was unable to fall asleep. Even though neither of the recent crimes had touched her personally, the proximity of violence and death had shaken her to her core. She felt emotionally spent.

She stared up at her bedroom ceiling, her mind buzzing, body unable to settle. Tomorrow she must pass along to Sheriff Bailey the incident with the kids that Jennifer had witnessed. The nerve of that scamp Morgan! Stashing his stolen hoard in the linen closet so he could gloat over it like a mini-Midas and impress his little sister. She supposed she shouldn't be surprised. Sneaking into guests' rooms and pilfering stuff was just one step up from his usual MO of purse diving. That child was destined to a life of crime!

Another vexing thought pushed itself to the front of her mind. It seemed very odd to her that no one in town had seen or heard anything of Jennifer's attack. Or, at least, they weren't admitting it. Was it possible the grisly nature of Rudy's fatal beating had frightened the town's citizens into silence?

Verity rolled onto her side and pulled a pillow over her head, as if goose down could smother fears and roiling emotions.

Not working.

Then there was the ghosts' strange dilemma. Anna Louise and Percy pretended to be brave but their inability to control their own specters must terrify them. At any moment, their fragile existence in this world might come to an end. She could tell from the way Percy guarded his words and stole nervous glances at his wife that he was trying to say nothing that would make her worry even more. If ever there was a ghost disposed to hysterics, it was Anna Louise. And, as troublesome as they could be, she hated the thought of their disappearing from her life. She'd grown, well, rather fond of them.

As if all these concerns weren't enough to set her head spinning, there was the matter of her cat.

How could she even call the animal hers when it had been in her care for only a few days before going AWOL? Obviously, she was to blame for that. She must not have been feeding it properly. Was she supposed to brush her, cuddle her, play with her? Did barn cats expect special attention in return for job-well-done mousing? Lady Macbeth was probably offended! No wonder she'd left.

"Oh, bother!" Verity pounded her fists into the mattress and grumbled herself into a restless sleep.


The next morning, as soon as she'd opened the metal cattle guards to let the cows out into their pasture, Verity returned to her kitchen, poured herself a coffee and started checking her emails and phone. She was surprised to see she'd received a phone call the previous night while she was taking Jennifer to the train station. Somehow, she'd missed it. The sheriff had left her a message.

"With all that's been happenin' lately," Bailey's bass droned, "I wanna know Mizz O'Halloran caught her train and you made it back home safe. Call me soon's you get home."

Annoyed with herself, she punched the sheriff's number. He picked up on the first ring.

"Sorry!" burst from her mouth before he could scold her. "We got to the station seconds before her train arrived. And I'm fine."

"Glad to hear it. Hold on a sec." She could hear him giving muffled instructions to someone. Two voices responded. His deputies, she imagined. She heard retreating footsteps. Bailey continued their conversation, "Not sure now whether it's a good or a bad thing that woman has left Evansfield."

Verity froze at the serious sound of his voice. She set her coffee mug down on the kitchen table. "Why? I thought you agreed she would be safer back home."

"After you left, I kept thinkin' 'bout the O'Hallorans. Somethin' has never added up."

"Like what?" She hitched a hip onto the edge of her kitchen table, retrieved the mug and sipped her steaming brew, for some reason more curious than worried.

"Still not sure, but somethin's been kickin' the back of my brain like a cantankerous mule."

"Well, I have other news for you," she said. "Maybe a solution to the recent thievery."

"Am I gonna thank you or cuss you out?" he grumbled.

"I'm not sure I'll deserve either." And then Verity told him about their young witness's stash of stolen items in the linen closet.

"Why that little bugger!" the sheriff fumed. "If I were his daddy, I'd—"

"I'm not sure I want to know," she interrupted. "I also have been thinking about Rudy and Jennifer." Throughout a very long and very restless night. "It's just that he, Rudy, was so incredibly obnoxious and cruel, while Jennifer seems like such a normal and nice person. I keep wondering what she ever saw in the jerk that made her want to marry him."

"I ask myself that question all the time," Bailey chuckled low in his throat. "Why hasn't Penny booted me out all these years?"

"I'm sure she knew you were a good person deep down, Sheriff. A man who wants to help people."

"Maybe." She imagined his big shoulders shrugging, the mysteries of love beyond him. "Any-who, after you drove off with Mrs. O'Halloran to the station last night, I dropped Penny off at the house and went back to my office. I knew I wouldn't sleep until I figured out what it was about those two that was troubling me. So, I did a little online investigatin'. Guess what I found."

"I have no idea." She sipped her coffee and sighed, knowing he liked playing guessing games about as much as she hated them.

"Nothin'. Zero. Zilcheroo." He paused a beat.

"I'm not sure what you're trying to say, Sheriff."

"I searched the National Crime Information Center and DMV databases. I couldn't find a match. It's like those two never existed."

She breathed in sharply and nearly choked on a mouthful of coffee. "That's just not possible." Turning her head away from the phone, she coughed and tried to catch her breath. "You're sure you didn't make a mistake when you entered their information? Not everyone has a criminal record but nearly everyone has a driver's license. You must have transposed a number in an address or misspelled their names."

"I may be technologically thick-headed but any idiot can do a simple search on a DMV site. And accessing a criminal record on the FBI's NCIC is easy-peasy."

"Jennifer might have kept her maiden name," Verity argued.

"Then why didn't she correct us all the times we called her Mrs. O'Halloran? She signed her statement: Jennifer O'Halloran. And according to the drivers' licenses I saw, they were O'Hallorans."

Verity put down her suddenly empty mug, puzzled because she couldn't remember drinking the rest of her coffee. "There must be an explanation."

"Of course there is. Obviously, their IDs were fake," he groused. "But I can think of only one reason why the woman would give me fake contact information when she claimed she wanted me to let her know when she could take her husband's body."

Verity considered this. "Maybe she—no offense, Sheriff—doesn't trust you and your deputies to keep her information private. You told her she might still be in danger, and this could be her way of protecting herself."

"Christ a-mighty!" he bellowed, causing her to hurriedly back the cellphone away from her ear. "Are you accusin' my department of leakin' a victim's information?"

"Sorry!" Fearing he was going to hang up on her she rushed on with what she needed to say. "Listen, Sheriff, there may be another reason why she gave you fake information. Just now I told you about the two kids in the linen closet, supposedly playing with things Morgan stole."

"Right." He could make one word sound impatient.

"But didn't your people already search the inn for those missing items?"

"Of course, we did. If anything had been in that closet that shouldn't have been there, we'd have found it," he said defensively.

"So-o-o-o," she thought out loud, "that must mean the stolen items were moved to the closet from another location, after your search." She could almost hear the man's mental gears begin grinding away.

"Ri-i-i-ight," he said.

"Jennifer said she intended to tell you, but it slipped her mind when Rudy was killed."

"Understandable. But you're tryin' to tell me that since the woman's been lyin' to me from the get-go, she might also be fibbin' about the two kids. Like she thought she could frame young Morgan for the thefts?"

She heard a sandpapery scraping sound through the phone. Bailey scratching his unshaven jaw? She let him dwell for a moment on this new, possibly deceptive Jennifer O'Halloran. Or whoever she really was.

"I was with my guys the whole time. I'm sure they searched all the closets." He sighed. "I don't know if this means the thefts might a been connected to the murder or not. What a God-awful mess."

"I know you'll figure it out, Sheriff," she said encouragingly. In a way, she felt as though she'd been part of the problem. She had believed in Jennifer O'Halloran's grief and trusted everything the woman had confided in her. Now, Verity couldn't help wondering if she'd been played.

She startled when the sheriff started speaking again.

"Would a few of your Nancy Drews help with a second search of the inn?"

Verity hated his favorite way of referring to the EPIs. "I'm sure I can arrange for a few volunteers," she said coolly. Admonishing him for making fun of them never seemed to do any good.

"I can't let civilians search occupied guest rooms," he continued. "I'll personally deal with those. But the public areas aren't a problem. I need to know that we're not missing other critical evidence."

"When do you want us to start?"

"Soon's you can. I'll be at the inn within the hour, after I try a few more ways to locate the tricky Mrs. O'Halloran." He made an exasperated sound, a little like a horse's lip snuffle. "I could kick myself for not runnin' ID checks on those two sooner."

"Well, you didn't know then what you know now, so don't be too hard on yourself. I'll gather up my search party and meet you at the inn."

She had meant what she said. It wasn't fair for Bailey to second-guess himself. The thefts had taken place before Rudy O'Halloran was killed, before his wife was attacked. No one had realized back then that anything worse was going to happen than the disappearance of a few valuables from travelers' rooms and some street-salable drugs from a medical office.

No one, that is, except for the one person who held a dark secret back then. They were already intent on murder.

# CHAPTER 28

VERITY PHONED Sunny at the café and explained the sheriff's need for their help.

"I can't leave the café until after closing today. Will seven o'clock tonight do?"

Verity had already guessed this might be a problem for the busy café owner. "Sorry, he's expecting us in less than an hour."

"Oh, dear. Well, at least I can split the EPI's phone list with you. I'll see if Mary Beth and Fumiko are free and tell them to meet you at the inn."

That left Verity to summon Denise, Kate, and Chaundra. She dropped a voice mail on Denise's phone, knowing she would check her calls as soon as she was free of customers at the candy shop.

Kate sounded thrilled with the request. "The girls are in swim camp at the community pool," she reported, cheerfully. "Your timing is perfect. My staff can handle the bookstore and I just need to pick up the girls by five o'clock. Should I wear anything special? Like a black catsuit?"

Verity laughed. "Katie dear, we're searching the inn with

permission of the sheriff in broad daylight. Jeans and t-shirt will do."

"Oh, psshaw! I always wanted to dress up like that actress in To Catch a Thief."

"Another time," Verity promised her.

Chaundra didn't treat their mission like something out of a movie. "This is on the up-and-up. You're sure? We're allowed to do this?"

"Sheriff Bailey's request. His official staff is spread too thin, as always. And he wants to get the search done as quickly as possible."

"Then count me in. Business at the Emporium has been slow today anyway. I think everyone's wallet is a lot thinner after our July Fourth festivities."

Verity's cellphone rang before she could tuck it back into her jeans pocket. "What's up, farmer gal?" Denise shouted into her phone to make herself heard above a loud grinding noise in the background.

Verity explained the situation.

"I'll have my two helpers stay on to serve customers after I finish this batch of fudge. Can't let it cool down before I throw it into pans or it'll be just one huge chocolate rock."

"But a delicious rock, I bet."

"Humph!" Denise said. "You've never had to rescue a batch of botched fudge."

"What kinds did you make today?" Verity couldn't help herself. Her mouth watered at the mere mention of fudge.

"This morning, we made maple-walnut and macadamia-white-chocolate. This batch is double-dark chocolate."

Verity moaned with pleasure. "Name your price for a half pound of each."

Denise laughed. "Unfortunately, the rest of my customers aren't as generous as you, Veri—or I'd be a very wealthy woman.

I'll charge you just the regular price. Deduct it from my next egg delivery and I'll bring you the two flavors that are already cooled and cut."

"Deal."

Within minutes after Verity arrived at the inn, her team had assembled on the inn's veranda behind a curtain of gorgeous red geraniums and hot-pink impatiens in hanging baskets. It turned out that Fumiko was out of town on a buying trip for her yarn shop—which Verity decided was just as well, given her previous interview techniques. But Mary Beth was there in a vivid paisley kaftan, expounding 'expert' tips from her favorite CSI series.

"Listen up, everyone!" Mary Beth announced before Verity could say a thing, "I've taken the liberty of bringing zippy bags— sandwich-, quart-, and gallon-sizes. Any evidence too big to fit in the largest ones, we'll need to inform the sheriff so he can dust for fingerprints *in situ* and safely remove the item from the premises."

Verity drew a breath to speak but Mary Beth rushed on. "And here's a packet of non-latex gloves, size large. Sorry, Kate and Verity, your itty-bitty hands will just need to make do. I can't stuff my elephant paws into anything smaller."

"I didn't know elephants had paws," Denise teased, elbowing Mary Beth.

"Oh, do shut up, Denise." Mary Beth held out the carton for each team member to take two thin blue gloves.

An elderly couple who looked dressed for something special were seated in a porch swing. They stared at the five investigators in their gloves with open curiosity. Verity heard the woman say, "They must be the cleaners. Rooms sure could use a good scrubbing." Verity didn't correct her. The less said to anyone the better.

They found the sheriff on the second floor, pulling stacks of towels and bedding, cleaning products, and vacuum cleaner attachments out of the hallway linen closet.

"Anything?" Verity asked.

"Not yet. One of my guys is strippin' down the third-floor closet, just in case. But so far, nada."

"Sheriff?" called one of the deputies from deep inside the second-floor closet. "You need to see this."

"What's going on?" Mary Beth squealed. "Let me see."

"It's too dark in there to see much of anything." Chaundra was front and center, shoulder to shoulder with Verity. "Looks like the overhead light bulb is burned out."

"Wait!" Mary Beth rummaged through her enormous tapestry tote. "I always carry a hi-intensity torch in my handbag."

"Of course, you do, MB!" Kate giggled. "Doesn't everyone?"

"I bet she keeps yellow crime-scene tape in there, too," Denise whispered.

"Stop it, you two," Verity snapped. She took the flashlight from Mary Beth and stepped into the closet to hand it to Bailey.

"That's better," he said. "Don't know why I didn't think to bring one. What you got there, Dennis-my-boy?"

The deputy dragged a small cardboard box from behind a row of air-freshener spray cans and toilet paper rolls. "I felt something inside there—like a watch, maybe jewelry, too." He set the box down on the closet floor and the sheriff aimed the torch's blinding white beam into it.

"I'll be damned," muttered Bailey.

The deputy pulled a clear baggie from his chest pocket. The sheriff used his gloved hand to drop a man's watch into it.

"Verity," Mary Beth whined, bouncing up and down on her toes, "what's going on? We can't see a thing with you and our favorite Amazon in the way."

Chaundra grinned at the mythical reference to her height and African heritage.

Verity turned away from the closet and herded her investigators farther down the hallway. "Let's give the guys room. We'll know soon enough if they've found anything that has more to do with the thefts or the murder. Meanwhile, we can start searching the parlor."

Minutes later, Bailey looked into the inn's posh parlor and crooked a finger at Verity. She joined him in the hallway.

"I'm sendin' what we found back to the office. We can dust for prints there." He tugged a red bandana from his pocket and swiped at his forehead. "There was also money in the box, but nowhere as much as was reported stolen from the guests' rooms."

"Could the kids have spent some of it?"

"Possibly. Or they might be holdin' onto it elsewhere. I'm gonna have another serious talk with the Denton boy, I can tell you."

"What about the other items reported stolen?" Verity asked.

"Jewelry. Most of what's in the box appears to be cheap costume stuff. I need to ask the people who reported the thefts to identify the items. This is another reason for findin' Mrs. O'Halloran. See if she's somehow involved in this theft and was just tryin' to lay blame on the kid." He frowned. "Just remembered. Two credit cards and an ATM card went missin', too. They aren't in the box."

Denise stepped out of the parlor and straight into their conversation. "I heard one of my customers at the chocolate shop say they are reporting the loss of two rings and a necklace to their insurance broker. People don't insure cheap costume jewelry."

"True." Bailey looked thoughtful. "So maybe the thief left mostly junk behind. Absconded with the good stuff. Mrs. Cade, can you have your Nanc—" she leveled a warning glare at him "—your, um, searchers do the kitchen after you finish with the parlor?"

"I'll be happy to," she said sweetly.

Dealing with Bailey was like training a new puppy that needed constant reminders to not soil the carpet. She wondered how long it would take before he gave the EPIs the respect they deserved.

# CHAPTER 29

"WELL, that was a waste of two hours," Denise complained.

"No, not a waste." Verity re-plumped the cushions on one of the brocade-covered antique loveseats in the room Henry called the library. Although there were only two small shelves of books, and most of these were paperbacks he had picked up at a used bookstore. "We've eliminated possible hiding places for clues and stolen items in the parlor, kitchen and library, and saved Sheriff Bailey and his department time they can use elsewhere."

"I guess," Kate said. "But it's sort of like being invited to a cool scavenger hunt and coming up emptyhanded." She plopped down on a loveseat and made a face. "How did people ever get comfortable on furniture like this? The seats are like concrete slabs!"

"Furniture built in 1860's predated foam rubber," Chaundra said. "If I reupholstered that loveseat, I'd use much softer padding than horsehair. This piece has good bones." She smoothed a hand up the wooden arm, then leaned down to examine the graceful brass claw-and-ball feet. Chaundra was their local expert on all things old.

Verity wondered what might be considered a valuable antique in Chaundra's birth country, Ethiopia. She wished she knew more about African civilizations. She recalled Chaundra once showing her a ceremonial mask and carved wooden deity, saying they were worth thousands. But whether or not they were old, she had no clue.

Out of the corner of her eye she saw Henry descend the stairs to the lobby from the upper floor. Resting over one shoulder, was what looked like a leather bomber pilot's jacket. He carried a red-white-and-blue U.S. Post Office mailing box. She dashed out of the library after him.

"Henry!" He seemed not to have heard her and continued on. She caught up with him in the kitchen. "What are you doing with that jacket?"

"Putting it in the mail." He unceremoniously stuffed it into the box. "One of my guests, uh—" he began awkwardly "—let's just say he left it behind."

She reached into the box before he could close the four flaps and pulled out the jacket. "This looks like the jacket Rudy O'Halloran was wearing in the café the night before he died."

Henry sighed, looking miserable at the mere mention of the man's demise. "His wife called early this morning, if you must know. She asked if I'd found it in their room. I guess she didn't realize she'd left it behind."

"Where are you mailing it to?" Verity asked, a bubble of excitement rising inside her.

He gave her a puzzled look. "To her residence in New York City, of course." He pointed at the postal label he had already filled out.

"Oh?" She read the label. "Is this the same address she gave when she registered at the inn?"

"Actually, no," he said." I guess she's moved."

"Huh." She hadn't seen the addresses Jennifer gave to the

sheriff just before she left town, and so, was unable to compare them. Verity copied the address from the box into her Notes app on her phone but had another thought. She thrust a hand into one of the jacket's front pockets.

Henry flushed and stammered, "What are you doing? That d-doesn't belong to you!" He looked as though he might faint.

"Sheriff's orders," she lied, just a little.

"But...b-but, Mrs. Cade!"

Nothing in either front pocket. She huffed her disappointment.

"What's up?" Kate stepped into the lobby, followed by the other investigators.

"I thought I might have found a clue, but there's nothing. It's just Rudy's jacket, left behind by accident. Both pockets are empty." Verity started to hand the garment back to Henry.

Denise snatched it away. "Hold on!" She flipped open the jacket's lapels. "I had a coat like this once. Look, there's a hidden pocket in the lining." She stuck her fingers down inside. "Something's in here." She pulled out a folded piece of paper.

Verity held out her hand. "Let's see what it says."

"Oh, I really don't think you should," Henry objected nervously. "If the sheriff finds out—"

But she had already opened the little paper square, which she now saw was stationary size, with the inn's logo at the top. As Verity read the words beneath the elaborate letterhead she sucked in a sharp breath. The blood in her veins turned arctic cold.

"What does it say?" Mary Beth cried, hopping up and down and sending her belly jiggling. "Don't just stand there, Verity. Read it to us!"

Verity refolded the note. "I think Henry's right. We shouldn't be doing this. Unfortunately, both the jacket and the note need to go directly to the sheriff." She could hear her voice trembling, pitched an octave too high. But she was unable to control it. Her hands shook, making it hard to tuck the little piece of paper into her jeans pocket. *I'm probably destroying every single fingerprint*, she thought, frustrated that she hadn't considered being more cautious a moment earlier.

Henry cast his carefully prepared mailing box an exasperated look, threw up his hands and stomped out of the room.

"Verity?" Kate moved up beside her. "You don't look too good. You okay, hon?"

"If that note has anything to do with our investigation," Denise said in a much less sympathetic tone, "we deserve to know what it says."

Verity hesitated.

Denise squinted at her. "C'mon, Verity. Fair is fair. You wouldn't have found that note and whatever it says if it weren't for me."

*She's right*, Verity thought. But she couldn't very well divulge the contents of the note to Denise without sharing it with the others.

"OK, but then it's going straight to the sheriff." *Even if what it says destroys the life of one of the nicest people I know.*

She sucked down a shaky breath and read it to them. "It says: 'This ain't over yet, O'Halloran. Meet me in the alley.'"

"O-M-G!" Mary Beth squealed. "That must be how the killer lured Rudy outside, behind the inn."

"It's as good as a confession," Kate said, blinking excitedly. "If it's signed, that is."

Stealing a trick from child-prodigy pickpocket, Morgan Denton, Denise pinched the note with two fingers from Verity's pocket and flipped it open. The candymaker's eyes saucered. "Oh, no," she breathed, staring at Verity. "It *is* signed—*Jason*." She looked around at the others. "Do we really need to show this to the sheriff?"

"We do," Verity said, her heart already in pieces. She gulped. "We don't have a choice. It's evidence."

Verity turned toward the stairs to the upper floors. Above, she could hear the sheriff and his deputies searching guests' rooms.

"No, no...no! Listen, it could be another Jason, couldn't it?" Kate was, all of a sudden, crying and hiccupping at the same time. The young mother was only a few years older than the twins and had always been particularly close to the two young men. She chased up the stairs after Verity.

"Katie," Mary Beth shouted after her, "of course it's him. Jason and Mr. Rude Rudy were *fighting* in the café. Everyone knows that. There must have been like a hundred witnesses."

*More like forty*, Verity thought. But even just four would be too many for a jury to dismiss. Verity felt her eyes burn at the thought of a trial. People were bound to view the note as damning evidence.

She tried to tune out the frantic chatter of her friends on the stairs behind her. Her heart drummed an erratic rhythm as she climbed the long, curving stairway. Her hands slick with sweat. Her mouth tasting like battery acid. She told herself that Jason's note could just have been intended to wind up O'Halloran. Just an empty dare.

Jason and Jerry—her protectors. Such fine people. The two young men were the only family she had in Vermont—at least among the living. Surely Jason wasn't capable of killing anyone!

More than anything in the world, she wished she could put a match to the horrid letter.

Then, an even worse thought oozed through the sticky mire of her mind. What if it actually *was* Jason who faced off with Rudy in the alley...but he wasn't alone? What if Jerry accompanied his brother that night, and the two of them confronted O'Halloran.

*Don't even go there!*

Of the twins, Jerry was the saner, more rational. Surely, if he had realized what Jason intended to do, he would have tried to talk him out of challenging Rudy. Whoever had attacked that horrid man, it surely must have been someone else. Someone who knew about the note and used it to cover his own crime, knowing Jason would be blamed.

Now she could hear the sheriff snapping orders at his men from just above her. Her body moved up the staircase of its own volition. Her perspective felt oddly contorted, as if she were floating somewhere above her own body, looking down on herself. She sensed her friends still on the stairs below her.

The sheriff and two of his deputies turned toward her as she stepped up onto the landing and then moved into the room. Bailey's expression changed from business-as-usual to wary, as soon as he saw her face. She thrust out the note, the paper jittering between her fingertips.

Bailey frowned. "You alright, Mrs. Cade?" He took in the other women standing close behind her. "Ladies, what's up?"

"Take the goddamn note!" Denise snapped. "Can't you see this is killing her?"

The sheriff's eyes hardened. "I don't know what this is all about but..." He reached out and removed the white square from Verity's outstretched fingers.

Her arm dropped limply to her side. She didn't wait for him to read what it said. She knew what he'd need to do. Her friends parted on the landing to let her pass. She clomped in misery down the inn's stairs.

From the room above she heard Denise ask, "What are you going to do, Sheriff?"

"Only thing I can do—arrest the boy," came Bailey's abrupt answer. Followed by a burst of angry protests from her friends.

Verity crossed the inn's foyer and flung herself out through the front door. She envisioned herself jumping into her truck and trying to beat the sheriff and his men to her farm. She'd warn Jason. Tell him to run! But wouldn't that make him appear all the more guilty?

She still didn't want to believe he had intentionally killed O'Halloran. Maybe there was another explanation. Jason had lured the man to the alley intending to give him a piece of his mind, but things got out of hand. The two men fought and Rudy was badly injured. Jason panicked and left his opponent on the ground and bloodied, not realizing he'd been badly hurt and was dying. Or was already dead.

She bolted for her truck, climbed in but didn't start the engine.

*Coward!* she berated herself as her heart ached at the thought of what she'd just done.

She couldn't go home now. Couldn't bear to watch Jason being taken away in handcuffs.

Feeling numb, her legs as wooden as fenceposts, she climbed down from the driver's seat and hobbled back across the street and into the Cat's Cradle, the only place she knew she could count on for comfort.

# CHAPTER 30

THE CHEERFUL ATMOSPHERE of the café felt like an annoying intrusion on Verity's morose thoughts. She stalked across the dining area—nearly empty at this between-mealtime hour—to the window-table favored by the Evansfield private investigators. She dropped into the first chair she came to, jammed elbows down on the tabletop and buried her face in her palms.

The cocoon of her hands was soothing. If she stayed here in the darkness long enough, maybe the whole horrible mess would go away.

"Am I allowed to ask what's going on?" a gentle voice came to her from close by. *Sunny. Of course it was her. Sunny the healer, the calm and logical one of us.*

"N-not. Just. Yet." Her throat felt raw. She pressed the heels of her hands into her burning eyes.

The café's bell tinkled. Hushed voices approached, talking among themselves. No one said a word to her, as if they knew she'd shatter like fragile crystal at a soprano's high C.

"Mary Beth," Sunny said, "in your simplest wording, will

you tell me why our friend here looks as if someone died? Has someone died?"

"I'll explain," Kate volunteered.

"No. I'll do it," Mary Beth claimed the honor for herself. For there was little Mary Beth liked better than talking about law enforcement. She cleared her throat. "We found an incriminating note—"

"I found it," Denise corrected her. "In the pocket of a coat that belonged to Rudy O'Halloran."

"I. Am. *Talking*," Mary Beth announced forcefully. "The note said something that might be construed as a challenge to O'Halloran, asking him to meet the writer in the alley."

"Might be *construed*?" Denise bellowed, causing Verity to finally drop her hands and look up. "It said *exactly* that, Mary Beth. It also said the writer would beat the crap out of Rudy. Well, not in so many words, but it implied as much. And it was signed—"

"—by Jason Grimalski!" Verity admitted wearily.

She noticed that the few customers who had been there minutes earlier had left, leaving only the EPI members in the dining area. Sunny's staff must have retreated to the kitchen; she could hear the clanking of pans and murmur of voices from beyond the beaded curtain.

Sunny waved the investigators not already seated into chairs before leaning over Verity. "Sweetie, this can't be right. Honestly, Jason? Are you going to show the sheriff this note?"

"She already has," Chaundra said. "We couldn't very well keep it from him."

"No, I suppose not. So, what did Sheriff Bailey say?" Sunny asked.

Verity shook her head. Her throat had closed up, making speech impossible.

"He and his deputies have gone off to the Cade farm to

arrest Jason," Denise explained in the softest voice Verity had ever heard her use.

"It's just awful." Kate sniffled. "The poor guy."

"Justice can be a cruel mistress," Mary Beth intoned philosophically.

"Oh, please, MB!" Denise snarled, back to her old self.

Sunny looked into Verity's eyes and squeezed her hands. "You can't blame yourself or protect Jason. I know how close you feel to those two young men. But if Jason had anything to do with that man's death, even if he didn't intend to kill him—he needs to explain exactly what happened. And the sheriff must do his job."

"My first instinct was to call Jason to warn him," Chaundra confessed, echoing Verity's earlier desperate thoughts. "Then I realized I didn't have his phone number."

Mary Beth's eyes brightened. "That would be aiding and abetting a felony."

Denise's entire face turned a virulent crimson. "One more word, MB, and I swear I'll—"

Sunny smacked the flat of her hand down on the tabletop. "Stop it, you two! Let's use our energy to think through this situation and see if we can come up with a way to help Jason. I can't honestly believe he did this."

Verity wiped at her nose. She hadn't been aware it was dripping. "Then you think this started with an empty threat?"

"Or some version of a taunt. Jason trying to get the guy's goat. Toying with him. Maybe." Sunny stared into the distance, miles away. "What if someone knew that Jason wrote to O'Halloran and took advantage of the note's incriminating wording for their own purpose?" Which matched one of Verity's theories.

"Like, someone framed Jason?" Kate whispered. She clutched a balled-up napkin. "But who would have seen the note other than Rudy?"

"The only person I can imagine Rudy showing a note like that to, other than his wife," Chaundra said, "would be the sheriff. The man doesn't sound like the kind of person to keep complaints to himself."

"I don't know." Verity pictured the scene in the café when O'Halloran had ranted at her and Sunny, then dared Jason to come at him. It seemed like ages ago. "I think O'Halloran was getting off on the outrageous scene he was making in town, hoping for a fight."

"Agreed," Sonny said. "I was sure he wanted to thrash poor Jason just for the fun of it in the café. The man was a nasty piece of work. Dangerous."

"Probably beat his wife," Denise muttered under her breath.

"I didn't see any evidence of that," Verity said.

Kate frowned. "I wasn't at the café that day, but if he was as awful as people are saying, how could she have married him?"

"Women don't always know what they're getting into when they hook up with a guy," Denise said.

Verity looked at the chocolatier. Was there something of a personal nature in that statement? But Denise being Denise, Verity was sure she would stand up for herself or walk out on any man who didn't treat her right. Jennifer O'Halloran was a very different sort of woman. A softspoken, fragile-appearing person, she seemed more likely to avoid provoking her husband than defy him.

"She must really have loved him." Mary Beth gazed dreamily into the distance. "To overlook his faults, I mean. Most people don't know it, but the mayor has faults, too. He doesn't always appreciate the time and effort I put into baking for him. Just yesterday, I made his favorite four-layer fudge cake and—"

"It's not the same thing, MB," Sunny interrupted gently. "Let's get back to our Jason. Is there anyone other than Jason who might have had a bone to pick with O'Halloran?"

"A man like that would have collected lots of enemies," Denise said.

"And it's going to include people who aren't locals," Chaundra added. "Folks we don't even know about. I guess we could call his wife and ask."

Verity shook her head. "We can't. The sheriff tried the numbers she gave him, and they aren't hers. He has no way to contact her."

"That's strange," Sunny mused. "If I had a husband and he was murdered, I'd be all over the police to find his killer. I'd demand hourly reports!"

"She may just be frightened," Verity said. "After the assault on July Fourth, she admitted she couldn't get out of Vermont fast enough."

Sunny shook her head. "Poor thing. I'm sure her opinion of our town's law enforcement, isn't exactly glowing."

"I drove her to the train station last night and we talked a bit," Verity said. "I got the impression she believes that someone here is responsible for her husband's death, and that same person attacked her. If that's so, then going into hiding sort of makes sense."

"It actually does," Sunny agreed. "Ok, so we won't get any help from her. But we still need to do something to help Jason." She turned to Verity. "The note you gave the sheriff. Could someone have forged it, putting Jason's name on it?"

Verity shrugged. "I don't know. Who would do such a thing? Everyone in town loves Jason. And no one among Ervin's tourists, other than Rudy, had any connection with Jason. There's just no motive for trying to frame him."

"I like Chaundra's idea," Mary Beth said. "Someone from O'Halloran's past could have driven into town in the dead of night and attacked him. Without anyone ever realizing they'd been here."

Everyone looked at her. For once, she was making sense.

"But how would this outsider know about the note?" Verity said. "That is, if Jason actually wrote it. And if the outsider forged it, how would a stranger have known to sign it with Jason's name? Wouldn't this person need to have witnessed Rudy and Jason's verbal sparring at the café?" She shook her head. The pieces to the puzzle of the tourist's murder still refused to fall into place. In fact, not one clue had turned up that might help them prove Jason Grimalski's innocence.

The café fell silent for long minutes.

"Here's another thought," Denise suggested. She looked at Verity. "Do we know for sure that the person who killed Rudy and whoever attacked Jennifer are the same person?"

"No," Verity said. "And that has bothered me for some time. I can't imagine Jason assaulting a woman."

"If Jason had an alibi for both nights, we could all stop worrying." Mary Beth glanced at the pastry display case, on the far side of the room. Everyone knew that her ability to think without benefit of sugar was measured in minutes not hours. "Then the sheriff wouldn't have grounds to continue holding him."

"Good thinking, MB." Verity felt a fragile thrill at the thought, butterfly wings of hope. "His brother Jerry still lives at home with their parents. But Jason has his own apartment now. He doesn't seem to have an alibi for when Rudy was killed. But on the night someone jumped Jennifer, Jason took a date to the fireworks. If she gives him an alibi for the whole night, he couldn't have attacked Jennifer."

"Still doesn't eliminate him from suspicion for the murder." Mary Beth looked around the room at the unhappy faces. "Just sayin'."

"Even if we can't absolutely prove Jason's innocence, I think we need to somehow show our support for him," Verity stated.

"I'll ask the sheriff if we can visit him at the jail. Maybe bring him something to eat."

"Oh, that's easy." Sunny smiled. "I supply breakfast, lunch, and dinner for the prisoners—when there are any. We can take turns bringing his meals to him."

"They might move him over to the county lock-up," Denise said.

"We'll hope not," Verity shook her head, feeling emotionally drained. She didn't want to think about what Jason's parents must be feeling. By now, they'd have heard he'd been arrested. Jerry certainly would have told them.

"I'm sure the sheriff will find the real killer soon," Kate murmured. "I mean, he's got to, right? Our Jason isn't a killer."

Verity closed her eyes, cradling that precious thought in her heart. Justice would prevail. Since Jason was a good person, he would be proven innocent. But she feared the many ways in which the situation could turn out badly.

# CHAPTER 31

SHE RETURNED HOME to find Jerry running the mower around her front lawn with a grim set to his mouth, daggers in his eyes. As if every blade of grass was the enemy. She wanted to talk to him about his brother, reassure him that all would be well. But his body language telegraphed his need to be left alone, and so she threw herself into her own chores.

After gathering eggs, she siphoned off four gallons of raw milk from the collection tank for making butter. Molly glared at her over the top rail of the pasture's fence as Verity walked back toward the house. Some people—well, everyone she knew—maintained that cows didn't have personalities. But Molly had a way of letting her know when she wasn't pleased. Those soulful, chocolate-brown eyes drilled unrelentingly into her.

"Been waiting long, Molly-Moo?" Verity called out to her. "Patience. I'll be there soon."

The cow watched her walk across the yard carrying the heavy milk pails. Molly looked even more perturbed when Verity reappeared from the house, only to veer away from the paddock in the direction of the kitchen garden. The day before, Verity had discovered a nasty infestation of tiny black thrips sucking the life out of her bean vines. Now, she spent half an hour spraying the plants with horticultural soap—a safe alternative to harsher solutions—to kill the little bugs.

Her neighbor, Carl Claiborne, had advised her, "Just shake a good snowstorm of Sevin on them; it'll kill anything." Which was true. But she knew the chemical would also kill the 'good bugs' and possibly the birds that ate the poisoned insects. She tried to stick with organic solutions, even though this often meant more time spent repeating the applications.

Verity returned her equipment to the back porch. "Alright, Molly, it's your turn now."

The cow seemed to understand and immediately ambled down the gentle slope behind the old milking parlor. She seemed to prefer the privacy and quiet of this subterranean level of the barn while Verity milked her the old-fashioned way, by hand. Although the Robo-Milkers weren't noisy, at least to Verity's ears, they constantly hummed and made other mechanical sounds that seemed to spook the sensitive Molly. This dim, earthy-smelling space was also Verity's favorite place to think about particularly horny problems.

Like murder.

She never needed to tie the animal to hold her still. Molly set down her hooves as if plunging them into quick-dry cement. She wouldn't budge an inch until Verity signaled her with a friendly pat on her buff-colored rump that they were done.

Verity pulled over the milking stool and a clean bucket. She wiped down the cow's udder with disinfectant and began the rhythmic motions with her hands, drawing down the cow's creamy white milk from her teats into the bucket. She always kept Molly's milk for herself. It just seemed special to her, a gift from her prima donna. Although, she had to admit that it probably tasted no different than the rest of her herd's milk before it was sent off to the co-op for pasteurization. She preferred the rich, buttery flavor of raw, whole milk to the rather flat taste of processed.

As she milked, Verity hummed to herself. Long ago, she had decided that Molly enjoyed a little musical accompaniment. Occasionally the cow released a contented 'hu-umph-ph' down deep in her throat. But mostly she just chewed her cud and bobbed her big tan-and-white bovine head.

Verity considered calling Sheriff Bailey to ask if she could talk with Jason. Maybe bring him reading materials, a soft quilt or pillow, anything to make him more comfortable in his cell. How long would it be before he could get out on bail?

She was sure his spirits must be low.

Sunny undoubtedly knew what Jason liked to eat and would provide some of his favorite meals. She wondered if the Grimalski parents had already spoken with the sheriff or Jason. Maybe Jerry would know—if she dared ask him. Did Jason have a lawyer yet? Or would he think he didn't need one?

Someone should tell him that he definitely needed a lawyer!

She hoped he didn't assume he could just laugh off that incriminating note. She still believed he was innocent. Rudy's murder might, on the surface, seem like the logical follow-up to their row in the café, taken to a more violent level. But if the assault on Rudy's wife had been carried out by the same person —then Verity knew without a smidgeon of doubt that Rudy's killer couldn't possibly be Jason. He was not now, and never could be, an abuser of women. Surely the sheriff must realize that!

"Done, Molly," she said softly, after again cleansing the cow's teats. She tapped the cow on her soft flank. Molly answered with a low appreciative moan. "You're welcome," Verity said.

She carried the bucket of frothy, warm milk into the house, looking around for Jerry as she walked. The roar of the lawnmower had stopped. Jerry was nowhere in sight; his truck was gone. Leaving for the day without telling her wasn't like him. She felt stung by his silent message: *you're the enemy*.

She wished now that she had spoken to him earlier, even if it meant becoming a convenient target for his anger. Did he really blame her for his brother's arrest? Did he think she could have said or done something to convince the sheriff that Jason wasn't involved in Rudy's death?

It didn't seem fair!

She had no influence over the law or the facts of the murder investigation as they now knew them. *That damn letter*! Of course it made Jason the prime suspect. And she couldn't prove that Jason hadn't fought with O'Halloran in the alley. All she had to offer her farmhand was a character reference. He was honest, hardworking, polite, and kind to her animals. What good would that do him in a courtroom? If convicted of the man's murder, the young man might well spend the rest of his life in prison.

She tried to push from her mind the darkest of these thoughts. But they relentlessly returned.

Back in her country kitchen with its blue-tile floor and perpetually sunny yellow walls, she poured Molly's milk through a fine sieve then into a jug to be refrigerated. She saved out a glass of milk for herself to drink with the last two chewy oatmeal-raisin cookies from her cookie jar.

Verity was rinsing out her glass in the sink when she heard an odd crackling sound, like static electricity only much louder. When she turned around, a pale, flickering image of Percy, in full dress uniform, appeared. The air around him snapped with bright blue electrical charges.

"Percy, oh my God, what's wrong? I didn't know your visibility problems were this bad."

"I th-thought...same...don't know." His voice alternately cut out and screeched as if coming to her through a malfunctioning microphone. "Have you see-see-seen A-anna Louise?"

"Why no. I haven't seen either of you since—" she had to think for a minute. "Not since you told me about the bus driver's conversation with Jennifer O'Halloran."

The ghost peered around the room but his eyes seemed unfocused, as though he wasn't actually seeing his surroundings, or her.

"Tell me what's going on." She had a horrible feeling. Was she losing them forever? Was this how it would end? A slow disconnect with the living world as the two ghosts transitioned to whatever awaited them after death?

"That's the problem." His voice had a tinny echo, reaching her as if from a great distance although he stood no more than three feet from her. "Nothing happened. We were together at the café. Anna Louise and I. Collecting evidence, as you...ask... asked...asked us to do."

Which was to say that the couple had been doing what they always did for entertainment—eavesdropping on the unsuspecting living. If the circumstances had been less dire, she would have laughed.

He continued. "My darling br-r-ride started fading. She gave me a strange look. Told me-me-me I was diminishing, too."

"Just like at the fireworks display?" Verity said.

"Worse, much worse. We ducked out the ba-ack-ack door of the café." His voice kept cutting in and out, sounding like a bad old-time radio broadcast.

"Did anyone see you?"

"No. Don't think so." His voice seemed steadier now. "But by the time we reached the alley, Anna Louise had nearly disappeared. She was so very frightened—shaking and weeping. I tried to comfort her."

Verity's legs felt suddenly rubbery. She steadied herself

against her table for a moment then dropped down into a chair. "Where is she now, Percy?"

"I don't know!" he groaned. "She suddenly was no longer in my arms. I hoped she came back here, to the house."

"No." Verity swallowed over the golf ball-size lump. The back of her throat tasted like sour milk. "Oh, Percy, I'm so sorry. I haven't seen her. Are you absolutely sure she didn't intentionally disappear? You know how she likes playing tricks."

His image momentarily brightened at that thought, but just as quickly dimmed again. "She would never intentionally frighten me. She knows how desperate I would be if I believed I'd lost her."

"Yes," Verity nodded her head emphatically, "I believe she would know." Anna Louise was terrified after learning they had been seen at the fireworks. "Is there any way you can think of to locate her?"

"Not if she has already passed over," he said wretchedly.

As a child attending Sunday school classes at her parents' church, Verity had been taught that there were no more worries in heaven. All was bliss. She could be assured of a reunion with those she loved who had passed on before her. And perhaps that was true. But what if it wasn't? What if those promised reunions never happened? Percy and Anna Louise had been inseparable in life and so much in love. If any couple deserved to be reunited after death, it should be them.

"Listen, Percy, you're still here." She studied his shade, which was even less substantial than it had been two minutes ago. "She still might come back. Perhaps this is just a temporary relapse. Sort of—" she searched for a comparison "—like the electrical short circuit you described to me the other day. Let's not panic yet. We need to find a way to stabilize the two of you. That is—" she hesitated "—if you *want* to stay in this world."

"I never thought we had a choice in the matter," he admitted. "But if we do, I believe that is what my Anna Louise wants. To be here with me. And with you." He smiled a little.

Percy's words warmed her heart. "I'm flattered. Still, it is natural to die and leave this physical world. Everyone does, eventually."

"Yes but—" His eyes, though fading now to the faintest blue, twinkled with tiny iridescent sparks. "I have an idea. We've never found out how or why we died. Maybe the reason we're still here is because it wasn't our time to go. That's what has held us here."

"But for over one hundred fifty years?" She shook her head. "That doesn't make sense. Unless..."

He looked at her with anticipation. "Yes?"

"Unless whoever is in charge of such things has simply lost track of the two of you. What I mean is—you kind of slipped through heaven's cracks."

He gave her a wry half-smile. "I don't think the Almighty loses track of souls."

"Assistant to the Almighty? An incompetent angel?" Percy didn't seem to take that possibility seriously either. "Well, it's the best I've got," she sighed.

"What should I do?" he pleaded.

She thought for a moment but didn't have a clue. For the time being, all she could do was try to keep him calm until they came up with a plan. "Wait here at the farm," she said. "If Anna Louise is able to return to the world of the living from wherever she is, this is the obvious place she'll look for you."

He stared at the square tiles beneath his officer's black boots, the picture of misery. "What if I've lost her forever, Miss Verity?"

"Oh, Percy. I would miss her, too. A lot. Although not as much as you would, I'm sure."

What remained of his image wavered, then dwindled to no

more than blue mist. Only his sword and medals seemed more solid. Perhaps because they reflected the light from the kitchen's overhead lights.

Verity wished she could reach out and give him a hug but sensed that might make things worse. Touching what remained of his fragile image might cause it to vanish entirely. "I've just had an idea," she murmured.

"A way to reach her?"

"Not quite. But something that might help. For the moment, I think we need to concentrate on controlling *your* visibility. If we can stabilize you, we may discover a way to bring back Anna Louise."

He frowned. "But that will take time. We may be too late to reverse her shade's disappearance." That didn't sound good at all.

"Ok, so it's a risk. But let's try to look on the bright side. Isn't anything worth a try?"

His blue-gray haze seemed to draw a shuddering breath as if agreeing with her.

# CHAPTER 32

JERRY GRIMALSKI TURNED his brother's truck into her driveway just as Verity was walking back across her yard toward the farmhouse. She felt a mood-lifting surge of relief. With time to think things over, he must have realized she was his brother's ally, not their enemy. She approached the driver's side of the vehicle with a tentative smile.

Jerry did not return it. "I came for our week's wages," he said. "Jason can't pick up his own since he's in f-ing jail!"

She stopped short of the truck's door, her face burning at his accusing tone. "Oh. Alright." Apparently, she alone was to blame for his brother's arrest. Never mind the provocative note Jason wrote. Never mind his threatening the man in the middle of a crowded café. "Jerry, I just want to say how very sorry I—"

"Just give me our pay. Please." He looked away from her.

She turned toward the house. What on earth would she do if both young men left her employ? Instantly, she felt a twinge of guilt for even thinking about her own problems. But the fact remained, not many locals wanted to labor on someone else's land. She was sure the pair had stayed with her only because of their continuing loyalty to Mark. Their father certainly could have used their help on his own land.

Standing at the old rolltop desk in her living room, she wrote two checks then brought them out to Jerry. He hadn't left the driver's seat; the engine was still running.

"Thank you, Jerry. I hope you and your brother know how deeply I appreciate your working for me." She passed the checks through the open window. "I absolutely believe Jason is innocent," she quickly added. "I'm sure the sheriff will become just as convinced very soon. He'll get to the bottom of this, please don't worry."

He looked at her as if he knew she was sugarcoating the situation. In reality, she had no idea when, how, or if Bailey would find Rudy's murderer. And there was one more thing.

Although she steadfastly refused to believe that Jason had intended to kill Rudy that night, there remained the possibility that, in a moment of reckless rage or purely by accident, he had ended the man's life. Either way, Jason Grimalski would be tried for the man's murder.

With a heavy heart, she watched Jerry drive away.

Verity made herself a glass of iced tea and brought it out to her front porch. Sadness weighed her down, making every step feel like work. Fear for Jason's fate, and for his family, destroyed any chance of productive action or thought.

Whenever she was stressed or mired in misery, she craved sugar. Today, she longed for one of Sunny's butterscotch brownies to go with her tea. The dough of butter, brown sugar and fresh eggs guaranteed a moist, chewy bar cookie. Sunny always added walnuts to the dough and a dash of maple syrup, making the treat special. Verity only ever bought one bar at a time, knowing she would devour as many as she brought home, often at one sitting.

She rocked on the porch swing, her hands curled around the

icy-cold glass. Since there seemed to be nothing she could do for Jason at the moment, she tried to focus on ways to resolve Percy and Anna Louise's problem. But where did one go for information about technical issues in the afterlife?

There were two churches in Evansfield. She could talk to Father Coyne at the Catholic Church or Tom Sanders, pastor at the Congregationalist Church. But how to explain *why* she needed their advice? "My resident ghosts have lost control of their corporeal selves." *Right, Verity. Like they won't pack you off for psychiatric evaluation.*

Maybe she could find something in the library about spirits that have lingered in the earthly world. But even if such a book existed, it would take her forever to hunt it down. Combing through magazines, journals, and newspaper articles also might take months. Carolyn Hurt, the head librarian, would know where to look. The woman's natural curiosity about virtually everything made her a research marvel. Still, offering a reasonable explanation for why she needed the information was impossible.

No. The safest way to research the problem was to do it on the Internet. The chance of anyone checking the browsing history on her home computer was unlikely.

Verity spent over two hours on her laptop. She Googled every possible combination of words that might generate the information she needed. She came up with an intriguing list of titles for articles and books:

*Ghosts and Their Ability to Appear to the Living*
*Verified Hauntings: 1950–2000*
*Stuck Between Heaven and Hell: A Soul's True Story*
*Séances: Bringing Back the Dead*
*Reincarnation for You and Me*
*Good Ghosts, Bad Ghouls*
*Spooks the World Over*

This last book on her list, she discovered, was actually about clandestine operations and international espionage.

Much of what had been written about ghosts, hauntings, and the afterlife sounded like the product of highly imaginative minds. There seemed little real proof that spirits walked among the living. And yet, she was darn sure she hadn't invented Anna Louise and Percy Putnam. They were as real to her as any of her living neighbors.

What she really needed was information tailored to her own ghosts' specific problem. *What sorts of research do writers do, when reading what other writers write won't do?* She chuckled at her silly tongue twister.

Moments later, the answer came to her: *Letters!*

Authors of historical fiction consulted anything written by real people of the era—artists, scientists, clergy, the wealthy and the poor, the educated and self-taught, celebrities and ordinary folk.

She had read an editorial in the Rutland Herald calling letter writing a lost art. People today texted, emailed, Instagrammed, or Facebooked—but few wrote paper-and-pen letters these days.

Then another thought occurred to her that set her heart to racing.

On the second floor of the farmhouse, connected by a rear flight of stairs leading up from the mudroom, was an addition to the original house that had been closed off from the rest of the house for years. She had investigated the room only once, while Mark was alive. The wing spanned the width of one end of the house and was twice as large as any of the other three bedrooms. Mark told her it had been added on before his grandparents' time, when farming families often produced large families. More hands to accomplish the hard labor of farming. His parents and grandparents used it rarely, to accommodate transient fieldhands and visiting relations.

She recalled seeing iron bedsteads without mattresses and an old chifforobe along with trunks and one or two small chests of drawers. There also had been knee-high piles of dusty books and stacks of cardboard boxes with God-knew-what in them. She remembered pulling open a carton of letters and jerking back at the stench of mildew.

It occurred to her that the Putnam family had been in residence at the farmhouse since before the American Civil War. So, at least some of the stored correspondence might be theirs. Anna Louise and Percy had met with their deaths—when? She couldn't recall exactly what Percy told her. But based on what she knew of their courting and marriage, their demise must have occurred sometime during the 1870's.

It occurred to her that, after their deaths, they might have revealed themselves to other living people, just like her. If that was true, the observers might have written about seeing them. Percy said their visibility issue happened once before, a long time ago. That was where she might find a clue to resolving their problem.

She made herself a sandwich for supper—creamy tuna salad and leaves of buttercrunch lettuce from her kitchen garden on Sunny's crusty sourdough bread. Yum! She brought the sandwich on a plate upstairs with her. Having found the key she had used on her earlier expedition, she unlocked the door to the abandoned room.

Verity wrinkled her nose at the first whiff of stale air. Vaguely musty with a hint of—euuuwww!—*dead* something. She didn't remember it smelling this bad when she'd been up here before. Perhaps a rodent or bird had gotten inside and died. She threw open windows on both ends of the room to air it out. A cooling breeze wafted through. She pulled a few cardboard boxes into the middle of the room and sat down on the floor with her lunch. Using a napkin to hold her sandwich and avoid contaminating it with dusty fingertips, she ate while sorting through their contents.

Before long, her sandwich was gone and she had become mesmerized by the wealth of material she was finding. Postcards and photographs from across the country, as well as exotic foreign locales. Sepia and water-color prints of locations revealed where people had traveled. Letters, crisp and yellow with age, were sent to the farmhouse from nearby towns. One stack of messages bound in a blue ribbon had come from France, during World War I. Another bundle arrived from England during World War II. She gasped at each new discovery in this treasure-trove of history.

Verity dug into yet another box, so tattered and water-stained the cardboard was falling apart. Her hands closed around an old cigar box. She held it to her nose; it still smelled of spicy, sweet tobacco. Inside were the cherished letters from a Civil War soldier to his mother. It took her a moment to realize that the soldier was Percy Putnam.

She felt drunk on his descriptions of another century, lost in the young officer's words. Traveling just a hundred miles in the mid-nineteenth century must have been like entering another world, another culture. The young Vermont farmer marching through Tennessee, North Carolina, and eventually into West Virginia, encountered geography, plants, insects, people, and places that he described to his mother back home. She sensed that these colorful observations were his way of staying connected with her while avoiding the bloody details of the battles in which he was engaged.

After she finished reading Percy's letters, she found remnants of more recent lives at the farm. A book of receipts for the farm's expenses, invitations to parties, wedding announcements, and more letters. Verity glanced up at the window that overlooked her kitchen garden and was surprised to find it had grown dark outside.

She reluctantly forced herself to stop reading every scrap of paper, every ledger entry she came across. She needed to focus on finding correspondence related solely to Percy and Anna Louise. What she wouldn't give to find their death certificates! Then she might discover how they'd died, and a clue to why their spirits lingered in the twenty-first century.

Verity sat on the floor, surrounded by paper trails of dozens of lives. Exhausted, her eyes burning, she gave up. A part of her felt guilty for spending time on her ghosts' problems while Jason languished in jail. Shouldn't she be concentrating on proving his innocence? Only as she was stuffing the last of the letters back into a box did she notice the delicate script of a female hand on faded-pink stationary. The letter was written by a woman in New Hampshire to her sister, here in Evansfield.

It was dated December 30, 1919. The writer referred to a recent Christmas visit to her family at the Vermont farm—Verity's farm. She thanked her younger sister for the lovely holiday but asked not to be given the "back bedroom" on future visits.

She wrote: "As I slept one night, I felt a presence in the room and awoke to see a beautiful woman with golden curls standing beside my bed. So alarmed was I, my throat went dry as sand and I was unable to cry out." The visiting sister went on to explain that she said nothing about the apparition to anyone the next morning, fearing the rest of the family would think she had gone mad. But then she added: "And yet, dear sister, I swear to you, the creature was real."

Her fingers trembling, Verity read on, eager to learn more. The mysterious woman wore a long full-skirted lavender gown and held in dainty gloved hands a reticule and fan; the description could easily have been of Anna Louise. Near the end of the letter, Verity found what she had been looking for.

In a postscript, the writer added: "Please, do not tell Ma or Pa about my experience. You know how they fuss over me. I believe this specter never meant to harm me. I swear to you, dear sister, that ethereal being looked just as shocked as I was when she realized I was able to see her!"

Could this be the incident Percy referred to when he and his wife lost control of their abilities so long ago?

Verity snatched up more letters from the same box, taking them with her back to her bedroom to read. But her eyes burned fiercely and she was covered in dust. Lacking the energy to drag herself into the bathroom for a shower, she stepped out of her jeans and pulled off her t-shirt. Sleeping in her underwear would have to do. She'd wash herself and her sheets in the morning.

Her aching muscles began to unknot as she sank into the soft bedding. Minutes of pure bliss passed. She was nearly asleep when she heard a sound that made her go rigid.

Rapid scratching sounds came from somewhere inside the house. Bolting upright in bed, she listened, trying to remember if she'd locked up before coming upstairs earlier that evening. She thought she had. Then again...maybe not. A ribbon of fear wriggled through her.

Throwing off the light patchwork quilt, she snatched her dusty jeans and t-shirt from the floor. Pulled them on and slipped her cellphone into her hip pocket, just in case someone, or some*thing* had broken in. After all, living in an already haunted house, one couldn't discount the possibility of new, less-friendly spooks invading her home.

Downstairs, she checked the front door. Locked. A barefoot dash through her front parlor, the living room and dining room and kitchen reassured her that all windows were properly shut and latched. On summer nights, she left only her bedroom windows open to catch the cool night breeze and pungent scents of pine, creek, and mown hay.

She stood at alert in her dark kitchen, breathing hard. The strange sounds she'd heard from her bedroom seemed to have stopped. But she still didn't feel safe.

She hesitated to return to her bed. *Might as well finish the job!* Last stop, the mudroom.

No sooner had she set foot on the top step leading down from the kitchen than her back door rattled loudly in its frame. Harsh scraping sounds chilled her.

Someone outside her door was determined to get into her house. Oddly, they didn't seem to care how much noise they made.

She reached to her right for the iron shovel. Holding her breath, she stepped gingerly across the raw planks of the mudroom while trying to identify the intruder. Not a wall-penetrating ghost, obviously. Surely, a burglar would be cagier about gaining entry. If a raccoon, fox, or something even bigger had crawled out of the woods, it would eventually give up and go away. Animals weren't stupid. They didn't waste energy when easier sources of food were available.

But the clamor renewed with even more determination. Now the intruder was digging urgently at the very bottom of the wooden door panel, as if it believed it could burrow its way into her house. If it happened to be one of the rare bears reported by locals, it might eventually succeed!

*Oh boy!*

Verity flicked on the porch light. Holding her breath— shovel blade aimed—she counted to three and cautiously cracked open the door.

Something whammed hard against the door, knocking it wide open. A shadow scuttled past her.

"A-a-a-ach!" Verity screeched.

Before she could recover her balance, the mystery beast flew through the open kitchen door and out of sight. Verity stood shaken. Her brain trying to make sense of the little she'd seen in the dim light.

*Lots of fur. Much bigger than a mouse or rat. Raccoon size? But the wrong color.*

Something clicked.

"Lady Macbeth, is that you?" She tossed aside the shovel with a clang and tore up the kitchen steps after what she hoped was her wayward cat.

Turning on lights, she stood in her kitchen and looked around while trying to catch her breath. Where did the silly thing go? It must be Lady M.

"Good grief, cat, isn't the barn good enough for you?"

A flash of motion caught her eye. In the glare of the overhead kitchen light, a cat—yes, now she was sure of it!—burst from her living room, dashed back across the kitchen floor and zoomed down the steps.

"What the—!"

Verity chased after it, tripping over her own bare feet and stubbing her toe on the wooden stair treads. She pitched off the steps landing hard on the mudroom floor but, miraculously, on her feet. A yellow tail whisked out through back door and disappeared beyond the circle of orange porch light, into the darkness.

Verity slammed the door shut.

She bent forward, hands on knees, sucking down air. What had sent the animal on such a wild tear? If something outdoors had frightened it, surely it would have remained in the house for protection. She hobbled across the room, favoring her injured toe. She heard sharp squeaks coming from somewhere inside the house.

Verity narrowed her eyes suspiciously. What had that crazy cat dragged into her house? She envisioned a half-dead, mutilated mouse. Now she would have to dispose of the poor thing. With a groan of frustration, her foot throbbing now, she plodded back to the kitchen. She grabbed a fistful of paper towels with which to handle the no-doubt bloody thing, and oven mitts to protect against possible bites, then followed the mysterious cries.

It didn't take her long to locate their source in her living room. Snuggled down in the cherry-red worsted yarn in her knitting basket was a tiny, nearly hairless kitten. Its eyes were not yet open.

"Oh my," she breathed. "Lady M, you're a mother!"

Reaching down, she gently picked up the squirming pink body. "It's okay, little one. I bet your mom will be back soon."

Just then, an angry howl erupted from outdoors. Verity gently returned the kitten to the basket, rushed back to the rear door and opened it. Crouched on the porch, Lady Macbeth looked up at her with glowing topaz eyes. Another kitten lay between her front paws. The mother cat picked it up in its mouth.

"Go ahead," Verity said. "*Mi casa es su casa.*"

Verity wondered what had prompted the animal to move her family into the house, despite the mild temperature and complications of rousing the resident human to open the door for her. Had a coyote or fox threatened her brood?

She followed the cat to the living room and watched her deposit Kitten #2 in the yarn basket before dashing away again.

On impulse, Verity seized a wicker harvesting basket from her pantry. She rushed outside just in time to see the cat's butt disappear into the tractor shed. Moonlight sliced between the weathered boards, providing just enough light to reveal Lady M squeezing behind a plow blade.

"Hold on, Momma!" she cried. "How many more have you got in there?"

She knelt down on the dusty planks and gently moved the big cat aside. Three more squirming bodies came to light. Verity scooped them up in her two hands and plopped them in the basket. Lady M squinted at her apprehensively.

"I'm not going to hurt them. Promise." She hooked the basket over her arm and stood up. "Come on, let's get this little family of yours all safe and cozy inside." But when she moved toward the shed door, the cat dove back into the darkness. "Really? Did I miss one?" Hopefully, not more than one. What was she going to do with all these little critters?

There was indeed one more, which the cat proudly carried in her mouth. Halfway back to the house, Verity heard the *scree-scree* of a hunting owl. "Guess we're just in time," she whispered. Together, they moved with more urgency toward the house.

Verity closed and locked the door behind them. She set the basket on the living room floor. Lady M dropped the kitten from her mouth into the fluffy mound of yarn with its sibling. One by one, the cat transferred the other three from the basket to the yarn nest. This accomplished, Lady M climbed in with her babies and favored Verity with a satisfied blink from her amber eyes.

Verity could almost hear her saying, *Job well done, human. Now we can get some rest.* The mother cat lay down with her kittens, and they began to nurse hungrily.

Verity collapsed into Mark's big leather armchair and watched them. The little family's contentedness washed over her. She sighed. How beautiful they were. Babies of any species were a gift of love. For the first time since Mark's death, she didn't feel a pang of bitterness or burning regret that she had no babies of her own.

This was absolutely lovely.

Finally, she stood up and walked into her kitchen. She had noticed that her once ginormous ginger cat was now much slimmer. Which, of course, now made sense. She had been carrying at least six babies. How had she been feeding herself since their birth? She wouldn't have dared leave them for long to hunt for her own food. She must be starving.

Having assumed the cat had permanently left the farm she'd stopped putting out food for it. She poured a cupful of dry cat food into a bowl, filled a second bowl with water and brought them into the living room.

"See?" she said, bending down to give Lady M a good head scratch. "I can be a good cat mom. Just give me a chance."

Wearily, she climbed the stairs to her bedroom. She swore she could hear Mark laughing at her. He had been right. She couldn't resist bringing her barn cat inside. *Cats*, she amended. They were welcome to stay for as long as it took to find good homes for them.

*Or maybe*, she mused drowsily, as her head sank into her pillow, *maybe Lady M and I will keep one or two babies for ourselves.*

# CHAPTER 33

THE NEXT MORNING when Verity checked on her new family, six velvety heartbreakers lay atop one another, sound asleep. She assumed their mom had just finished nursing them. She opened the back door to let Lady Macbeth out. The cat took off like a shot. Verity left the door cracked open then carried the yarn basket from the living room and down into the mudroom.

"What are you doing?"

She nearly dropped her kitten nursery. "Percy! How many times have I told—Oh, never mind. Our barn cat has returned to us with a gift of a litter of kittens. I'm moving them down to this room."

"You are keeping them in the house?" the ghost asked.

"I am."

"Mr. Mark was right. He knew you couldn't resist bri—"

"I know...I know. Technically, though, they aren't cats yet. They are kittens. And it wasn't my decision to bring them inside. It was their mother's."

Percy snorted and crossed his arms over his medal-decorated chest. He wore his Northern blues, saber strapped to his hip, brimmed felt hat cocked rakishly over one eye, just as he did whenever he wanted to flirt with Anna Louise. He was not flirting now though. He was glaring at Verity in stern reprimand.

He puffed up his chest authoritatively. "You cannot treat an animal like—"

"Stop it, Percy. My house, my rules. Here's the latest one: cats are allowed in this house."

He shook his head and frowned at the tips of his boots. "I apologize. Of course, you are right. I'm just not myself today. I can't stop thinking about Anna Louise."

"She's not back yet?"

"No." His gaze shifted restlessly around the rough plank floor and unfinished wall studs. "Something terrible has happened to her. I feel it in my bones."

"You no longer have bones," she said, then kicked herself for sounding so callous. "I apologize, Percy. You have every right to be worried." It wasn't like Anna Louise to be away this long.

Verity plumped the skeins of soft red fibers around the sleeping kittens. The yarn would undoubtedly be ruined by kitten spit and pee and poop; she didn't care. They were so adorable. So tiny and helpless. She stroked a perfect little head between two perfect little ears with the tip of one finger. The kitten's fuzz looked as if it had grown overnight; the pink skin seemed slightly less visible.

*I'm in love.*

Lady Macbeth came in through the back door, stopped dead still and looked up at her.

"Now don't have a hissy fit," Verity said. "I haven't hurt them. We're just relocating your babies to a more appropriate part of the house. See?" She tipped the basket to give the mother cat a view of her babies.

"Grr-eep!" the cat said, which Verity interpreted as—*alright, have it your way but I don't like it one bit.* However, after patrolling the mudroom for hidden dangers and lurking predators, Lady M climbed grudgingly into the basket with her babies. The matter seemed settled.

Verity honestly hadn't felt this relaxed and happy in a very long time. Maybe it was true, pets were good for your emotional wellbeing.

Apparently the same wasn't true for ghosts. Percy ignored the domestic scene and paced the mudroom, his spit-polished military boots marching across the floorboards, although they made no sound at all. She still couldn't get used to that.

"Madam," he said with military solemnity, "have you forgotten that you have a murder to solve, your farmhand's honor to clear, and my missing wife to find?" He stopped his agitated pacing and stood at attention in front of her. "Your immediate action is required on all fronts!" He sounded as though he was chewing out one of his enlisted men.

She sighed. "No, Percy, I haven't forgotten any of that. I guess I just needed something positive to focus on for a change." She waved a hand toward the basket. "They are beautiful, aren't they?" He squinted at her. "Alright," she continued, "I understand that we need to prioritize. Let's first focus on Anna Louise's disappearance and what might have caused her to go missing."

"I fear the worst," he stated dismally. "What if she is... dead?"

"Well, she *is*. You both are. We can't get around that fact. But at least she can't die again or be in pain, so that's good. Right?"

"You don't understand. I fear she has been transported to heaven. Without me."

"A possibility, yes. But then we must ask—why haven't you been likewise summoned?" She hesitated; not sure she wanted to say aloud what she'd just now thought. "I need to ask you something, Percy."

His nod of consent was stiff.

Here, she mused, is the tricky part. She took a deep breath. "During your natural life, did you do anything that might, you know, result in your being sent to *that other place*? You know, the not-heaven place." She couldn't bear to say 'hell.'

Percy turned a whiter shade of pale. "I have thought long and hard on that very question," he admitted gloomily. "It's true, I served as a soldier in a horrifically bloody war. Men died in my arms, more by my hand. But I never harmed a woman, child, or civilian."

She nodded her head. "Then let's assume you'll make the cut," she said.

"The cut?"

"It's a sports term. Unless every person who has ever fought in a war is denied a place in heaven, I can't imagine a good man like you would be refused." She thought for another minute. "For the sake of argument, let's assume Anna Louise hasn't been swept into the afterlife ahead of you. Can you think of any other reason she might be unable to return to you?"

"I truly don't know," he said miserably. "Unless it has something to do with the recent unpredictable nature of our luminosity."

"Ah." She considered this. "So, tell me, when you realize you're either becoming visible or fading from sight without intending to, does anything else happen?"

He looked away. "Now that you mention it, the last time my control faltered, I was trying to pick up my hat off the bedpost in the spare room. I couldn't. My hand kept slipping through it. And that's definitely not normal."

"Anything else?"

"I lost my ability to move through a wall. Ran plumb into it."

She would have liked to have seen that! Somehow, she managed not to laugh. "What if Anna Louise entered a room, then she or someone else closed the door. If she suddenly lost her ghostly powers, she might be unable to grasp the doorknob, and she couldn't escape from a room through a wall."

"Mercy!" he cried. "That surely is a possibility." He resumed pacing, his white-gloved hands clasped behind his back. "I feel lighter of heart already."

"It's just a possibility," Verity stressed. "We still need to find her. Where did she say she was going the last time you saw her?"

"We talked about reconnoitering the café per your request, but she also mentioned visiting the inn and the town green."

"I think we can eliminate the town green. Nothing there could have trapped her. But if a room at the inn is empty and the door's shut, it might stay that way for days."

"Thereby confining her," Percy agreed.

"The café seems less likely," she mused. "All Anna Louise needs to do is wait until a customer opens the door. She can slip out as they pass through, and they'd never notice."

"I'll search the inn," he said.

"No, Percy. You really should stay here at the house and work on the mystery of your visibility."

"But as you can see, I'm quite lucid at the moment. No short circuiting! And I am able to make myself unseen to others. See?" He demonstrated by flickering in and out of sight.

"Excellent. But it never lasts, does it?" she reminded him. He looked crestfallen. "Listen, if you insist on searching for her, we'd best go together. That way, I can warn you if you start to become visible while people are around."

He gave her a sharp salute. "Agreed, madam!"

# CHAPTER 34

ALTHOUGH VERITY truly cared for Percy and Anna Louise Putnam, they were sometimes more trouble than help when it came to lending her a hand. So, it was with mixed feelings that she set off with the youthful, one hundred and fifty-year-old soldier to locate his missing wife.

Case in point: there was the day the ghostly couple volunteered to help bring her cows in from the field. The ghosts' sudden appearance in the herd's midst—an ill-conceived attempt on their part to get the cows moving faster—terrified the normally docile animals. They stampeded, taking down a thirty-foot length of fence. Half of her ladies made it across the creek bordering the Cade farm before Verity and the Grimalski twins could stop them and bring them home. Mending the fences required hours more work.

Today, however, she sympathized with Percy's desire to participate in the search. While alive, he had been a man of action. Ordering him to remain in the farmhouse and do nothing would be cruel. On their way into town, she again reminded him to stay close to her, consciously remain invisible to the living world, and listen for any sound that might lead them to Anna Louise.

Together, they combed the inn, room after room. As it turned out, the unoccupied guest rooms were easy; Henry apparently made a habit of leaving the doors into empty rooms open. Perhaps this was a savvy advertising tactic. Out-of-town or local visitors who peeked into the lavish, antique-furnished rooms might become future customers.

With the doors into the hallway already ajar, Anna Louise could have come and gone freely. But just to be sure, Verity opened closets, bathroom doors, antique wardrobes, chifforobes and cupboards throughout the building. Percy looked beneath beds, behind couches, inside bureaus and chests and drawers. Together they investigated the linen closets on each floor.

"Where do these go?" Percy asked pointing to steps leading up, she assumed, to an attic.

"Let's see," she said.

The immense space beneath age-darkened rafters was jammed with old trunks, boxes and bins—all thick with dust. Sticky curtains of cobwebs brushed against her bare arms and snagged in her hair, making her shiver. But they found nothing to indicate Anna Louise had ever been there. Next came the basement. The musty cellar stored excess building materials— ceramic tiles, carpet remnants, tubes of caulking, five-gallon buckets of paint—leftovers from Henry's renovation of the inn. Any object, space, or container that could possibly trap a curious spirit, Verity carefully inspected.

She was glad Percy had come along. Without him, the search would have taken forever. She couldn't have asked EPI members for help. What could she possibly have said to them? "My ghost has gone missing! Please help me find her."

Having exhausted all other possibilities, Verity was about to start knocking on doors of occupied rooms when she ran into

Henry on the staircase. "What are you up to now?" he demanded brusquely. "Back to bother my customers yet again?"

"I, ummm, I'm doing a favor for the sheriff," she fibbed.

From the empty look Henry gave her, she knew she had to provide a better explanation than that, even if it meant doubling down on her lie. "He thinks he left his notebook here the other day. You know...when he and his guys were looking for—"

"Evidence and clues. Ridiculous!" Henry snorted. "I've never seen such a fuss over a common accident."

She didn't bother to correct him. As far as the sheriff's department and the EPIs were concerned, O'Halloran's death was no longer considered an accident of any kind. Even her mother—an avid fan of Agatha Christie's mysteries—would definitely have said 'foul play' was involved.

"I'm sorry you've been inconvenienced, Henry." She looked around on the landing for Percy. No ethereal glimmers. *Good!* "Honestly, we...I'm trying to handle everything as sensitively as possible."

"Why doesn't Bailey look for his own notebook?" Henry planted his feet, fists on bony hips as if challenging her to get past him. The man looked so frail she envisioned blowing him out of her way with one hard breath.

"I'm sure you know how busy Sheriff Bailey is," she said as patiently as possible. "A death in our community followed by the attack on a woman requires—"

"Ha! Pretending to be a hotshot lawman, that's what he's doing. You can be sure he's enjoying every minute of this so-called investigation!"

She chose to ignore his rants. "Well, if *you* would rather hunt for his notebook and return it to him when you find it."

Henry's palms shot out toward her, rejecting the possibility. "Please, you go right ahead. But I want no complaints from my customers. You hear?"

She smiled. There was no easier way to keep a job for oneself than by asking for volunteers.

"Most suspicious," Percy whispered in Verity's ear after Henry had left. "He refuses to acknowledge the man's murder. Do you suppose he's hiding something?"

"I'm beginning to think *everybody* is hiding something," Verity muttered under her breath.

By the time they finished searching every inch of the inn for Anna Louise, Percy's mood had dimmed from worried to morose.

Verity led him down the inn's curving stairway and out through the deserted kitchen to the rear door.

"Where are we going?" her still-invisible companion asked.

"I don't know," she admitted tiredly. "I just need someplace quiet to think. Anna Louise must be somewhere. I'm sure if she'd left this world you'd know it, Percy. Might she have traveled outside of town?"

Percy appeared dimly before her. His translucence told her that she alone could see him. "She never goes far without telling me." He pounded the hilt of his sword with the heel of his left hand. "If someone has done her harm, I swear by Lincoln's soul I shall cut them to pieces."

"Percy," she said gently, "how can anyone harm her?"

"I know. I just miss her so much." He turned away, but she had already seen his eyes go glossy with tears.

"Let's go back to the house," she suggested. "She may have returned and be looking for us. I wish I'd left a note saying where we'd be."

"Two days," he muttered. "Two days she's been gone. I know something terrible has—"

"Shut up!" Verity shouted.

Percy glared at her. "I beg your pardon, Mrs. Cade."

"Sorry, I didn't mean...it's just something people say when

they're surprised, in a good way. Look over there." She pointed across the alley. "Do you see that?"

"What?"

"That little wooden shed." In fact, it was so small, the wood so faded and warped, that it had entirely escaped her notice until now. "That's the one place on this property we haven't looked."

He shook his head and landed a playful punch on her shoulder—which she hardly felt, as ghosts generally don't have much weight to put behind their touch. "That's not a shed, my dear woman."

"Well, it sure looks like one. Although I doubt you could fit much more than a shovel in there."

"*That*," he informed her, "is an outhouse."

"Oh, is that what it is? A bit before my time, but—" She stared at the splintery structure. "Hey! Do outhouses move?"

"Not in my experience."

"Because that one is really rocking." She started running toward it. Percy must have realized what she was thinking and outpaced her.

"Anna Louise is that you?" he shouted, his figure suddenly glowing brightly.

Verity frantically looked around to make sure nobody was nearby or looking out through the inn's rear windows.

"H-help me!" a weak voice came from inside the wobbling structure.

"Oh, my darling!" Percy cried. "Be brave! We're almost there."

A rusty iron latch held the door shut. He flipped it up and the door flew open. A vision in blue taffeta and ruffles plummeted into him, knocking him off his feet. The two ghosts landed on the dusty ground, Anna Louise on top.

"My precious," Percy cooed, unfazed by their mishap.

"Oh, Percy darlin'!" Anna Louise clung to him. "I was so frightened. And, my word, it smelled something awful in there!"

Verity stood over them, relieved at their reunion but concerned that their current state of visibility might be observed through any of the shops' rear windows.

"In-vis-i-ble!" she hissed in warning.

The two ghosts cast her an apologetic look, crackled with blue-and-white sparks, and disappeared.

# CHAPTER 35

"WHAT ON EARTH were you doing in an outhouse?" Verity said as soon as they were all back at the farmhouse and in a much calmer frame of mind. "Don't tell me ghosts require a toilet!"

"We do not," Anna Louise replied, with a delicate pout to her rosy lips. She turned to her husband, standing at her side in Verity's living room. Percy hadn't released his bride's hand since rescuing her. "I was in the inn's kitchen watching Henry try to make cookies for his guests' teatime. That man has no idea how to bake anything, I can tell you! Not that I was ever much of a cook, but I watched my mother and sisters turn out a loaf of bread or pretty peach cobbler now and then."

"The outhouse, Anna Louise," Verity gently reminded her.

"Ah yes, I was just getting to that. Patience, dear Verity."

"I'm trying."

"It was while I was in the kitchen," Anna Louise continued, "and being ever so careful to remain invisible, when I heard voices outside in the alley. They sounded like children squabbling. And you know how I just adore little children." Anna Louise batted her long blonde lashes at Percy.

He blushed and gave her waist a squeeze.

"And was it children?" Verity said.

"It surely was. A little boy and a girl. From the way they were scrapping, I'd say they were brother and sister."

"The boy a little older? Maybe five or so?"

"Why yes. How did you know?"

"Let's just say I've seen him in action. How did seeing them end with you in the outhouse?"

"Well, that's just it." Anna Louise touched a fingertip to her chin in deliberation. "You see, the boy was teasing his sister after he took a red ball away from her. He threw the ball across the dirt yard, and it rolled toward my feet so I naturally looked down...and I could see them!"

Verity narrowed her eyes. "See what?"

"My feet, of course! If the children hadn't been so busy arguing, I most certainly would not have been able to rush into the outhouse before they caught a glimpse of me."

"Such a close call," Percy sympathized.

"Oh yes, my darling!" Anna Louise flipped her hand in the air and an ivory fan, with a gold silk tassel dangling from it, appeared. She gracefully snapped open the fan. "I'm sure the poor little things would have been terrified."

"I wouldn't count on it," Verity muttered, but neither ghost seemed to catch her sarcasm. "I think I can guess what happened next. You were visible when you hadn't intended to be, so you must have also lost control of your other abilities. Like manipulating a door latch."

Anna Louise made a sour face. "It was ever so frustrating. The door had been open but after I rushed inside the wind blew it closed. By the way, I don't believe that thing has been properly cleaned in decades. I waited for someone to come and use the commode, but no one ever came."

Why would they? Verity thought. Indoor plumbing had

been around for over a hundred years. She smiled affectionately at the pretty ghost. "How awful for you."

Anna Louise snuggled up to her husband. "You came to my rescue though."

"I did, my sweet. I never would have given up looking for you."

They rubbed noses, kissed on the lips. Verity felt like a third wheel. She turned to leave the room.

"Wait!" Anna Louise cried. "Don't you want my report?"

"If nothing important happened, I guess it can wait," Verity said. To be honest, her heart ached just a bit. Seeing the couple so in love made her think of Mark. How could it not? If he were alive and here with her, they'd be rubbing noses. Or doing something even more intimate. She sighed. Such beautiful memories.

"We'll talk later," she said, just a little mistily.

"Don't you want to hear about the Widow O'Halloran?" Anna Louise looked disappointed.

Verity turned back to face the ghost. "What about her?"

"I saw her last night while I was trapped."

Obviously, Anna Louise was still confused about her lost days in the outhouse. "Actually, Jennifer was already back in New York City last night. So, you couldn't have seen her, at least not last night."

"Well then," Anna Louise huffed, clearly annoyed at being corrected, "since I most definitely saw her and it most definitely was last night, she must have come back. And she was with someone."

"You're absolutely sure it was Jennifer that you saw? While shut inside the—"

"There were rather large cracks between the boards and I have amazing night vision. Do I not, Percy dear? He calls me his kitty-cat." Anna Louise demonstrated with a low purring sound and flashed her husband a mischievous smile. "Because I can see in the dark."

Verity took a deep breath. Conversations with ghosts could be so frustrating. "You're absolutely certain it was Jennifer O'Halloran?"

"Of course. I recognized her right away. But not him. I must say, I didn't like the looks of that fellow at all. Quite sinister he was." She shimmied her ruffled shoulders.

Verity sighed. "Anna Louise, sweetie, it's just not possible. Are you sure you weren't overcome by fumes? Or dreaming? I drove Mrs. O'Halloran to the train station myself."

Percy stepped closer to Verity with a serious expression. "I would be inclined to believe her, ma'am. My wife has the eyes of a c—"

"I know, I know—cat's eyes, sees in the dark. But after what happened to her and her husband, she swore she'd never set foot in Evansfield again. So, why would she suddenly return?"

Percy stared across the room grimly. "That indeed is the question."

# CHAPTER 36

VERITY'S MIND tossed and tumbled, constantly revisiting the events of the past week. Nothing made sense to her. They were still no closer to knowing who had murdered Rudy O'Halloran or who attacked his wife. She refused to accept the possibility that Jason had anything to do with either attack. And yet, she couldn't prove his innocence.

Verbalizing a problem often helped her begin to understand it and work toward a solution. She decided it was time to call another meeting of the EPI. She phoned Sunny to see if they could meet at the café, but its owner sounded less than enthusiastic.

"To be honest," Sunny said, "I've had a really rough day. I can't wait to get out of this place, soon as I close up. Can we please meet at your house?"

"Ummm, well..." Verity wanted to keep visitors out of the farmhouse until her housemates found a way to control their visibility. She couldn't risk the Putnams sneaking into their meeting and being seen. "Ordinarily, that wouldn't be a problem," she began, but wasn't immediately able to come up with a good excuse.

All this subterfuge had become exhausting!

"There's been a problem with the sump pump ever since that last heavy rain," Verity said at last. Which was true, it had been unreliable recently.

"Did your basement flood?"

"Yes. That's exactly what happened. And the pump clogged," she said. "And, well, the whole house stinks of mildew. It will take days, maybe weeks to air out." Which was not true.

"I guess that might spoil our thinking processes, not to mention our appetites," Sunny agreed. What good were meetings if they didn't include sweets? "What about Mary Beth's place?"

"Not a good idea. Remember what happened last time we met at Mary Beth's? If the mayor is in the house, he'll hijack the meeting."

"You're right," Sunny agreed. "Let's avoid that nightmare. Denise's shop?"

"She barely has enough room for half a dozen customers waiting in line to buy their fudge and truffles."

"Didn't she add seating behind her shop?" In the background, Verity could hear Sunny ringing up a customer's bill. The café sounded busy—conversation and laughter, the clink of cups and plates, her servers delivering orders.

"You're right, I'd forgotten. And it's supposed to be warm and clear tonight; no chance of rain."

"I'll give her a call," Sunny offered. "If it's okay with Denise, I'll let you know and summon the others. We close early today, thank goodness! Can we say, seven o'clock?"

All seven members of the EPI—Verity, Sunny, Mary Beth, Denise, Kate, Chaundra, and Fumiko—arrived within minutes of each other at Denise's Chocolate Designs. Although Verity would have loved to be able to ask her friends for advice on her ghosts' personal dilemma, she still couldn't think of a way without giving away the fact that deceased individuals lived in her house.

Meanwhile, Percy had admitted his worst fear to her. The increased instability of their spirit selves might well be a sign they were finally nearing the end of their time in the living world. If that were true, she might well lose them forever.

There had been a time when she believed this was what she wanted. A normal ghost-free house. But the immediacy of their departure tore at her. She had grown accustomed to having their company. In the strangest of ways, they had become quite dear to her.

Sunny plopped a pastry box on the picnic table behind the candy shop, startling Verity out of her melancholy. "My contribution to the meeting," Sunny announced. "Day-old donuts, muffins, bear claws, and apple fritters. They're on the house tonight, ladies."

Mary Beth chortled. "Day-old, schmay-old. They're still better than anything from a grocery store." She unceremoniously ripped open the box. "I should test a few, just to be sure."

Kate elbowed her. "MB, the polite thing to do is take one at a time. That way each of us will have at least one."

"Oh, right." Mary Beth frowned. "Sorry."

"Kate, she's not five years old!" Sunny said. Verity smiled fondly at them.

Kate, a former teacher, sometimes reverted to elementary-school rules in adult settings.

Mary Beth seemed unfazed. "It's okay, Katie. You're right. I get carried away sometimes. Look at all this yumminess!"

After Denise made a few runs back inside the candy shop for everyone's coffee, they all settled on benches at the long wooden picnic table in the secluded courtyard.

"I assume we're meeting to compare notes about what we've found out so far?" Chaundra said. "To help with the murder investigation."

"Or attack on woman," Fumiko added, squeezing her fingers around her own throat and making demonstrative gurgling sounds.

Verity winced at the pantomime. "Correct. Does anyone have new information that should go to the sheriff?"

"It's not exactly new," Kate said meekly when no one else jumped in. "But that bus driver is making me very nervous."

"Why?" Verity asked.

"Yesterday, I brought my girls to work with me at the bookstore for Storytime." Kate owned and managed A World of Stories bookshop. "My youngest is fascinated, God knows why, with tattoos. The bus driver was standing on the sidewalk smoking. Tabitha approached her and asked what the pretty picture was on her arm."

"Oh, how cute!" Sunny said. "She probably thought it was a decal or wash-off paint, like the face-paint artist used at the July Fourth festival."

Kate made a face. "The woman acted like this little kid had insulted her. She jerked her arm away when my daughter reached out to touch the tat. Tugged down her shirt sleeve and refused to answer my daughter."

"Mean," Fumiko muttered. "So, *so* mean! I give her slice of my mind."

"Piece," Sunny corrected with a gentle smile. "Piece of my mind."

"Yours, too?" Fumiko said. Verity hid a smile behind her hand.

Kate resumed her story. "The look she gave my child—it frightened me. Luckily, we were just a few feet away from the bookstore door. I pushed the girls inside before they had time to think about what had just happened."

"I believe I know what that might have been about." Heads turned to Verity. "I'm sure the sheriff wouldn't mind my sharing this information with you, as long as we keep it within the EPI." She took a deep breath. "Susan Brown, the bus driver, served time in prison. Breaking and entering, thefts, nothing violent. It's possible that tattoo has something to do with her incarceration. She probably wouldn't want attention drawn to prison tats—which Tabitha was innocently doing."

"Oh, my!" Kate's eyes were huge. "Do you think the woman's dangerous?"

"I hope not. But I'll tell the sheriff what happened in case he thinks there's cause to worry. The bus is scheduled to return to New York City tomorrow."

"I, for one, will feel much better when they're gone," Kate stated firmly. She picked up her raspberry jelly donut, eyed it with uncharacteristic indifference, then returned it to the napkin in front of her. "Every horrible thing that's happened in the past week started when those people arrived in Evansfield. Robberies, murder, a fight, and a violent attack on a grieving woman. And now Jason's in jail! It's all because of *them*!"

"It would seem," Verity agreed, keeping her voice calm. "But we can't blame folks just because they are outsiders."

"My turn," Chaundra jumped in. "It may mean nothing but I saw Henry and Ervin arguing this morning, out in front of the Emporium. Lots of finger-pointing and shouting. I have no clue what it was about, but they sure were up in arms over something."

"We need to interrogate them, separately," Mary Beth proposed.

"Good idea!" Denise said with so much enthusiasm it made

Verity nervous. "If one of them has dirt on the other, he might rat on him without us needing to use force."

"No one's using force, Denise," Sunny said, nailing her with a look.

"Agreed." Verity took a bite out of her bear claw. Swirling through the soft, sweet dough was just the right amount of cinnamon and sugar. The vanilla glaze was heavenly. She chewed and swallowed. "But we should get the sheriff's permission before we talk to either of them. He needs to be made aware that something's going on between those two. He might want to be the one to have a conversation with them. Anything else?" She consulted the faces around the table.

No one seemed to have anything more to add.

"Alright then," Verity said, "I need to ask you something. Has anyone seen or heard from Jennifer O'Halloran at any time today or last night?"

Sunny narrowed her eyes at Verity. "Veri, dear, you're too young to be having a senior moment. You told me yourself that you drove Jennifer to the train station. I even saw her getting into your truck with you, right in front of my café."

"True. But today—" how to say this? "—I received an anonymous tip that she was seen last night in town. In the alley behind the shops, with a stranger."

Mary Beth hooted. "Someone's got an imagination!"

"The whole tragedy has been on people's minds," Kate pointed out. "I bet it was just someone who looks like her."

"She *is* the kind of woman who would blend in just about anywhere," Chaundra added.

Denise barked a laugh. "Next thing you know, people will be swearing they saw ol' Rudy walking the streets, even though we know he's dead."

"Could be his ghost." Sunny grinned. "Come back to haunt my café and complain about my slow service."

"Ah-o-o-o-o-w!" An eerie howl made everyone jump and peer around looking for its source.

"Sorry, I couldn't resist," Kate admitted meekly. "My girls do that to me all the time."

"What are you—ten years old?" Denise snarled. "You scared the bloody crap out of me, Katie!"

Verity drew a deep breath to calm her shredded nerves and waited for the others to settle. "The thing is," she began again, "if there's any chance Mrs. O'Halloran did return to Evansfield after making such a big deal about wanting to leave, we need to ask ourselves why. Why come back to a place she claimed to hate and never wanted to see again?"

"She liar!" Fumiko burst out, her black eyes flashing fire. "I never, never trust this woman."

"Maybe she just forgot something," Chaundra suggested more calmly. "Or there's another perfectly innocent explanation."

Mary Beth cleared her throat. "The detectives on my CSI shows always say—"

"Do you know who the anonymous informer is?" Sunny interrupted her, turning to Verity.

"I, well, yes but I'm not at liberty to reveal their identity." Verity got skeptical looks from both Denise and Sunny. Chaundra studied her with the solemnity of a judge. Mary Beth just looked confused, as she often did. "But my source is reliable, I can absolutely vouch for them."

"So-o-o," Fumiko said, slowly, "you get phone call from this mystery person?"

"No."

"They came to your farm?" Kate guessed.

"Yes." That, at least, wasn't a lie.

"Were they young? Old?" Denise asked. "A local resident or someone from out of town?"

"Local," Verity said, glad she could be honest on that point, too. After all, the ghosts had lived—so to speak—in Evansfield far longer than anyone at this meeting.

"This isn't a guessing game," Sunny scolded, throwing up her hands in frustration. "What's happening here is really serious. Verity told us that the tip was anonymous. We should honor that person's wish."

"Somebody needs to question Henry and Ervin," Chaundra stated. "If Mrs. O'Halloran returned to retrieve something she left on the bus or at the inn, they'll know."

"The sheriff's the one who should ask them if they've seen her," Sunny said.

"Absolutely," Verity agreed. "I'll tell him about the reported sighting."

"Well, the whole thing sure sounds shady to me," Denise muttered.

*If you only knew*, Verity thought.

# CHAPTER 37

LOOKING Sheriff Bailey in the eye while outright lying to him was more than Verity could handle. She chose to deliver the news that Jennifer had been sighted by phone.

"That's a bunch of baloney," he snapped when she was done. "I'm not wastin' my time chasin' down rumors. And Henry and Ervin have been pestered enough. You leave those boys alone, hear?"

"But don't you think the possibility Jennifer has suddenly returned is at least suspicious?"

"It's not information, it is *gossip*, Mrs. Cade. You have no idea how many nuisance calls my office gets every day."

"Wait!" she shouted, sensing he was about to hang up on her. "I know you're terribly busy, Sheriff. Please, will you just give the EPI permission to ask Henry and Ervin if they've seen her? I promise, we won't bother them, or you, again."

He muttered a few expletives she tried not to hear. "If it'll get you off my back, go for it." The connection died.

She shook her head and sighed. She'd angered him, but at least she had his permission, even if it was grudgingly given.

Because Sunny couldn't leave the café during the most popular mealtimes and Verity was so far behind in her chores, it was decided that Mary Beth and Chaundra should ask Henry if he knew anything about Jennifer returning to town, and Kate and Denise would question Ervin. Verity hoped that Chaundra would temper MB's habit of spontaneously erupting into CSI jargon. Polite and reserved Kate had at least a fighting chance of reining in Denise's tendency to go ballistic. Meanwhile, Sunny, Verity, and Fumiko would keep their ears open for other rumors of Jennifer's return.

Time was desperately short. The tour group was due to leave town at 11:00 am sharp the following morning. Any important news needed to be passed along to the sheriff before the bus sped out of town.

Delegating jobs had always been hard for Verity; she wanted to do everything herself! At least then, if something went wrong, she had only herself to blame. But she desperately needed a morning free for her farm chores.

With Jason in jail, she had to ask Jerry to assume as many of his brother's jobs as possible. The rest would fall on her. But Jerry was so furious with her he hadn't said a word to her since picking up his pay—obviously, because he believed she had betrayed his brother. Tomorrow, if the sheriff let her, she would visit her jailed farmhand. Hopefully, she'd find a way to clear the air between herself and Jason. Maybe that would make Jerry feel better about her, too.

Before the end of the day, her investigators turned in their reports. Neither Henry nor Ervin had seen the widow O'Halloran in the past twenty-four hours. So, was Anna Louise mistaken? Verity was never sure she could entirely trust the ditzy ghost.

As she lay in bed that night, she kept thinking about Jason, alone and in a jail cell. Poor guy. In her heart she knew her young farmhand couldn't have killed Rudy. At least, not intentionally. And not in the way little Morgan had described— repeatedly pounding the man's head with such awful rage. She slept little that night.

Before morning's first light and Verity's first cup of coffee, her phone rang. It was the sheriff.

"You keep some kinda ledger or reports in your barn?" he asked. "Somethin' where your boys might make notes about your critters and such?"

Her head felt foggy, without its usual wake-up jolt of caffeine. "Huh? Yeah, of course. But why?"

"Bring it down to the café. I'll be there by seven." He hung up without further explanation.

By 6:50, she was parking her truck in front of the Cat's Cradle. The other shops along the street wouldn't open for another two or more hours. However, Sunny's café already boasted a full complement of regulars in search of food, the latest gossip, and coffee—not necessarily in that order. Toast and lots and lots of strong java were high on Verity's list of priorities.

A table at the very back of the café's dining area was traditionally reserved for the town's old-timers who gathered every morning for maple-syrup-drenched pancakes, hickory-smoked bacon, and a schmooze. Sheriff Bailey sat there with three of his poker buddies. She caught the sheriff's eye. He hitched his head in the direction of a free table and strode across the room to join her.

She noticed his buddies' eyes slyly following him and shooting her curious looks. No doubt speculating about their reason for privacy.

"Children!" she huffed, more amused than bothered. *Did men never grow up?*

"What did you say?" Bailey dragged a chair from beneath the table.

"Nothing. Here's my daily work log, although how it might help with your investigation I have no idea."

He was already flipping pages, grunting now and then. Verity eyed the plates piled with food on neighboring tables. Her stomach growled.

"Here!" he said abruptly, clamping his big hand down on a page.

She frowned. "What about it? It's a dairy pick-up receipt."

Bailey hurriedly rifled through his jacket pockets and pulled out a clear plastic evidence bag. Inside was Jason's note to Rudy O'Halloran. Bailey removed it from the bag and laid it beside the open page of her log. She watched, intrigued as he pulled a small optical lens from his shirt pocket and examined each of the two sheets of paper.

"Dang," he breathed.

"What?" The man was frustrating!

He passed her the hand lens. "Check out what Jason wrote there." He pointed. It was a note to her about Molly, letting her know that the cow was being obstinate—no surprise there!—and wouldn't let him milk her.

"So?"

"Now use the lens to look at the note to O'Halloran."

She did as instructed. The two samples of Jason's handwriting appeared identical. Her heart clenched. For a moment she'd thought he was trying to show her evidence of Jason's innocence.

She handed back the little magnifying glass. He was silent for a moment, observing her so closely her skin began to itch.

"Don't you see it?"

She gave a mournful shrug.

One corner of his mouth twitched. "It's Jason's get-out-of-jail-free card." He looked smug, which made no more sense than his words. What the hell was the man saying?

"Sorry. I-I don't get it."

"Look again at the evidence letter. Closely." He shoved the lens back into her hand.

So, she did. After experimenting with the distance between the lens and her right eye, she found the best focus. And she thought she saw what he meant.

"You got it now?" He grinned at her.

"Maybe. It's almost as if some of the letters in the evidence note have very faint shadows." She shifted the lens to Jason's log entry. "No shadows here, though."

"Exactly, Mrs. Cade!" he bellowed. A woman at a nearby table cast him an annoyed look. Bailey lowered his voice. "It's like someone was trying to pass off their own writing as Jason's. They must have traced a sample of Jason's handwriting in pencil, then inked over the indentations in the paper. It's a good trick, but almost impossible to do perfectly."

"Thus, the shadow lines," she mused, looking up at him. "I'm impressed, Sheriff."

He wobbled his head side to side in a modest way. "Mind you, I can't ignore Jason's threats to O'Halloran in front of witnesses, right here in the café. We need a lot more than wonky handwriting to clear that young man."

"Like solid evidence someone else murdered Rudy O'Halloran?"

"Right." His satisfied expression with his recent discovery turned abruptly serious. She followed his gaze toward the street door. It flew open forcibly, the silver bell above jangling loudly.

One of his deputies careened between tables like a slalom skier, moving toward them.

"Sheriff," the man gasped, trying to catch his breath, "something's...well, *happened*." His eyes flicked sideways at Verity.

Bailey waited a beat. "Well, Cunningham? You gonna keep it a secret?"

"No, sir. No, Sheriff, sir. It's, well, one of the tourists has gone missing." Another flick to surrounding diners, as if concerned about speaking in front of an audience. He lowered his voice. "Just up and disappeared."

Bailey's body language altered from irritated to alert. He smiled. "Now, here's a little detail we might use," he said with renewed energy. He turned to Verity. "Whoever's gone on the run has givin' himself away. Town's gotten too hot for our murderer. Dang!" He pushed himself back from the table, chair legs screeching and hitched the waist of his pants up over his big belly. "Who is it, Cunningham? Who's done a runner?"

"A little kid. Boy named Morgan."

Verity felt as though her body temperature dropped twenty degrees. The saying 'as if someone walked across my grave' flashed through her mind.

The sheriff's face reddened. His jowls quivered. He ratcheted bloodshot eyes toward the ceiling as though searching the tin tiles for strength. "You're talkin' 'bout the same boy Jimmy is s'posed to be watchin'? Our only witness has disappeared?"

Deputy Cunningham gave a stiff nod and backed away a step. As if he wanted to be out of range of the flames should his boss spontaneously combust. "Ah, yes, sir."

The sheriff stood motionless, at a rare loss for words.

"How long has the boy been missing, deputy?" Verity asked.

"Parents said they went down to the inn's dining room for an early breakfast. The boy was still sleeping and they didn't want to wake him. But when they finished eating and returned to their room, he wasn't there."

Bailey shouted, "And how in the name of sweet Jesus did that child get past Jimmy?"

Cunningham hesitated. "You see, sir, Jimmy says he had to take a leak—sorry, ma'am—but swears the kid was sound asleep on his bed when he peeked in at him."

"Probably fakin' it," Bailey muttered. "Waitin' for his chance to vamoose."

Verity checked her watch. "He can't have been gone for long."

"Right," Bailey said. "Where are the parents? I need to talk to them."

"Yes, sir!" The deputy looked as though he was starting to enjoy the drama. "Mom and Dad are outside in front of the inn, demanding Mr. Ervin keep the bus from leaving until they find their son."

Bailey was already on the move, his deputy jogging behind him, no longer bothering to keep his voice down. "Bus driver's yelling, too! Says she' wants to leave early. Not her problem they can't control their kid. And...and, Sheriff, Mr. Ervin's standing between driver and parents, trying to keep 'em from killing each other. Poor old guy looks 'bout to toss his breakfast."

Bailey nearly trampled over a customer to get to the café door. "Sure woulda made my life simpler," he complained under his breath, "if our fugitive had been the killer."

Verity hurried after the two lawmen, two of her running steps to each of the sheriff's galumphing strides.

The tour bus idled like an immense chrome whale in front of the inn, bleeding diesel fumes and doing a good job of forcing all southbound traffic on Main Street to squeeze past it. Its driver was waving passengers on board while yelling something at the missing boy's parents.

All along the street was mayhem. A crowd had gathered on the cobblestone walkway and wooden steps in front of the

Historic Wayfarer's Inn. The sheriff plowed between them toward Sue Brown.

"You," he roared at the bus driver, "stand down! You're going nowhere until we locate your missing passenger."

"You got until ten," Sue sneered. "Another job's waiting for me back in the city."

Bailey jabbed a thick finger at her face. They were nearly the same height, but Bailey won in weight if not in muscle. "You leave without my permission, and I'll toss your sorry ass in jail."

"I ain't done nothing wrong!" Sue complained but then squinted apprehensively at the mad-dog distortion of the sheriff's face and shuffled back a step.

"Go sit on your damn bus until I tell you otherwise. And shut down that engine before you pollute the whole county!"

Sue glared at him, but after a moment dropped her gaze to the ground and slumped onto the bus.

"Now," Bailey said turning to the boy's parents, "Mr. and Mrs. Denton, do you have any idea where your son might have gone? I don't want to hold up the tour's departure, seein' as how so many of us have been lookin' forward to it all week."

Verity bit her bottom lip to stop a spontaneous laugh.

Mr. Denton either didn't hear or ignored the rebuff. "You promised to protect my son! What the hell happened? We left him asleep in our room trusting your man to guard the door."

"He's been kidnapped!" the boy's mother wailed, stepping between her husband and the sheriff. "Whoever killed that man must have found out my boy witnessed the murder. If that monster has taken my son, I—"

"We will sue your honky-tonk department," her husband broke in. "Hell! We'll sue this whole town!" Mr. Denton glowered. Mrs. Denton sobbed.

"Ma'am," Verity said, touching the woman's arm before the sheriff could respond, "I'm sure your son is fine." Which was a flat lie, but these were the first words that came to her and all she could think of to calm the woman. "Isn't it more important that we put our energy into locating him? He seemed fascinated with the farming equipment and animals on my farm. Maybe he went off to investigate one of the nearby farms on his own?"

"Don't be ridiculous," the woman snapped, pulling her arm away. "I knew this would happen. His lies and fantasies have finally resulted in disaster." The woman spun away to continue haranguing the sheriff.

Verity looked around at the other tourists, taking in every word of the spectacle. She noticed the missing boy's younger sister sitting on the inn's steps, playing with a cellphone. Her eyes locked on the screen, unconcerned with the fuss around her. Wasn't that the way with siblings when they were young? If the drama wasn't about them, it wasn't worth their attention.

Meanwhile, none of the adults appeared capable of doing anything useful. Morgan's mother shouted increasingly wild threats of legal action. Sue had turned off the bus's engine and was lounging in the driver's seat, heels kicked up onto the dashboard; Verity thought she caught a smirk on the woman's face. What was so amusing? Why look so smug? The former inmate puzzled her. Was it possible Sue Brown played a role in the boy's disappearance?

An explosion of activity drew her attention back to the Dentons. Mr. Denton was stomping up and down the sidewalk, throwing his arms in the air, cursing the ineptitude of all law enforcement agencies. Henry and Ervin stood on the inn's veranda, shoving fingers at each other's chests, trading accusations. Fisticuffs might well ensue, although she doubted either retiree had ever been in a real fight. They were more likely to strain a muscle than land a decent punch.

Verity gave up hope of placating anyone. She walked over to the little sister—Bethany, she reminded herself. The little girl looked no more than four years old. Verity sat down beside her on the steps. Bethany didn't look up or even seem to notice that she was there. Verity watched her play with an app on the phone. It was an inane video game—something to do with popping colorful bubbles shaped like little lambs—but it seemed to enthrall the child.

"What are you playing?" Verity asked, trying to make herself heard above the racket of swapped insults and threats.

"Sheepsbaby." Bethany's lips barely moved. She didn't look away from the screen for even a second.

"Looks like fun."

"'Tis."

Verity smiled, a woman of few words. "May I have a turn?"

Bethany giggled. "I don't think so, silly. You don't even know how to play."

"True. But you could teach me."

"Don't have time."

"Ah. Busy schedule. I understand." She paused to let the obsessed player sink deeper into her game, hoping to get her talking about her brother. "You don't happen to know where Morgan is. Do you, Bethany?"

She shook her head, eyes fixed on a fat pink sheep jumping a fence.

"Oh, well that's too bad, because I'd really like to find him. He could be in danger."

Still no reaction. But a second later... "I know," Bethany murmured.

Verity froze. "You *know* that Morgan's in danger? How?"

"'Cause he told me, silly"

Verity's heart gave an out-of-sync thumpety-thump. "Ah, of course." She tried to keep her voice free of emotion. "Brothers sometimes tell sisters their secrets, don't they?"

Bethany nodded in agreement. "He tells me shtuff."

"If he didn't tell you where he was going, did he say why he was in danger?"

The little girl shrugged and flashed Verity an annoyed look, as if the Q&A had become tedious. "He *had* to leave. They was gonna kill him."

*What?*

Verity forced herself to count to ten before trusting she could speak calmly. If she jarred the child out of her fantasy world, she feared the girl might stop talking altogether. "Bethany, who is going to kill Morgan?"

"Dunno." A weary sigh.

"Do you know *why* they want to kill him?"

Bethany's fingers stopped tapping. She looked up at Verity with unswerving gray eyes, her patience exhausted by this meddlesome adult who needed the simplest things explained to her. "'Cause he knew who killed the man. And killers kill waitresses and my brother was a waitress so he had to run away."

For a full minute, Verity sat stunned and totally clueless. *Killers kill waitresses?* "Oh, you mean witnesses?"

Bethany's eyes returned like heat-seeking missiles to the phone's screen. Two little pink thumbs flew over the keypad.

Verity scooted off the step and twisted around in a crouch facing Bethany at eye level.

"Would you tell the sheriff what you just told me about your brother? He really needs to find Morgan." If this kid was as clever and sneaky as her sibling, she might know exactly where he was, in spite of her assertions to the contrary.

"Can't."

"Why not? Sheriff Bailey is a very nice man and he very much wants to help your brother," Verity coaxed ever so sweetly.

Finally, Bethany broke her concentration on the phone and

jumped to her feet, compelling Verity to stand and fall back a step or be knocked aside by the little dynamo.

"It's a *secret* of course!" Bethany shouted, fists on hips. The child's frustrated expression telegraphed how incredibly stupid the nosy woman in front of her must be. *Primary rule of childhood: you don't tell secrets.*

And yet, it somehow didn't occur to Bethany that she had, indeed, told at least one secret. Just not to the sheriff.

# CHAPTER 38

MORGAN DENTON WAS able to identify Rudy's killer. That was why he'd run.

Verity looked around frantically for Sheriff Bailey. She finally spotted him still standing on the sidewalk, trying to talk the Dentons out of killing their fellow tourists, who apparently still wanted the bus to leave early. She needed to tell Bailey what the boy's sister had just revealed to her.

However, she was reluctant to pass along Bethany's information in front of half the town and a busload of visitors, including the missing boy's parents. She tried to move closer to Bailey and wave to get his attention. He glanced toward her, shook his head then mouthed: *Not now!*

A tap on her shoulder made her whirl around.

"I just opened the emporium and left my helpers in charge. What did I miss?" Chaundra said, eyeing the crush of people around the sheriff. She wore a gorgeous African-print sarong. Against the rich, earthy hues of the fabric, the Ethiopian woman's skin positively glowed.

"I wish I could say 'not much.'" Verity sighed. "Come with me, Chaundra. I don't want to talk here. Too many ears."

Just then she caught sight of Denise rushing out through the front door of her candy shop. She motioned to Denise and led the two women away to a quieter spot beneath one of Main Street's beautiful old maples.

"There's been a development," she explained. "I need to talk to the sheriff in private but, as you can see from that mob scene over there, he's occupied. One of the kids on the tour bus has gone missing."

"Let me guess." Denise smirked. "Your favorite little boy from the farm tour?"

"Got it in one," Verity said. "His little sister says he ran away, convinced someone is going to kill him because he witnessed the murder. I think he's figured out who the killer is."

Chaundra's dark eyes snapped with fury. "Then why aren't all these people searching for the child?"

"From what I've overheard," Verity explained, "most of them seem to think he's just hiding, trying to get attention. Except for the parents who are sure he's been kidnapped. I just need to get the sheriff alone for two minutes to tell him what the boy's sister said."

Denise tipped her head and scrutinized the crowd. "I think I can help with that." She hitched back her shoulders and marched straight toward the thickest part of the crowd.

"Oh, no," Chaundra moaned. "There she goes. Someone's going to die."

Verity pressed a hand over the sinking feeling in her stomach. With Denise, you just never knew. She held her breath.

Denise stopped walking and stuck two fingers in her mouth, producing an ear-splitting whistle. "Hey, everyone," she shouted, "free samples of fudge at Denise's Chocolate Designs!" All arguments ceased. Heads turned. "Ten flavors to choose from and a whopping ten percent off all purchases for the next hour!"

Denise played Pied Piper, leading a swath of customers down the sidewalk and up the steps into her shop. Even more soon followed.

"Impressive," Chaundra commented.

Within minutes, the lawn and sidewalk in front of the inn had cleared considerably, leaving only the sheriff, the Dentons and a few hangers-on.

Verity strode up to the sheriff, no longer trying to be subtle to get his attention. She gripped his forearm. "A word, Sheriff. Now!"

He cast her a bellicose look, but when she didn't back off, he excused himself from the boy's parents, who appeared to have pretty much shouted themselves into exhaustion.

"Unless you know where the little b-r-a-t is," he said, "whatever you have to say can wait."

"I think they can spell." Verity slid her eyes toward the Dentons, but they were oblivious to their conversation. "And *no*, Sheriff, I don't know where Morgan is yet. But I've just interrogated his little sister, at no small cost to my nerves, and she—" he opened his mouth to speak but she steamrolled him "—and she claims her brother told her that he had to run away because, and I quote the young lady, 'they are going to kill him.'"

He squinted at her. "You're serious?"

"Deadly. I suspect Morgan actually thinks he knows who the killer is. He believes his life is in danger and may think he can keep himself safer than the adults in his life will."

Bailey raked the fingers of one hand through his hair, forgetting he was wearing anything on his head. His uniform cap flew off his head. Verity caught the shiny black brim before the hat hit the ground.

"Good grief," he muttered as she handed it to him. "This is one holy mess. Oh, alright. I'll organize a town-wide search party. He can't have gone far. My department will be out in force." (And by that he meant all six people including his office staff.) "And I'll have a word or three with that little girl. See if I can get any more out of her about her brother's whereabouts." He thought for a moment. "Meanwhile, you round up as many of your ladies...ummm, investigators as you can. I'll inform the parents what we're doing."

"Will you tell the Dentons what Morgan said to his sis?"

"Lordy, no! That's all they need—more ammunition for lawsuits!"

# CHAPTER 39

FUMIKO VOLUNTEERED her yarn shop for an emergency meeting of the Evansfield Private Investigations. On a carpeted area at the rear of her shop, she had set chairs in a circle for her knitting and crochet classes. The arrangement suited the EPI equally well.

"This so exciting!" Fumiko yipped as the investigators chose seats. "I think you call this hide-and-seek. Boy hides, we seek. In Japan we have similar game. We call it *Huko Onna*. It is a survival-horror board game. Bloody and disgusting. Just right for that little monster-boy."

"We're not playing any kind of game today. This is serious," Chaundra said. "Verity thinks the child is in real danger."

"So, we need to come up with a list of the most likely places he'd hide," Verity explained. "Then we'll pair up and search for him. The parents are out of their minds with worry, convinced he's been abducted. If we don't find him first, that might actually happen."

"How horrible." Kate pressed her fingertips to her lips, no doubt thinking of her own girls.

"The good news is," Verity continued quickly, "there's no

evidence that anyone broke into the place where he was sleeping. The deputy tasked with watching the room swears that the windows, three floors up and not easily accessible to begin with, were locked. He saw no one going in or out after Mom, Dad, and his sis went downstairs for breakfast. And anyone dragging a screaming child downstairs through the lobby would certainly have attracted a lot of attention."

Sunny frowned. "Then how—?"

Verity rolled her eyes. "Jimmy Fender, the deputy in question, took a potty break. That's when the boy must have snuck out."

"Fender's an Idiot." Denise shook her head. "How does Bailey find these guys?"

"Well," said Mary Beth, "I always say, when ya gotta go—"

"Sure, but you'd think the deputy would call someone to relieve him," Sunny reasoned.

Verity held up both hands: *Enough!* "We need ideas for where Morgan might have gone. If his sister knows, she's not saying. And the parents are no help."

"I remember one time when my friends and I were playing hide-and-seek," Mary Beth recalled wistfully. "I squeezed into a teeny-tiny cupboard beneath the hallway stairs, and no one found me for hours and hours, and when I finally tried to get out, I was stuck like Pooh Bear in Rabbit's hole. Then," she rushed on breathlessly, "I realized all my friends had gone outside when the rain stopped—did I say it was raining?—so, no one heard me crying for a really long time."

"MB, this isn't about you," Sunny chided gently.

Kate turned to Verity, her eyes glassy and frightened. "Kids sometimes do dangerous things when they're scared. Like, hide under a bed when there's a fire. Or in an old refrigerator while playing with friends."

"Exactly," Verity said, "the sooner we or the sheriff's search team find him, the better."

"Do you really think the *perp* might hurt him?" Mary Beth looked a little too pleased with her use of a favorite CSI word.

"We just don't know, do we?" Verity hesitated. This was all so complicated. "I told the sheriff about the anonymous tip I got." AKA, Anna Louise's sighting of Jennifer O'Halloran. "The big question is, why return? If Jennifer came back to innocently retrieve something she'd left behind, like her husband's bomber jacket, why make such an effort to stay under the radar? And why ask Henry to mail it to her?"

"Most sus-s-spicious!" Fumiko hissed.

"Discover the motive," Mary Beth stated with authority, "and you'll find the killer!"

"Oh, good grief, MB!" Denise groaned.

"Is it possible that Jennifer O'Halloran's return to town and the disappearance of the boy are connected?" Chaundra asked. "You said the parents suspect kidnapping."

"Here's what I think." Denise leaned in, fists jammed down on her knees. "If a criminal wants to silence a witness who is an adult, the bad guy can threaten them or pay them off. But if the witness is a kid—well, kids are unpredictable. How do you guarantee a child's silence? Scare them? Maybe. Bribe them?" She shrugged. "He sounds like a gutsy little guy. I think he's a loose end and the murderer will want to—"

"Don't say it!" Kate begged.

"We can hope that nothing like that will happen." Verity studied her trembling hands, a lump growing in her throat. "But Denise is right. Morgan Denton likes drama; he gets a kick out of feeling important and clever, and most of all—outsmarting adults. Like filching money from Mom's purse without getting caught. It's a game to him. And he likes getting attention, too. What better way is there than by outing a killer?"

"He'd be a hero," Kate whispered. "At least in his own mind."

"Verity, you said at our last meeting that the bus driver told Jennifer there was a witness," Sunny pointed out. "Are you thinking that either one of them, or the two women working together, might have killed Rudy O'Halloran?"

Verity frowned. There were just too many variables, too many unanswered questions. "I don't know. I just keep coming back to the fact that Jennifer appears to have returned secretly to town—which doesn't make sense." She paused as another thought from days earlier returned to plague her. "I wonder if there might be a reason for Jennifer shutting herself in her room after Rudy's death. Grieving could be part of it. But what if she was in the alley with her husband the night he was killed? Maybe she witnessed his murder. Or she might be worried someone saw her and would think she had something to do with his death."

Sunny frowned. "So, you're saying she could have stayed out of sight to reduce the chances of being identified by a witness or by the person who killed her husband?"

Verity shrugged. Put into words, her theories sounded a bit lame to her own ears.

"Maybe we should just come out and say it." Chaundra looked around the circle of her friends. "It's possible that Jennifer murdered her husband."

"Man, that's cold," Denise laughed. "But I like it. As a theory, that is," she added quickly.

"The fact is, we have no evidence to put her at the scene, and no motive." Verity sighed and checked her watch. They had been talking for nearly ten minutes, but they needed to get organized and move on with the search for Morgan Denton.

"What about attack on Jennifer?" Fumiko burst out before

Verity could get the conversation back on track. "If she kill no-good husband, who attack her?"

Verity recalled the details of the July Fourth assault vividly. The terror in Jennifer's eyes. The vicious red mark made by her necklace when her attacker pulled it tight around her throat. The woman's trembling.

"Is it possible," she said very slowly, thinking through each word as a new idea began to gel in her mind, "we've been viewing events of the past week all wrong? Maybe we've been manipulated into assuming certain things that aren't true?"

"Manipulated?" Kate asked, looking lost. "By whom?"

"And why?" Chaundra added.

"Oh, oh, oh!" Mary Beth sang out. "I know the answer!" They all stared at her. "Rudy O'Halloran isn't really dead!" She shot Verity a triumphant smile. "Like you just said, we assumed—"

"MB, Verity discovered his stone-cold dead body. The sheriff and Doc Evans examined it." Denise stared at the mayor's wife in disbelief. "*And* there's already been an autopsy."

"Oh, right." Mary Beth looked down at her lap. "Slipped my mind, I guess. Embarrassing."

Verity checked her watch again. Another critical five minutes had passed. "I think we can all assume that Rudy's death is a sure thing. What I meant by looking at things the wrong way has to do with what happened *after* he died."

"I do not understand." Fumiko tucked strands of silky black hair behind one ear and chewed her lip. "This more and more confusering me."

"Confuses me," they all helped out.

"You too? We no good detectives, always mixing up."

Sunny patted Fumiko's arm. "We'll get there," she assured her. "Verity will help us. Just like last time."

Verity was touched by her confidence, which was not something she shared. Nevertheless, she plunged on.

"Here's what I've been thinking," she said. "After Rudy died, Sheriff Bailey started his investigation. He was taking the case seriously, even though, at first, he considered the man's death an accident." Verity took a breath to steady her jangling nerves. "Let's say, Jennifer was somehow involved in her husband's death, maybe she got nervous. She wouldn't want to be considered a suspect, so she came up with a way to emphasize her role as victim."

"You're saying she staged the assault on herself?" Sunny said doubtfully.

"She choked herself with her own necklace. To make her story of being attacked more convincing." Denise sounded more impressed than shocked. "Clever."

Verity nodded her head slowly. "No one witnessed the attack. So, it's possible she faked it."

"Why?" Sunny asked. "To what purpose?"

Verity leaned forward, feeling more and more sure of her theory. "To make the point that a killer was still on the loose and—"

Mary Beth interrupted excitedly, "And if everyone thought the same person who killed her husband also attempted to kill her, then *she* couldn't have murdered him!"

Verity smiled sadly at her friend. "Exactly so, MB."

There was a moment of silence while they all processed this.

Then Sunny said, "But she seemed like such a meek, ordinary sort of person. Wouldn't it take a sharp criminal mind to pull off something so...I don't know, so evil and devious?"

"None of us really knows who Jennifer O'Halloran is, or what she's capable of," Verity said sadly. Because she'd honestly liked her.

The next part made her feel a bit icky. "Jennifer is a lot smaller than Rudy was. But we know from the pathologist's report that Rudy was struck from behind with a hard object. I don't think it would take a great deal of strength for a person to hit another person hard enough to at least stun them."

"And once Rudy was down on the ground, unconscious or at least dazed," Chaundra added, "his killer wouldn't need to be particularly strong to finish him off."

Denise slid down in her chair, eyes narrowed, arms crossed over her chest. "I'm thinking Verity may be right, at least about the choking. It would be easy enough for someone to drag a thin chain across her own skin and leave a mark, like rope burn. Then she could have planted the necklace in the road for someone to find."

"We've gotten off track," Kate said, echoing Verity's earlier thoughts. "Our priority needs to be finding Morgan. Once we know he's safe, then we can try to figure out the rest of the mystery."

Her reminder that a child's life was at stake immediately settled the group. They quickly agreed on a plan for searching the town by divvying up areas. Sunny offered to help Verity search her property for the boy.

# CHAPTER 40

VERITY STEERED the Ridgeline into her farmyard. Sunny followed in her own car since she wanted to return to the café as soon as they completed their search of the farm for Morgan. Verity sighed, thinking she should have refused her help. What she really wanted to do was talk to the Putnams about the missing little boy.

"Guess we should split up to make the best use of our time," Verity said, wiping the sweat from her forehead with a shirt sleeve. The day had turned hotter than she'd expected. "If you find the little scamp, grab him and shout for reinforcements. Jerry should be somewhere around here, too."

"Where do you want me to start?" Sunny looked around at the dairy barn and surrounding sheds.

"Do you mind taking the garage, tool sheds, and crawl space under the front porch of the house?" Verity said. "The cow barns and chicken coops would be a lot more fun for you, but the cows sometimes spook when a stranger comes too close to them, and you'll get filthy in the coops."

"I'm not a big fan of chickens," Sunny admitted. "My parents kept a half dozen hens as layers, but they often got broody and pecked at my ankles when it was my turn to collect eggs. Beaks like daggers those birds had."

"Your ankles shall remain unblemished today." Verity smiled. "Do you need a flashlight?"

"I have one in my car, I'll get it."

Sunny reached into her car for a flashlight the size of a battering ram. The café owner headed off across the yard toward the garage. As soon as she was out of sight, Verity ran inside her relatively cool house.

"Percy! Anna Louise! Are you here?" she called from her kitchen.

"What did we do now?" Anna Louise whimpered from nearby.

Verity scanned the room but neither ghost was in sight. "Nothing. I need your help. Both of you."

A rose petal-pink image jittered into view. Soon Percy appeared in a subdued dark blue shirt and canvas pants. Neither ghost seemed stable; they flickered weakly.

"Still haven't fixed your fine tuning?" she guessed.

"I think I may be getting closer to an answer," Percy said. "Although, I can't be sure. Can we still help?"

"Do you remember the little boy during the farm tour who tried to ride off on my tractor?"

"I surely do." Percy made a sour face. "The little rogue. What's he done now?"

"His name is Morgan Denton, and he may have bitten off more than he can chew this time. His life is at risk."

"Oh dear." Anna Louise fluttered her fan.

"What may we do to help, Miss Verity?" Percy asked.

"If the person who killed Rudy knows Morgan was a witness—which is likely since that information has leaked to the public—the killer may do something rash. Kidnap the boy, or..." She couldn't make herself finish that horrific sentence.

"According to Morgan's sister, he has run away to protect himself."

"You want us to hunt for the lad?" Percy said.

"I think the EPIs have that part covered. Here's what I most need from you two. Go into town and keep your eyes peeled for Jennifer O'Halloran. Either on her own or in the company of the man you saw her with before, Anna Louise. If you see them —one of you must keep them in sight while the other alerts me." It was times like this she really wished the dead carried cellphones. Coming to her with their report would eat up valuable time. Time that could cost the boy's life.

"We will gladly do our part." Percy snapped into a gallant military salute.

"Please be careful," Verity called out urgently to their dimming shades.

Verity made her way from one chicken coop to another, crawling inside henhouses to peer into dim corners, eyes peeled for any sign of the truant five-year-old. It was dirty, disgusting work, but had to be done.


An hour later, Verity and Sunny had eliminated every barn, bin, stall, cellar, shed, cupboard, and coop as possible hiding places for Morgan Denton. Wherever he was, it wasn't on the farm. Sunny returned to the café. One by one—Denise, Kate, Fumiko and Chaundra phoned in their reports to Verity. Not only did her investigators fail to locate the missing boy, no one in town had seen him. Her uneasiness was fast plummeting toward desperation.

On a positive note, no one other than Anna Louise seemed to have seen Jennifer or her mystery man since Verity deposited her at the train station. Therefore, a chance remained that the ghost was mistaken about whom she'd seen while trapped in the outhouse. *One less thing to worry about*, thought Verity. But there was still the problem of a missing little boy.

She paced her yard, agitatedly plucking weeds from her flower border. Denise was right—the little guy was gutsy, he enjoyed taking risks. And messing with adults. But his mischievous nature didn't make him less deserving of their help.

She turned toward the milking barn, normally a place of tranquility for her. But not today. The analytical part of her brain kicked into overdrive as soon as she stepped beneath the heavy, old timbers, into the dark interior. She pictured Morgan alone in the family's room at the inn, an intruder slipping inside while Deputy Jimmy was off relieving himself. But with no idea how long it might be before the deputy returned, wasn't the killer taking a huge risk? No, that didn't sound right. She'd already eliminated that theory.

Any scenario in which the killer dragged the boy out of his parents' room and down through the lobby didn't make sense. Morgan, being Morgan, wasn't likely to go quietly. In a TV crime show, kidnappers chloroformed their victims. Was it really so easy to get hold of that stuff? Anyway, a stranger carrying an unconscious kid out of a busy inn was sure to raise an alarm.

*Think, think...think!* Something in particular made Morgan run for his life. What was it?

Maybe Morgan happened to look out the window and saw someone who *looked like* the person he'd witnessed attacking Rudy. To her knowledge, Morgan and Jennifer never had reason to meet, unless he'd noticed her on the bus from New York. After that, she'd stayed in her room to avoid being spotted by possible witnesses. But if, in the light of day, he was suddenly looking down on the alley from the family's room, and he happened to see a person who resembled Rudy's murderer... And if that person now looked up at his window and saw him staring down at them, he'd of course be terrified. That might explain why he'd run.

But why not tell his parents if he believed O'Halloran's murderer was coming for him?

Because he didn't trust adults; they never believed him. Not even his own mom and dad. And now, his bodyguard had left his post. So, he had to do something to protect himself. She could appreciate this reasoning.

Her phone rang in her jeans hip pocket. She pulled it out. The sheriff.

"Did you find him?" she gasped, her heart doing a marathon under her ribs.

"Me and my guys got nothin'. I'm thinkin' I'll call the state police. They got sniffer dogs." She tried to interrupt him but he plunged on. "Wish I'd got them involved sooner, but I was sure by now, with half the town lookin' for the boy—"

"Sheriff!" she shouted into her phone to stop his rambling. And then she told him her theory of Morgan's disappearance.

Verity had returned to her chores feeling little better for the promise of additional support from the region's law enforcement. The nerves in her hands and arms alternately burned and went numb, as if complaining that she should be doing something other than shoveling grain into her cows' feed troughs.

"I'm on it!" Bailey had said before hanging up. Exactly what he intended to do, she didn't know. At least he seemed to have taken her seriously. Now it was out of her hands.

Minutes later, her phone rang. It was Sunny.

"Hey, what's up?" Verity said, hoping for good news. She laid aside her shovel and again swiped sweat away from her forehead.

"Where are you?" Sunny rasped.

Her body tensed another notch at the urgency in the café owner's voice. "Still at the farm. Why?"

"I can hear a lot of shouting down in the alley behind the café," Sunny said. "But I can't get a good look at who's out there or what's happening without stepping outside on my landing and being too obvious about it. Do you think I should, you know, investigate?" She sounded frightened. Verity couldn't blame her, after all that had already happened.

"No. Stay inside and call the sheriff."

"I tried!" Sunny choked out. "No one at his office is picking up."

"Stay where you are," Verity said. "I'll be right there."

"Veri?"

"What?"

"I—ummm—think one of the voices is Mary Beth's."

*Dear God!*

If Mary Beth was involved, it couldn't be good. Verity broke into a run toward her truck.

Just then, Jerry came around the corner of the tractor shed. "You're leaving me with all this work again?" Jerry yelled bitterly.

She had entirely forgotten about him and felt a twinge of guilt. "The kid who claims he witnessed the murder has gone missing. I don't know how you missed hearing about it." Even to her own ears, she sounded annoyed.

"I've had my head stuck in that damn milking barn's refrigeration system," he retorted.

"Oh, right." She frowned. "Sorry, Jerry. I know you've been working twice as hard since—"

"Since you got my brother thrown in jail!" he sparked at her.

"I didn't...oh bother!" But she sorta did. She blew out a long breath—the kind meant to induce calm but rarely did. "Listen, the sheriff now has another suspect for O'Halloran's murder.

Good news for Jason." She climbed aboard the Ridgeline and started the engine. "But I'm really scared something's happened to that little boy. And now something strange is going on in town."

Jerry's face lost its angry flush. He stared down the road toward the center of Evansfield. "Need me to come with you?"

She didn't give it a second thought. "Hop in."

# CHAPTER 41

VERITY WIGGLED her cellphone out of her hip pocket as she pointed her little blue truck down the middle of Main Street. Jerry kept asking her for more information. She gave him one-word answers. Her head buzzed with too many questions of her own. She held out her phone to him.

"What am I supposed to do with this?" he said. "Man, do you know how old this model is?"

"It works, that's all I care. Find the Evansfield Private Investigators group on my contact list. Text them to meet us at the inn." Something terrible was happening, she felt it in every cell of her body. "Tell them it's urgent."

"Got it." Jerry typed, punctuating thumb punches with grumbling. No doubt aimed at the antiquity of her technology. "Done."

Ignoring the speed limit, Verity scanned the street ahead as she drove. *Where exactly did those shouts that Sunny heard come from?* She couldn't hear anything. For some reason, the silence was scarier.

Her phone pinged.

"You got a message," Jerry said. "No, wait, three messages. Four. Man, these ladies don't waste time, do they?"

"Read them to me."

"Ummm. Right. First one—Sunny—'out the door now.'"

"Keep going. All of them."

Jerry scrolled down. "This one's from Miss Kate." He smiled. "She's nice. Kinda cute, too. Oh, she says she will bring her girls. Doesn't have a sitter."

"She really shouldn't." Verity worried her bottom lip with her teeth. "There's no telling what might happen if Jennifer and the guy she's been seen with—"

"What guy?"

"Never mind. Other messages?"

"One from the Japanese lady—Foo-meek-oh?" he stumbled over the pronunciation of her name. "Says she's already in front of the inn."

"Good. Any others?"

"Just one more, so far. From the mayor's wife. Huh, wonder what she means by that?" Verity glanced across the cab and motioned impatiently toward the phone. "Oh, sorry. You can't see the screen. She says: 'Got him!'"

"She's found Morgan, the missing kid? You go, MB!" Grinning, Verity fist pumped in triumph. "Call her, Jerry. Find out where she is and what's going on." She drove past Denise's Chocolate Designs and the Cat's Cradle Café, then swerved into the first free parking space she came to. The truck barely rolled to a stop before she jumped out.

Jerry jogged behind her, her phone to his ear, apparently still waiting for Mary Beth to pick up his call. "Hey, hold up!" he shouted.

Verity came to an abrupt stop on the sidewalk in front of the long white railing of the inn's veranda. Fumiko stood on the porch steps, talking so excitedly with two of the guests she didn't seem to notice their arrival.

"What's Mary Beth saying?"

"Uh, nothing. She picked up the call but hasn't said a word. I'm just hearing background voices." Frowning, he stared at the phone's screen. "Ma'am!" he shouted into Verity's phone. "Mrs. Mayor, are you there?" He looked at Verity and shook his head.

"Oh no!" she gasped. If MB had found Morgan, why wasn't she telling them where she was? This was bad. Very, very bad! "Did you lose her, Jerry?"

"I don't know."

Verity snatched the phone from him and switched it to speaker mode so they both could hear. "Mary Beth, it's Verity, what's going on? Do you have Morgan or not?" The woman could be such a ditz. What was she playing at now?

Finally, her friend's familiar voice came through loud and clear. "No! I told you, he's staying with me. I'm taking Morgan to his mother."

*Who*, thought Verity, *is she talking to?* She didn't ask, fearing Mary Beth might not have muted her phone so that others wouldn't hear incoming voices.

"Don't be ridiculous!" a different voice snapped angrily.

Verity's heart bumped to a stop. She *knew* that voice. It belonged to the woman she had felt sorry for and sheltered in her own home. But now Jennifer O'Halloran sounded very different indeed.

Jennifer's tone had turned coaxing and silkily dangerous. "He needs to come with us. We spoke with the sheriff a while ago. He told us if we found the little guy to bring him to his office."

"Oh, that's so nice of you to offer." Mary Beth's voice sounded equally saccharine but with unmistakable resolve. "Thanks anyway, *Jennifer*. I'll take him with me. You and your friend are so kind to offer. But since we're *already here in the alley*—" and Verity instantly knew this bit was for her benefit "—and the sheriff always has his afternoon coffee and slice of pie this time of day, I'll just run Morgan inside to him and—"

"Shut up, you stupid bitch!" A man's shout echoed simultaneously through the phone and from the direction of the alley. "The brat's coming with us. Or else."

*Or else?* Verity swallowed, pressing a trembling hand to her chest. Jerry's eyes widened.

Obviously, Mary Beth had left her phone on, wanting them to know where she was and who was with her. *Clever girl!*

Not only had she found Morgan, she was protecting him. Or trying to. But for how long would that be possible?

Verity lunged forward. Jerry's hand flashed out, grabbing her arm and wrenching her to a stop. "Let me go!" she hissed. "She needs me."

With his free hand, he snatched his own phone from his back pocket and punched a stored button. "Calling 911," he whispered.

She hesitated, unsure what to do. She needed to get to Mary Beth before the situation got worse, if that was even possible. But would her sudden appearance in the alley only complicate an already precarious standoff? Probably a moot point since Jerry showed no signs of releasing her.

He was whispering into his phone, his free hand still wrapped around her arm like a tourniquet. She focused on indistinct noises coming from her own phone. Weird scuffling sounds, like someone fighting.

Suddenly, frantic cries spilled from the alley. "Oh! I really d-don't think you want to *shoot* anyone!"

Verity side-glimpsed alarmed expressions from Fumiko and the guests on the inn's porch. Fumiko guided the guests inside the inn.

"If you fire that gun," Mary Beth was screaming now, "it's going to make a really, really loud noise! A whole lot of people will come run—"

*Bang!*

Nobody could mistake the nerve-jolting crack for anything but gunfire. The following silence was just as chilling. Sickening consequences flooded Verity's mind.

Jerry's eyes flew wide with horror. "Shots fired!" he barked hoarsely into his phone, unconsciously releasing her arm. "Behind the inn."

In Verity's mind she was already running down the path toward the rear alley, but seconds flashed by before her feet finally obeyed. Then she was racing between shops. Jerry's steps pounding behind her.

"Dammit, Verity, stop!" he shouted. "Wait for help!"

But her body was driven by a cocktail of fear and adrenaline. She wouldn't...couldn't stop. Because now, no voices, no sounds of any kind were coming from her phone. Which was so, *so* much worse.

*N-no! Oh, God, please! Mary Beth...Morgan!*

Acting on instinct—unfortunately, the kind that got one into situations which often didn't end well—she ran *not* away from the gunfire but *toward* it. Gasping for air, she burst into the rear alley behind the café. An appalling tableau brought her to an abrupt halt.

Jennifer was wrestling with Morgan Denton, attempting to drag him by one skinny bare arm and a fistful of shirt toward a black sedan. A bearded man in a plaid shirt held open the rear door of the car to receive them. In his other hand he gripped a pistol. So focused were the two of them on Morgan, they didn't seem to realize they had company.

Verity frantically searched the area for Mary Beth, but she was nowhere in sight. *Thank God!* A moment of delirious relief came over her. Although something about that didn't feel right either.

Jerry caught up with her. "Don't even think about it," he breathed in her ear. "He's got a gun. We've got nothing! Come on." He tugged her toward the shadows behind the café. She knew he was right. Stay out of sight. Wait for help to come. She could at least describe the car, maybe get the license plate.

*But the child!* her heart wailed. They had to do something to stop the two kidnappers, didn't they? However, if she and Jerry rushed the car, they definitely would be shot. And the little boy might be further imperiled in the mayhem.

Playing amateur detective was one thing. Pulling a Jack Reacher would just get people killed, and Morgan would still be taken.

Reluctantly, Verity turned toward the rear wall of the shops. That was when she saw the mound of vibrant fabric heaped on the ground. A plump, beringed hand peeped out from beneath a swirl of red and orange silk. Verity's heart broke into little pieces.

"Oh, Mary Beth," Verity breathed, rushing forward. She dropped to her knees in the dirt. Sour bile rose into her throat. She stared, alert to the slightest sign of life—a breath, a shudder, a cough or whimper. *Anything. Please!* All she could see of the woman was one side of her wan face and the hand. A dark red rivulet was trickling across the ground from beneath the kaftan's fringed hem.

*Please, please...please don't be dead!*

By then, of course, the kidnappers had noticed her and Jerry. When Verity turned her head, she met the man's eyes and saw only emptiness. No soul existed behind those cold, black eyes. It hadn't bothered him in the least to gun down a defense-less woman. As if to make this point clear, he raised his pistol toward Jerry in warning. Verity shivered; ice water had surely replaced the blood in her veins.

Everything was happening too fast. The day had gone so horribly wrong. Nothing would reverse the bullet that had struck down this dear woman, whose life was bleeding away beside her.

An ironic thought crossed her mind. *If this were a scene on Mary Beth's favorite CSI show, she would have loved it.*

And then...

Three things happened with almost magical synchronicity.

One: The beleaguered Morgan kicked Jennifer O'Halloran in the shin so hard she shrieked in pain and grabbed her leg, thereby releasing her hold on the boy.

Two: Sheriff Bailey's SUV appeared at one end of the alley, blocking the would-be kidnappers' vehicle.

Three: Sunny Whitaker appeared at the rear door of the Cat's Cradle Café, waving Morgan toward the wooden ramp and safety.

Then Bailey levered himself out of his vehicle, holding a rifle. "It's over, folks!" he shouted. "You can't gun down everyone. Mrs. O'Halloran, best you encourage your buddy there to put down his weapon and give himself up."

Jennifer stared in bewilderment at her partner. Verity easily read her thoughts: *What do we do now?*

The man in plaid brushed Jennifer aside. "Stupid bitch!" he raged at her. "I'm done cleanin' up your messes!" He slammed shut the car's rear door and flung himself into the driver's seat.

"No. Wait!" Jennifer frantically slapped at the driver's-side window.

The engine revved loudly, and the black sedan reversed around 180-degrees, kicking up a dust storm and forcing Jennifer to jump out of its way. The car sped off in the opposite direction from the sheriff's one-man roadblock. Jennifer stood alone in the middle of the alley, limp as a ragdoll, looking lost.

For a man of his considerable size, Sheriff Bailey moved like a rocket when necessary. Within seconds he had clapped handcuffs on Jennifer O'Halloran and sat her down in the dirt. *Right where you belong,* Verity thought bitterly.

Shouts came from deputies who appeared out of nowhere. One stood watch over Jennifer even though she showed no inclination to move. Two others reacted to a jerk of the sheriff's head and took off at a run, presumably for their cruisers, in pursuit of the gunman.

Verity stayed where she was, kneeling beside her wounded friend. She couldn't see where the blood was coming from, and she didn't dare try to move her to search for its source. She scooped up Mary Beth's hand, still warm, and held it gently between hers. Mary Beth lay on her stomach; head twisted to one side. Verity gently pulled aside a fold of the silk kaftan revealing one closed eye, purplish lips. Still no reassuring movements. No visible breaths.

The sheriff was calling for an ambulance, adding details of their location. "Pronto!" he barked into his phone.

Verity was only vaguely aware of Denise, Kate, and Chaundra when they ran into the alley. All three stopped dead still, clutching each other when they saw Verity on the ground and the unmoving shape beside her. Jerry hovered silently over her.

Bailey moved in closer to Verity. "How is she?" he asked gruffly.

Verity shook her head, acid tears burning her eyes. "I d-don't know." She moved her fingertips gently along the wrist extending from the kaftan's loose sleeve. "I-ummm-I can't find a pulse," she sobbed. She knew there was a better place to find a heartbeat. Where the hell was it? Her brain refused to work.

She really wanted to shift Mary Beth to her back, to make her more comfortable. But what if that made things worse?

Bailey must have been thinking the same thing. "Best to let the EMTs..." He coughed, cleared his throat. "Aw, hell...I'm not waitin' for them." He jumped into triage mode.

Down on his hands and knees, the sheriff pushed his hand beneath Mary Beth's torso then moved on to her limbs. He gently pulled Mary Beth's right arm out from under her body, finally exposing the bullet's entry point in her upper arm. Using his big hands, he pressed firmly over the bleeding wound.

Without turning to look at Verity, he said, "You go on inside to Miss Sunny. Ask her to make you a cup of tea."

Verity shook her head violently. "No. I can't leave her." Tears splashed down her face, blurring everything around her like a horrific version of a funhouse mirror. She was aware of Jerry shifting his weight, foot to foot to foot. When she glanced up, his mouth was moving without producing words.

Verity felt as though a piano had fallen on her chest, making it impossible to breathe.

*Oh, God. Mary Beth, don't you dare.*

She had just been trying to protect a child. Why did he have to shoot her? Verity stroked the inside of the limp wrist.

It might have been a sudden breeze or the sheer power of her imagination that made a corner of the paisley fabric seem to flutter.

"Mary Beth?" Verity whispered, her voice rough with emotion. "Are you alright?" How dumb was that! *Of course,* the woman was nowhere near alright. She'd been shot!

"Oh, wow," came a response from ground level.

"Wow?" Verity repeated, leaning in.

Mary Beth's left eye flicked open, and Verity could have sworn it winked at her. The hand she'd been holding curled around her fingers.

It was all Verity could do to not throw herself bodily on top of this dear, crazy woman with relief. "Oh, geez, don't try to move! Help will be here soon. Hey, Sheriff! Where's your damn ambulance? Good grief, MB! I thought for sure you were—"

"Stop fussing, Veri dear. It's just a flesh wound."

"Wha-a-at?" she yipped.

The corner of Mary Beth's lips lifted. "I've always wanted to say that."

**CHAPTER 42**

VERITY THANKED Dr. Frank Evans for calling and set down her cellphone on the bistro table in the Cat's Cradle.

"Well?" Sunny prompted.

Five pairs of eyes fixed on Verity in anticipation. Sunny, Denise, Fumiko, Kate, and Chaundra sat with her in the sunny bay window. Outside, Verity could see the cobbled sidewalk lined by lofty maples. Across the street on the town green, proudly stood the white Victorian bandstand. Red-white-and-blue banners fluttered in a soft summer breeze. A little mob of cheerfully screaming children played on a panoply of Crayola-bright slides, swings and ride-on animal characters. Her town's harmony restored, Verity felt a surge of inner peace.

She turned back to her friends. "She's coming home soon. It's official."

Cheers erupted, causing diners to stare at them with curiosity. The EPIs now knew that it was Mary Beth who had found Morgan hiding in one of the big commercial trash bins behind the café. She was taking him to the sheriff when Jennifer and her boyfriend intercepted them, causing the violent standoff that resulted in the man shooting her.

"Doc Evans actually called you in person?" Kate's cheeks pinked. "I guess he must consider you a VIP." They all knew Kate had a crush on him since her high school days. She still did, despite now being married with two little kids.

"Least he could do," muttered Denise. "He threw us out of the hospital, didn't he?"

"That was after all six of us had been camping out in the waiting room for two days," Verity reminded her and took a bite of her cinnamon-sugar donut, still warm from the fryer. It literally melted in her mouth. "Frankly, Deni, I think you scared the staff half to death."

Denise honored this with a dramatic huff. "Don't be ridiculous. All I did was tell those nurses—and well, yeah, that one night-shift doctor with an attitude—that they damn well better give our friend the best care ever or they'd be sorry!"

"You should talk attitude, Denise," Fumiko giggled and risked nudging the chocolatier with her pointy little elbow.

Denise narrowed her eyes. Fumiko leaned away and gave a little shudder.

"Details!" Sunny cried, providing just the distraction they needed.

"Yes, of course." Verity smiled around the tables at these women who had come to mean so very much to her. She would trust any one of them with her life. "Doc apologized for not filling us in sooner on MB's status. He says the bullet, luckily, missed the bones in her upper arm and also the brachial artery. However, while passing through her flesh it did cause some damage that required surgery. He's keeping her for two more days, in case she shows early signs of infection. But as long as she continues to do well, she can come home on Wednesday."

"That's such good news," Chaundra said with fervor, tears glistening in her dark eyes. "Gunshot wounds can be so very, well, let's just say things might have turned out so much worse."

The anguish in the Ethiopian woman's face made Verity wonder if she might be thinking of a personal memory. Chaundra so rarely talked about her years growing up in Africa.

Sunny passed around the plate of donuts a second time, giving everyone something less macabre to think about.

Chaundra smiled—white teeth flashing, eyes bright—dispelling whatever dark thoughts had briefly haunted her. "We will throw our dear MB a welcome-home party, shall we?"

"Absolutely," Sunny agreed. And so did the others, with joyful enthusiasm.

Kate set down her teacup and glanced around at her friends. "I've heard so many rumors in the past two days about Rudy O'Halloran and his murder. But I have to admit, most of them sound farfetched. I don't know what to believe."

"For sure," Fumiko agreed, then dropped her voice to a whisper. "I hear man tell buddy—gangs come from New York and kill him in cool blood!"

"Cold blood," Chaundra corrected her. "It's cold blood, dear."

"Oh, that even worse!" Fumiko shook her head dolefully.

Verity smiled. "There will be plenty of rumors, I'm sure. But you can forget about last week's excitement having anything to do with gangs. Here's what I've learned since talking to Sheriff Bailey a few hours ago." As a sign of his gratitude for her help getting to the bottom of the murder, Bailey had shared as much information as he could with her.

"Rudy O'Halloran and Jennifer Schultz—not O'Halloran," Verity explained, "because we now know they were never married—were a con-artist team. One scam involved booking space on large cruise ships or land tours, then robbing their fellow travelers and planting false clues to make other people appear to be the thieves. By the time a trip was over, the police or private security people still hadn't figured out who was to blame. Meanwhile, the couple had disapp—"

"That doesn't make sense," Denise interrupted. "They'd need to steal an awful lot of money to offset the cost of a pricey cruise."

"Ah!" Verity grinned, enjoying her role as storyteller. "So, here's the interesting part. They always included themselves as robbery victims by filing a formal complaint with whoever was responsible for the investigations. On a cruise ship, that would be the ship's own security department. On a land tour, it was local police. Meanwhile, Rudy was making a big scene about the poor service."

"Like he did at The Cat's Cradle," Sunny commented. "Bad mouthing my poor staff!"

"Right. His goal was to get a full refund of the trip's costs. If he was initially refused, he threatened legal action or trashing the company on social media." Verity continued, "It's my understanding that companies often prefer to settle out of court as a cheaper solution to lawsuits and negative press. They want to protect their reputation."

Chaundra frowned. "I can see that kind of scam working if it's a big cruise ship with thousands of people on board they could steal from. But Ervin's tour group had like fifty people."

"Exactly," Verity agreed. "I think Rudy was the one who ended up being hoodwinked. Ervin advertised his debut tour as offering 'luxury accommodations' and 'platinum service,' and he priced the tour accordingly in his brochures. Any thief worth his lockpicks would assume Elite Vermont Tours attracted wealthy travelers. Which promised a crook good spoils for just a week's work. But O'Halloran apparently didn't realize how few people would be traveling with him and his partner."

"As soon as he got on that bus in New York City, he must

have realized the trip was a mistake," Sunny said. "He definitely wasn't a happy camper when I first saw him here in the café."

Denise leaned back in her chair with a steely look in her eyes. "Let's get to the elephant in the room. Who killed Rudy the Rude?"

"We all know Jennifer has been arrested," Sunny said. "But seriously? She's like half that man's size!"

"It's beyond doubt now," Verity said. "She's signed a confession. Admits she struck him down with a rock in a fit of rage."

"Oh, my!" Chaundra breathed.

"That's not so hard to believe, I guess," Denise mused. "Give anyone enough reason to kill, if there's a weapon handy, they'll be so pumped with so adrenaline, size won't matter."

Kate added, "Haven't we all heard incredible examples of superhuman strength? Like a mother actually lifting a car off her child after a wreck?"

"Jennifer must have hated him even more than the rest of the world," Sunny murmured with a shake of her head.

"Oh! Do you think it was O'Halloran who broke into Doc Evans' office and stole drugs?" Kate said.

"The sheriff says it was. Rudy knew which drugs he could easily sell on the street," Verity said. "Apparently, he also planned to break into houses in town to supplement his meager takings from the tourists, whose pockets weren't nearly as deep as he'd expected. Maybe that's where Jennifer drew the line."

"Or maybe he not give her big enough cut of loot," Fumiko laughed. "He too greedy. Got what he deserved!"

Verity shook her head. "It seems he worked with a string of female partners before Jennifer came along."

"No surprise there!" Denise bellowed. "Who'd stay with an idiot like that?"

"I still don't understand one thing," Chaundra said. "Where did that other man come from? The one who shot Mary Beth."

Verity sighed. "According to Jennifer, the gunman is—*or was*—her actual boyfriend. I guess he still hasn't been caught."

"Let me get this straight." Sunny sipped her coffee thoughtfully. "She called on this guy to help her kidnap Morgan because the little boy witnessed her killing O'Halloran? How awful!"

"Jennifer told the sheriff that the kidnapping wasn't her idea. And she admits to planting the watch and money Rudy stole from the inn's guests, then blaming Morgan for the thefts. But I feel like something's still off about this whole picture. Don't know what," Verity admitted, pushing around leftover donut crumbs on her plate with the tip of one finger. "Maybe I'm just stuck on the fact that we immediately eliminated her as a suspect. In retrospect, that was a huge mistake. We got sucked into the idea that poor little Jennifer was a victim. She seemed so utterly distraught after Rudy died. And she seemed even more upset after the July Fourth incident. She sure made a believer of me!"

"Don't feel bad. We all fell for her act," Kate said. "Mary Beth will never let us forget that mistake though. She's always going on and on about how the investigators on her CSI shows make the victim's spouse or lover their primary suspect." Kate smiled, her eyes softening like melting ice cream. "I know MB's goofy sometimes. But we really should listen to her more often."

"I second that," Chaundra said.

There was an agreeable pause in the conversation while they finished their coffees.

At last, Verity pushed aside her empty mug and looked at Sunny. "Is it ready?"

The café owner's aster-blue eyes blinked a yes as she stood. "I've been keeping everything warm until you were ready to leave. I'll bring it out to you."

Fumiko looked at Verity, curiosity leaking from every pore. "Something new on menu?"

Verity shook her head. "I'm taking Jennifer her breakfast, to save Sunny a trip across the way to the jail." But that wasn't her real reason. Jason had been released from jail, and that was a huge relief to them all. But she still had questions in need of answers. Delivering the prisoner's meal would be her get-into-jail-free card. Whether or not Jennifer would be willing to supply those answers, she had no idea.

# CHAPTER 43

VERITY THANKED Sunny for the insulated bag holding the prisoner's breakfast. She left the café and walked across the town green to the dark-red brick town hall. The cells in the building were rarely used, and then mostly for the purpose of providing a safe place where an intoxicated individual could dry out without harming themself or others. To her knowledge, never before had one been occupied by someone arrested for murder, theft, *and* attempted kidnapping.

Harriet wasn't at her desk, so Verity stuck her head into Fred Bailey's office to let him know she had arrived with the prisoner's meal. The room still smelled faintly of cigar smoke, even though Harriet had instituted her no-smoking rule months ago. Bailey sat at his desk, glaring at a storm of paperwork.

"How are you, Sheriff?" Verity said. "I assume your world is a lot calmer today." Ervin's tour bus had departed town, reducing the flurry of activity around Main Street and pretty much emptying out the inn.

"You'd think," Bailey grumbled. "Ms. Schultz's boyfriend is still in the wind. She's given us his name. Quince Franklin.

There's an all-points bulletin out for him. The U.S. Marshals Service is coordinating the search across state lines."

"And Jennifer? How is she doing?" She stepped the rest of the way through his doorway, the thermal bag dangling at her side.

He leaned back and studied the web of cracks in his ceiling. "Hard to say. The woman's a puzzle. I expected her to be as close-lipped as when I tried interviewin' her in the inn, after O'Halloran died. Figured her for the hardened con artist he was."

"Do I hear a *but?*"

"She waived her right to an attorney. Like I told you, made a full confession. I can't be sure everythin' she's sayin' is the absolute truth, but she's been cooperative. And what she's told me so far makes sense." He scratched his head and frowned. "Sorta."

"You think she's still holding back something?" Verity said.

"Maybe, maybe not. I'm inclined to believe the woman got herself in too deep with O'Halloran and she's just relieved to be rid of him. Asked me right off the bat if acceptin' responsibility for his death and helpin' us locate Franklin would make any difference in court. I told her that it might mean a lighter sentence. No guarantees though."

"Either she's smart enough to own up to her crime now that she's been caught," Verity said, "or she's still trying to con us."

"Exactly my thoughts."

She sighed. "Well, here's her breakfast." She held up the carrier by its straps.

"Thanks, I'll let my deputy know. You can just leave it there on the file cabinet."

She hesitated. "Could I bring it to her, Sheriff? I'd like to chat with her for a few minutes, if she's willing. And if it's alright with you that is."

"We already have her taped and written statements and

confession. I don't see that it's a problem." He looked steadily at her. "Anythin' strikes you as new information, you'll pass it along to me, hear?"

"Of course."

"Deputy Fender will take you to the cells and let you out when you're finished." Apparently, Jimmy Fender of the weak bladder had been forgiven and, she was glad to see, remained a member of the department.

The deputy led her through part of the building she'd never seen before. The bare walls of the musty smelling corridor were painted an institutional gray. He unlocked the first door on the right.

"Ma'am, you have a visitor," he called out and waved Verity inside. "I'll be right out here if you need me, Mrs. Cade. You just give a shout if it's necessary." He laughed self-consciously. "I mean, of course it'll be necessary if you want to be let out of a locked jail cell. I'm just saying, in case anything happens that—"

"I understand, Jimmy," she said, feeling as though she should pat him approvingly on the head. *Good boy.*

The prisoner was lying on a narrow cot, her back to the door when Verity stepped into the cell. "I hope I'm not waking you, Jennifer," she said softly.

Jennifer O'Halloran turned over and slowly sat up. Her mousy hair was tousled, one side of her face stamped with pillow wrinkles. "Oh, it's you," she said dully, making a point of not meeting her guest's eyes.

Verity set the insulated foil sack on the bed. There was no other furniture in the cell. Only a small sink and toilet. The barren space was, thankfully, clean but reeked of disinfectant. A temporary depository to hold a troubled human being. A sad place.

Verity stood uneasily beside the cot and motioned toward her delivery. "There are styro- clamshells and cups in there with a full breakfast from the café. Sunny told me it's scrambled eggs, maple bacon, sage-pork sausage, hashbrown potatoes, OJ, and coffee. Oh, and she said she knew you liked her croissants, so there's one of those instead of toast. I hope that's ok."

Jennifer sat forward on the edge of the cot, hands clasped between her knees. She was wearing the same clothes in which she had been arrested. For some reason, Verity had expected an orange jumpsuit.

Jennifer glanced at the bag. "Thank you," she said softly.

"I can keep you company while you eat. If you like."

"Oh?"

"Or," Verity said, "I can leave you to your meal. Whatever you—"

"No, I'd like for you to stay," Jenniver said quickly. "I just... just don't understand why everyone is being so nice to me. After what I've done."

Verity let out a long breath. "Well, I've never been one to judge. No one is perfect." As soon as she'd said it, she thought how ridiculously lame that sounded. *No one is perfect?* The woman had murdered a man and very nearly kidnapped an innocent child! Well, not so innocent. After all, it was Morgan. But still.

Jennifer side-eyed the bag again. "Guess I should eat that before it gets cold, huh?" She pulled the sack over to her lap and unzipped the top. The cell immediately filled with the aromas of bacon drippings, sweet pastry, and eggy goodness. Comforting morning smells.

"Oh, my," she whispered. "I'm sure going to miss the café's lovely meals."

Verity felt a sharp twinge of sadness on behalf of the young woman. She would spend years, maybe even the rest of her life in prison for what she had done.

"Sit," Jennifer said, finally looking up at Verity and patting the cot beside her. "It was rude of them not to bring in a chair for you."

"There's probably some rule about that."

"Oh yeah. Like I'm gonna use it to clobber you or that goofy cop?"

"Well," Verity pointed out, "you've done some pretty violent stuff."

"There is *that*." Jennifer bit off the end of a strip of bacon and closed her eyes, savoring it. Verity could almost taste the crisp, briny meat. The maple aroma was to die for. Jennifer chewed and swallowed. "I still don't understand how things got so crazy."

"You don't have to talk about it, if you don't want to." But, of course, Verity was dying of curiosity. One of her questions for Jennifer, she couldn't even put into words because her thoughts were still all a-jumble.

"You want to know why I did it. Don't you?" Jennifer guessed.

"Only if you feel comfortable telling me."

Jennifer unwrapped her plastic utensils and dug into the container of scrambled eggs. For several minutes all she did was eat. Verity waited impatiently.

After Jennifer finished her hot food, she popped the lid off the coffee cup, added packets of cream and sugar then took a long swallow. "Go-o-o-od."

"Yeah, Sunny's joe is the best."

Jennifer's gaze drifted past Verity or, more accurately, *through* her as she continued to sip. For another minute she remained silent. Only the subtle changes in her angular features revealed passing thoughts. Verity wondered if she had changed her mind about telling her anything at all about the previous week's crime spree. But then—

"It started out so simple. Me and Rudy. I guess that's the

way life is. You think, hey, I've got a handle on this. It's just a way to pocket a little money. No one gets hurt." She shrugged. "And at first, we were so-o-o damn good at it. Rudy had some great schemes."

"You've done this sort of thing before?" Verity asked. "Signing up for a tour with the intention of robbing people?"

"Nothing as rinky-dink as this Elite Vermont Tours thing." She laughed. "Mostly big cruise ships. The ones you see advertised all the time. Man, they're so huge they're like freakin' cities!"

"I've never been on a cruise," Verity admitted.

"Oh, you'd love it. You should go!" Jennifer smiled at her then shrugged. "They have security on board, of course. But with thousands of passengers and nearly as many crew, we found plenty of ways to grab cash, credit cards, jewelry. Rudy, he even came up with a con to get our money back for the fares we had to pay to get on the ship." Which was what the sheriff had already told her. "Ol' Rudy, he'd throw a fit over some little thing one of the crew did or forgot to do, make a big deal about it —and threaten to sue the cruise line."

"Like the way he acted in the café?" Verity suggested.

Jennifer nodded. "Exactly. One thing you could say for Rudy, he was a really good actor."

"And you went along with his plans because you loved him?"

Jennifer exploded with laughter. "Him? No way. I might have been his partner in crime, but I didn't *sleep* with him. I have or rather *had* a boyfriend. You saw him in action when he was trying to snatch that kid."

"Oh." Verity didn't know what to say, but Jennifer said it for her.

"I guess you're thinking I sure know how to pick 'em. Right? They're cut from the same cloth, Rudy and Quince. But I didn't know Quince would shoot your friend and try to snatch that little boy. I swear, I didn't want anyone to get hurt." She stared somberly into her coffee. "To be honest, I never really liked Rudy. But hell, I was making more money than ever in my life. It was hard to say no to him."

Verity looked at her until Jennifer finally lifted her head and met her gaze. "But you finally did say no...to Rudy?"

"I tried to." Jennifer wrapped her fingers tightly around her cup. "See, I screwed up by booking us into this Vermont trip. So, the fact we were even here was my fault. I thought it would be a change of pace from the mega trips. I was worried some of the companies were beginning to get wise to us." She let out a soft sigh. "And Quince wasn't happy about me being gone for weeks at a time and pretending to be married to Rudy."

"He was jealous?" Verity guessed.

Jennifer nodded. "Big time. Quince never trusted Rudy. I thought if I found Rudy and me a few short trips closer to home, Quince and I could spend more time together. See, he lives just across the Massachusetts border, not thirty miles from here. Anyway, I sold Rudy on this Vermont trip with a new company that claimed to be for posh travelers. Super exclusive. Loaded with rich old people carrying cash or high-limit credit cards. Easy to fleece."

"But small numbers made the two of you more visible," Verity guessed, "which was riskier."

"I hadn't thought about that until too late. Stupid me!" Jennifer shook her head. "Anyway, the wealthy marks we expected didn't exist. The minute we stepped on the bus in New York, it was pretty obvious the idiot running the show had booked a bunch of old pensioners and families. Not a diamond ring or AE card in sight! Rudy was steamed, so he started taking chances. Breaking into rooms at the inn and the town doctor's office. Then he told me he planned to hit some of the shops and houses in town, too. I warned him he was taking too many risks. If he got caught, I figured I'd be going to prison, too."

"So, you told him to count you out?" Verity said. "You quit as his partner."

Jennifer nodded solemnly. "Yeah. That night in the alley I laid it on him. Man, he was furious." Jennifer blinked at the memory and her whole body shuddered. "I told him I wanted nothing more to do with him. But he said if I quit, he'd find a way to make it look like all the thefts had been my doing."

"How awful!"

"Yeah." She gazed off into an invisible distance, as if trying to teleport herself beyond the cell's walls. "I didn't know what to do. He laughed in my face, Verity! Then he turned and started walking away. Like I was nothing! Like he could do anything he wanted and there wasn't a thing I could do to stop him." She gritted her teeth, her eyes sparking fury. "But he was wrong."

*He sure was*, Verity thought. His arrogance cost him his life. "Oh, Jennifer. You could have gone to the sheriff."

"No. It would have been Rudy's word against mine. Like I said, he was a really good actor. He could make you believe anything."

Something about that fateful night still bothered Verity. Why couldn't she put her finger on exactly what it was? She changed the subject. "Then the July Fourth attack was all an act?"

A nervous smile flickered across Jennifer's lips. "Sure was. Did I really fool you?"

"You did. I was worried for you. Really worried."

"Sorry. You were so nice to me. But I was scared that cop, Bailey, would immediately suspect me of killing Rudy. I didn't trust my ability to convincingly act like a grieving widow. I kept wanting to laugh out loud, totally relieved that Rudy was gone and could no longer control me."

*Ah,* Verity thought as another piece of the puzzle fell into place. "That's why you shut yourself in your room at the inn? To avoid talking to the sheriff or anyone else."

"Right. But the sheriff wouldn't leave me alone. So, when he brought you to my room, I thought—well, maybe I can fool this little farmer lady. Worth a try!"

Verity winced. After all, the woman had succeeded in pulling the wool over her eyes! Not for a minute had she believed the innocent-looking woman sitting disconsolately in her room was a fraud and a murderer. How wrong she'd been! The evidence collected at the scene of the crime and in the morgue—not to mention Jennifer's own confession—proved otherwise.

But *something* kept clawing at the back of her soggy brain.

Verity observed Jennifer, who was now well into her second course. She took bites of the buttery croissant between sips of coffee.

"Jennifer, when you gave your statement to the sheriff, did he ask you about your intent when you confronted Rudy in the alley?"

"Intent?"

"Did you seek out Rudy in the alley with the intention of killing him that night?"

Jennifer shook her head. "No. I knew he'd gone outside to smoke since he wasn't allowed to in the room. I wanted to tell him I was quitting. But like I said, he just flipped me off."

"Oh, Jennifer."

She popped the last bite of croissant into her mouth and chewed thoughtfully. "When he told me he'd make sure I was blamed for the thefts, I stood there, crying and staring at the ground. Feeling sorry for myself, I guess. And angry too."

"Of course, you were," Verity said.

"Then I saw this big old hunk of rock or cement on the

ground. I don't even remember picking it up, but I guess I did. Next thing I remember, Rudy was lying there in the dirt and... and I knew he was dead."

Verity rubbed her forehead, frowning. "*How* did you know he was dead?"

"I told you, I just...well, for one thing, he wasn't moving. Duh!"

Verity stood up from the cot and turned to face the young woman "How many times did you hit him, Jennifer?"

"Why would you ask me something like that?" she groaned miserably.

"Just think really hard. Tell me how many times."

"I don't know. Once, I think."

"You're sure?" Verity felt wired. Her head buzzed like a whole hive of angry bees.

"Pretty sure. Soon as he hit the ground, I snapped out of my rage. I saw blood on the back of his head. I felt dizzy and sick. I threw the rock over the fence and ran back inside the inn. I was shaking so bad it was all I could do to climb the stairs to my room without falling down. Hey, where are you going?"

Verity was already at the cell's door, shouting for Jimmy Fender to let her out. "I need to tell the sheriff what you said just now."

"Did I say something wrong?" Jennifer called after her.

"No! You said something right."

# CHAPTER 44

HARRIET WAS BACK at her desk. "Good morning, Verity. Have you recovered from last week's excitement?"

"No, but—" she felt out of breath "—I need to see the sheriff again."

"Oh now, dear, I really wouldn't bother him. You know how he is about paperwork. He's got a ton of it due after the murder investigation."

"I'm about to make his life easier," Verity said. *Or more complicated.* It could go either way.

Harriet frowned. "Mercy me! You are a glutton for punishment."

But Verity was already halfway through the door into Bailey's inner sanctum.

His big bull of a face tilted up from a sea of forms, photographs, file folders, and transparent evidence bags. "Had a good visit, did you?" he muttered.

"A useful visit. I think I've just now learned a critical piece of information neither of us was aware of."

He observed her warily. "Go on."

"You said the coroner reported multiple blows to O'Halloran's head, four or five I think it was?"

"So?"

"Did you ask Jennifer how many times she struck Rudy?"

He rolled his eyes in exasperation. "Mrs. Cade." She stiffened. He called her that when he was angry or irritated with her. Or about to throw her out of his office. "The woman *confessed* to the murder. She described striking her husband with a rock. She killed the man and admits it."

"But Jennifer says she struck Rudy just once—*don't interrupt me!*—and she dropped the rock over the fence."

"So?" He shook his head, glaring at her. "This may have been a mistake, letting you talk to her."

"No, please. Listen, Sheriff, you already know she wasn't married to Rudy. It was a charade—them acting as a couple. And the guy who tried to take off with Morgan, Quince Franklin, was her boyfriend."

"I *know* that!" He huffed at her. She imagined an angry bison, like in those videos when some idiot visiting a National Park decides he's going to pet the huge beast.

"Wait! Listen! Quince lives only half an hour or so from here. She told me the Vermont trip was their idea—hers and Quince's—a way for them to see more of each other. But she also said that Quince and Rudy never got along."

"*No one* got along with Rudy," he muttered, his fingers moving back toward the nearest stack of papers.

"But this was more than the two men not being buddies. He hated that Rudy was stealing all his girlfriend's time for his scams. He was jealous. Quince wanted her back."

"Alright. That's at least a theory. How does this change Jennifer's confession? You're sayin' the woman's still not tellin' the truth? Well, big surprise there!"

Verity nibbled her bottom lip, mulling over every detail of

everything they knew. "No. What I'm saying is that she's telling the truth as far as she knows it. Yes, she clobbered Rudy and left him for dead. She admits that much. But what if he wasn't dead? What if someone else finished the job?"

The lawman's normal beer-flushed complexion took on a record level of redness. Each and every broken vein on his nose looked near to popping. "Gimme a break, Mrs. Ca—"

"Listen to me, Sheriff!" She threw herself at his desk and banged down both fists, intent on getting across her theory before he called Harriet to haul her out of his office. Harriet was even more formidable than a buffalo.

"From everything Jennifer has just now told me," Verity continued, "it's clear that she and Quince planned to meet up while she was on the Vermont tour. Even if Rudy didn't like it. We also know that Quince turned up in town, at least twice. Once, when he tried to snatch Morgan and shot Mary Beth. But remember that anonymous sighting of Jennifer and a stranger after I left her at the train station?"

"I do."

"What do you bet that man was Quince? And what if he came to town another time, to check on Jennifer—to reassure himself that she wasn't cheating on him with Rudy?"

Bailey frowned. "I don't know—"

She was on a roll now and wasn't about to let him cut her off. "Say that Quince arrives in time to see Jennifer and Rudy arguing in the dark alley. He watches, unnoticed by either of them. He sees her smash the guy over the head, then run away in a panic."

"How the hell do you come up with such falderol?" Bailey slapped his big palms down on the opposite side of the desk and leaned in aggressively. "I know you're fond of the woman, but—"

"Listen to me!" she screamed. "Jennifer said something a

few minutes ago that made me remember something that happened just before Quince Franklin drove away. He yelled at Jennifer, 'I'm done cleaning up your messes.'"

Verity stopped talking long enough to give Bailey's brain time to catch up with her.

"Think, Sheriff. *Clean up her mess*—which is, now, the matter of Rudy lying there bleeding. So, what does he do? He doesn't help a stunned Rudy get up off the ground or seek medical attention for him. *What does he do?*" she repeated.

Bailey leaned away. He straightened his broad shoulders and stared at her. The pupils of his eyes shrinking to black pinpoints. "So-o-o-o, you're sayin' Quince Franklin was there that night. The night O'Halloran was murdered."

She held her breath and gave a stiff nod.

"He sees everythin'," the sheriff continued. "But unlike his girlfriend, he don't trust that Rudy's dead. Maybe notices him twitch, moan, or try to get up, after she's run off." With great effort, Verity held back from saying anything, fearing an interruption would return Bailey to his natural state of pure obstinance. "If she disappeared inside like she claims," he went on, "Quince might have picked up where she left off, continued battering the guy until he'd killed him."

He finally got it. Three people in the alley. Jennifer stunned Rudy with one blow. Quince finished him off. What a sleepy Morgan had witnessed that night from the window above had been two different people attacking Rudy O'Halloran.

"What do you think?" she asked.

Bailey narrowed his eyes at her. "Much as I hate to admit, it's just possible."

# CHAPTER 45

BACK AT THE FARM, the morning fog still hadn't fully burned off. Verity turned her blue truck into the gravel driveway. Her lovely buttercup-yellow farmhouse had never looked so inviting. She longed for a cup of tea and a few minutes alone to quietly reflect on the past week. But first, she needed to find her farmhands.

Their truck was parked in its usual spot between the milking barn and the house. She went in search of Jason and Jerry.

Verity was worried this first meeting with the brothers since Jason's release from jail would be, at the very least, awkward. She could easily imagine the bitterness and anger Jason might feel toward her. There had been moments when she doubted his innocence—and he knew that. In his eyes, she had abandoned him to a jail cell and perhaps to an even worse fate.

And Jerry? Their last words had been sharp and accusing. He had remained loyal to his brother and couldn't understand why she didn't stand by him. All this had left a nasty taste in her mouth. As far as she knew, the twins might be working their final hours on her farm before officially giving notice. Leaving her to struggle on, alone, managing a farm that had always been meant to be a family's work and legacy. Her heart wobbled.

After looking through two of the outbuildings, Verity found the brothers in her kitchen garden, the last place she expected them to be. Rounding the corner of the farmhouse, she spotted the two young men through the pea-soup fog, their baseball caps poking up above rows of corn. At first, she couldn't figure out what they were doing. They never hoed weeds in that plot or picked vegetables for her. The kitchen garden was her domain. In fact, it seemed so strange to see them there that she approached cautiously, not knowing what to expect after the past few tumultuous days.

Their heads turned, eyes taking in her approach. After giving her a hurried glance they turned to each other and exchanged sly smiles.

"Hey, guys," she said with forced nonchalance, "what's up?"

"Well," Jason said, "we were just now discussing the possibility that you might have made a mistake in the choice of herbs for your garden."

Jerry snickered and looked away.

She swallowed, unable to tell where this conversation was going. "Oh? And why is that?" she asked, defensively.

Now that she was standing with them in the middle of her patch, she could read their body language. Jason rocked back on his heels, hands in pockets, looking smug. "You may just want to yank out that row of plants over there." He pointed.

Only at that moment, as the gray mist finally began to lift a few inches from the ground and she dropped her focus away from the two young men's faces, did she see the problem.

In the grassy verge between rows of lush green leaves a foot high, dozens of cats sprawled in her beloved garden. Some rolling around beneath the growth, others munching on low-hanging leaves while still more dozed contentedly.

There were orange cats and white ones. Slate-gray kitties. Striped tabbies. Calicoes. Torties. Sleek, black miniature panthers. Cats with markings reminiscent of a wild lynx. Two, at least, with the luxurious long fur of an elegant Persian. A few looked like what she, a novice to the cat world, supposed were Siamese. And an immense amber-and-tan creature that resembled the cat her grandmother had kept as a pet when Verity was a very young child. She thought she remembered her grandmother calling him a Maine Coon cat. Three-year-old Verity had called him Puppy when she visited, because he was as big as many dogs and followed her grandmother everywhere.

"What on earth!" she gasped.

"You've drugged the entire town's feline population," Jerry laughed.

"It's catnip," Jason stated. "You planted catnip. And from the looks of things, I'd say it's a pretty powerful variety."

"Oh bother," she moaned. "I thought I'd planted mint in that row. I wondered why it didn't look right to me. Or smell right."

"Took them a while to discover your cache, I guess." Jason grinned. "But as long as you keep growing it in such tempting profusion, I'd say you'll never have to worry about needing more cats on your farm."

"Or having a rodent problem," Jerry added.

"They don't look much in the mood for mouse catching," she observed of the creatures' extreme lethargy. "Guess you're right. I'll need to dig up that whole row. At least I'll still have Lady Macbeth and her litter."

"Want us to pull it up for you?" Jerry asked.

She gave this some thought. She had begun to feel an unexpected warmth toward felines. But overpopulating her property might cause territorial squabbles. "Let's allow them to enjoy themselves for a few more hours. Then please dig up all but a few plants. I'll keep some in a pot on my porch for Lady M, if she likes it."

She shifted uneasily between her feet and looked out across the field of chicken coops, then beyond to the line of soaring pine trees and, above them, the evaporating mist. She could see glimpses of blue in the summer sky.

"I need to apologize," she murmured, before losing her nerve.

"For thinking I was a murderer?" Jason said.

She blinked up at him. He sounded angry, but she was almost certain she'd seen a momentary twinkle in his eyes. "I never believed you would intentionally set out to kill anyone, Jason. Truly, I didn't."

"Maybe you didn't want to," Jerry said. "But you were afraid of what he might have done. Because of that business in the café."

"Yes, because of that. You really were fit to kill, as they say."

"I was," Jason admitted. "And I would have punched the guy's lights out if you hadn't stopped me. So, I should thank you for that. I was out of line, even if he was a total jerk."

"He was more than just a jerk. And I'll explain everything I've learned about Rudy O'Halloran and the woman we thought was his wife, but first—"

"Thought?" they echoed, staring at her.

"We'll talk later this afternoon, after you've finished the day's chores." She hesitated then added, "If, that is, you forgive me and want to continue working on the Cade Family Farm."

"Oh, we're staying," Jason said, and his brother nodded his agreement. "Dad told us he would be glad to hire us to work his farm. But when we told him what you were paying us, he just about had a conniption."

Jerry made a face. "He offered us what he calls 'the family rate.' Half of what you pay us."

"Well," she choked on a laugh, "does that mean you're staying? You'll keep working for me even though I—"

"You didn't do anything we wouldn't have done," Jason said with a straight face. "Next time *you* are accused of murder, we'll need to seriously consider the facts of the case before accepting that you didn't do it."

She grinned at them. "I'm so glad you're staying, guys. I really wouldn't know what to do without you." And it was true. Because—the necessities of labor aside—they were, in every way but blood, family.

It was nearly dark when she finally completed the last of her own work and dragged her tired self into her cozy kitchen to prepare a simple supper of homemade tomato soup and grilled cheese sandwiches to eat at her kitchen table.

As she munched her first warm, gooey sandwich half and sipped the soup, tangy with ripe tomatoes from her own garden and laced with Molly's cream, she thumbed through a seed catalogue. Although she usually ordered the same varieties each year, she sometimes enjoyed trying out a new hybrid tomato, squash or corn.

"You can't go wrong with Menomonie," a voice stated with solemn authority. "No sense bothering with any of those newfangled corn breeds."

Verity giggled. "Oh, Percy, I'm not sure that old-time seed still exists." She peeked over her shoulder at him.

The handsome young soldier had donned his blue dress-uniform again, this time displaying a field of ribboned medals across his chest, marking his valor in various battles. He wore white cotton gloves and his left hand rested smartly on his sword's hilt, his other hand at his side. He studied the open catalogue with a look of bewilderment.

"Has farming changed this much?" He shook his head in consternation at the mindboggling array of plants, bulbs, seeds, tools, fertilizers, pest control options, and soil conditioners as she flipped pages.

"Indeed, it has, Lieutenant Putnam. And where, may I ask, is your lovely bride? I hope you haven't lost her again."

"Oooo-whoo! Here I am, sugar!" called the lady in question. "I was just changing into attire more appropriate for the celebratory occasion."

A vision in aquamarine tulle flashed into view. Anna Louise shimmied her bare shoulders flirtatiously for the benefit of her husband, her lavender eyes dancing behind a matching embroidered fan. Three strands of perfectly matched white pearls looped gloriously around her slender throat. As lovely as Anna Louise was in her departed form, Verity could only imagine how beautiful she must have been in real life.

She studied the young couple, aware that something about them seemed different. "A celebration, you say?"

"Why, of course!" Anna Louise's trills of laughter echoed through the house. "You have yet again solved a murder! We are so very proud of you, my dear Verity."

"Indeed, we are," Percy added. "Our only regret is that we were not present when the villainous Mr. Franklin shot your friend and threatened you. It was most unfortunate that we were occupied."

"Occupied?" She would never get used to the idea that the dead appeared to have lives as busy as the living. At least the two she knew did.

"Why yes," Anna Louise said, giving her voluminous skirts a

swirl and looking pleased with the effect. "You entreated us to focus on discovering the reason behind our visibility issues."

"And have you made any headway?" Verity asked.

She still worried about their leaving her. But slowly, she was coming to accept the natural order of life...and death. Eventually, they must move on. Just as her lovely Mark did. Just as she must, some day. Meanwhile, she would enjoy all this young couple from the past brought to her life.

Verity allowed herself a maudlin sniffle but quickly recovered. "And have you discovered the cause of your problems?"

"No," Percy admitted, "I'm still quite perplexed by our unpredictable loss of control. However, I believe I have found a temporary solution."

Verity smiled. "Do tell, Lieutenant Putnam.

"Chocolate."

She stared at him, then at his wife—certain he was joking. But they stood before her with solemn expressions.

"I-I'm afraid I don't understand," she said.

"Shall I?" Anna Louise fluttered her long eyelashes at her husband.

The man looked as though he was literally melting. "Of course, my dear."

"You see," Anna Louise explained, "at the slightest indication that our shades are about to fade or become visible without our willing it, we always become terribly anxious. Admittedly, I am more inclined toward panicking than my dear Percy." Which was something Verity knew from experience. Anna Louise was clearly a high-strung and emotional ghost. "And, you see, our anxiety seems to make our situation worse."

"That's when we really lose control," Percy explained. "Then it becomes impossible to focus on recovering our powers. We're no longer able to grip things like doorknobs or move through walls. Or—"

"Or open your mail. Ooops!" Anna Louise ducked behind her fan.

"But *chocolate*?" Verity said.

"Our research at the library taught us many things. For instance, we learned that certain foods affect human behavior," Percy explained. "It seems that chocolate has been found to have benefits for mood enhancement. It can calm as well as energize. It's really quite magical."

"B-but you can't *eat*," Verity objected. "You're ghosts. You're dead!"

"This is true," Anna Louise cooed, "but it's rather rude to keep pointing this out to us, don't you think?"

"Sorry." Verity sighed.

"It appears," Percy continued, "that we don't even need to *eat* the chocolate. The mere aroma of cacao—the bean that sources cocoa powder and chocolate—when intensified by warming it, soothes us."

"You mellow out?" she said, still trying to grasp the logic behind this odd reaction. "Like the living do after drinking a glass of wine or cup of tea?"

"In a manner of speaking," he agreed. "The fragrance of cacao takes the edge off our anxiety. Then, feeling more relaxed, we are able to reestablish our powers and either dim or increase our visibility according to the situation."

"Amazing!" Verity said. "You do seem to appear, ummm— well, brighter than the last time I saw you."

They sparkled at her.

"Then you're not leaving for, you know where?"

"Not at this moment," Percy said.

Anna Louise cuddled up to him happily. "We do so wish to stay with you, Miss Verity, for as long as our spirits or—" she directed her gaze toward the kitchen ceiling "—the powers that be allow."

"And I am very happy to have you stay with me," Verity assured them. She felt like giving them each a big, warm hug. But, as close as she often felt to them, actually touching a ghost still felt a little woo-woo to her.

Instead, she observed them fondly and offered, "Anyone for a whiff of hot chocolate?"

# ABOUT THE AUTHOR

Kathryn Johnson (aka Mary Hart Perry/Nicole Davidson) has authored over 40 thrilling mystery, suspense, and historical novels for adults and young readers. Her books have been nominated for the prestigious Agatha Award and won the Heart of Excellence and Bookseller's Best Awards presented by the American Library Association.

Kathryn loves teaching the craft of fiction writing at The Writer's Center (https://writer.org), in the Washington, DC area, as well as throughout the world via live workshops on Zoom. She has developed seminars for and spoken at the Smithsonian Institute, Library of Congress, Mystery Writers of America, International Thriller Writers and many regional writers' conferences.

As the founder of a writer's coaching and editorial service, https://KathrynJohnsonLLC.com, Kathryn is bursting with pride for her amazing author clients as they pursue their own publishing careers. Her nonfiction book, The Extreme Novelist is based on her popular 8-week course for fiction writers.

Kathryn is thrilled to be joining the Oliver-Heber Books family and introducing the Haunted Farmhouse cozy mystery series, featuring the intrepid Verity Cade, two ghosts who have lost their way to the Afterlife, and a cat named Lady Macbeth.

A small press bound by the belief that every voice matters.

Sign up for our newsletter to learn about new releases and more.
https://oliver-heberbooks.com/subscribe/

Follow us on social media:

facebook.com/oliverheberbooks

instagram.com/oliverheberbooks

amazon.com/oliverheberbooks

youtube.com/@OliverHeberBooksPublisher